MARVOLENE

A Fall to Darkness Novel

SUMMER SULLIVAN

MARVOLENE

To my friend Ana,
For reminding me that life is about a lot more than just surviving.

Author's Note:

This book is a prequel to the events of 'The Last Heir' and 'The True King', the first two installments of Fall to Darkness. This book, however, can be read as a standalone novel. Please be aware it might spoil certain parts of 'The Last Heir' and 'The True King'.

Chapter 1

Could this day possibly get any worse?

Marvie posed the question to herself as she watched the angry customer storm out of the bakery. No, she decided, biting her lip to hold back tears. It could not get any worse.

The day had started out all right, she supposed. Marvie had slept in until her aunt pounded on her door, yelling that breakfast was getting cold. Marvie had dragged herself out of bed and slipped into a tunic, before stumbling downstairs, still half-asleep. Sienna was smiling happily at her, gesturing to a plate of eggs, toasted bread, and two links of sausage.

"Look who's finally up!" she exclaimed. "You know, my dear, they say the most successful people are the ones who are up before dawn."

Marvie tried for a smile. "I'll never be one of those successful people, then." She slipped into the chair in front of the plate and glanced around their small apartment. She had called this place home for almost her entire life. It was small, yes, but there was something cozy about their modest kitchen and wooden table. The room adjacent held old but durable furniture sprawled around a fireplace. The window in that room had a view of the city streets and the brick buildings that were identical to theirs. Upstairs was her bedroom and the one her aunt and uncle shared. It had never felt cramped or crowded.

To Marvie, this was home, even though she had been born in Auntica. Her parents died when she was young; she had no memory of them. Her aunt and uncle had taken her in, moved her to Orinth, and raised her as their own. Though she never called them mother or father, they had filled that role in every other aspect. In almost every sense, Marvie was Orinthian, besides the Auntican accent that never went away.

Marvolene Pere was her full name, but she had always gone by Marvie, a nickname her aunt had given her from the time she could walk. There was not a single person who called her Marvolene. To her friends at school, her fellow workers, and her acquaintances, she was Marvie.

"Oh, Marvie, don't say that," Sienna chided, her tone light. Her aunt was in a bright mood this morning. "You're going to be a very successful woman. I just know it."

"Whatever you say, Sienna," Marvie replied, shoving a bite of the eggs into her mouth. "Where's Uncle Hewes?"

"He left before dawn. They're working on a project for a rising businessman. His name was Vacci, I believe. You should ask your uncle about it. It's quite interesting." Sienna slid into the chair across from her. "I'm glad, though. It gives us a chance to talk."

Marvie froze, her spoon halfway to her mouth. "Talk?"

Sienna gave her a look. "Yes, talk. Nothing too serious, don't worry."

This is when the day started to get slightly bad. Not terrible, but enough to throw her off balance.

"What's this about, then?" Marvie asked, setting her utensil back on the plate.

Sienna shifted in her seat. Marvie' s chest tightened in anticipation. Her aunt had possessed the same mannerisms for as long as Marvie could remember. When she was nervous, she didn't stop moving, shifting, tapping, blinking. Sienna could not sit still when there was something on her mind. Hewes had always laughed at the habit, managing to relax his wife by rubbing her shoulders or kissing the top of her head. For Marvie, it filled her with more anxiety than she could handle, and she often mimicked her aunt's movements.

"I just want to know, Marvie…" Sienna paused and shifted once more. "Are you happy?"

Marvie blinked once. "Am I happy?" she repeated.

Sienna nodded, staring at Marvie's mostly untouched food. "Yes, dear. Are you happy?"

Marvie dropped her hands to her lap and slid them underneath the table, biting her lip. "What kind of question is that, Sienna? Of course I'm happy."

Her shoulders sagged in relief, but there was still tension as her aunt spoke. "I'm just wondering, dear. It just seems like you don't spend as much time with your friends as you used to, now that the term is over. You have a few months before you could start university. You don't go out as much. You work and come home and then work again. I just want to make sure you're happy. Did something happen with your friends?"

Marvie's mind was spinning as she tried to think of ways to answer these questions. "Sienna...yes...I...it's just that my friends are busy." Lie. Her friends had asked her multiple times to go out with them, to some tavern or another, but she always had some excuse not to. "They work, too. It's hard to find time outside of the school term to do things with them now that I'm working." Another lie. Her shifts weren't terribly long, and she honestly didn't have to work at all. She chose to work to fill the void that had become her life.

She was seventeen years old and had finished her primary education. The time had come to choose a university to attend. There were a few of them in Orinth, a few in Auntica, even some across the sea. But Marvie had no interest in them, despite her aunt and uncle's prodding. She couldn't bring herself to tell them just how little she was interested. That was a conversation for another day. She had four months before she had to make a choice, and Marvie would use every second of those four months to think of an alternative.

Sienna raised an eyebrow. "Even Isla? She's your best friend and I haven't heard you say a word about her for weeks."

That was because Marvie had been actively avoiding her friend, but Sienna didn't need to know that.

"Isla is busy. We are all busy." Marvie tried to keep her voice level, and not indicate to her aunt that she was vocalizing her biggest insecurities.

Sienna seemed satisfied by the answer. "Okay, Marvie, if you say so. I just wanted to make sure. These are supposed to be the best years of your life. You're so young and I don't want you to waste this time away working. You don't have to have the job at the bakery. Hewes and I can give you money. We want you to have a fun few months before the stress of university starts."

Marvie closed her eyes, taking a deep breath to calm her racing heart and racing thoughts. *Don't freak out*, her mind screamed at her. *Do. Not. Freak. Out.* Releasing that breath, Marvie opened them, and managed to smile at her aunt. "I know, Sienna. And I appreciate that. But I like working. It gives me something to do. I like working for my money. You're right, I should be doing more with my friends. I'll go visit Isla tonight and set something up for this week."

Sienna nodded, smiling. "Good. Bring Isla over for dinner one of these nights! I miss seeing her!"

Marvie looked down at her plate. The food on it suddenly seemed unappetizing and she was no longer hungry. "I will, Sienna," she replied softly.

That conversation had started the downward path her day had taken. It wasn't her aunt's fault; Sienna was being the kind, thoughtful person she was. Marvie had wrongly assumed that she was successfully hiding the changes in her attitude from her aunt.

Was Marvie happy?

No. Not in the slightest.

It was a weird realization to come to, realizing you weren't happy. It hadn't been gradual for Marvie either. One day, things had been perfect, and she loved her life. No, she wasn't worried about where her life was going. She didn't care about the future; she cared about the moment. She was young and carefree, and she wanted to make the most of it before life caught up to her.

Then in the blink of an eye, it had fallen apart.

Nothing had caused it, necessarily. Marvie had woken up and the realization had hit her. I am no longer happy. She had racked her mind for a reason, some event or person that had caused this. Had one of her friends made some rude comment that stayed with her subconsciously? Had she been embarrassed at school, and it caused her to spiral? No, it was none of those things.

She just wasn't happy anymore.

As Marvie searched for a logical reason, she gradually began to notice things, little things, but things nonetheless. Her friends seemed happier without her. She had a large group of them, boys and girls, and they had been together for a long time. Less than a month ago, she had passed them on the street after a late shift at the bakery. They hadn't noticed her as they walked, laughing together, the light of the streetlamps casting a glow around them. Isla was leading the group, and Marvie watched as she spoke, the whole group quieting, before bursting into another round of laughter at her words.

Marvie had stopped in the street and watched them, until they turned a corner and disappeared, probably to some tavern to have the night of their lives.

They hadn't even invited her.

It was something so small and she was immediately racked with guilt at even being bothered by it. So what if her friends hadn't invited her to a single night out? They probably thought she would still be working. It was such an insignificant matter. There were people in their country, on the continent, who were starving, who had no home, who had no love or life. There was a war happening in the Wilds, people giving up their lives for Orinth. How could she possibly feel hurt by something as trivial as this?

But their faces. Their smiles had been so large, their laughter so loud. Did she ever make her friends laugh like Isla did? Was she as entertaining as the girl she had called her best friend for so many years? Marvie realized, of course, that she could turn around and follow them into whatever tavern they were going to. They would cheer when she walked in and she would probably have a good time, but her legs started moving and she was on her way back to the apartment. Marvie didn't want to be with them; she would be dead weight.

And that night, as she laid in bed, imagining the memories her friends were creating, Marvie compared herself to Isla for the first time in her life.

Isla had been beautiful for as long as she could remember. Her hair was a dark auburn, and she had deep green eyes that were akin to emeralds. She was built like a goddess and when she smiled, people couldn't help smiling back. When she talked, everyone listened, drawn in like they were watching a magic show. Isla wore the brightest clothes, as if her raw beauty wasn't enough to attract the eye of every passerby.

Isla was everyone's favorite person. The more Marvie thought about her, the more a deep pain filled her stomach. She denied what the feeling was, but it was obvious.

She was jealous of Isla.

They had met long ago, when they had started school together at a young age. They had been inseparable. Isla had become like the sister Marvie never had, the sister she never knew she needed. Things were so easy when they were young. No one cared about what they looked like or what they possessed. Everything was routine, there was no worrying about tomorrow or the next day. It was so…easy.

The older they got, the more it all changed. Marvie hated change.

After that short but damaging conversation with her aunt, Marvie had gone to the washroom, closed the door tight, and stared at herself in the mirror. Her blue eyes stared back at her, and she wondered what they would look like if they were emeralds. Her blonde hair hung across her face, falling down to her back. She had never cut it. Isla's hair was short and she was the only person Marvie knew who could have hair to her chin and still look like a princess. Marvie's facial features, depending on the day, seemed too little or too big for her face. She was small and short, and she hated her proportions. She hated everything about the reflection that looked back at her.

With that happy thought, Marvie climbed back into bed and laid there for as long as she possibly could before she had to get dressed for work.

It had been a long walk to the bakery and she kept her eyes glued to the brick streets. She had lived in Tenir long enough to know how to navigate through the perpetual crowds. Marvie had never felt unsafe there. Her aunt and uncle lived a long way from the harbor district, where there were rumors of substantial criminal activity, but it had never affected Marvie. As she wove in and out of the masses, she prayed to the gods that she wouldn't see anyone she knew.

The gods must've been listening because she reached the bakery without incident. She glanced up at the painted wooden sign hanging from a black bar: 'Olga's Bakery'. It was between a store and a tavern, made of brick like the rest of the buildings in the city, with large open windows that she loved staring out of when work was slow. There were a few apartments above that Marvie secretly monitored, waiting for one to come up for sale. Then she wouldn't have to make the fifteen-minute walk to work anymore. Not that it mattered. She was content living with her aunt and uncle, but a small part of her wondered if she would upset them with her growing unhappiness.

With a deep breath, Marvie had walked into the bakery and began the monotonous routine of her job.

And immediately, more things went wrong.

She had always worked at the front counter, selling the different pastries, cakes, breads, and other items they offered, but today, the kitchen was behind schedule. They had managed to get the bread baked and out on the racks, but none of the pastries were even close to being ready. One of the kitchen workers explained that a delivery had gone wrong, and they hadn't gotten the correct ingredients. Marvie tried to calm him down because she was absorbing his stress, and she could not afford to be stressed while working. She explained that they could take their time on the pastries, and she would tell the customers that there was a delay, and they would be ready in a few hours.

It seemed that every living, breathing person in Tenir wanted a pastry that day.

Dozens of people walked in demanding pastries. Being as polite as she possibly could, Marvie informed them that it would be a few hours. Some of them were kind about it, and left with a smile, while others shouted in her face. Marvie couldn't comprehend it. She was a seventeen-year-old girl, and grown adults were screaming in her face for something completely out of her control.

"I COME HERE EVERYDAY FOR THE PASTRIES!" one woman seemed to screech. "WHY AREN'T THEY READY TODAY?"

Marvie inhaled deeply before responding. "We had some problems with the delivery, and they won't be ready for another few hours," she explained, attempting to keep her voice level, but it was rapidly rising in pitch.

The woman threw her hands into the air angrily. "This is absolutely ridiculous. I want to speak to the owner!" And it continued from there.

It took about two hours before Marvie snapped. The last man she served in line had cursed at her before storming out, and she watched as he slammed the door behind him. Holding back tears, she ducked into the kitchen and sought out the owner of the bakery, Olga herself. The woman was about the same age as her aunt and uncle, with gray hair and a smile that seemed to be plastered to her face.

"Olga, you're going to have to take over out there," Marvie told her, pressing her palm to her forehead. "I can't do this anymore today."

She had been working at the bakery for almost two years and was close with Olga. Marvie had a feeling other employees wouldn't be able to talk to the owner like this.

Olga shot her a smile. "I'm sorry, dear. They're being brutal today, aren't they? Well, you can take a break, but I need you to make a delivery. I was going to do it, but I'll take over for you, and you can do this instead."

Marvie breathed a sigh of relief. "What's the delivery?"

Olga bit her lip. "Well, I guess it's not a delivery. There's a shop a few doors down from us, called The Wooden Barrel. The owner gives me a discount on flour in exchange for some pastries every day and well..." She cast a look to the kitchen, which was in a state of absolute chaos before turning back to Marvie. "It doesn't look like he'll be getting any today. Just let him know for me and tell him I'll make it up to him."

Marvie stared at her. "You want me to go to this man and tell him we have no pastries?"

Olga frowned. "Yes. Can you handle that?"

Suppressing the urge to burst into tears and stomp her feet like she was four years old, Marvie nodded. "I can handle that." No, she couldn't. But facing one man was better than facing the onslaught of angry people who let something as simple as a pastry bother them. He could scream in her face and then it would be over with.

Olga beamed. "Good. Now, I'll handle the front and you go let him know. It'll take less than ten minutes and then I can find something else for you to do."

Marvie ran a hand through her hair. "I'll be right back," she mumbled as she turned around and started towards the door. As she left, a large group of patrons were entering, and she felt a small pang of relief that it wouldn't be her responsibility to deal with these angry pastry people.

The late morning sun seemed to beat upon her as she walked down the street. She hoped the bustle of Tenir would distract her from the terrible day thus far, but it didn't. Echoes of the conversation she had with her aunt floated around in her head, bits and pieces of it repeating over and over again. She saw flashes of Isla's face, her smile, her laugh. Marvie wondered where her friends were at that moment. She was the only one of them who worked this much. They were probably spending time with one another, making more memories that Marvie would be absent from.

Are you happy?

I'm not.

It didn't take long to reach The Wooden Barrel, and as Marvie walked in, she crashed into a man who was walking out. Of course, the man had been holding a flask and managed to spill half the contents onto Marvie's green tunic and apron. The liquid was freezing and Marvie yelped as it met her skin, soaking through the fabric. The man shot her an apologetic frown but said nothing as he pushed out into the street. Marvie watched after him with her mouth agape, trying to think of something to say. Holding the door open, she glanced down at her now soaking tunic and back at the man, who had disappeared without an apology. She closed her eyes, once again holding back tears as she stepped into the shop.

She was the only person in the room except the boy behind the counter, who had watched the entire encounter with one eyebrow raised.

It took one second for Marvie to notice the rest of him and she stopped.

He was beautiful, this boy, and it had been a while since she had appreciated the pure beauty of someone in a way that wasn't fueled by jealousy. He was leaning against the counter, elbows resting on the surface, staring at her. He had the curliest black hair she had ever seen and it hung below his forehead, falling just above his eyes. The boy was wearing a black shirt, but she couldn't help noticing how perfectly formed he was. Sharp was the word she thought of as she took in his angles and edges, from his jawline to his forearms resting on the counter. His eyes were green, she could see their brightness from across the room, but not green like emeralds. Green like the forest and the trees that graced it. Green like the outside world Marvie had barely seen. With one look at him, she wished she would've seen more of it. Gods, she could lose time just staring into those eyes. Wait, how long had she been standing there staring at him?

Marvie snapped out of it almost immediately at the thought of what he was looking at in return. A blonde girl wearing a dirty apron that was soaked with water, gaping at him like some sort of crazy person. She was relatively sure there was flour in her hair too, which did not help matters. Clearing her throat, Marvie crossed the space between them, intently focused on not stumbling in front of this beautiful boy.

"That was rude of him," the boy said before she was even at the counter, still leaning across it, looking up at her with those eyes. His accent was as Orinthian as a voice could be.

Marvie shrugged. "It's been one of those days, to be honest." Her heart was in her throat as she spoke and she was suddenly aware of how fast it was beating. Why in the world was her heart pounding? It was so unlike her to be fawning over a boy in some small shop filled with supplies. She saw boys every day. She didn't care about them, didn't care about being in a relationship. Isla had a boy she was with, and maybe that was the reason Marvie was so opposed to the idea of it.

"Oh?" the boy said, not straightening up even as she stopped at the counter.

"One of those days where every person seems to be spilling their water on me. Not literally."

"I think we all have those days," he replied thoughtfully.

Marvie couldn't think of anything else to say because she had forgotten how to be a human being in the presence of this boy. Without thinking, she blurted out, "I don't have any pastries!" She realized she yelled the phrase at him in this shop that was silent, her voice echoing throughout the room, and she wanted to hit her head against a wall.

There was the hint of a smile on the boy's face as he cocked his head in confusion. "Excuse me?"

Marvie took a step back. "I don't have any pastries for you."

"I wasn't asking you for pastries."

Marvie shook her head, pressing her hand to her forehead. "No, I'm sorry. I work at the bakery down the street and my boss sent me over to tell the owner of this store that she didn't have any pastries for him today. She normally brings him some, but we weren't able to make any this morning, so she said she'll make it up to him tomorrow. That's what I'm trying to say." For gods sake, was she a toddler? She was babbling incoherently like one, speaking as fast as the words would come out of her mouth.

The boy nodded. "I see. Well, my boss just had to step out, he'll be back in ten minutes. Would you like to wait so you can tell him yourself?" he asked kindly, too kindly, and Marvie groaned internally. He was probably wondering what he had done to deserve such an absurd person walking into the store where he worked.

"I can wait, yes," Marvie said quietly, taking a deep breath to calm herself. She avoided looking at the boy now, observing the rest of the store instead. He was making her look foolish. It wasn't her fault, she tried to tell herself. It had been a long time since she had a conversation with someone so attractive.

She would wait ten minutes, tell the boss, depart, and pretend this had never happened. This day could not possibly get any worse. If she had to choose a word to describe it, it would be mortifying. And the worst part about it? The day wasn't over yet. Taking two steps back, Marvie turned away from the boy and pretended to be observing the different spices on the shelves.

"So, you work at the bakery?" he prompted, and she was simultaneously despaired and ecstatic that he was still speaking to her.

She answered without looking. "I do. I have for a while."

"I've never been to that one before. Olga's, right?"

"That's right. You're missing out. Some people say we have the best food in Tenir. Others claim it's all of Orinth."

"Really?"

"No."

The boy laughed softly, and the sound was music to her ears. Marvie wanted to make him laugh again. She looked over her shoulder at him and her heart skipped a beat as she realized he had been watching her. When he met her eyes, he looked away quickly, as if he were the one embarrassed and Marvie bit back a smile.

He was nervous, too.

"I'll have to stop in sometime, then. My boss has given me some of the pastries, but if it really is the best food in Orinth, I should probably try something else," he said in reply.

Marvie shrugged. "I don't make the food, I sell it. But I have faith, it's the best food in Tenir."

"I believe you," he said, and there were traces of laughter in his voice.

"What about you?"

"What about me?"

"You work at this shop?" she asked before realizing what a stupid question it was. He was standing at the counter of the shop. He had referred to the owner as his boss. Obviously he worked at the shop. Marvie had forgotten how to speak to another human being.

The boy didn't draw attention to it as he answered, "Yes, I do. It's my first job in a while. I like it, I like Tenir."

"Me too," Marvie agreed, grateful for the fact he hadn't laughed in her face.

"Where are you from?" he asked.

"You can tell I'm not from Orinth?"

He smiled again. "I think the accent gives it away."

Marvie turned away from the spices, facing him fully. "I'm from Auntica."

"Your Orinthian is beautiful."

Marvie inhaled sharply but hoped it wasn't noticeable. She hoped a lot of things weren't noticeable, from her hand tapping her leg too quickly and the constant biting of her lip she resorted to when she was nervous. Beautiful. He had just called her beautiful. No, he had called her Orinthian beautiful. It wasn't about her; it was about her knowledge of his language. No, it was more than that. What was happening to her right now?

"Thank you," she managed to get out without her voice cracking. "I learned the language when I was very young."

"You're welcome…I didn't get your name," he breathed, and his gaze had settled onto her again.

"It's Marvolene," she told him, and she didn't know why she used her full name. She never went by it. But she wanted him to know every part of her, starting with her given name. "But I go by Marvie."

"Marvolene," he repeated, as if he were trying out the syllables. "Marvolene," he said again, and she wanted him to keep saying it. She liked the way it sounded coming off his lips. She found herself staring at those lips for longer than a moment. They looked soft. She wondered what they would feel like pressed up against her skin. Marvie immediately scolded herself for the thought only minutes after meeting this stranger, but her gaze hadn't moved.

He smiled a little bigger and Marvie managed to rip her eyes away from his mouth, heat suddenly creeping up her neck and flushing her cheeks. This boy had caught her shamelessly staring at his lips. They had met less than five minutes ago, and she had managed to ruin it in less than that time. Her face grew hotter, and she prayed to the gods it wasn't visible.

Marvie spit out her next words. "What's your name?" She shouted the question at him. Why did she get so loud when she was embarrassed? She tried not to think about how Isla would handle an interaction with an extremely beautiful person such as this one. Probably perfectly. She would sweep him off his feet and have him wrapped around her finger in record time. Jealousy rose in Marvie's throat like bile at that thought.

"It's Auden," he said quietly, as if he were afraid someone would overhear, though they were the only two in the room.

"Auden," she murmured, liking the way it sounded when she said it. "Auden."

He ran a hand through his black curls and Marvie had a hard time not fawning over the movement. There was something about it that was so undeniably attractive that she found herself staring at those lips again. "Auden who?" she asked, trying to distract herself from the overwhelming wave of enthrallment coursing through her.

"Frae. My name is Auden Frae."

"Auden Frae," she repeated.

He smiled at her. "I like it better when you say it."

Marvie beamed back at him, the embarrassment falling apart piece by piece in an instant. "It's nice to meet you, then, Auden Frae."

"And you as well, Marvolene."

"You can call me Marvie if you want."

"It's nice to meet you, Marvie."

She opened her mouth to respond but before she could, the door of the store opened, and both of their heads snapped towards the person who had walked in. It was an older man with dark hair, who stopped, glancing at Marvie and then at Auden.

Auden spoke before the man could. "Kalen, this is Marvie. She has a message for you from the bakery down the road."

Kalen observed Marvie before walking behind the counter next to Auden. "You have pastries for me then? Normally Olga brings them herself."

Marvie shook her head. "I'm afraid not. We're out of pastries today because of an error with the delivery. Olga sent me to tell you that she would make it up to you tomorrow, if that's alright."

Kalen shrugged. "It's no problem. Tell her thanks for me." With that, he ducked into a room behind the counter, leaving the two of them alone once more. Why was there a slight thrill from that notion? She glanced after his boss, before dragging her eyes back to Auden, who was studying her. It certainly did not help the redness of her face, being the center of his attention. She took a step back.

"I guess I should get back to the bakery."

"I have a question for you," he said, ignoring her former statement. Something flashed behind those green eyes and Marvie suddenly had an avid desperation to find out every single detail about this boy and crash into his life with no regard for caution. There was something so alluring about him, and it made her want more. More what? She didn't know, she just needed more.

"What's the question?" Marvie blinked, her heart racing to the point where she could feel her pulse in her fingers.

Auden stepped out from behind the counter, and leaned against the front of it, crossing his arms in front of his chest. His expression was unreadable as he spoke. "Have you ever met someone for the first time, but deep inside of you, you know it's not the first time at all? That somewhere, at some time, your paths have crossed. You just can't remember where or when. But you just know." He paused. "Has that ever happened to you?"

She was surprised she stayed upright. For a few minutes, she thought it might only be she who noticed the connection between the two of them. Marvie was imagining it because she was unhappy with her life and needed something to change that. But it wasn't just her. His words had confirmed that. Why else would he ask her such a question?

And why did it make so much sense?

Marvie's voice trembled as she responded. "I think it has, now."

Without waiting for a response, Marvie spun around and left the shop.

Chapter 2

Thoughts of Auden Frae consumed her.

She had barely made it through the rest of her shift because her head was in the clouds and the floor kept spinning under her feet. She received more than one look from Olga, who had never seen her best employee like this, but Marvie couldn't help herself. Her heart had not ceased pounding in her chest and she avoided the desperate urge to walk back down the street, go into the store, and talk to Auden for a few more hours.

There was a lightness in her soul that had not been there before, and his words kept repeating in her head over and over again. What had just happened? She replayed the scene of meeting him dozens of times, from the first word to the last. The logical part of her brain tried to say it wasn't real. Her mind had over-exaggerated everything about Auden because she was bored and unhappy. Marvie found herself denying that adamantly. It had been real, the attraction she had for him. And, well, she hoped he might have it for her too.

Has that ever happened to you?

I think it has, now.

Marvie worked the counter for the rest of her shift and not a single angry person yelling about pastries could ruin the indescribable sensation. When they screamed, she smiled at them. Every time the door opened, her head snapped up, hoping it was Auden coming after her. He now knew where she worked.

Would he seek her out? Or would their first conversation be their last? That question dimmed Marvie's elation but only slightly. What if Marvie had distorted the encounter, and Auden had only seen a bumbling, embarrassed teenage girl who forgot how to act like a human being when she saw a good-looking boy? What if their conversation meant more to Marvie than it did to Auden? What if that was it?

She tried to shake those thoughts away, but they lingered in the back of her mind.

The shift seemed to fly by after her encounter with Auden. As soon as Olga told her to go home, she was out the door. But she stopped, in the middle of the street, the crowd surging around her like she wasn't there. She stood, facing the direction of the shop, and pondered whether or not she should return. Every fiber of her being told her to go back and simply ask Auden what had happened between the two of them, ask him if he had been referring to her with that last question. She should just return and do...something.

Marvie took a deep breath. "Hi, Auden. I was wondering what you were doing tonight, and also, every single night for the rest of your life," she muttered to herself. Maybe there was a better way to approach it than that.

But she didn't walk toward the shop. Instead, she turned around, and began towards the apartment. Marvie was tired and she was sure that she smelled like the inside of a bread oven. There was still flour in her hair and dried sweat had begun to crust on her forehead. It was time to call it a day. She swallowed back a lump of disappointment as she stared at the cobblestones.

That night, she dreamed of Auden. They were standing on the edge of a roof, and he was smiling at her. He was saying something, but she couldn't hear what it was. She could only stare at him, despite her urge to run her hands through his black curls or press a kiss to his jaw. Tell me everything about yourself, she wanted to shout. Tell me every detail, the major ones, the minor ones, the funny, the painful, the beautiful details of yourself. There isn't a detail too small for me, I want to know it all.

Her voice returned in the dream, and she managed to spit out one question. "Where have we met before?"

Auden just smiled at her, and for some reason, that was better than an answer.

Marvie awoke from the dream at the sound of someone pounding on her door and she groaned. She never wanted to wake up from that.

"MARVIE!" her aunt yelled. "Breakfast is ready!"

"I'm coming, Sienna," Marvie grumbled, pulling her covers over her head, a desperate attempt to escape back into the dream of Auden Frae. After a few moments of squeezing her eyes shut to meet nothing but darkness, Marvie rolled out of bed.

This time when she went downstairs, her uncle was sitting at the table. He gave her a smile. "She's finally awake."

Marvie pressed a kiss to her uncle's cheek as she slid into the chair across from his. "I'm surprised you're not at work, Hewes. I thought you were working on your big project."

Hewes looked exhausted, but his face always brought her comfort. He was a large man, with gray hair and traces of a beard on his face. There were slight wrinkles around his mouth, but a youthful light behind his eyes. Her uncle had always been a quiet man, but being in his presence instilled a sense of peace. This was a man who had a long life and wisdom to give if you only asked for it.

"The project has been delayed for a few days, Marvie," Hewes said as Sienna rounded the corner and smiled at Marvie, pressing a kiss to her head before continuing into the kitchen. "There have been some…issues."

"Issues?" Marvie said, leaning back in her chair with her eyebrows raised. "That sounds ominous, for the construction business."

"Well, it is. This Vacci man…" Hewes tapped his fingers on the table, looking thoughtful. "He's powerful."

"More like he's dangerous," Sienna chimed in from the kitchen, with a hint of disapproval.

"I won't deny that," Hewes mumbled as Sienna set down three plates of the same breakfast they always had: eggs, toast, and sausage.

"What does he do?" Marvie asked. Unlike yesterday morning, she had an appetite, and immediately began to dig into her food. Despite the fact that she had eaten this every morning of her life, it still tasted delicious.

"Well, he owns a lot of taverns in Tenir, but people say they're fronts."

"Fronts?" Marvie questioned.

Hewes leaned in closer, as if they were going to be overheard in their own apartment. "Fronts for his immense smuggling operations."

Marvie raised both eyebrows. "Do you know for sure?"

Hewes shrugged. "I have my suspicions. Damon Vacci isn't as wealthy as he is from taverns alone, that much I can say. We had to stop construction because apparently, he ran into some trouble from the throne. Queen Natasha sent some soldiers to investigate his operations more thoroughly. We can't work until the investigation is finished."

"Is he upset?" Sienna asked, sliding into the other chair and taking a large bite of toast.

"He's furious, or so I've been told."

Marvie shook her head, shoveling another spoonful of eggs into her mouth. "If I were you, Hewes, I would stay out of it."

"Believe me, my dear, that's what I'm trying to do."

There was silence after that, but it wasn't a tense or uncomfortable silence. They often ate in silence, the three of them, and it was only ever peaceful. Marvie realized that the sign of a strong relationship wasn't constant communication, but rather, the comfort they could draw simply from being in one another's presence.

She wondered where Auden was at this moment. Had his shift at the shop already started? Or was he sitting down eating breakfast with his own family? Maybe he was still sleeping. The idea that Auden was a late sleeper, such as herself, made her smile a little. Thinking about him made her smile. Everything about him made her smile.

Marvie internally reprimanded herself. She met this boy yesterday, for less than ten minutes. Their conversation had been so brief, an introduction more than anything, and there was no indication that she would ever see him again. She had no right to think about him and wonder what he was doing. There was no reason she should be questioning whether he had thought about her as much as she had thought about him. Was Marvolene Pere consuming his mind like Auden Frae was consuming hers?

No, she wasn't the type of girl who people thought about.

Still, the smile lingered on her lips.

Marvie realized her aunt was staring at her with narrow eyes. She quickly tried to wipe the smile off her face and continue eating nonchalantly, but Sienna had already caught on. She pointed her fork at Marvie and asked, "Why are you smiling, Marvolene?"

Oh gods, she had used her full name. Sienna hardly ever did that. Marvie gave her a look. "Do I have to have a reason to smile? Can't I just enjoy breakfast with my aunt and uncle?"

Sienna rolled her eyes. "Normally, you're barely awake when you come down here. What's going on? Did you make plans with your friends for tonight?"

There was a quick surge of pain in her chest from that question. Marvie would not see any of her friends tonight, but the possibilities of where they could be haunted her. They would be together, no doubt, without her. It didn't matter. She was unbothered, or at least, Marvie convinced herself she was.

"No, I didn't make plans with my friends for tonight. I just had a good shift at work yesterday, that's all," Marvie said quickly.

Hewes furrowed his brow. "I thought you said every customer screamed at you because there weren't enough pastries."

"Yes, they did. I meant I'm glad that shift is over with and I'm going to have a better shift today than I did yesterday." Marvie's attempt at a cover-up was truly pathetic. She had never been good at lying, especially to her aunt and uncle.

"Marvolene," Sienna said seriously, though a grin had crept onto her own face. "What is going on with you?"

It was just like Marvie to be giddy over a boy she had talked to one time. She would probably end up planning their wedding the next time she saw him. After that, she would choose the names of the children they would have together. She honestly hated herself.

"Nothing, Sienna," Marvie insisted, standing up suddenly. "I just remembered I have to go into work early. I'm going to go get ready."

"Marvie!" her uncle called after her, but she was already racing up the stairs. She closed the door to her room and slid down into a sitting position. Pressing her face to her hands, she smiled again. *Stop it!* A voice in the back of her head screamed at her. *You're getting your hopes up for nothing and you're just going to be disappointed. Stop it right now and spare yourself the regret.*

But she physically could not rid herself of the euphoria from thinking about Auden Frae.

It was a lie that her shift started early. But Marvie got dressed anyway as she was overcome by a sudden wave of confidence. She wanted to see Auden again, because he had made her feel something she had never felt in her entire life. She wanted to feel it again, the intoxication of being around him.

Marvie slipped into a blue tunic she frequently wore to work and tied her hair back. She frowned at her reflection in the mirror. She was not pretty. What would Auden even like about her? She shook the thought off and ran down the stairs, yelling goodbye to a very confused Uncle Hewes and Aunt Sienna.

She had an hour to spare, and she knew exactly where she would spend it. Marvie strode past Olga's without looking toward the place. Marvie practically skipped down the crowded streets of Tenir before she stopped in front of The Wooden Barrel. She closed her eyes, taking one deep breath before entering the shop.

Her heart dropped. Auden was nowhere to be seen. Instead, the same man who she had denied pastries was standing at the counter. He gave a small nod at her. "Hello," he said, and his eyes flashed with recognition. "Oh. You've brought me pastries then?"

Marvie bit her lip. "Um, no, sorry. I'm not working right now, but I'm sure Olga will bring some to you today. I...actually...um..." she stumbled over her words before managing to say, "is Auden here?"

Kalen raised an eyebrow. "Auden? Oh, you mean Frae? No, he doesn't work today. I can give him a message if you'd like."

Marvie shook her head. "No, that's alright. I'm sorry to have bothered you," she said quickly, turning around and attempting to swallow back the massive discouragement.

"You're a friend of Frae's then?" Kalen called after her and Marvie stopped, looking over her shoulder.

She hesitated, before replying, "Yes, I am."

"I've never met a friend of Frae's before."

This time, Marvie turned around fully to face the man. He was studying her thoughtfully.

"Oh?"

Kalen nodded. "He's been working for me for almost a year, and I've never met a single friend of his. No family, no acquaintances. You're the first one."

Marvie tried for a smile. "I'm honored."

"He's very private, that one. I might even go as far as to say he's an enigma."

"I guess he is," Marvie replied, turning back around and walking toward the exit. "Have a good rest of your day." She pushed open the door and left, without waiting for a response.

A new wave of questions about Auden arose, the most prominent asking if Auden already had someone in his life. What if he had a woman at home waiting for him? What if Marvie was fantasizing about a married man? She wasn't sure how it was relevant to what Kalen had said, but the thought still plagued her. Private? An enigma? He hadn't come off that way to Marvie. Then again, their conversation had been short. Maybe she was overthinking this.

No, she was definitely overthinking this.

Exhaling, Marvie fell back into the moving crowd, and decided to head back to the bakery and go in early. Maybe Olga would let her go home before her shift was over. The disappointment about Auden's absence remained and Marvie tried to push it away. So maybe she had embellished their interaction a little...no, a lot. She wasn't happy, she knew that, and her brain was trying to give her something to look forward to.

It was an illusion.

Chapter 3

As Marvie walked into the bakery, she decided to avoid thoughts of Auden altogether.

Olga greeted her with happy surprise and put her to work straightaway. The issues that had afflicted the bakery yesterday had been resolved and Marvie fell into the mundane routine of her job, only semi-conscious as she took order after order. She recognized several patrons as the angry customers who had felt the need to scream in her face. She fought the urge to spit in theirs, at their desire to belittle a young girl who had done nothing wrong. The suppressed anger of the day before, for Marvie, had returned in full force.

Unsurprisingly, Olga did not let her leave early, citing that they were much too busy to let her go. Marvie didn't care; where else did she have to be? It wasn't as if a group of friends were waiting for her to be done.

She had her back turned to the door, counting how many pastries they had left, when the bell rang to signal someone had entered. Marvie didn't turn around, as she didn't want to lose her count. They could wait an extra moment or two.

"Marvolene?"

Marvie froze. Her heart burst into a million rays of light because it was him! She whirled around to see Auden standing at the counter, a half-smile on his face as he looked at her. He was dressed in all black, his curls pointing in countless directions, his hands tucked into the pockets of his pants.

"Auden!" Marvie exclaimed, praying she didn't sound too eager, despite the fact she was almost shaking with excitement at seeing him again. This time in real life, not in her dreams or thoughts or imagination.

He gestured to the bakery around them. "So, this is it?"

Marvie followed his gaze. Why did she suddenly grow self-conscious about the state of the bakery as he observed it? It was old and the paint on the walls was beginning to fade. She hoped he wouldn't judge her for working here.

"This is it," she said in reply. "It's not much, but this is it."

"I like it," Auden said. "It's very…Orinthian."

"That it is."

He leaned up against the counter, resting his elbows on the edge like he had done yesterday at the shop. A single curl fell out of place, resting on his forehead, and it took all of Marvie's willpower not to tuck it back herself. "I thought I would come see for myself. That is, see if the food is truly the best in Orinth."

Marvie beamed at him. "Is that the only reason you came?" The words were out before she could stop them, and she wondered if they were too straightforward.

Auden smiled back at her. "Honestly, it's not even the real reason I came."

Marvie raised an eyebrow as her heart hammered even harder in her chest. "Oh?"

"I came because I heard the service here is so exceptional."

She threw her head back and laughed. "Is that right?"

He nodded eagerly. "That's what they all say, anyways." Auden glanced around the bakery. "The service is exceptional, the food is good, there's a great view of the Tenir streets. And," he seemed to lean in a bit closer as he finished, "the girl who works there is beautiful."

Marvie immediately felt heat rush to her face, and she set her elbows on the counter, matching his position, their faces only inches apart. "Is she?"

"I can confirm," Auden murmured mischievously.

Marvie grinned. "I'll let Olga know you hold her in high regard."

Auden burst into laughter and the sound was music to her soul. She decided right then that her new aspiration in life was to make Auden laugh as much as possible. Imagine what Hewes would say to that, the next time they had a conversation about the future. *I want to make Auden laugh, Hewes. That's all I want to do.*

"While I'm sure Olga is a treasure, she's not who I was talking about," Auden said, the smile still on his face.

Marvie blushed even harder as she stood up straight, asking him, "What would you like to try?"

"What do you recommend?"

"I like the cherry tarts the best," Marvie said, voice still shaky from Auden's words. From the smile on his face, he could tell, and it made her all the more flustered.

"Then I'll take two cherry tarts," Auden said, and Marvie was glad for the opportunity to turn around and retrieve them from the shelves, a chance to calm herself down and regain her cool. Who was she kidding, she had never been cool. As her shaking hands reached to get the tarts, Marvie just accepted that fact.

She placed the two of them into a bag as Auden paid her. He made no move to leave even after she handed the tarts to him. A small thrill went through her.

"How much longer do you have to work, Marvie?" he asked her.

Marvie glanced at the old clock on the wall, before looking back at Auden. "I'm done any moment now. Why?"

Auden held up the bag with the tarts. "I happen to have an extra tart, and I don't think I'll be able to eat both myself. I was wondering..." He cut himself off, looking down at the ground then back up at her, taking a deep breath. Marvie hid a smile. He was nervous again. It made him seem more human, which somehow transferred into him being that much more attractive. He managed to spit the rest out. "I was wondering if you wanted to go for a walk after you're done working...with me."

"I would love that, Auden," Marvie said, barely able to keep her excitement from bubbling up to the surface. She glanced down at her clothes. The tunic she was wearing was stained with sweat and her apron was covered in food. "I guess I should go home and change beforehand," she mumbled.

Auden shook his head. "There's no need. You look lovely."

"Don't lie to me."

"I promise I'm not lying," he said with a smile and Marvie couldn't help but return it. His smile alone made her more than giddy.

"Well, alright." Marvie glanced toward the back. "Let me go check with my boss and see if I can get out of here early." Without waiting for a response, she entered the other room, found Olga, and asked if she could go. Her boss, taking a quick look at Auden, gave Marvie a knowing smile before allowing her to leave. Marvie hung up her apron and grabbed her bag before returning to where Auden waited for her.

"Are you ready?" she asked him, coming around the counter to stand next to him, not entirely convinced that this wasn't a dream.

"Absolutely," Auden said, taking her hand. The moment their skin touched, Marvie's senses sharpened and everything around her became clearer. For the briefest of moments, she stared into Auden's green eyes, wondering if the same sensation was happening for him. Holding his hand was so…right. It was like her hand had been made to fit in his; she never wanted to let go.

Gods, Marvie, calm down! Some logical part of her brain screamed at her. *You met this boy yesterday. You don't even know him. He's a stranger! He could be dangerous!* The warnings she gave herself just seemed to fade away as Auden smiled at her again, leading her out the door.

The crowds were pouring down the street, but she didn't seem to notice as Auden guided them through the merchant area. He shot her a smile as they finally found an emptier section of cobblestones.

"Where are we going?" Marvie asked him.

Auden shrugged. "I don't really know." He gestured to the people around them. "They all seem to know where they're going."

"Probably some tavern or another. That's all people seem to do in this town." As Marvie spoke, she stepped closer to Auden to get out of the way of an oncoming couple and without saying a word, he let go of her hand and wove his arm through hers. Marvie inhaled sharply but hoped it wasn't audible over the lull of the crowd. Being so close to him made her heart race faster and a part of her wanted to pull away because it was too much for her senses. Another part of her wanted to kiss him just to see if it felt as good as she imagined it would.

"Not a tavern-goer?" Auden asked her.

Marvie shrugged. "I guess not. I used to be when…" She cut herself off before she could continue. *When I had people to go with* was how she was going to finish the statement. But she was sure Auden didn't want to hear those details of her life, how she was retreating further and further into her own world every day.

"When?" Auden prompted her.

She shook her head. "I used to be a tavern-goer," she finished, hoping he didn't ask her anymore about it.

Thankfully, he didn't. "Where's your favorite place in the city, then?"

Marvie took a deep breath of the salty air as she answered, "I love the harbor district. I know it can be dangerous to go there, but it's always been my favorite place. It's so loud, but at the same time, it's peaceful. I like the sound the ships make when they're just sitting there, the waves lapping up against the wood, the creaking, the wind. It's simultaneously calm and chaotic all at once. I don't know, I just love it. Does that make sense?"

"It does," Auden replied. "I can see why you love it."

"It's a little close to Southside, which I try to avoid for the most part." Marvie glanced over at him as she spoke and watched his eyes flash at the mention of Southside. For a moment, a shadow seemed to pass over his face, and then it was gone. Marvie wasn't sure if she had imagined it. She asked him quickly, "Have you been to Southside?"

Auden nodded, the movement slow and deliberate. "I have," was all he said in reply.

Marvie had a feeling she shouldn't ask another question about it. His voice hadn't changed, but her instincts told her it was a sore spot for Auden. The Southside was the worst part of Tenir, where most of the crime occurred. It was broken down and in constant need of both repairs and authority. There were also rumors that most underworld operations were conducted from the Southside. Her uncle constantly reminded her to stay away from the place, not that she would even consider going there on her own.

"Are we going anywhere specific?" Marvie asked him, hoping the mention of Southside hadn't ruined the mood. She hadn't forgotten what his boss had said to her. Auden had been working for him for a year, and Kalen had never met a single friend or family member. He had referred to him as mysterious. Was Auden...dangerous?

Honestly, Marvie didn't care if he was.

"Well, the harbor's a bit of a walk from here." They had gotten a distance from the bakery and started onto a stone bridge that went over a small creek that ran through Tenir. Auden stopped and leaned over the edge of the bridge. Marvie leaned next to him, studying the slow way the water moved. Streetlamps on either side of the bridge cast low light over them and something about it was so romantic that Marvie wondered if he had led her this way on purpose. "Where do you want to go?"

Her answer was automatic. "Anywhere with you." Marvie clapped her other hand over her mouth and rushed to correct herself. "I mean, anywhere you want to." She tripped over the words and mentally scolded herself once more. *Anywhere with you, Marvie? You met him yesterday!* She wouldn't be surprised if he took off running into the crowd after hearing her say that.

Auden was smiling at her, and the panic disappeared. "There's a bench down by the creek. We can sit there and eat the tarts, if that's okay with you, Marvolene."

"That's perfect, Auden," Marvie replied, and his smile grew wider at the sound of her saying his first name again. She avoided the urge to repeat it over and over again. He took her hand again and within minutes, they had turned down a street parallel to the creek. It was less crowded than the main street and dimly lit by lanterns. Moments later, the bench he had been referring to came into sight. There was no one else near them. Marvie sat down first, and Auden sat next to her, close enough that their shoulders were touching.

Auden took out one of the tarts and handed it to her. Marvie took a bite and savored the delicious, sweet flavors of it. She was tired of most things at the bakery, as she ate them almost every day, but the cherry tarts would never get old. She watched as Auden examined his carefully before taking a small bite.

Marvie raised an eyebrow at him as he chewed and swallowed. "Well?"

"It's delicious," he said, taking another bite. "You were right."

She observed him once more, this time closer than she ever had. His black curls were tousled from the slight breeze and Marvie once again avoided the strong desire to run her hands through them. His skin was clear and smooth, and his eyelashes were dark and long, somehow enhancing his beauty. And beauty was the word she would use, not 'handsome' or 'cute'. Auden was beautiful, as if he were from the pages of a story, some prince or great warrior. And she adored his eyes, that green color that hadn't strayed far from her mind since the moment she had seen them. As she watched them in the dim light of the streetlamp, she noticed there was a sort of seriousness behind them. It was almost like the wisdom she saw in her Uncle Hewe's gaze but not quite. His seriousness came from age and Auden couldn't be much older than she was.

"Can I ask you something?" Marvie spoke without thinking.

Auden looked at her and he almost appeared worried. "Of course."

"How old are you?"

A smile crept onto his face as he responded. "How old do you think I am?"

Marvie tapped her foot and looked at the creek. It calmed her to watch the water slowly flow through the rocks, ebbing and weaving around each obstacle so peacefully. She replied, "You can't be much older than I am, and I'm seventeen."

"You're close," he told her, finishing off the tart with a final bite. "I'm eighteen years old."

"You act older than you are," Marvie informed him, and Auden looked amused by this.

"It's not the first time I've heard that."

"I imagine."

"How long have you been in Orinth?" Auden asked her.

"My whole life," Marvie explained. "My parents died when I was very young. My aunt and uncle raised me, moving from Auntica to Tenir when I was a toddler. I live with them still."

Auden's eyes lingered on the cherry tart in her hand. "Do you have any brothers or sisters?"

She shook her head. "No, I don't. Sometimes I wish I did. I love my aunt and uncle very much, but it gets lonely." Of course, she used to have a friend who was like a sister to her, but they didn't see much of each other these days. Marvie almost wanted to open her mouth and tell Auden about Isla and the rest. She wanted to tell him everything. The desire to give him every part of her life was immense.

"Do you have any brothers and sisters?" Marvie quickly asked before she lost her mind and started spilling the most minor occurrences in her life to him.

"I do not," Auden replied, saying nothing else. Marvie wanted to ask him more about his family, but she had a feeling she shouldn't. His demeanor hadn't changed, but she recognized her own kind. Auden was an orphan, like herself, and maybe his story didn't end the way hers did. She had her aunt and uncle. Did Auden have anyone raising him, helping him?

They weren't questions to ask during their second conversation ever.

Marvie looked down at her cherry tart and then back up at Auden, whose eyes lingered. She offered it to him. He met her eyes, smiling a little. "You can have it," Marvie told him. "I'm not that hungry."

"I bought it for you, though."

"I eat them every day, Auden," Marvie laughed, holding the pastry out to him. "It's yours."

He took it, grinning. "I appreciate it. You were right about them; they're fantastic. So Olga's has amazing pastries and a beautiful girl. My kind of bakery."

Marvie felt herself blushing and turned to look at the creek so he wouldn't see. "I don't know if I would say that," she said and her voice cracked mid-sentence. She bit down on her lip to prevent from smiling.

Auden laughed softly and for a moment, there was silence. But it wasn't an awkward silence by any means. In the distance, the soft lull of the crowd could be heard. The sound of the creek babbling intertwined with it, the music of Tenir. Marvie took a deep breath, her shoulder just brushing Auden's and savored this moment. There was something about it so peaceful and perfect. She sneaked a glance at Auden, who stared at the ground, his green eyes contemplative.

There had never been anyone in her life so easy to share silence with, not even her aunt and uncle. But here he was.

It was a long time before either of them spoke again.

"Can I ask you a question, Marvolene?"

Marvie shifted on the bench, suddenly worried. She wasn't very interesting. Gods, they had just spent the last five minutes in silence. Marvie had enjoyed it, but had Auden? If he asked her more questions about herself, she would have to tell the truth and the truth was just boring. Still, she answered him. "Anything."

"Why," he struggled to find the right words, "why did you come with me?"

She bit her lip. "What do you mean?" The anxiety must have been apparent in her voice because Auden rushed to correct himself.

"I'm glad of it. But I guess I'm just trying to figure this out…" He took a breath and Marvie could hear his voice shake. "I don't know what I'm trying to say, Marvie. I know we just met, but why do I feel like I've known you my entire life? Why, when you walked into the shop yesterday, was it like I was seeing someone who had been apart from me for a long time? Why is that I can barely breathe when I look at you, Marvolene? Gods, I'm nervous just sitting here next to you. Can you explain it to me?"

Marvie didn't move; she thought she might pass out if she did. She pressed her hands together to prevent them from shaking. She wasn't sure if she had heard him correctly. Was her mind playing tricks on her? Was she still in a dream? How had he described the exact sensation that had overcome her upon first seeing him? She couldn't bring herself to look at him, though she felt his gaze on her.

"I don't know, Auden," she whispered, surprised her voice was even audible. "I can't explain it."

"I don't want to scare you."

"You're not scaring me," Marvie rushed to say.

"I think I am," Auden whispered.

Marvie remained still. Then, slowly, she turned to face him fully. His green eyes bore into her and there was so much behind them that she didn't understand. Who was this boy, and how was it possible that he had consumed her life so fast? In stories, she had read about loving someone the moment you saw them, but that wasn't real. Things like that just didn't happen.

And yet, the longer she looked at him…

With a trembling hand, Marvie reached up and ran a hand through his black curls. He inhaled sharply but didn't pull away. Instead, he leaned his head against her hand, so she was cupping his cheek. She kept it there, the corners of her lips upturning slightly. There was a tension that hung in the air and an energy coursed through her body, a sensation unlike anything she had ever known. She wondered if Auden could feel it too.

"I have to say," Marvie whispered, "this is the strangest conversation I've ever had with someone I met yesterday."

Auden smiled at her, and she was quite sure it was an image that would stay in her mind forever. He gently took her hand from his face and intertwined it with his own. "Me as well."

"I wish I had answers for the questions you asked me. I wish I knew, because I feel it too, Auden. I don't know what it is, and frankly, it's a little terrifying. I don't know you and you don't know me. If this is some sort of ploy to rob me, I'll tell you now, I don't have much to take," Marvie said, trying to force a chuckle, but it was getting hard to breathe with his hand in hers.

"I don't normally say things like this," Auden murmured, using his thumb to stroke her palm. The movement almost paralyzed her. "I can't help it with you. I feel like I need to tell you everything, starting with how I can't take my eyes off you."

"Auden, I'm not special," Marvie mumbled. "I'm just a normal girl from Tenir who works at a bakery and has no hobbies. I'm just trying to figure it all out."

"I think everyone's trying to figure it out, Marvie," Auden breathed, and his voice was uncertain as he continued stroking her skin. Everything about this was uncertain, and Marvie wondered if she should just get up and leave.

Without thinking, she stood, releasing his hand. "I should go," she said, voice wavering.

Auden was on his feet immediately. "I'm sorry. I'm so sorry." He tripped over the words, rushing to get them out. "I didn't mean to frighten you."

"You didn't," Marvie insisted, but the hammering of her heart said otherwise. But she wasn't scared of him. She wasn't afraid that he was going to hurt her or anything of that sort. No, Marvie was afraid of what was happening to her, the way her chest felt like it was imploding on itself, heart beating too fast. She feared how her head was spinning and her whole body was trembling. More than anything, Marvie was afraid of what these feelings were and what they meant and why they were happening around a complete stranger.

And why didn't he feel like a complete stranger?

Marvie stepped away from him, turning around as he called after her, "Marvie, please!"

She stopped.

"When can I see you again?" Auden asked, desperately, though he made no move to stop her from leaving.

Marvie closed her eyes. She wasn't scared of him, but rather, what she had begun to feel for him. She was seventeen years old and giving into these feelings might be her demise.

You don't know him, her brain screamed at her. *He's a stranger and he's going to hurt you.*

But he isn't, another part of her mind told her. *You know he isn't. You know him.*

There was only one way to know for certain.

Before she realized what she was doing, she turned around and crossed over to him in three strides, her lips colliding with his as she wrapped her arms around him, pulling his body against her own.

She had been kissed before, but never like this.

As his lips traveled against hers, every single part of her lit up and each of her senses responded more vividly than they ever had before. She breathed him in as they kissed, his scent that she couldn't find the words to describe. His hands moved up her back and wove into her hair, gently tilting her head to kiss her once more. He pulled back, pressing a kiss to her cheek and then her jaw, before meeting her lips again. Marvie wrapped her arms around him tighter.

He pulled back, his lips pressed against hers as he spoke, "I shouldn't be doing this."

She was too absorbed in the kiss to process what he said. "Why?"

"I…" Auden began, but his words were drowned out as their lips met once more.

Time had stopped for her, the world around them had disappeared, and Marvie hoped to the gods the moment would never end. He was what she wanted now. She wanted Auden, every part of him, every mistake, every triumph, every painful memory, every joyous one. She wanted it all. And she wanted to give him the same thing of her own.

"Marvolene," Auden whispered as he pulled away fully, grasping onto her. She was breathing heavily, her heart pounding against her chest that was pressed against his. He could probably feel it. Without realizing what she was doing, Marvie reached and touched his own chest, feeling for his heartbeat. She felt its pulse against her palm, beating as fast, if not faster, than hers. She moved that hand upwards and brushed another piece of hair out of his eyes.

Auden was staring at her intently, and she couldn't decipher what was behind his gaze. It certainly wasn't the elation that coursed through her. It wasn't regret, thank the gods, but something else, some expression she couldn't decipher.

Marvie forced herself to take a step back, releasing him. He didn't move, even as she took another three steps backwards. Without a word, Marvie turned around and started walking towards the street, her legs, no, her whole body shaking from the kiss. She didn't look back at him, couldn't bring herself to do anything but walk away.

She made it down three streets when she finally exhaled, stopping and pressing her hand to her lips that had just been passionately pressed against Auden's. She stumbled out of the middle of the street to avoid the crowds and used the wall of a building to brace herself. Marvie took long deep breaths as she repeated each and every detail of the scene, trying to understand it, but none of it made sense.

One thing was for certain, though: Marvolene Pere was in serious trouble.

Chapter 4

After managing to make her way home, Marvie crashed into bed but didn't sleep whatsoever. Instead, she relived every single moment she had shared with Auden, trying to put the pieces together. She was certain she had never met him before. More than certain, because there was no way she would've forgotten him. And yet, their connection had been instantaneous, something that shouldn't happen between two strangers.

So why did she have the urge to spend as much time as possible with this boy?

Marvie tried not to think like that, yet those thoughts had been frequent. They were not good thoughts, because she did not know Auden. She knew nothing about him, besides where he worked and how old he was. She refused to be the girl who ended up mugged in an alley because she trusted a random stranger.

But he wasn't random. Kissing him…kissing him had been the most wonderful sensation she had ever experienced in her entire life. Auden was a good kisser; she supposed that was another fact she knew about him.

Yet it had been he who stated, "I shouldn't be doing this." Doing what? Being with her?

After the tenth time of going through the same thought circle, Marvie dragged herself out of bed and put herself to doing something useful. The morning came and the hours ticked by slowly. Sienna tried to make her talk, noticing her strange behavior, but Marvie didn't speak a word of Auden. Gods, what would her aunt and uncle say if she told them? *Sorry I was late last night, Sienna and Hewes, I was kissing a boy I met the day before.* There was no way.

Marvie left for work an hour before she needed to. She was tired of trying to put the pieces together on her own. It was time to just ask Auden what was going on, where they stood, and what it meant. And if he asked never to see her again, then she would never see him again. The thought of those words coming out of his mouth made her sick to her stomach. Still, she walked through the streets of Tenir with her chin up, taking deep breaths to combat the rampant panic. When she reached the shop he worked at, she stood outside it for a solid five minutes.

"No," Marvie said, taking a step back and turning around. "No, I don't need to do this."

She walked three steps forward before cursing under her breath and charging into the shop.

Auden was in there, and immediately her words were caught in her throat as images of their kiss flashed before her eyes in rapid succession. The entire speech she had prepared seemed to disappear from her mind and she stood there, trying to stay on her feet, mouth hanging open.

Auden looked concerned. "Are you alright?" he asked her.

Marvie closed her mouth before turning and running out the door. She had made it only a few steps when Auden caught up to her.

"Marvie," he said, grabbing her hand.

She stopped, exhaling slowly, and turned to face him. Desperately, she tried to keep her gaze from lingering on his lips, but her body betrayed her as her vision locked on them. She let go of his hand, taking another step back. "Auden, I…"

"Marvie," Auden began at the same time as she, before stopping. He smiled at the ground and immediately the fear that had overtaken her mind disintegrated. She could not resist his smile. Some great artist needed to paint a picture of it or create a sculpture to capture its likeness. People would pay large amounts of money just to stare at it; Marvie knew she would.

"I'm sorry I left last night," Marvie said, tripping over the words as she blurted them out. "I was just confused and a little scared…" She tried to cut herself off before speaking the word.

Auden shook his head. "Don't apologize, Marvie. I'm sorry if I came on too strongly. I'm sorry if I scared you."

"You didn't scare me," Marvie rushed to correct him.

Auden raised an eyebrow. "But you just said…"

"It wasn't you," Marvie interrupted him. "It was," she gestured between them, "this. I wasn't lying when I said this is the strangest thing that's ever happened to me. Every logical part of my mind is telling me this is some sort of trick. Tenir is a city of criminals and part of me is convinced this is a ploy. There must be some ulterior motive. If that's the case, you're good at your job, Auden." Marvie tried to laugh, but it came out as a breathless grimace.

Auden picked up her hands once again, and this time she let him. He held them in his own as he spoke, staring into her eyes. "It's not a trick. I don't have ulterior motives. I'm the last person in the world who is going to hurt you, Marvolene. But what I said last night…" he trailed off.

"I shouldn't be doing this," Marvie repeated the words, and even now, they made her chest ache.

"It's not you," Auden said quietly. "My life is complicated."

Briefly, Marvie thought back to his boss, who had informed her she had been the first acquaintance of Auden that he had ever met. Did the complications have something to do with that? "Everyone's life is complicated, Auden. That's a part of being alive."

He shook his head once again. "Not like my life is."

Marvie released his hands, crossing her arms in front of her chest. "What do you mean?"

Before he could answer, someone called from behind them. "Frae!"

They both turned. Auden's boss, Kalen, was standing in the door of the shop, scowling. "We have customers. I need you in here." Marvie bit her lip, pressing a hand to her forehead. Now she had gotten Auden in trouble. She should've just waited until he was done with his shift.

Auden spoke loudly and clearly to his boss. "I need five more minutes, Kalen."

Marvie tried not to outwardly gasp at his tone. It was not the respect that an employee should show their superior, and for one panicked second, Marvie wondered if she were about to witness Auden get fired. How could he speak to his boss in that way? She was more than prepared to take a step back and let him get back to work. She swallowed back the guilt and braced herself.

It never happened. Kalen nodded and replied, "Five minutes." He returned inside. Marvie gaped, staring at the door and then at Auden.

He didn't give her a chance to ask any questions. "Marvie, I want to spend time with you. As much time as I possibly can. I want to get to know you, every single detail, because no detail about you is too small for me. I've spent most of my life alone by my own will, but suddenly I want to spend my time with you. My life is complicated in ways I don't know how to explain. But if you're willing to give me a chance, I think we'll be able to figure out what this," he gestured in between them as she had done only moments ago, "is."

She opened her mouth to respond, but no sound came out. Marvie watched him instead, his black curls blowing chaotically in the wind, green eyes staring intently at her. For a brief moment, she lost herself in the beauty of them, before snapping out of it. "What are you asking?" she finally managed to say.

"I'm asking if you want to go to dinner with me tonight," Auden said, a small smile dancing on his lips.

Gods, she should say no, and walk away. The last thing she needed right now was more complications. Auden had openly admitted to being one. He had denied being a criminal, but how could she know that for sure? She couldn't.

But what Marvie did know was that being around him brought her a genuine happiness she hadn't felt in a long while. His smile alone did a number on her. When she looked at him she wasn't looking at a stranger, but rather, someone she had known for a long time, someone she might have loved a long while ago and couldn't remember. There was a familiarity in the deep green of his eyes she found nowhere else. Looking at him now, she could see a future, their future. It was ridiculous and preposterous, and most people would probably accuse her of being young and stupid, and maybe she was.

But she was young, and now was the time to be stupid.

It could've been the most foolish thing she had ever done as she responded. "I'll see you tonight, then," Marvie whispered, unable to contain her grin as she turned around and began walking the other direction. She could feel his eyes on her back as she walked, and she prayed to the gods she didn't trip and fall.

Her entire shift through the bakery dragged out, and her mind rested on Auden alone. She couldn't stop smiling, even as the doubts nagged at the back of her mind. Marvie ignored those doubts. At one point, Olga asked, "What's gotten into you, Marvolene?"

Marvie could only smile and shrug, which earned an eyeroll from her boss.

The moment the bakery closed, she grabbed her cloak and ran out the door.

Auden was leaning against a streetlamp, arms crossed, waiting for her. His eyes lit up when he saw her and a part of her melted. No one had ever reacted that way to seeing her. A grin spread on his face, and he started towards her, weaving through the people before reaching her. He took her hand, intertwining their fingers, and without a word, started leading them down the street.

"Where are we going?" Marvie asked him, her voice higher than usual. It made sense, considering she felt as high as the stars themselves.

"Dinner," Auden said to her, squeezing her hand once and shooting her another smile.

"Where?"

"A tavern down the street, if it's okay with you," he replied.

"Anything's okay with me," Marvie responded, squeezing his hand in return. They fit perfectly together. The first time they held hands, she had considered that maybe they were made for one another. Marvie mentally slapped herself for the thought a second time, but it lingered. Made for one another. What a silly little phrase.

"Did you have a good day today?" Auden asked her, leading her through the crowd. As they walked, Marvie was overcome by a sense of peace as she took in her city. The cobblestone streets packed full of people, the tall brick buildings, the waves crashing in the distance, the smell of salt lingering in the air, and best of all, a beautiful boy holding her hand, looking at her like she was worth something.

"I'm having a good day now," Marvie answered, and this time, she didn't care how it sounded. She could be honest with him. It was hard to be honest with anyone these days but not Auden. She could tell him anything.

Auden didn't hide his smile at the answer. "I can't imagine why."

"I think you can."

He looked down at the ground, and then back at her. "Maybe."

"What about you? Did you have a good day?" Marvie asked him, swinging their hands back and forth as they walked. With her other free hand, she pulled her hair down from where it had been pinned up, shaking her head back and forth, letting it fall. She ran her hand through it a few times, before glancing back at Auden, who was watching her.

"I am now," he responded, and Marvie knew there was no turning back from this.

They walked the rest of the way in comfortable silence, listening to the sounds of their city, the talking, the laughter, the footsteps on the streets, the music pouring from nearby buildings, and Marvie basked in the perfection of it.

Being with Auden made her want to see the beauty in everything.

He finally led them into a tavern. It had no outward sign and was housed in a typical two-story building of brick. The place was crowded, and Marvie couldn't spot a single open table. Auden kept a tight grip on her hand as they moved. A waiter suddenly appeared in front of them, a young man who looked exasperated. "There's a wait for tables," he snapped.

Marvie took a step back. "We'll come again," she told Auden, but he didn't move.

"We'd like a table now, please," Auden said to the waiter and Marvie blinked. The waiter looked slightly stunned.

"Auden, there are no tables," she said, tugging on his hand. The tavern was ridiculously hot, and there was a stench of sweat mixed with some sort of delicious-smelling meat. She could barely hear over the music that was coming from the stage on the other side of the room. Most of the patrons stood at the bar, a long one right near the door. Between the bar and the stage were the wooden tables, and they were completely full. Maybe Auden had misheard him, though the waiter had been pretty damn clear.

"Auden..." she said again when he didn't respond.

The waiter spoke before he could. "I'll go get a table ready for you," he said quickly, ducking away from them.

Marvie raised both eyebrows. She stuttered, "W...what?"

Auden looked at her and shrugged. "Sometimes you have to ask twice. These Orinthians can be rude."

She had never seen anything like that before, and she had spent a lot of time at taverns with her friends. "I can't believe he changed his mind like that," Marvie yelled over the music.

"I guess we're lucky," Auden shouted back.

"I guess," Marvie replied, still slightly confused about what had just happened.

The waiter reappeared, and he looked dazed. "I have a table near the back for you." He gestured at them to follow. He led them away from the stage, against the wall opposite the bar. It remained loud, but they didn't have to yell over one another. Auden pulled out a chair for her and Marvie sat down, unable to hide another grin. He sat down across from her and thanked the waiter, who walked away with a confused expression.

Marvie reached across the table and picked up Auden's hand. "Maybe I'm not the only person affected by your charm."

Auden laughed, pressing a kiss to her palm. "I'm just good with people," he told her.

Another waiter came by and took their drink order, explaining tonight's meal was chicken and potatoes. Auden ordered two plates of it before turning his attention back to Marvie.

She cursed under her breath. "I don't have any money on me."

Auden rolled his eyes. "Don't worry about money."

Marvie protested. "I don't want to make you pay for me."

"I want to pay for you, Marvolene," Auden said, tracing circles on the top of her hand with his thumb. "I want to make you happy."

"You barely know me," she laughed, turning in her seat to watch the performer, a single man playing a fiddle and singing. The crowd had begun to clap along with him and there was a swell of joy in her chest as she glanced at Auden again.

"I want to get to know you," Auden responded. "Tell me something about yourself, Marvie."

"What do you want to know?"

"Anything."

"Well…" Marvie took a deep breath, racking her mind for something interesting to tell him. She bit her lip. She was not an interesting person, which brought her back to the same question she had been asking herself for the last two days: why her? Why would this beautiful boy be interested in her? She ignored her question and tried to find a way to answer his.

"I don't know how to swim," Marvie finally said and immediately regretted it. She had the chance to tell Auden something special or fun about herself, and of course, she chose something disappointing.

Auden raised both eyebrows, not in mockery but in surprise. "You don't?"

Marvie buried her head in her hands. "Don't make fun of me."

Auden was hiding his laughter as he grabbed her hands again. "I'm not! I'm just surprised. I thought all children in Orinth learned to swim at an early age."

"I'm not Orinthian," Marvie pointed out, as if it was a strong defense. Her cheeks were starting to grow warm, and she rushed to explain. "My aunt and uncle tried to teach me when I was young. They tried to raise me as an Orinthian. But being an only child…not even their child…they had a hard time telling me no. And after three failed attempts at swimming, I didn't want to do it anymore. Well, they didn't protest me giving up." Hearing the words aloud made her realize how truly pathetic it was. Seventeen years old and unable to swim. Her cheeks grew warmer.

"Marvie, it's okay!" Auden exclaimed, though she could tell he was holding in laughter. He pressed a kiss to her hand once more. "Swimming isn't all it's cut out to be."

"Don't lie to me," Marvie said, rolling her eyes at him. Before he could respond, their server dropped off two glasses of Orinthian wine. Marvie immediately took a long drink to calm her rapidly increasing nerves.

"I'll teach you to swim, okay?" Auden said, beaming at her as he took a drink of his own wine.

"No way," Marvie said, shaking her head, though secretly thrilled at the idea of planning another occasion to see him. "I'm not embarrassing myself like that in front of you."

Auden threw his head back and laughed, while simultaneously brushing the hair from his eyes. Marvie wondered if he had any idea how attractive he was. Probably not. She had met a lot of boys who knew they were and used it to their advantage. Auden seemed completely oblivious to the fact he was the most beautiful in the room.

"I wouldn't laugh at you," Auden promised, trying and failing to keep a straight face as laughter seeped through the cracks.

"You're a bad liar," she said, though she couldn't help smiling back at him.

"Maybe," he shrugged, taking another drink of the wine.

"Okay, your turn."

"My turn for what?"

"Your turn to tell me something about yourself," Marvie said, giving him a look. "You know more about me than I do about you."

"I like it that way. I heard some people like mystery." Auden cocked his head. "They say it's attractive."

"You don't need any help there." Marvie spoke before she realized it and clapped a hand over her mouth. Auden started laughing, and she buried her face in her hands once again. She was so bad at this.

"Good to know," Auden said, gently grabbing her chin and making her look at him. He wove his fingers through hers and appeared thoughtful. "Something about me? I've never been to Auntica."

Marvie raised both her eyebrows. "Really?"

He nodded, pursing his lips. "I've never had much desire to leave Orinth. But now," he paused, meeting her eyes again, "now, I feel like I want to go there."

"Why is that?" Marvie asked, leaning forward to rest her elbows on the table as she finished the last of her wine. It was so delicious and had already gone to her head, making the music louder and the colors brighter and the world better. She wanted to signal for another glass, but she didn't look away from the boy sitting in front of her.

"I don't know, really," Auden said, tearing his gaze away from her and signaling at one of the nearby servers, who collected their empty glasses and replaced them with two full ones.

"Do you live with your parents?" Marvie blurted out the question before thinking about it. She had been wanting to ask it since the night before but was afraid to, given his reaction to the question about having siblings. Her curiosity seemed to have gotten the better of her after the first glass of wine, and she was already halfway through the next one.

Auden's expression didn't change, but something behind his eyes darkened. He took a long drink before answering. "I live alone. A few blocks from here, actually."

It was an answer, but it wasn't an answer. She had been trying to ask whether or not he had parents at all. Marvie had a feeling he had purposely avoided the question, and it fueled her interest even more. But the darkness was there, and it was apparent. Even as she looked at him, she subconsciously leaned back into her chair, smile disappearing from her face. It was intense, the pain that flashed behind his eyes, and Marvie had never seen anything like it before.

Then, in an instant, it was gone.

"What do you do when you're not working?" Auden asked, interrupting the tension. His voice was light, as if the last few seconds hadn't happened.

Marvie tried to shake off the foreboding feeling as she answered. "Not much," she replied, thinking suddenly of Isla. She glanced around the room, searching the faces to see if she recognized any of them. She had been to this tavern a few times, with Isla, of course. It was dark in the room, but none of the patrons looked like her old friend. Marvie turned her attention back to Auden, trying to think of something interesting she did. "I spend a lot of time with my aunt and uncle," she finally said, and it was the best she could do.

"That's wonderful," Auden said cheerfully. "What are they like?"

Marvie smiled without realizing it. "They're amazing. They are like my mother and father, but I call them by their first names. My childhood was so good, I have so many memories with them. Sienna and Hewes were never strict, though I guess I didn't do that much to warrant discipline. We traveled. When I wasn't in school, they would take me back to my home country, sometimes other cities in Orinth like Abdul and Lou. They're easy to get along with and I know they would love you."

She didn't mean to say the last part, but by the way Auden's face lit up, she was glad she did. "They sound incredible," Auden replied.

"You can meet them." Marvie drained the last of her second glass, glancing at Auden. She reached across the table and ran a hand through his black curls again. He was smiling, slightly uncertain, and Marvie continued, "You can come with us on our walk tomorrow."

"Walk?"

"We always go for a walk by the harbor on the days I don't work," she explained. "We go right before the sun starts to set. That way we can watch it while we walk. Come with us." Was it hasty to invite Auden to meet her aunt and uncle when it was only the third time they had met themselves? Yes. Did she care? No. Was she starting to get a little tipsy? Yes.

"Are you sure?" Auden asked. He was probably just as confused as she was. Marvie waved their server down for another glass of wine before responding.

"I want you to meet the people I love," Marvie said, touching his cheek.

He set his hand on top of hers. "I want to meet them, Marvolene. But do they want to meet me?"

Well, they don't know you exist, Marvie thought to herself. Before she could reply, the server returned with two plates of food and another glass of wine for Marvie. The question was forgotten as they dug into the delicious dinner, clapping each time the performer ended a song, occasionally commenting on one thing or another.

It was perfect. He was perfect. Auden was easier to talk to than anyone she had ever met in her entire life. He listened to her intently when she spoke, making her feel like she was the only person in the world. He knew the right things to say. Every time he picked up her hand, it sent shockwaves of joy through her body, and she lost another small bit of her heart. Every doubt, every warning was gone; not even a whisper of it remained.

There was only Auden.

They stayed for hours after they finished eating, Marvie going through multiple glasses of wine. When they cleared the tables for dancing, she didn't even ask, only grabbed Auden's hand and pulled him onto the floor. Song after song, he danced with her, smile not leaving his face. At one point, the entire tavern sang the same song, an Orinthian folk tune that Marvie had learned when she was young. Auden wrapped his arm around her and sang, his beautiful voice music to her ears.

It was only when she could barely stand that they left the tavern.

The streets were still crowded, but Marvie couldn't see straight. She leaned up against Auden, not able to stop laughing or smiling. She was giddy, absolutely elated because it had been the best night she had had in a while. No, it might have been the best night of her entire life. Drinking and dancing and eating and laughing and Auden Frae.

He had his arm wrapped around her, holding her up as they walked. She had managed to give him directions to her aunt and uncle's apartment, unable to make it there herself. It had been a long time since she had been this drunk.

It had been a long time since she had been this happy.

When they turned down an alley to take a shortcut to her apartment, Marvie stopped them.

"What's wrong?" Auden asked, tucking a piece of her hair behind her ear.

Marvie didn't respond but kissed him instead, wrapping her arms around his neck and pulling him as close as she possibly could. Auden kissed her deeply in return, walking until her back was pressed against the wall of the alley. He planted one hand behind her neck, the other braced against the brick behind them. He tasted like Orinthian wine and Marvie slipped her hands underneath his shirt, feeling his bare skin that was hot to the touch. Auden exhaled against her mouth, laughing.

"Marvolene, I have to get you home," Auden managed to get out in between kisses.

Marvie gasped as his lips moved down to her neck. She wove her hands through his curls and was barely able to reply. "We're not far from your apartment, you said?" The last place she wanted to be was in her own bed, alone.

"Marvie," Auden was chuckling as he pulled back. She tried to kiss him again, but he kept both hands on her shoulders, rendering her motionless. "I have to get you home."

"Why?" Marvie groaned, her head suddenly spinning. The ground was moving beneath her, and she tried to remember how many glasses of Orinthian wine she had.

Gods, she was in an alley with a boy she had met three days ago, drunk. Was she stupid? Yeah, she was stupid. But there wasn't a single part of her that felt like she was in danger. On the contrary, holding onto Auden was so incredibly safe.

"Because," Auden replied, taking her hand and pulling her away from the wall. She managed to stay on her own two feet this time, but she laid her head on his shoulder, sighing. "I'm meeting your aunt and uncle tomorrow, and I want to be well-rested for that."

Marvie looked up at him. "You are?"

"Isn't that what you want?"

"Absolutely it is," Marvie smiled.

"Then let's get you home. And when you go to bed, you'll close your eyes. When you open them, it'll be tomorrow, and tomorrow, we'll be together. You see?" Auden was chuckling as he spoke, but he was breathless. Marvie had a feeling there were other choices he was debating rather than taking her home.

"But we're together now," Marvie protested, swinging their woven hands back and forth again.

"And now is perfect," Auden answered. "But tomorrow will be better, so long as you and I are together, Marvolene."

The words filled her with an exhilaration that was so incredibly powerful, she leaned back against Auden for support, unable to muster any words, just a smile.

She didn't remember whether he walked her to the door or up the stairs. She only remembered collapsing into her bed alone, smile still across her face as she tried, through her foggy brain, to remember every moment she had shared that night with Auden Frae.

As she drifted to sleep, his words echoed in her brain, lulling her into a peaceful slumber.

Tomorrow will be better, so long as you and I are together.

Gods, let them be together for the rest of her tomorrows.

Chapter 5

He had done a lot of bad things in the last four years.

He had killed a person to start it off, a reality that continued to haunt him almost every day. The image was imprinted in his mind: a boy in an alley, laying on bricks that were stained with Auden's own puke and blood. He hadn't killed since then, but his sins were still egregious. He had stolen. Almost everything he owned had been stolen. Well, was it stealing if he had simply asked and was given what he wanted? Yeah, it still counted. His horse, his large stash of money, his apartment, his clothes, his wine, his food; all of it had been given to him. It was only last year he decided to get a job, if only to keep him somewhat entertained. He had stopped the manipulating afterwards, as he had enough of everything to last him awhile. But he didn't stop using his powers. Auden just used them for little conveniences now, but using them was bad enough.

But the worst thing Auden had ever done was letting Marvolene Pere into his life.

As he laid in his bed, the same bed he had used his shadow to get, it was the only thing he could think about. She was too good for him. No, that was a drastic understatement. She was worth more than him by an infinite amount. Marvie was good, pure, innocent. Marvie was some sort of superior being, as if all the loveliest things in the world had manifested themselves into a single person.

There used to be a spot in his room at the orphanage where the carpet was clean enough to lay. The sun would come in the window just right, its beams resting on that exact spot, and Auden would curl in a ball, soaking up the warm rays in a place that could grow very cold. In those brief moments when he lay in the sun, the horror of his life just faded away, and his chest would fill with this glowing energy. For just a moment, he could convince himself that everything might be okay, that his life wasn't a waste, that he wasn't doomed to the life of misery that had been carved out for him. In the sunlight was a freedom he could find nowhere else.

Since that day in the alley, there had been nothing to make him feel that way again.

Until he saw her.

Marvie had stumbled into that stupid shop he worked in, some stupid man spilling water all over her without an apology, before she turned to him, her face going pale and her mouth opening wide, like she was seeing a ghost. Auden had been paralyzed for the slightest of seconds, as that sensation of the sun slammed into him like a wave crashing to shore. An inexplicable joy filled him with warmth and the shadow disappeared. He was a normal person, a regular man who just set eyes on the person he wanted to spend the rest of his life with. That void where the darkness lingered had ceased to exist and that warmth had filled the cracks and holes of brokenness and pain inside him. That demon that lived in his skin was gone.

He waited for the feeling to go away, but it didn't, as she stood there talking to him, and Auden racked his brain to figure out where he had met her before. There was no possibility that this could be the first time they had met. He recognized her, this beautiful girl with her golden hair and her dazzling blue eyes, her soft features and smooth, almost-glowing skin. He recognized her quiet demeanor, reserved but curious. Her sort of beauty didn't fit with someone who was reserved; she had to have spent the majority of her life with people's eyes on her, because Auden found he couldn't stop staring.

The words had bubbled out from him before he could stop himself, words about having met her before, and he cursed himself. He would terrify this girl with his stupid questions, his assumption that maybe she was feeling this as powerfully as he was. No, Marvolene was seeing some crazy man behind the shop counter and would probably continue to look over her shoulder to ensure he didn't follow her. He was a fool to have said anything at all, but maybe that was for the better. She would run away and never come back, and he couldn't hurt this girl with the dark reality of who he was. She would be safe from him and live a good, long, happy life.

But Marvie hadn't run.

She had stayed and suddenly his entire purpose in life had shifted. Before her, the only reason to keep living was...well, he didn't have one. There was just something inside him that forced him to keep going, to not look back, to survive, survive, survive. It had been his mindset since his childhood in the orphanage. Just survive. What was the point of surviving? It didn't matter, just survive. What was his purpose? What was keeping him here? What made him get up in the morning? What made him keep breathing? It didn't matter. Just survive.

In the blink of an eye, every single one of the questions had answers, and the answer was Marvolene Pere. She was the point of surviving. She was his purpose, what was keeping him there, what made him get up in the morning. Marvolene Pere would keep him breathing.

He had known her for so short of time, but he belonged to her, every broken bit of him.

They had spent time together, and it had locked into place, much to his simultaneous joy and despair. Joy, because he already knew he loved her, though he wouldn't say it yet. He wouldn't scare her off, even though she should be scared. Despair because being near him was a dangerous game.

He was a disaster, and he was going to ruin her life. Auden possessed a dark, demonic power that he barely knew how to control, and most days, it seemed to control him. Danger followed him around like a disagreeable companion. The darkness that resided in his heart would no doubt attempt to overtake Marvie too. The safest thing for her was to stay far away from him.

But it was already too late.

Auden saw the way she looked at him, the way her smile never seemed to fade when they were together. As much as it filled him with an indescribable joy, he wanted to scream at her to run away. For a moment, he thought she would. When she walked away from the bench on the creek, he wondered if that was it, if the safe haven that had crashed into his life was leaving as quickly as she had come.

Yet, she had turned around and kissed him, and it had sealed his fate.

His purpose was no longer to survive. It was to make Marvolene Pere happy. It could be the worst decision he had ever made, but there was nothing he could do now.

Auden didn't go to work the next morning. Kalen might yell at him, but he would forget about it, because Auden would make him. The idea of having to stand in that shop all day before seeing Marvie was laughable. Working was a part of surviving, and now that he didn't have to survive anymore, Auden wondered if he should just quit the job. He would ponder on it before making any sort of decision.

Yesterday was the best night of his life. Nothing came close. He had been frightened, at first, when Marvie ran into the shop only to run right back out. He followed her, despite the customers, while a part of him wondered if maybe he should let her go. But Auden wasn't capable of it.

He had tried to warn her though. *"My life is complicated."*

"Everyone's life is complicated, Auden. That's a part of being alive."

If only his life had those typical life complications, instead of a darkness that was rooted in his soul and gave him the power to do terrible, terrible things.

The rest of the night had been perfect, every part of it. Drinking and dancing and talking with Marvolene, listening carefully to each of her stories, watching that smile never leave her face. Auden wished he could relive the entire night because the shadow had disappeared once more. Well, he had used it to get them a table, but that didn't count. He occasionally bended people's minds to get what he wanted. Was that necessarily evil?

Yes, and he was a fool to pretend it wasn't, but he didn't think about that; he thought about Marvie.

If their time at the tavern wasn't enough to seal his fate, the walk back to her apartment had done it. And now, she wanted him to meet her aunt and uncle. Once again, he was in the predicament of experiencing overpowering happiness and intense anguish. Happiness because Marvie spoke extremely highly of the two people who had raised her. The fact she wanted to introduce them to him was telling in the best and worst way. He was becoming important to her. Not. Good.

Auden was powerless. For the first time in his entire life, he had found something that brought him some semblance of light. His world had been consumed by darkness for so long, and he had let it. The hatred he possessed for the person he had become was intense. A chance to pull himself from this fog? Auden had to take it.

Auden glanced up at the antique clock on his wall that he had stolen/been given from a store in Tenir. He had about three hours before he had to be at the harbor to meet Marvie, her aunt, and uncle. That was three hours to figure out how he was going to answer the questions they would assuredly ask, the questions that Marvie had asked herself. He had managed to dance around them, but that probably wouldn't work on the two people who raised Marvie as their own.

Their first question would probably be along the lines of "what do you do?".

Auden cleared his throat, speaking to the emptiness of his apartment. "Well, Mr. and Mrs. Courtright, I work at a shop that sells items to travelers, different sorts of rations and such, called The Wooden Barrel."

The next question would probably be along the lines of "what do you want to do?".

"I want to be a normal person who doesn't have the capability to destroy with just a thought. I want to go through my day without using my powers to manipulate and use other people to get what I want. One single day without tapping into the shadow, but I don't think I'm capable of it. I want to love someone without plunging them into the danger that seems to follow me. There are people watching me, sometimes. I think they might know about what happened in the alley and I think they might be plotting something, but it's always out of the corner of my eye. If I were a normal boy, this wouldn't be a problem. I want to be free of the shadow, but at the same time, I wonder if I could survive without it. I don't think I could."

Auden stood up, straightening the blankets on his stolen bed, before he changed into a pair of pants and a shirt that a merchant had handed to him a few weeks ago. Auden glanced at his reflection in the mirror on his wall, a long one with gold trim. His hair stuck up in every direction and he tried to smooth his curls with one hand, to no avail. Auden stared at the green eyes that looked back at him. The darkness within them was so apparent, how couldn't Marvie see it? Or maybe she did and chose to ignore it. For now, that's what he would do. With a sigh, he walked out of his room.

He poured himself a large glass of water as he thought of the next question. "What do your parents do?"

"Well, Mr. and Mrs. Courtright," Auden answered, returning the bottle to the ice box that wasn't his. "My father is a soldier. He knew I was in that nightmare of an orphanage, but he didn't care enough to do anything about it. I haven't seen him in years. I don't know if he's alive or dead, fighting that War in the Wilds, and I can't find the will to care. And my mother," he sucked in a breath, picking up his glass and resisting the urge to throw it at the wall, "my mother abandoned me so early on, I can't remember a single thing about her. Not her face, not her voice, not her laugh, nothing. I don't know how it's possible for a baby to be so revolting, but apparently, I was. Maybe she knew, Mr. and Mrs. Courtright. Maybe she looked into my eyes after holding me for the first time and saw the darkness there, saw the shadow that ran through my veins, and realized she could never love this child. I can't say I blame her, but I'll never forgive her. I guess what I'm trying to say is I don't really know what my parents do, and I don't care to find out."

He took a long drink of water, the cool sensation trickling down his throat and chest. Auden walked over to the window that his sitting room faced. The view was immaculate, a direct view of the sparkling blue sea, the sun hitting it perfectly. He was on the top floor of the building, with a room that would typically cost his entire month's wages to rent, but it cost him nothing. The landlord couldn't understand why his profit was so low with a room like this. Auden wouldn't be the one to explain it to him.

"What are your goals, Auden? What are your dreams and your aspirations?"

Auden leaned his forehead against the glass, closing his eyes, before murmuring to himself. "I never want to kill someone again. Once was enough, more than enough. He was going to kill me, but I hate myself for it. I think about it every day, replaying it in my mind. Was there something I could've done differently, protecting myself and sparing him? If I never have to kill someone again, I'll be happy about it."

Auden opened his eyes, glancing out at the sea once more. "But even if I don't kill another person, it'll never leave me, will it? It's a burden I'll have to bear for the rest of my days. I will never exist as a person free of darkness. It's a part of me. No matter what I do or who I become, it will always be there. And that is the cold reality I will never be able to face."

He turned around, the shadow suddenly a living, breathing, flaring thing, coursing within him with as much intensity as it could, feeding off his anger, desiring to be put into use at that very moment. "I bet you want to know, Mr. and Mrs. Courtright, why I would be good for your niece, the girl you raised as your daughter. Well, the honest to gods truth is, I'm not. While she's the best thing that's happened to me, I'm the worst thing that could've possibly happened to her. I'll try to keep my darkness hidden, of course, but it likes to reveal itself. I'm not sure I'm strong enough to stop using it, as much as I want to, for her..." his voice trailed off.

Auden slipped onto one of the stools in his kitchen, letting his head fall onto the counter. "I'll become good for her though," he whispered, thinking once again of the previous night. "I'll stop using my powers. I'll stop manipulating people, even in small ways. I'll act as human as I can, for her sake. Will that make me good enough for her? Not even close, but I can still try."

He would have to keep working to pay for this apartment. He couldn't use the shadow on the landlord anymore. He could never use it on Kalen to make his workload lighter or to take longer breaks. Auden would have to carry money wherever he went; he couldn't just ask a merchant to give him some product and get away with it. He would limit every single possibility of growing angry, the time the shadow thrived the most. Let it drain out of him, slowly, until he was as human as possible.

Would that be enough? No, it would never be enough. He would never be enough for Marvie, but gods, he couldn't let her go. Was he capable of it, not using the shadow when it was such a part of him? He used it every day, in one way or another. Auden didn't know, but he would try, for Marvolene Pere.

"I know I'm probably not what you imagined for her, Mr. and Mrs. Courtright," he said softly into the counter. "But there's no one in this entire world who's going to love Marvie more than I will."

For the first time that morning, he felt some semblance of relief course through him, numbing the shadow until there was nothing left but Marvie.

Chapter 6

The hours went slowly, too slowly, waiting for the sunset. As the time grew nearer, Auden realized his heart was pounding, and a small amount of sweat coated his skin. He quickly changed clothes again. Gods, he was nervous. When was the last time he had been nervous about something? Maybe never. But meeting Marvie's aunt and uncle for the first time was incredibly daunting, like he was meeting a king and queen. Auden went into his washroom countless times and splashed water from the basin on his face. With one final look in the mirror, he left.

His apartment was about a twenty-minute walk from the harbor, and he took every shortcut he could. It was a dangerous part of Tenir, but danger didn't seem to register with him anymore. What could anyone possibly do to him? Even if they jumped him, had the element of surprise, had every advantage in the book, he would beat them. Nothing had ever happened while walking the backstreets, and Auden pondered about whether people could sense the air of darkness around him.

For one petrifying moment, Auden wondered what would happen if Marvie's aunt or uncle sensed the shadow within him, if they subconsciously feared him. What would happen then? Marvie loved her aunt and uncle. If they told her not to see Auden anymore, he had no doubt she would respect their wishes. Now, Auden sort of wished they would, to protect her. It might destroy him, but she would be safe from him.

The thought strengthened the shadow, and he took deep breaths to calm it. He would not meet Marvie's family while reeling in the darkness, despite the fact it made him feel alert, alive.

Auden followed the streets without really looking. He knew them like the back of his hands. It was strange to think he had grown up in this city, that miles away, the same orphanage still stood. After everything that had happened, he had never gotten close to it. A part of him had wanted to leave Tenir completely, but he didn't; he knew nowhere else. So, he had moved across the city, praying he would never see the people of his past again. So far, he hadn't.

It seemed like an eternity before the tall masts of the ships came into view. Between the bustle of the sailors and the many booths vendors had assembled in the stone square beyond the docks, the harbor district was one of the busiest parts of Tenir. Right along the water was a wooden boardwalk that extended around the outskirts of the city, boasting a perfect view of the sea from any point. At that moment, a large crowd was mingling around each of the booths, and the smell of something delicious hung over them like a cloud. There was music coming from somewhere, intermingled with the sound of talking and laughing and cursing. Auden had always loved the harbor district, even as a child. It was a place where worlds collided. And now that he was about to meet Marvie's aunt and uncle, the sentiment was even truer.

He scanned each of the faces around the booths for her, but she was nowhere to be seen. He cut through the crowd with mumbled apologies as he bumped into a few people. His shadow was dangerously on edge with the crowds around him, a precaution he couldn't help but take. Auden took a deep breath through his nose and released it through his mouth as he made his way towards the start of the boardwalk, a short distance from the actual docks. He planted himself in place, leaning against the railing, continuing to scan the crowd for Marvie. Auden glanced at the sky. The sun was an orange dot resting on the water, the clouds an explosion of pinks and oranges, a painting by the gods. Auden exhaled softly as he took it in, appreciating the fixed chaos for the slightest of moments. He had always loved sunsets, ever since he was just a boy. In the orphanage, there had been very little to appreciate. Many days, the only form of beauty was what lay outside his window, and he would try to absorb it all before it disappeared.

For a moment, Auden grew immensely jealous of that little boy from his memories, face pressed up against the glass in wonder. Maybe his life was hard, but at least he was still innocent. There was darkness within him, but it wasn't a living, breathing thing with the strength to control him. Auden envied that boy who was free of the burden of the shadow; he would give anything, *anything*, to go back and be that boy again. The sunset was just another beautiful, painful reminder of who he was, a reality he could never escape, no matter how hard he tried.

"Auden!" a voice called from behind him, and he tore his eyes away from the palette of colors in the sky.

There she was. Marvolene Pere. Auden didn't even try to hide his grin.

She was walking towards him, smile glowing as her blonde hair swung back and forth with her steps. It hung down around her face, slightly curly, and perfect in his mind. She had on a white shirt and a blue skirt that somehow made her already beautiful blue eyes more vivid. The setting sunlight hit her face at the perfect angle, casting an orange glow on her skin, and Auden wondered why in the world this sweet girl was bothering with him.

"Marvolene," Auden said, dragging out each of the syllables, every beautiful bit of the word. He picked up her hand and pressed a kiss to it. A pink flushed her cheeks and she smiled at him, reaching up to brush one of his curls back. She had already made it a habit of doing that, and he absolutely adored the movement.

Auden glanced behind her, expecting to see two other people, but there was no one. He looked down at her, their hands now intertwined in front of their bodies. "I thought your aunt and your uncle were coming on the walk." For a moment, his stomach churned as he thought she had changed her mind and didn't want her aunt and uncle to meet him. Again, it would definitely be for the best, but it didn't make it any less painful if it was true.

"They are," Marvie assured him. She glanced over her shoulder at the mass of people in the square. "They wanted to stop to get whatever smelled so good. They're going to get you something too, so be prepared." She smiled at the ground, almost bashfully. "They want to impress you."

Auden raised both eyebrows. "I thought that's what I'm supposed to try to do."

Marvie shook her head. "No, they already love you. I told them about you and they're just so glad I'm seeing someone besides the two of them that..." She cut herself off, her cheeks growing redder as if she had unknowingly revealed some sort of secret. "Well, they're excited to meet you," she finished breathlessly.

Auden squeezed her hand once. He hadn't expected her to need reassurance, but by the tone of her voice, it was clear she did. Even though it felt like he had known this girl for his whole life, they had only met days ago. He didn't know everything about her, yet. "I'm excited to meet them, too," he assured her.

She gave him a grateful smile. "What did you do today?" she asked cheerfully, leaning up against the railing, staring out at the sunshine. Auden wanted to watch it too, but he found he couldn't take his eyes off her.

"Oh, this and that," Auden replied, holding back a bitter laugh. He had spent his day thinking of what lies he could tell Marvie, her aunt, and her uncle so they wouldn't discover who he really was. It wasn't exactly the best use of his time. "What about you?"

"Oh, this and that," Marvie repeated his words, laughing as she turned to face him. When she met his gaze, she quickly pulled away and looked down, blushing. She dragged her eyes up to his again, smiling shyly. Auden smiled back at her. "What?" he asked.

"Nothing," Marvie said, shaking her head. "It's just hard to breathe around you sometimes."

Auden barked out a laugh. "I promise you I washed today, Marvolene."

She scowled at him, but the smile leaked through the cracks. "You know that's not what I meant," she chided.

"What did you mean, then?" Auden asked, squeezing her hand once more, unable to hide his amusement. It was funny, to him, how she tried to hide her feelings. He was more than prepared to tell Marvie absolutely everything she had become to him. Marvie, on the other hand, was more reserved about it, almost embarrassed when she slipped up. For him, it was the opposite of embarrassment.

"I mean," she stuttered, biting her lip. "Well, I mean…"

"Marvolene!" a voice called from behind them.

They both turned to see two people approaching, their hands full of food in paper bowls. One of them was a shorter, older woman with blonde hair that could've once been the same color as Marvie's, but now had a good amount of gray in it. There was a large smile on her slightly wrinkled face, and she had skin that was tanned, probably from years living in the Southern Orinth heat. The other was a large man, taller and broader than Auden, with a serious face. Auden could immediately tell he was less enthused about Auden than Marvie's aunt and another swell of nerves overcame him. Subconsciously, he straightened his shoulders and stood taller.

Marvie released Auden's hand, clasping her own together. "Sienna and Hewes, this is Auden Frae. Auden, this is my aunt and uncle."

There was a shifting of the food from their arms to Marvie's as Auden extended his hand to shake theirs. "It's a pleasure to meet you," Auden said, hoping his voice wasn't trembling as they shook his hand in return.

"You as well, Auden!" Sienna exclaimed. "Marvie has told us so much about you!"

Marvie immediately blushed as she held the food to her chest. "Not that much," she mumbled, and Auden shot her a smile.

Hewes looked Auden up and down, assessing him. Marvie told him last night that her uncle was a builder, and right now, he inspected Auden as if he were some sort of structure he was working on. "It's nice to meet you, son," Hewes said, his voice quiet and deep.

At the word 'son', Auden's heart lurched in his chest and for a split second, the shadow flared. It had been a long time since anyone had called him 'son'. The implications of the word were somewhat painful, given his father's extended absence.

Sienna clapped her hands together. "We weren't sure what you liked, Auden, so we got a few choices," she explained, taking two of the bowls from Marvie. She extended them to him, the smell of the contents overwhelming his senses. "One is pork and the other is chicken. Which do you prefer?"

Auden gave her a kind smile, trying to suppress the growling of his stomach. He hadn't eaten the entire day, mostly because debating the morals of spending time with Marvie made him sick. It finally hit him how hungry he was. "Whichever one you don't want, I'll take," Auden answered. He gestured towards his pockets. "I can pay you back as well."

Sienna scoffed. "Don't be ridiculous. This is our treat." She gave him another wide smile and Auden decided he liked Marvie's aunt. She exemplified some of the same warmth that made Marvie so wonderful. He looked at Marvie, whose eyes were darting between Auden and Sienna.

"I'll take the chicken then," Auden said politely, taking the bowl from her hands. It was an Orinthian specialty, meat atop a bed of rice with different vegetables and spices. It was especially popular in Tenir, and it had been a while since he had eaten it. "Thank you so much," Auden said, nodding to Sienna and then Hewes.

"Don't mention it," Hewes said quietly, and Auden's stomach lurched again. *Calm down*, his mind told him. *You have all night to show him that you're a good person who's worthy of Marvie.*

But you're not a good person. And you're not worthy of Marvie, another voice chimed in and the thought sent chills down his spine.

"Shall we walk and eat?" Sienna asked, looking at each of them as she clutched her bowl.

Without answering, Hewes started walking on the boardwalk the opposite way of the docks, spooning rice in his mouth as he did. Sienna shrugged and followed him. Marvie gave Auden a look that could only be described as apologetic. He waved her off as they started behind her family.

"So, Auden," Hewes began as they fell into place behind him. "What is it that you do?"

Auden answered automatically. "I work at a shop that sells items to travelers, different sorts of rations and such, sir. It's actually where Marvie and I met," he added, smiling at Marvie, who smiled back at him.

"Oh, very good! Do you enjoy it?" Sienna asked him without looking back. It seemed that the four of them had split their time equally between eating the rice bowls and watching the sunset. The colors of the sky had intensified, the purples becoming deep lilacs, while the oranges had melted into burning reds. Occasionally, Hewes looked over his shoulder at Auden, the assessment continuing.

"It's a living," Auden said with a shrug and Sienna laughed. It wasn't necessarily true. He made his living by manipulating people into giving him what he wanted. Not anymore though, he would make sure of it.

"What about you? Marvie tells me you're a builder?" Auden directed the question towards Hewes. One thing he knew for certain, people loved to talk about themselves. For the first time in a long time, Auden was scared. Not of any imminent danger, but of the fact Marvie's uncle might not approve of him.

Hewes nodded and there was pride in his posture as he spoke. "Indeed. I've been doing it for almost forty years in this city."

Auden whistled under his breath admirably. "I'm impressed, sir. That's quite an achievement."

"Well, it keeps food on the table," Hewes chuckled. "If I may ask, Auden, what is it you want to do? Do you go to school? Is there any career in particular that you see yourself doing?"

Auden chewed his food, careful not to choke on it, his first instinct after hearing the questions. He didn't know why he was surprised; he had expected and attempted to prepare for this. But as Marvie's uncle asked them, the questions churned in his stomach like acid. He swallowed and took a deep breath before answering. "I'm not exactly sure yet, sir. I don't go to school. I'm still figuring out what it is I want to do."

Auden hoped his voice didn't sound as shaky as it felt. His tone was noncommittal and slightly withdrawn, but it was the best he could do.

"What do your parents think about you not going to school?" Hewes asked nonchalantly, not looking back at him.

"Uncle Hewes!" Marvie choked out. Auden saw out of the corner of his eye that she was blushing a furious red, not her typical slightly embarrassed pink. His shadow flickered like a candle in the dark, not necessarily at Hewes, but at the fact his "parents" didn't care about him at all, much less whether or not he went to school. Hewes was simply protecting Marvie, an ambition that Auden shared.

"Hewes," Sienna scoffed. "We've only just met the boy."

"No, it's okay," Auden rushed to say. He only had this one chance to make a good first impression. "My parents aren't in Tenir, or Orinth really. I wanted to go to school, but I didn't get the chance."

"I'm sorry," Hewes murmured.

Auden looked over at Marvie again, who was shaking her head and avoiding his eyes. He tried to shoot her a smile, but she wouldn't meet his gaze. Auden cleared his throat. "Don't apologize. As far as a career goes, I enjoy reading a lot. I know how to write," he offered meekly, as if that was something special. "Maybe someday I could be a scribe. Right now, Mr. Courtright, I'm just trying to survive."

The silence after his statement was heavy, too heavy, and he cursed himself. Auden had been trying to avoid using the word 'survive', and two minutes after meeting her aunt and uncle, he had already let it slip. They would force themselves to be civil for the next hour and then demand Marvie never see him again.

"That's a worthy goal, Auden," Hewes finally said. "I think everyone is just trying to…survive."

He had blown it so fast. All of that planning in his head and within minutes, it was ruined. It shouldn't surprise him, but it still made him feel like someone was plunging a sword through his heart. Auden wasn't meant to get close to other people. Maybe Marvie was an exception, but clearly Hewes could sense that something was wrong with him.

Another period of silence occurred, stretching out torturously long. *That's it then*, Auden thought to himself as he took the last bite of his food. It tasted like ash in his mouth now. He had met Marvie, fallen in love with her in a ridiculously short amount of time, changed his life priorities for her, and a stupid slip of the tongue had ruined it. Again, it was for the best. Marvie would be safer without him in her world, but it would be excruciating for Auden. His existence would continue to be one dark, agonizing misery.

Sienna cleared her throat. "What do you like to do, Auden?" The words were forced and unnatural, and Auden's heart fell even further. Marvie was looking at him, but he couldn't bring himself to meet her eyes.

"I...um..." He struggled to find an answer. What did he like to do? He couldn't say he liked to use his dark shadow-power to manipulate people into doing his will. Was there anything in this world he actually enjoyed? Besides spending time with Marvie, there was nothing. Surviving didn't enable one to have enjoyments. "I like to swim?" Auden phrased it more as a question than a statement. He tried to correct it. "I read, like I said. When I was a kid..." he cut himself off once again, thinking of the orphanage and trying not to say the wrong thing. "When I was a kid, I enjoyed fixing things." He didn't mention that he had learned from the sheer amount of things Lola had him fix in the orphanage. "It's nice because when something breaks in my apartment, I know how to fix it myself." Another lie. When something broke, he simply threw it out and stole a new one.

"That's a great skill to have," Sienna complimented him. "Marvie doesn't know a hammer from an axe, to be quite honest."

Hewes and Sienna both laughed in unison at this and there was a spark of hope in his chest as he looked over at Marvie once more, who was the same shade of dark red. Her eyes flashed between Auden and her aunt as she began to protest. "That's not true!"

Hewes snickered. "Oh Marvie, you think you would be better at it considering I've been a builder for so many years." He looked back at Auden, a hesitant smile on his face. "We tried teaching her, but when Marvie gives up on something, there's no talking her back into it."

"Oh yes," Sienna added, over Marvie's protests. "Remember swimming?"

"She told me about that," Auden laughed.

"I told you in confidence!" Marvie exclaimed, but she was laughing too.

"Tell me more about Marvie as a child," Auden said, shooting her a grin. She glared back at him, but she grabbed his free hand that wasn't holding the bowl and squeezed it tight. Auden squeezed hers back. For one glorious moment, he was laying there on that carpet in the sun again, filled to the brim with warmth and joy. With the sunset framing Marvie's perfect face, he could've been right there.

"She was stubborn," Sienna told him, slowing her pace as she stopped to watch the final moments of the sunset. Marvie still held his hand tight, like she was afraid he was going to disappear. "From the time she could talk, she was stubborn. But Marvolene was the best child. She never got into any mischief, serious mischief, that is. As long as you could handle a little girl who thought she was always right."

Strangely enough, Auden could completely see that. Marvie seemed the type that would stand firm in her beliefs for as long as she possibly could. "I would've loved to hear some of the discussions you had in your house," Auden said with a smile.

"Believe me, there were many," Hewes replied, winking at Marvolene, who scowled at him. She was unable to keep the mask of anger and giggled into her hand. There Auden was again, on the carpet. Her smile took him there immediately.

It occurred to him, suddenly, just how different he was from Marvie. She had come from a home, while Auden had come from…not that. She had two parents, or two people who acted as her parents, who had loved and cherished her, had given her the best childhood possible. Of course they had. How could you look at Marvie and not want to give her the world? He, on the other hand, was from a broken orphanage, given up by broken people. In what world would he have a happy childhood from that?

"What were you like as a child, Auden?" Sienna asked, chuckling, before immediately stopping. She exchanged a glance with Hewes and then attempted to correct herself. "I mean, if you want to talk about it."

They had probably figured out, by now, how damaged he was, which he had wanted to avoid. He had to make this lie good. "I was very resourceful," Auden told them, and that was actually true. "I learned at an early age to take care of myself, and I think that was appreciated. I did get into a decent amount of trouble," Auden added, forcing a smile as if it was a funny joke. "But don't we all?"

Most people's childhood "trouble" didn't include a dead body in an alleyway.

"Most definitely," Hewes agreed.

"I know I did," Sienna mumbled.

"Not me," Marvie whispered under her breath, and they began laughing again.

The rest of the walk proceeded peacefully, with small chatter about trivial things Auden could make up answers to. The shadow had quieted, but he couldn't shake the feeling that he had failed tonight, that he had failed Marvie in some way. There was a lingering despair that this might be the last night they spent together. For that reason, as they walked back towards the square by the light of the street lanterns, Auden tried to remember every detail about the way Marvie's hand felt in his, her soft, smooth skin against his calloused hands. He memorized the way her blonde hair curled and swung, as if it were being moved by its own wind. Auden wished he could paint the way the soft light of the lanterns cast shadows on her face, accentuating her beauty to a level he did not know was possible. And when she laughed, he tried to tuck the sound deep down in his heart, where it would never leave him, even if Marvie would.

By the time they got back to the square, most of the vendors had closed their booths, but the band was still playing, a slow Orinthian song Auden was familiar with. A few couples were swaying to the music on the cobblestones, and Hewes smiled at Sienna, offering her his hand. "Shall we?" he asked, and Sienna blushed as she took it. Together, Marvie's aunt and uncle made their way to the crowd of dancers.

Auden looked at Marvie, tight with anticipation, mentally preparing for a goodbye despite the fact her hand was in his. Sienna and Hewes had given them some space, and now Marvie was going to give him space, by telling him she never wanted to see him again.

The funny thing was, if she told him that, Auden would obey her wishes until the day he died. Nothing mattered more, now, than Marvie's happiness and safety. If his absence would ensure those two things, then absence it would be.

"I am so sorry," Marvie said, her voice filled with pain as the words rushed out of her mouth. "I told them not to ask any questions like that and they did anyway." She let go of his hand, turning away from him as she rested her elbows on the railing, her head in her hands. "Please forgive me, Auden. That was a nightmare."

Auden opened his mouth to respond and then closed it. She was asking for his forgiveness? Marvie, who was perfectly blameless, sounded like she might cry. But why? She had done nothing wrong. He picked up both of her hands, pulling them away from her face. She wouldn't look at him, but her eyes were filled with tears.

"Look at me, Marvie," he said softly, squeezing her hands.

She took a deep breath, looking up at the sky and blinking, before turning to him.

"You have absolutely nothing to apologize for," he told her, pressing a kiss to her forehead. Her shoulders sagged in visible relief. "Of course your aunt and uncle are going to be asking questions like that. They love you and they want to make sure you're safe. I only wish I would've answered the questions better." He sighed, glancing at where her aunt and uncle were now dancing, enveloped in one another's arms like there was no one else in the world. "It's me who should be apologizing."

"Don't say that, Auden," Marvie pleaded with him, touching his face and forcing him to turn back to her. She was still blinking rapidly to keep the tears from falling. "It's not your fault that…" she stopped herself.

Auden raised an eyebrow. "That?"

She shook her head. "Never mind."

"No, say what you were going to say."

It was as if all the other sounds and sights had faded away, leaving only the words coming out of her mouth, rushed and frightened. "I've been trying to piece it together, and I think I finally understand. I'm technically an orphan, so it's easy to recognize when other people are orphans too. I was going to say it's not your fault that your parents are gone, and they left you on your own. Please don't be upset with me, Auden."

For a brief moment, while holding her hands, the shadow wavered with intensity, as a sudden burst of memories overcame him: the orphanage, Lola, the boys, the alley, the body, his father. Auden closed his eyes, inhaling sharply as he tried to coax it away. His hand was intertwined with Marvie's, and beneath his skin was a power so deadly he could destroy her.

Maybe it was best to walk away. Maybe her uncle's words had been a sign from the gods. Would the time they had spent together be enough to pull himself out of the darkness? Maybe not, but it didn't matter. Marvie had to be safe, and as his shadow flowed and ebbed throughout his body, she was the opposite of that.

Auden opened his eyes to see Marvie staring at him, concern painted over her beautiful face. "First of all, Marvolene," he said quietly. "I don't think I could ever be upset with you, for anything. Don't be afraid of that." There were a dozen other things she *should* be afraid of, but that wasn't one of them. "And secondly, I'm not an orphan, not really. My childhood was…messy. I don't like to talk about it very much because I'm here now. I don't want to live in the past. My life is what it is, and there's not a lot I can do to change it." He tore his gaze away from hers and let it land on the dark sea, trying to let the sound of the crashing waves soothe him, calm the shadow in some way.

"Oh," was all Marvie said in reply and the shadow filled his lungs once more.

Auden had utterly destroyed any chance of a future he could have with her. It really shouldn't have surprised him. His life was consumed by darkness. Someone who was the embodiment of light was not meant to live in a world of shadow, Auden's world. As much as this would damage him, he would take solace in the fact that Marvie would stay in her world. She would walk in the sun throughout her life, shining brightly wherever she went. One day, she would probably meet a man who was as luminous as she was, and together, they would create a family of beautiful, warm, blonde-haired children who were destined to bring joy to all those who crossed their path. That image of Marvie and her sunny future gave him exactly what he needed to walk away in this very moment.

He dropped her hands and cleared his throat. "I probably should get going." Auden couldn't think of an excuse for why, so he left it at that.

Marvie's face crumpled into an expression of pain. "Why?" she asked him, and the tears behind her eyes had returned.

"I don't want to hurt you," he whispered.

"Then don't," she whispered in return, taking his hands again and pressing her forehead against his. He didn't move to get away from her but tried to remember every detail of this moment once again, every single part of it, so when he walked away, he could relive it. The way her skin felt against his, the way she smelled, the way his heart pounded from being close so her.

"Marvolene..." he began.

"Auden, I don't care about your past. I'll never ask you about it again if that's what you want. But I do care about you a lot, maybe a little too much, but I can't help it. I haven't been this happy...no, I haven't been this alive for so long. Please don't walk away from this. Please don't," she inhaled, her voice quivering as she continued, "please don't walk away from me."

Every shred of willpower he had crumbled into dust as he wrapped his arms around her and pulled her into his chest. Another sigh of relief rippled through her body, and she buried her face in his shoulder.

He wasn't strong enough to walk away. And in all honesty, Auden didn't care. Even as a voice in the back of his head screamed at him to leave this girl and her innocent, bright life, he couldn't. Auden was laying there in the sun once more, and he refused to let it go. What waited for him in his solitude but darkness?

Marvie had become everything. Marvie was the sun, the moon, and the stars, all the bright things that graced their world in a single person, and so long as he was able, he would stay in her light.

"I love you," Auden whispered into her hair, soft enough to be inaudible.

Marvie pulled back, keeping her arms around his neck and her body pressed against his. A single tear rested on her cheek as she asked him, "What did you say?"

Auden used his thumb to brush the tear from her skin and made a silent vow; it would be the first and the last tear he ever made her shed. He kissed her forehead and replied, "I asked if you wanted to dance with me."

With a large smile on her face, Marvie grabbed his hand and led him towards the crowd. He exhaled, letting go of the remains of the shadow that lingered within him, opening himself entirely to the light.

Chapter 7

Auden had to rid himself of the darkness as much as he possibly could, because he couldn't walk away from her now.

The internal battle in his mind had almost torn him in two. The elation of being with Marvie contrasted the intense guilt of putting her in danger. As he walked back to his apartment, alone, he couldn't force the smile from his face. Auden clenched his fists to stop them from shaking and took calming breaths to slow his heart rate. No one had ever made him feel this alive. It was as if he were waking up for the first time. He had been sleepwalking his entire life, trapped in an inescapable nightmare.

Marvie had pulled him into a dream.

He couldn't bring himself to leave her, after what she had said. *"Please don't walk away from me."*

"Anything for you, Marvie," he whispered as he trudged up the steps to his apartment. The streets were quiet and dark, which would typically be intimidating, but he couldn't bring himself to feel anything other than exhilaration. "Anything."

As he laid in bed that night, he made a promise to himself; expel the darkness. It was that simple. There was a certain amount that he would never be able to get rid of, but Auden had accepted that. The rest? The burdens he carried, the dangerously harmful memories, the grudges, the hatred; all of it had to go. He had already decided to stop using the shadow, but it was time to go a step further.

He wasn't sure how to even begin that process. How was it possible to destroy the shadow within him, to end its hold on him? Auden might as well try to stop breathing, because using the shadow had become as easy as breathing to him; he needed to feel the power the way his lungs needed the air. Habitual and necessary.

It had been that way ever since he killed Conli, the moment his shadow had truly awakened.

After he walked out of the alley, four years prior, he had stumbled across the city until he no longer recognized the brick buildings that towered over him. With each step, he moaned in agony. Auden hadn't stopped, hadn't given himself a chance to treat his wounds, clean the vomit off his clothes, scrub the blood from his skin, wash away the scent of death. The crowds had become a blur as he ran past them, but whether or not they saw him was irrelevant. Maybe it wasn't uncommon in Tenir for teenage boys to be covered in blood.

His lungs ached so painfully he was forced to slow down. Auden had ducked into a different alley, and pressed his back up against the brick, trying to take slow breaths, but they were more like quick, choking gasps for air. It took a moment for him to realize the air wasn't reaching his chest and he grabbed at his throat, heaving as he fell to his knees. Auden didn't even notice the pain explode from his bones hitting the brick; he couldn't force himself to breathe. The agony was overtaking him. His ribs were assuredly broken, his nose too. His stomach had gone numb by this point, tingling from each and every kick he had taken. Once the pain settled in…gods, he was dying. He blinked rapidly, eyes searching for any bystanders, anyone who could help him, but he was alone in the alley. He tried to scream, but no sound came out because the air was choking him from the inside, the pain triumphant.

The last thing he remembered was a darkness overcoming him, a sweet release he assumed was death. He remembered distinctly not caring the moment of his demise was upon him, because at least the agony would end.

But Auden hadn't died. He had simply passed out. When he opened his eyes, he was lying in the same spot in the alley, overwhelmed by a stench so disgusting he gagged at his first breath. The heat of sun had made the smell of blood, sweat, and vomit more potent and before he could stop himself, he ripped his shirt off his body, leaving it in a heap on the brick. He glanced around again. Auden could hear voices from a distance, but no one had found him. He was grateful for it, because if Orinthian guards stumbled upon him like this…he didn't even want to know.

Auden had used the wall to get to his feet, the world immediately spinning, a blur of colors and sounds, and he closed his eyes, moaning as his stomach churned. His body was broken; it was the only way he could describe it. With a shaking hand, he gently touched his ribs. He flinched and held back a scream.

At least one of them was broken, if not more. If that wasn't proof enough, his wheezing breaths that hurt with each inhalation confirmed it. Auden ignored the warm tear that had fallen onto his bloody face as he touched his nose. He flinched again, then exhaled. It was covered in dried blood but seemed mostly intact. Those were the two injuries he was most worried about. Everything else, the bruises and scrapes, would have to wait.

The events of the day had immediately rushed back to him, but he ignored them. "Not now," he had whimpered to himself, his palms digging into the edge of the bricks. He was shirtless and covered in blood. His pants were torn, stained with puke and…urine. *Great, Auden, just great.* Another tear met his skin. He rested forehead against the brick and took another deep breath, which was simultaneously relieving and incredibly agonizing.

He couldn't go back to the orphanage. No, he couldn't go back to that side of town. A part of him wondered if maybe he shouldn't just leave Tenir altogether. But how? He had nothing but the clothes that he wore, which were a pair of urine-stained pants. Somewhere between the alley and where he was now, he had dropped his backpack; he had probably been in too much pain to hold tight to it. The few supplies and the money he had stolen from the boys were in there, and now, it was gone.

Auden had absolutely nothing.

Oh, except some sort of power to kill people with his mind.

And as the crystal-clear memory of murdering Conli suddenly came down upon him, Auden screamed into the brick. He fell to his knees again and unleashed a wave of sobs from the torment. It hurt to breathe; screaming was so much worse, but he couldn't stop, his throat burning as if he had swallowed fire. He pressed his hands to his face, the crusty dried blood only increasing his sobs. He needed to stop, because his chest was imploding on itself, his ribs throbbing, but he couldn't, because he had killed someone with his mind.

Conli's distorted screams seemed to echo in his head along with his own. Conli was in his mind, yelling in his ear, punching and kicking and beating him again. Conli was alive and he was coming for Auden to get revenge.

"NO!" Auden had screamed, slamming his head against the brick and crying out as he did it. "STAY AWAY!"

The pain had become a living force, moving throughout his body, stopping to pay particular attention to each part of him. The scrapes on his hands from fighting back, the bruises on his bones from the kicks, the fresh stream of blood dripping from his head, his ribs, his chest; the pain didn't spare a single part. *Let me die. Let me die. Let me die.* He held onto the wall, sobbing. *Let me die.*

The agony wouldn't end as he stayed there, clinging onto the wall. It was as if he lived a million lifetimes, each more painful than the last. The external torment was nothing compared to the anguish that lay within his head, the ghost of Conli shrieking in his ears. "Make this end," Auden whimpered. "Please, gods, make it end."

"What are you doing here, boy?" A sharp voice came from behind him, and for a moment, Auden didn't know whether it was real or an illusion the pain was creating. He didn't respond, but closed his mouth, going silent, letting the suffering ravage him. The voice asked again, "Boy, what are you doing?"

The voice was real. Auden didn't think about the consequences as he turned around, sobbing in relief. "Please help me," he cried out, falling to his mysterious savior's knees without seeing his face. He could barely see at all, as dark spots had clouded his vision. "Make the pain go away, please!"

"What in the gods names!" the voice exclaimed, stumbling back away from him. "What happened to you? You're covered in blood!"

Auden laughed, high-pitched and hysterical, at the idea of what his savior was seeing. A fourteen-year-old boy on his knees, battered, face covered in blood and tears, pants stained with urine. His shirt was in tatters, so every scar and mark on his chest was visible. His black curls were matted down by sweat, and now blood, with only himself to blame. Auden opened his mouth to explain, but could only utter, "Help me."

A pair of arms slid under his and Auden screamed as the savior attempted to lift him. Every bone in his body seemed to shatter at once, at least that was the sensation that rocked through him. Immediately, the savior released him, and Auden collapsed on the ground again, groaning.

The savior didn't move to help him as Auden laid flat on his back on the cobblestones, floating in the waves of torment. Even through the ringing in his ears, he heard the savior whisper hoarsely, "Whose blood is that?"

"Mine," Auden croaked, immediately knowing what was going on. His savior was suddenly questioning if Auden was a victim or a killer. Was it possible to be both? He was both. With a grunt, Auden lifted his head to see the man who had attempted to help him. Surprisingly, the savior looked to be only a little older than himself, with wide, frightened eyes and dark hair. The rest of the details were murky, and Auden had a hard time trusting any of his senses when they were all preoccupied with the pain. "My blood," he coughed.

The savior shook his head, taking a step back as Auden rolled to his stomach, careful to keep his ribs from the brick. Biting his lip to keep from screaming again, he stumbled to his feet, using the wall. This time, he breathed in the pain, managing to stay up upright as he stared at the savior, who had taken several steps back, shaking his head.

"What happened?" he asked, the tremor in his voice as obvious as it was frightened.

"I got into a fight," Auden managed, swallowing back the metallic taste of blood in his mouth. He used the back of his hand to wipe his face, eyes not leaving the savior. "I lost." It was a lie. Auden wasn't the one lying dead in an alley. He had certainly not lost, but as he bathed in a mixture of his own blood, sweat, and urine, it was hard to crown himself the victor.

"I should get a guard," the savior said, taking a few more steps back.

"No!" Auden had shouted, flinching again at the mere effort the sound exuded from him. "Please don't do that," he whimpered.

The boy was shaking his head. "I don't know what's happened, but you need medical attention. They can help you." He made a motion to turn around, but Auden had to stop him.

Several things happened simultaneously. Auden ran through every single scenario where an Orinthian guard got involved, and all of them led to him being executed for murder. It hadn't been long since he had killed Conli in the alley. The witnesses must've alerted the authorities; one look at Auden and it would be glaringly obvious he was to blame. Even if the guard helped him with medical attention, they would ask questions that Auden didn't have answers to. The savior couldn't get a guard.

As he began to speak, the same sensation that had overcome him with Conli overwhelmed his senses. There was a burst of power, the living darkness coursed through his veins and Auden blurted out. "Stop." The one word shot out of his mouth, the darkness swirling beneath his skin. In the most disturbing way, it brought relief to his hurts, temporarily soothing the pain. Auden watched as the savior abruptly stopped, as if frozen to the bricks. Auden was taken aback momentarily, in the fog of the darkness. He used one hand to prop himself up as the savior turned around.

"Okay," he whispered, so quietly Auden could barely hear.

Auden didn't move. The power roared with pleasure. His plan had been to run the other direction the moment the boy was out of his sight, but he had stopped, as if Auden had commanded it. As the darkness flowed, Auden wondered if he had. But that was impossible. He had used the power to kill and torment Conli. Perhaps the savior had heard the fervent desperation in his voice and didn't have the heart to ignore it; that was why he stopped. It had nothing to do with the energy consuming Auden's mind and body, right?

Feeling the darkness within his chest, Auden asked, "Do you live close to here?"

The savior nodded. His entire body had started to tremble, as if he could sense the waves of power radiating from Auden, power that was dangerous and deadly.

Auden didn't believe his heart had ever been intact. But staring at this boy and seeing the outright terror in his eyes seemed to shatter something deep inside Auden. This boy was looking at him like he was a monster.

You are, a voice in the back of his mind whispered, and Auden believed it.

Taking a shaking breath, Auden said, "I'm not going to hurt you." He had never had to make that clarification in his life. "I just need some clean clothes and food. Maybe some gauze and water. Supplies. Please," he pleaded. "I can pay you back once I get some money. I have none, now. But if you get me that, I'll get out of your way."

The savior's bottom lip quivered like he was going to cry. "I have to go," he whimpered.

"Please," Auden begged, and he resisted the urge to fall to his knees. The darkness surged in his chest and as he spoke once again, he felt the slightest release of that darkness in his words. "Please do this for me. I need supplies."

The boy winced as if he had been shocked. And then, his shoulders straightened, and without another word, he turned and walked out of the alley. Auden gasped for breath once again, the pain and the darkness colliding in his body and he held onto the wall. He didn't know what was happening to him. Hours ago he had killed someone, and now he was quite sure he was trying to kill himself. The deep breaths did absolutely nothing to lessen the pain or gain some semblance of control over the power. For one frightening moment, Auden wondered if he was going to explode. There was no possibility his senses could handle this much without breaking down. Another cold tear had fallen onto his cheek as he resolved he wanted it to happen. Anything to ease this burden.

Before it did, the savior returned, hauling a bag on his back. He had dropped it at Auden's feet, not daring to come any closer, before bolting out the other side of the alley. Auden didn't have the energy to thank him or stop him. Instead, he collapsed next to the bag and dug through it until he found a canteen. At this point, he didn't care what liquid was in it; he poured it into his mouth, gulping as if he hadn't had water in a century. Each swallow caused an agonizing shock through his body, particularly his ribs, but he didn't care.

And as he stopped drinking, using the rest to wash some of the blood from his face, a thought arose. Auden immediately rejected it, but it was too late. It was stuck in his mind. The boy had gotten him the bag of the supplies because Auden had commanded it. The savior had been fully prepared to seek an Orinthian guard and return with him to deal with Auden. Yet, he hadn't, because Auden had commanded him not to.

Or, more likely, the swirling power within him commanded it. It was the only way. The boy wouldn't have stayed, but Auden...willed him to. He had made the savior do his will with his words.

With a shaking breath, Auden had spoken to himself in a broken whisper. "I can control people with my mind."

Auden pulled himself out of the memory, forcing himself to snap out of it. He was laying in his bed in Tenir, not clinging to the wall of an alley, begging for death. His ribs were intact, there were no bruises and scrapes on him anymore, and his skin was clean of any bodily fluids. Hours ago, he had taken a walk with the girl he was in love with. He was safe.

Auden was still ashamed of the fact that only hours after using the shadow to kill, he had learned to manipulate with it. It was a temptation that a fourteen-year-old boy was too weak to deny. He might not be strong enough to deny the temptation now.

Everything he wanted was given to him. Everything. The "swirling power" in his chest made it so no single person could tell him no. And he used it. Every. Single. Day. Never for anything too sinister, or at least that's what he told himself. He never used it to hurt people. He did use it to gain every single thing he owned, all the money he had. Ask and you shall receive. It was especially true for Auden, and he couldn't deny that, sometimes, the extent of his powers thrilled him.

No one could ever hurt him again.

Well, that wasn't true anymore.

Marvolene Pere had the power to hurt him. She had the power to leave him, which would utterly destroy him. She had the power to make him smile, make him laugh, make him genuinely happy. For the first time since that day, there was someone who held more power than he.

And Auden found he was completely okay with it, so long as it was Marvolene Pere holding that power. He fell asleep after that thought. His sleep was normally plagued with nightmares fueled by the shadow and the memories, but that night, it was entirely peaceful.

When he awoke the next morning, light was streaming through the window. He sat up and stretched his muscles, before smiling to himself. Gods, he was in a world of trouble. He liked her so much that just *thinking* about her put a smile on his face. Marvie had to work today, but afterwards, he was taking her to a tavern across town where a popular musician was playing. The place would be packed, but it would be easy enough to get a table, just like he had the other night...

No. No, he couldn't do that anymore. He couldn't use the shadow to get them into a busy tavern. Auden couldn't use the shadow at all. A part of him protested; it wasn't evil if he was using it for that. It was cheating, sure, but not evil. There would be no harm done.

It didn't matter, Auden thought to himself as he changed into a fresh set of clothes. It was still the shadow, and he had sworn to himself yesterday that he was done using it. It didn't matter if it was for something as arbitrary as getting into a busy tavern. He wasn't using it.

The same part of his mind laughed at him. *Right. Like you'll be able to resist.*

"I will," he whispered out loud, but his voice faltered.

With a sigh, he left his room to find something to eat, before leaving for his own job.

An angry Kalen was waiting for him. The moment Auden set foot in the shop, his boss was yelling.

"Where were you yesterday?" he exclaimed angrily, slapping his hand on the counter.

Auden had forgotten about his skipped shift yesterday and he swallowed back guilt. He didn't mind Kalen. The man had given him this job without Auden even having to use the shadow. He was easy-going about his hours and seemingly respected Auden, despite him not deserving that respect. Auden had used the shadow more times than he could count on the older man to get out of lectures like the one he was about to receive.

"I'm sorry," Auden grumbled, ducking around the counter and falling into the routine of opening the store, setting different items out and sweeping the floor.

But Kalen wasn't done. "Sorry? Frae, it was ridiculously busy yesterday and you didn't show up! I almost had to close the doors! Where were you?"

The shadow swirled angrily in his chest and the instinct to use it was overpowering. One word and yesterday's mishap would be completely forgotten. It wasn't that harmful either, right? It was just Kalen. Auden took a breath, letting his guard down for a split second, before slamming it back into place.

Marvolene Pere.

He thought of her blonde, wavy hair as he responded, "I wasn't feeling well, but it's no excuse, Kalen. I'm sorry."

Kalen slapped the table as Auden continued to set the items out. "You're damn right it's no excuse. I lost sales because of you, Frae! I can't afford to lose those sales!"

Her blue eyes. Her smooth skin. Her soft lips. "I know. I know, and I'm sorry. I'll make it up to you, I promise."

Kalen wasn't satisfied. He ran a hand through his disheveled hair and grumbled, "I should fire your ass. I can't have employees that aren't reliable. Damn it, look at me, boy!"

Do it. Use it. End this stupid lecture. No. Her laugh. Her voice. Her shy smile where she looked at her toes and then back at him. Auden set down the pair of boots he was holding and turned back to Kalen. With a deep breath, he said, "You have every right to, Kalen. But it won't happen again. Don't fire me, please. I'm one of your best workers. You need me." His words were completely free of the shadow, and they felt ridiculously powerless.

Kalen's shoulders sunk in surrender. "Yes, you are, Frae," he sighed, putting his hand to his head. "You sell more than anyone else and you're typically very responsible. Just don't let it happen again." With that, his boss turned around and hurried into the back office, leaving Auden by himself.

He exhaled in relief and felt a strange thrill of triumph course through him. Auden had tackled the first battle of this new war against his shadow. Kalen had given him an earful, but he hadn't touched his power. He couldn't even credit himself; it was all because of the face that lingered on his mind almost constantly. With a slight smile on his face, he continued to set up the shop.

The next few battles were tougher than he anticipated.

Auden never realized how much he used the shadow during the course of a normal workday. Most of the customers who came into the store to purchase supplies were civil enough, but damn, there were a lot of rotten ones. Normally, when a particularly rude character charged in through the doors, Auden would use the shadow to shut them up or send them packing. This time, he let them scream right into his face. And gods, some of them liked to do just that. A particular woman, upon finding out they were temporarily out of oats, yelled for about five minutes straight before Kalen was forced to interfere. Once the woman had stormed out, Kalen gave him a look and muttered, "I've never seen them like this before."

Auden couldn't help but agree.

It took every bit of willpower he had to prevent himself from using the shadow. He should've been happy that he was resisting, but instead, he was slowly filling up with despair. Was this how far he had fallen? Was he seriously experiencing withdrawals from not using the shadow? He was barely holding on. Without Marvie's beautiful face in his head, he would've been doomed.

Fortunately, that same face came into the store a few hours after opening and saved him from his misery. Auden couldn't contain his delight when she walked in through the door. Thank the gods there was no one else in the shop.

"I am glad to see you," he groaned, leaning across the counter.

Marvie smiled, her eyes alight as she gripped a brown paper bag to her chest. "Oh? Rough day on the job?"

"You have no idea," he replied as she leaned over the counter and pressed her lips to his.

There hadn't been a question in his mind whether or not she was worth it. But as his lips moved against hers, it was reaffirmed. Every trace of the shadow disappeared, and his chest was filled with the same elation from last night. Marvie ran her hand through his curls as he cupped the back of her head, bringing her closer. She let out a soft breath against his mouth, and he kissed her harder.

When she pulled back a moment later, she asked him, breathlessly, "Better?"

Auden grinned at her. "Much better."

She beamed back at him, and his heart seized up again. He wondered if it was possible to freeze a moment. If it was, he would freeze this, Marvie smiling at him. It radiated the same light and joy that Marvie embodied, and it was quite possible he could stare at her forever.

He could be with her forever.

I could love you forever, Marvolene.

Auden was so desperate to tell her, but he didn't. She started speaking before he could work up the nerve. "I had a little break so I brought you something," she exclaimed happily, holding out the brown bag to him.

He took it and opened the bag. Auden took a whiff and grinned up at her. "Cherry tart?"

Marvie nodded. "Fresh out of the oven."

"I think I might be in love with you," Auden told her. Marvie was taken aback and opened her mouth, but Auden rushed to speak. "You were right about one thing; Olga's is the best bakery in Tenir."

Marvie hesitated before responding, "How do you know? Have you been to any of the others?"

"Well, no," Auden admitted, his heart suddenly racing from his accidental confession. "Maybe we need to amend that."

At the word 'we', Marvie broke into another smile. "That might take a long time, you know. Trying all the bakeries in Tenir, that is."

"Good thing we have a long time," Auden replied, leaning back over the counter and picking up her hand, squeezing it once. Forever. They had forever. Because Auden planned to love this girl forever. She didn't know it yet, but it was that simple. Maybe one day, he would work up the courage to tell her.

A slight pink had crept up into her cheeks, but her smile didn't fade. "I have to get back. You're still coming to meet me after work?"

Auden nodded. "I wouldn't miss it."

She pressed a kiss to his cheek and shot him one more smile before leaving the shop. He watched her until she disappeared into the crowd. Did she have any idea how much he loved her? Marvie looked at him and saw a man, but when he looked at her, he saw his whole world. Was he crazy? Yeah, he very well might be.

And he was okay with that.

After seeing her, the rest of his shift flew by. Even the angry customers who got particular joy out of screaming couldn't bring him down from the high he was on. Auden was sure he looked ridiculous with a permanent smile painted on his face. Kalen gave him a look at one point, rolling his eyes and muttering something along the lines of "foolish boy".

Auden practically skipped out the shop when he was done, rushing through the streets to get to Olga's. It was an eternity before he reached the familiar shop. Marvie was standing outside the doors, her hands folded in front of her. As soon as he came into view, her face lit up and Auden's chest lurched. He, Auden Frae, was the one who brought a smile to her face. He made her happy.

It was a responsibility he didn't take lightly. He planned to make this girl happy for a very long time.

"How was the cherry tart?" Marvie asked him in way of a greeting.

He didn't answer but wrapped his arms around her waist and kissed her. She melted into his embrace, pressing her body closer to his as their lips traveled against each other's. When Auden finally pulled back, he said, "That was my thank you. You know, for the cherry tart."

At her deep red blush, Auden laughed and pressed a kiss to her forehead as he wrapped one arm around her. "I'm going to start bringing you more of those," Marvie mumbled as she leaned into him, and together, they started walking.

When he was a small child, Auden loved to read. The orphanage's collection of books was pathetic, but a few of the old novels had captivated him. When he read, the world around him disappeared and he was completely and utterly sucked into the story. His entire focus landed on the words and their meanings, and he remained undistracted by his surroundings. Sometimes, hours would pass and he wouldn't even realize it. Auden would be so engulfed in whatever was happening in the story that everything else faded.

Being with Marvie resurrected that same sensation.

The crowds, the streets, the noise, all of it just disappeared when they were together. He found himself getting lost in her words, hanging onto every single one of them. Auden could only stare at her as she spoke, at her mannerisms, the way she used her hands to speak, her changing expressions, her smiles and laughs mixed in with each story and answer. Time just slipped away until there was nothing but Marvie.

At one point, as they headed towards the tavern, she caught him staring. Immediately, she flushed pink and asked, "What is it?"

"What is what?"

"You're staring at me."

Auden snapped out of his trance and glanced around. They were in a completely different part of Tenir, blocks away from where they had started, his arm linked through hers. He couldn't recall getting from point A to point B because he had been so absorbed in one of her stories from work. He grinned at her. "Can you blame me?"

She shook her head, rolling her eyes but biting back a laugh. Marvie's gaze rested on her feet. "To be honest with you, Auden, I don't get it."

"What don't you get?"

"You. Liking me. Wanting to spend time with me. I don't get it."

Auden stopped in the middle of the street, a feat that could be quite dangerous in a city like Tenir. The crowd wove around them, but Marvie looked back at him, tugging at his arm. He didn't move. "What?" she asked, puzzled.

"I'm trying to absorb what you just told me," Auden answered. "To be honest, Marvie, I don't get it." He repeated her words from moments ago.

She glanced at the ground and then back up at him, as if they weren't in the middle of the street. Maybe it was the same for her as it was for him: a disappearing act when they were together. "I don't understand why someone like you would ever want to spend time with someone like me. I mean, look at you," she choked. "You're...beautiful. Seriously, I could look at you all day. You're interesting and mysterious. You must have girls after you all the time, Auden. But for some reason, you want to be with me. It kind of scares me."

Auden didn't speak for a solid minute, just stared at her, absolutely astonished. Was this really happening right now? Was Marvie seriously asking him why he wanted to spend time with her? Had she ever looked in the mirror before? That was his first question, though Marvie's beauty went so much deeper than how she looked. Did she know herself at all? Did she recognize her own loveliness, the way that she lit up a room, spreading a sort of ethereal light to the world? It was so glaringly obvious to him, and yet, she was asking him why he bothered.

He must've been silent for longer than a minute because Marvie muttered, "Please say something."

Auden didn't say anything, but he grabbed her hand, leading her away from the crowd and into a somewhat familiar alley that was empty, two brick walls towering over them on either side. He turned around and placed two hands on her shoulder, looking straight into her blue eyes, that had gathered tears behind them. It broke his heart in two and he rushed to speak.

"Marvolene, I don't know how to explain this to you. But..." he stammered, "Marvie, you are my light." It was such a ridiculous thing to say, and he wouldn't blame her if she laughed in his face and abandoned him. He had never been good with words, and it was the first thing that had come to mind.

"I'm not trying to force a compliment out of you, Auden," Marvie insisted, and he could tell she was embarrassed. "I was just wondering out loud, I guess. Come on, let's keep going." She tugged at his hand, but Auden stayed in place. She glanced back at him, desperation in her eyes. "Auden," she said, exasperated.

"I don't think you understand, Marvolene," he said softly, drawing her in closer until his arms were locked around her waist. He pressed his forehead against hers. "I have lived with my eyes closed for a long time, in this fog of darkness, just trying to get by. When I met you, it was like I could finally see. The sun rose and I could see the beauty of the world. I know it's only been a little while, but a part of me thinks maybe I've been searching for you my entire life. I've been searching for," he exhaled slowly, "my light."

Marvie didn't speak for a long while and Auden took a deep breath, falling back to his habit of trying to memorize everything about her before she walked away. Could he do or say anything right when it came to Marvolene? No, he couldn't. No one had ever taught him the proper etiquette when you met someone who turned your life upside down. Lola might have taught him how to read and write, but nothing about this. Auden had a feeling you weren't supposed to profess your undying feelings a week after meeting someone.

But, as he had promised from the beginning, if Marvie walked away, he wouldn't follow her. He would let her go and try to pick up the pieces when she was gone. Which he already knew would be impossible. If Marvie left him, she was leaving behind an empty shell.

Marvie finally looked up at him with those thoughtful blue eyes. Using one hand to brush back his curls, she pressed her lips against his. The kiss was soft, a gentle whisper that made his heart pound harder as he cupped her face. It was as if every dark piece of himself was filled with a majestic glow, what was left of the shadow crumbling bit by bit. Auden wondered if passersby could see a physical glow radiating from his person, as that was how he felt.

When Marvie pulled back, she spoke in a shaking voice, "I'm not good with my words. I wish I could tell you how much you mean to me already, but I don't think I'm capable. Do you understand, Auden, how much I lo…how much I care about you? I can't stop thinking about you, ever. When I wake up, you're the first face I see and when I go to sleep, you're the last person on my mind. Auden, I…" she cut herself off, burying her face in his chest as she embraced him.

He glanced around as he held her, his hands trembling slightly from her words. The familiarity of the alley suddenly sunk in. For the first time in four years, he was back in the place where he had first learned the full extent of his shadow, where he manipulated that poor boy into giving him supplies, where he had clung to the wall and begged for death to give him salvation.

Somehow, Auden had found his way back, clinging to this woman he loved.

He thought he was going down a dark and dangerous road. Ever since that day in this very same alley, he had been. But Marvolene Pere had given him the light he needed to change his path. He owed her everything.

"I'm falling in love with you, Marvie," Auden whispered to her. It was a lie of extreme proportions because he was already so deeply in love with her, the magnitude of the feeling shocked him. He didn't want to scare her, though, more than he already had. They had met one another a few days ago. From an outsider's perspective, one would think Auden was insane.

Yet a part of him knew that this was not the first time his soul and Marvie's soul had met.

"I think I'm already there, Auden," Marvie murmured in reply and Auden felt the last bit of darkness within him disintegrate.

Chapter 8

It had been seven days since he had used the shadow.

That was, by far, the longest he had gone without using it since its initial discovery. Auden had expected to feel symptoms of withdrawal, but there had been none, because he had spent each of the seven days with Marvolene.

Some days were better than others, but the temptation was still there. Auden would be walking to work, and some stranger would knock into him without apology. He would stare after them, fists clenched, seething until they were out of sight. The Auden before Marvie would've yelled after them and used the shadow to force an apology. But he wasn't *that* Auden anymore. He was pretending to be a good person, capable of dispelling that darkness.

After refraining from using the power every day, seeing Marvie was a constant reassurance that this was completely and utterly worth it. The moment he saw her face, the light would fill him and the previous battles of the day would disappear.

He was expelling the darkness, just as he had planned. Auden had ceased using the shadow, which was the main component. But returning to the alley where the manipulation had begun? It had been a cathartic release that expelled the darkness a little more. Yet there was one more task he had to complete.

Auden had to make things right with Lola.

"Can you read it to me one more time, Lola?" a seven-year-old Auden had begged the woman who ran his orphanage. She favored him above the rest of the children, and for that reason, it was he who was getting to sit in her office after the others had gone to bed. She had scolded him for being awake but didn't protest him laying across her small sofa while she did work at her desk.

Lola had sighed, giving him a look. "Auden, you should be in bed right now, not bugging me while I'm trying to do paperwork."

"But I can't read it myself and none of the older kids will read it to me. It's my favorite story and I want YOU to read it to me."

Lola groaned, but she couldn't deny him much. He took care of a lot of them. He was seven years old, and he was already providing for the rest of the children stuck in this nightmarish place, helping to prepare their meals and clean their messes. He helped everyone spare the older boys who enjoyed tormenting him; they took care of themselves.

The head of their orphanage took a dark gray book out from below her desk and opened it to the first page. Auden relaxed into the sofa, closing his eyes.

With one final sigh, she began.

"This is the story of a man named Rider Grey."

He hadn't been back to see her since the day in the alley.

It broke his heart in two, but he had no other choice. Auden didn't even know if Lola was still alive, and that thought haunted him. There was no chance he would return to the place, even if it had been four years.

But he could write a letter.

Which was why he was bent over the counter at work, gripping one of Kalen's spare quills, staring at an empty sheet of paper.

It had been like this all morning. The moment Auden thought he had the right words, they disappeared or sounded wrong or got mixed up. This was the third sheet of paper Kalen lent him. Judging by his scowl, it was the last chance Auden got.

A group of girls had just waltzed out of the store and Auden once again had a revelation about the shadow. Marvie's words a week ago had confused him. She had called him beautiful and surmised that other girls were "after" him. He had pondered the expression a long time. Auden had never had eyes for anyone else but Marvie, truly.

It turned out he had used the shadow as a buffer.

Because a lot of girls were "after" him. They came into the store and said ridiculous things to him. Auden had gotten into the habit of using the shadow to let them down easy or direct their eyes elsewhere, but now, he was vulnerable to their pursuits. It was simultaneously the funniest yet most ridiculous thing to ever happen to him. Without the shadow, his response to them was always the same

"I'm sorry, I'm seeing someone right now," in a mumbled voice so Kalen wouldn't hear. The man would tease him until he went blue in the face and Auden did not want to deal with it.

As funny as it was, it made Auden realize all the more: Marvie was the only person for him.

That made it even more essential he write this damn letter, expel this last bit of darkness so he could be worthy of Marvolene.

Lola,

He wrote.

Auden stared at the paper so intently he was surprised there wasn't a hole burned through it. He was so focused he didn't even realize Kalen had come up behind him, staring over his shoulder. When his boss spoke, Auden jumped. "Is Lola the girl who you've been darting out of here to see every night?"

Auden glanced over his shoulder at the man. Kalen's arms were crossed, and his eyebrows raised. "No," Auden managed to choke. "I don't know what you're talking about."

Kalen snorted. "I've seen her in here too. The blonde. First time I've ever met any of your friends or family members."

Auden shrugged, returning to the letter. "She's just a friend." Even saying those words made him want to laugh. Marvie was most definitely NOT just a friend. A part of him was afraid she might shoot out from behind a shelf and scowl at him for even suggesting such a thing. But there was no reason his boss of almost a year needed to know the details of his personal life.

Kalen snorted for a second time. "Do you kiss all of your friends on the lips, or just the girl?"

This time, Auden turned around and gave him a look. "Say what you need to say, Kalen," he said, but he was fighting a smile.

Kalen sighed, walking around the counter and shuffling some of the items on a shelf mindlessly. After a few moments, he turned to Auden, scratching the back of his head. "You have been working here for almost a year, Auden Frae. I know nothing about you, besides the fact that you're a good worker and you have a certain way with people. You don't talk about your family; you don't talk about your friends. There's a heaviness in your eyes that shouldn't be there for someone so young. Is this an accurate description so far?"

Auden leaned over the counter, resting his arms on the wood, nodding. "You're not far off." One thing he appreciated about Kalen was his bluntness, though his description of things had been a little *too* accurate.

"But lately, within the last two weeks at least, something has changed. I have actually seen a smile on your face. You're happier. You're..." Kalen hesitated, searching for the right word, "...lighter. Forgive me if I'm crossing a line, Frae, but I'm glad for it. You worry me sometimes."

Auden held back laughter. He worried himself sometimes, too. "You're not crossing a line," he told Kalen.

"So, what's her name?" Kalen asked nonchalantly as he continued to straighten up items in the shop.

Auden grinned to himself as he looked back down at the empty letter. "It's Marvolene. Marvie." Saying her name out loud was addicting. It brought a rush of joy that was almost as intoxicating as seeing her smile.

"She's the reason for all of..." Kalen glanced at him and made a gesture with his hands, "this?"

Auden didn't answer right away, as he suddenly realized the first thing he needed to write to Lola. Using the quill, he wrote hastily.

I'm so sorry.

He looked back up at his boss. "This is the first time in my life things are going right and it's because of Marvie. So, yeah, she's the reason for all of..." he gestured at himself, "this."

Kalen seemed satisfied at the answer, and he mumbled to himself, loud enough so Auden could hear. "Then let's pray she doesn't go anywhere."

Auden laughed softly before returning to the letter. His laughter and joy quickly disappeared as he wrote the next few lines.

You did nothing but take care of me my entire life, and I didn't even have the courage to come say goodbye face-to-face. I'm sorry it took me this long to get in contact with you. I don't know how much you know about what happened. For your sake and mine, I hope it's nothing. But if you rip this letter apart after reading it, I'm not sure I could blame you. I guess the boys probably told you their version of what happened. Maybe you see me as a monster. Maybe I am one. But that doesn't change the fact that I still care for you deeply and want to find some way to say goodbye.

The memories rushed upon him like a wave, and he closed his eyes, inhaling slightly.

Lola kept reading. "Rider Grey had a power unlike no other; he was immortal. He could not die. How he came upon this power, no one knew. But while the rest of his friends and family grew older, Rider stayed the same."

"I wish I was like him," Auden interrupted, folding his hands across his stomach. "I don't want to grow old."

"Growing old is a privilege, Auden," Lola chastised him. "A lot of people don't get that privilege."

Auden grumbled under his breath as Lola continued, "People were envious of Rider Grey, but he basked in his newfound gift, cherishing it like a priceless treasure. Being trapped in the body of an eighteen-year-old was his dream come true. He had eternity to gain all the knowledge, all the riches of the world. For many years, he lived like this, in eternal youth. The bliss of his gift started to wear off, however, when he met a girl. He fell in love with her."

"Who is Lola, then?" Kalen asked, breaking him free of the distant memory.

Auden raised both eyebrows at his boss. "We're very curious today, aren't we?" This might have been the longest conversation he had ever had with Kalen. His boss was a man of few words and most of those words were related to the store. In fact, Auden realized he knew absolutely nothing about Kalen, spare that he owned and operated this place. Did he have a family? Did he have friends? Auden had never cared to find out.

Kalen shrugged, as if uninterested. "I guess we've never had a real conversation before, Frae. I'm just trying to hold one." He went back to stacking items on the shelves, but he was watching out of the corner of his eye.

"Lola was the woman who raised me," Auden said nonchalantly as he leaned back down and continued writing.

I'm not going to recount the situation for you, but I will tell you my actions were those of self-defense. I hope you trust me enough to believe that.

Auden stopped thinking about the memories of Lola as he crumpled up the paper and threw it into the waste bin. Kalen noticed the movement and raised both eyebrows. "Your mother?"

"No. Enough about me, Kalen. What about you? Tell me about your family and friends and life." Auden couldn't keep the irritation out of his voice. There was nothing he could say or write that would appease Lola. It would never be enough. What could he possibly say to obtain her forgiveness? Nothing.

Kalen grunted. "Point taken, Frae. I'm sorry I bothered you."

Auden sighed, pressing his forehead to the counter. "I didn't mean to snap at you. My childhood was a mess, Kalen. I don't talk about it to anyone, not even Marvie." She was the last person who would learn of it. He was more likely to tell his boss, who was once again studying him with narrow eyes.

"I'm sure she loves being kept in the dark," was his only reply.

"She does not," Auden snorted. "She hasn't asked me too many questions, but when she does…" he trailed off. "I don't know what I'll tell her. It's not something I'm proud of. She might leave me when she hears it…if she hears it."

At that moment, a few customers entered the store and Auden quickly straightened up and put on what Kalen called his "customer face". Once they had purchased their products and left, Kalen responded. "If she likes you, really likes you, your past won't change that. And if it does, well, maybe she's not the right one."

Auden laughed at that. It was laughable, considering the premise there might be someone else for him other than Marvie. It was absurd, actually. Marvie wasn't just the right one, she was THE one. But he didn't feel like explaining it to Kalen, who, up until this point, had never shown any interest in his personal life. Auden simply replied, "I'll keep it in mind." Kalen was quiet after that.

As the hours ticked by, it became crystal clear what he had to do about the Lola situation. Auden had to go see her.

Just the mere thought made his stomach churn. He wanted to see Lola; he really did. But the idea of returning to the orphanage was one fraught with terror. How could he possibly go back there, to that place where the nightmare began? It would haunt him, the choices he had made in that old building that was crumbling, like every person who lived there. How could he walk through the door, through those rooms that were so familiar but never felt like home? How could four walls shelter so much horror?

But Auden had to expel the darkness, and this might be the only way.

It had been four years. Four years. Conli's friends would be nineteen and twenty by now. There was no possible way they still lived at the orphanage. But some people would still recognize him, the children who had been there when he left. 'Mr. Auden' they had called him. They would recognize his black curls and dark eyes. What if they knew about what happened in the alley?

He would put everything at risk by going back, but there was no other choice.

Auden was so close to being a normal person. The temptation to use the shadow was barely there and he truly believed he had the will to never use it again, thanks to Marvie and Marvie alone. There was a lightness within him that had been void for his entire life. It seemed the last task he had to complete was allowing his wounds to turn to scars. The influence of his childhood would never go away, the pain of it would always linger, but he could still move on from it.

This was the last step of taking the first step into his new life, his life with Marvolene Pere.

Kalen seemed to sense the inner turmoil that Auden was facing, as the man let him leave an hour before his shift was supposed to be done. Auden didn't remember walking out of the shop or even down the streets of Tenir. His body had taken over his mind, seemingly knowing exactly where he needed to be to finish this last step.

Which was how Auden found himself standing on the outskirts of Southside.

"The girl Rider loved wasn't the loveliest or the funniest or the wisest that he had met before. But she was so beautiful to him, both on the outside and what was within. He fell in love with every single part of her, so much so that the gift of eternal youth paled in comparison. Her love for him in return was worth an infinite amount more."

"Rider married the girl, and it was the happiest day of his life. When his lips met hers and they sealed their matrimony with a kiss, his heart was full. But alas, a happier day arrived; the day his wife bore their first child, a beautiful baby boy. And then, years later, a baby girl. Together, Rider and his wife created a perfect life together, and he couldn't fathom what he had done to deserve such love."

"But such happiness for Rider Grey was never meant to last. What had once been an incredible blessing to him was slowly becoming the bane of his existence. As his wife begin to grow in years, Rider remained in the same body he had been trapped in for as long as he could remember, the body of an eighteen-year-old boy."

"And when his first son surpassed him in years, Rider began to despair about what the future held for him and his remarkable life." Lola sighed after she read that line. She always sighed at that part.

It hadn't changed a bit and Auden wasn't surprised. Of course, Southside hadn't changed. The rest of the city could create the most intricate buildings and streets, but the slums would remain the slums.

A bridge acted as the border between Southside and the rest of their city. Each step Auden took as he crossed seemed a mile. He couldn't bring himself to look up yet, staring instead at the dirty cobblestones that hadn't been cleaned in decades. Auden didn't have to look to know he had arrived; the smell was signal enough. Taking a deep breath in through the nose, he was transported back to his childhood with that unmistakable odor of smoke mixed in with something rancid and indescribable. He tried not to choke on it.

His hands were shaking as he lifted his head and took it in.

The main street of Southside led directly to a different harbor, one he prayed Marvie had never been to. He could see the sea in the distance. Lining the entire route were identical brick buildings that were a dark shadow of the ones in the rest of the city. They were old, centuries old, and it was apparent. Most of them were falling apart, broken bits of brick littering the ground in front of them. Auden remembered being in the habit of intensely observing the streets if he was walking without shoes, ensuring he didn't step on any shards of glass.

Even now, four years later, Southside felt the same. The general air of hopelessness was thick and unavoidable. Unavoidable because they were still here: the people of Southside.

Streets and alleys stemmed from this main street and even now, Auden knew them like the back of his hand. His eyes fell on certain buildings, mind connecting which alley was behind it. He was still a good distance away from *the* alley and with the gods as his witness, he would not return to it. This one final trip to the Southside was not to confront the ghost of Conli but to gain some sense of closure about Lola. How would Auden accomplish that? He had not a clue, but his feet began to move and he was on his way.

No one batted an eye at him as he walked, but of course they didn't. Auden laughed bitterly to himself at the cold reality: he belonged here. Southside was his home. He was raised here and was supposed to have died here. Even after moving across the city, putting the past far, far behind him, he fit in. The high of being with Marvolene Pere was slowly fading while his shadow gained more and more traction.

Auden couldn't avoid one simple fact: he had left Southside, but Southside would never leave him.

He couldn't bring himself to look into the eyes of passersby because he knew exactly what he would see there: Anguish. Desperation. Suffering. And above all, a primal, instinctive need to survive, the same need that he lived off until Marvie. No one had asked to be here, yet here they were, living in a crumbling city, more than likely turning to vice to survive. There was a reason the criminal underworld flourished in the Southside. People needed something to live for here, and the underworld gave it to them: Drink. Stimulants.

Companionship. Any vice one could possibly desire, they could find it in Southside.

It had amused Auden, in a cynical sort of way, when Marvie told him she avoided Southside. One day, he would probably have to tell her it was his home. Not any day soon; maybe she never needed to know.

Auden didn't watch where he walked; his body knew where to go. The route to the orphanage had become ingrained in the deepest depths of his memories. For the first fourteen years of his life, he rarely left Southside. Once in a great while, he would walk to the "outside world", or the safe part of Tenir, just to escape. More times than not, it ended up burdening him, seeing how some lived life so free of hardship, or at least the hardship he was familiar with.

The hair on the back of his neck was standing up. Auden was viciously aware of how intensely the shadow was coursing through him. It was right on the edge, begging him for use. Auden dragged a breath in through his mouth, but it did nothing. It was as if the seven days of not using the shadow hit him all at once. He forced himself to stop walking as he withdrew to a streetcorner, ducking into an alley and pressing his forehead against the cold brick of the wall, gasping for air. His entire body was trembling now as the shadow continued to flow through every part of him, punishing him for his disregard.

"Time became his most hated of enemies, because it was time that was stealing the woman he loved away from him. It was time that was abducting his children. The years passed too quickly and age descended on his wife as swift as an eagle. Her skin had wrinkled, her hair grayed; her eyes misted over like dew over the morning earth. His wife couldn't move on her own anymore, but it didn't matter. Rider carried her from their bedroom to the washroom, from their kitchen to the balcony, where they had watched the stars for so many years. She weighed nothing for Rider, whose body was still young and able."

"Eventually, her voice faded away, but her love for him never did. He could see it in her eyes, those eyes that had captivated Rider from the moment he saw her."

"And as he held her in his arms the day she died, he was filled with so much regret he thought it might kill him. How he would give anything to be laying there next to her, his skin wrinkled, his hair gray, his eyes misted over like dew over the morning earth. What he would've sacrificed to be holding her hand, departing for the Beyond surrounded by the family they had created, their children, their children's children. Instead, he watched the life drain out of her, looking like one of the youngest in the room."

"And as Rider Grey knelt by her grave, he swore he would never love a woman again, as he was as broken as a man could possibly be. He resented that past version of himself that had considered youth a blessing, as he now knew what a terrible, terrible curse it was. Rider had always believed he was cheating time, but he knew, now, that it was time who had cheated him."

Auden stumbled back onto the street, knowing he had to keep moving. If someone spoke to him in that moment, he might use the shadow just for the sake of satisfying it. He desperately tried to recall Marvie's face or voice or laugh or anything that could possibly distract him, but his mind wouldn't cooperate. Each of his senses were completely overtaken by darkness.

He didn't realize he was scanning the faces of people who passed him, but he was doing so intently. A few made eye contact with him, shooting strange looks. Auden couldn't imagine what they were seeing in return, and he didn't care. He was waiting to recognize one of them.

He *wanted* to recognize one of them.

He wanted to see one of the other boys who were in the alley that day. Just the idea of it put a bitter smile on his face. Auden wanted to see one of them and use the shadow to lure them into an alley, just like the one they had been in that day. He would instill as much fear and anguish as he possibly could into their minds before revealing himself to them.

And then he would smile, as Conli had smiled at Auden before beating him bloody.

Auden would allow the shadow to do whatever it wanted with the other boys. He had fooled himself into believing he was in control of the dark power, but it was, and had always been, in control. After seven days of not using the shadow, it had only grown more powerful, built like a wave ready to crash to shore. It was ready to devour. Devour who? Auden didn't know. Maybe himself.

Only strangers continued to pass him as he searched desperately. *Please, gods, if you're listening, let one of them come near me. Let me see one of their faces and destroy them the way they destroyed me my entire life. Please, let me let go of this burden.*

As Auden turned down the street that the orphanage was on, her voice cut through the fog like a knife. **"But I do care about you, a lot, maybe a little too much, but I can't help it."**

Auden sucked in a breath that felt like a jab through his stomach as he saw her in his head. Marvolene Pere. The girl he was in love with. Long, blonde hair and the most beautiful blue eyes he had ever seen. His lips pressed against hers, their hands intertwined in a perfect fit, her arms wrapped around him holding him to the face of the world. The way she smiled at the ground and then at him, radiating as much light as the sun. Marvolene.

His entire world.

"I haven't been this happy, no, I haven't been this alive for so long. Please don't walk away from this. Please don't walk away from me."

"Never," Auden managed to get out, shouting the word in the middle of some Southside street. He staggered down the cobblestones, apathetic to the fact people were now taking notice of him, this crazy man talking to himself and moving as if he were highly intoxicated. "Never, ever," he groaned. "I'll never walk away, Marvolene."

"Rider became a shell of the man he used to be, withdrawn from the world. He left the place that had been his home because he couldn't bear to watch his children die. He couldn't face the reality of death that wasn't his reality, no matter how badly he wanted it to be."

"He found work in a city hundreds of miles away from his home, far enough where his family would never find him. Rider threw himself into his job, avoiding every attachment he possibly could. He had no acquaintances, no friends, no lovers, no one. It was the way he wanted it to be. Affinity for somebody, anybody, would destroy him. How could he possibly enjoy someone's company, knowing he would eventually have to watch them die?"

"Rider Grey became the loneliest man in the world, and it was by his own choice."

Auden truly didn't know how he made it to where the orphanage was supposed to be. His vision had clouded over, specks of darkness dancing on the edge of his sight. He could barely feel his body anymore; the shadow had created a sort of numbness in him, a punishment for starving it for so long. His chest had blossomed with a pain only comparable to the first time he used his powers and he was acutely aware of a single bead of sweat dripping down the side of his head.

Auden bit down hard on his lip to prevent himself from crying out as he dragged his gaze up to look at the place that had been his childhood home...

...to find nothing there.

He squeezed his eyes shut, the ringing in his ears suddenly silencing. Auden slowly opened them once more, but he was seeing the same thing. It wasn't his imagination, some illusion the shadow was creating.

The orphanage was gone.

Auden was absolutely positive he was in the right place, as he recognized every single building that was near the empty lot. He could distinguish the exact street, identical to the one etched in his memory, the view he used to stare at from his window in the orphanage. But the orphanage itself? Once a three-story, crumbling, neglected brick building that housed so much pain and sorrow? It was gone.

He had taken a few steps forward though he didn't realize it. The remnants of the place were few, but they were there. A few lone bricks were scattered over the ground, as well as several pieces of broken glass. Already, weeds had begun to spring up among the dirt and rubble, a desperate attempt to create new life among the destruction. It was almost ironic. Hadn't Auden made the same feeble attempt to create something within the destruction that was his life? And yet here he was, one shred of will preventing him from letting the shadow explode like he so desperately wanted it to.

His mind was filled with questions, too many questions, but one rose above the others: where was Lola? If the orphanage was gone, where would she be? Another emotion seemed to slice through the power of the shadow, but it was somehow equally as painful: panic. Auden balled his hands into fists, gripping so hard that his nails began to cut into his skin. Where was Lola? What had happened to the woman who raised him? The orphanage had been her entire world. She had no one besides the children who had become her family, a dysfunctional, broken family, but a family, nonetheless. Had they taken the children away from her?

The panic disappeared as the shadow took over once more, the anger engulfing his entire being.

"The months faded into years and the years into decades, and yet, Rider allowed no one into his life. Loneliness became an old friend to him, one he disregarded but couldn't get rid of. His life had no purpose, but he didn't want to die. So Rider settled into the mundane routine of surviving and nothing more. The decades faded into centuries, and he still looked the same as he did on his eighteenth birthday."

"But love, as we all know, has no boundaries, follows no rules. Rider had created the tallest and sturdiest of walls around his life, but their infiltration was as

inescapable as love itself. He saw her, one day, walking down the street where he lived. She stopped, on her own accord, and turned to meet his gaze."

"It took only a moment for Rider to realize he was doomed once more."

Auden drifted in and out of memories and delusions, unsure of what was real and what was not. Was he even in Southside right now or was he in a dream? No, the shadow had never felt this real when he was sleeping. But his mind walked the streets of the memories that this very spot held for him, memories of the pain that had carved him into the person he was, a person unable to resist the power of the shadow.

Thinking only of that hungry, desolate little boy from his past, Auden knew he had to use the shadow in this very instant. He didn't care if it was on someone from his past or a complete stranger; he only knew he had to release it.

"I'm sorry, Marvie," he cried out, putting his head in his hands before pulling on his hair, trying to focus on that pain instead of the shadow. "I'm not strong enough." And it was the gods-given truth.

He had tried, for her sake, but he couldn't do it. Auden was destined to be alone; his fate was sealed. He realized exactly what he had to do. First, find someone to use the shadow on. He wished he could hold himself to manipulation. He would try, try not to hurt anyone, but he wasn't sure he was capable of it. The shadow had built up to such a magnitude that causing pain might be the only release.

And then, he would find Marvie and tell her goodbye. It would hurt, but could it hurt any worse than the shadow hurt him now?

Yes, it would. But the idea of Marvie seeing him like this, tormented and controlled by the shadow, was too much. She would be in so much danger. If Marvie was here, right now, there was a possibility that he would use the shadow on her. That hypothetical situation was enough to make him despise himself. Yet, it was enough to know he had to say goodbye before she got hurt.

Marvie would hurt, too. She would probably come to hate him. Though they had known each other for a short time, Auden could see exactly what he meant to her. She loved him, or at least he thought she did. Maybe he was wrong, and he prayed that he was.

But Marvie would heal. She would move on, find someone who was the opposite of Auden, someone who was strong and happy and would fill her life with the light that Auden could not. The thought of Marvie with another man gutted him, but at least she would be safe. That was a luxury he could not provide. The plan solidified in his head. Use the shadow. Leave Marvie. Use the shadow. Leave Marvie.

And as Auden went to stand up, a man's voice spoke up from beside him.

"It's a pity, isn't it?"

Every bone in his body froze. He didn't recognize the voice at all, and he couldn't bring himself to look at the stranger. Auden didn't want to see the face of whoever he was about to harm. He was planning on seeking someone out, but this would do. This unlucky stranger would be the victim of the power that was controlling him.

"What is?" Auden responded, his voice a low growl in his throat. If the stranger was smart, he would run the other direction.

He did not. "The orphanage being torn down after so many years. I still walk past it every day because I truly can't believe it."

Auden rested his hands on his knees. *Not yet*, he told himself. At least find out what happened to the orphanage, and then use the shadow on this man, this poor soul. The stranger happened to be in the wrong place at the wrong time, and Auden just prayed it didn't mean his death.

"Why?" was the only word he could utter in reply.

The stranger was looking at him, Auden could feel his gaze, but he wouldn't meet it. If he turned and looked at another human, the shadow would pounce like a cat. *A few more moments*, he internally screamed at himself. *A few more moments and you can do just that.*

"You didn't know? It was all a part of the Queen's new command. Natasha Lyn went through a few of the major cities in Orinth inspecting the orphanages. If they didn't meet her standards, the children were taken to much better ones, paid for by the throne. The old ones were torn down. Her majesty came by this one only months ago and declared it wasn't suited for raising children. They took away the kids and the place was torn down," the stranger explained.

How was it possible to simultaneously feel a kernel of hope and a wave of despair? Auden didn't know, but they were his two most prominent emotions. Hope for Lola, hope for the children, hope for the rest of the orphans in their country. The Queen of Orinth, Natasha Lyn, had saved them. With a single breath, Auden praised her name...

...and cursed it.

Where would he be right now if someone had come to save him from the orphanage? He certainly wouldn't be kneeling in an empty lot, begging himself not to kill a stranger. What if he had been swept away, taken to some place that was safe and secure? What if he would've been adopted? What if some man and woman would've chosen him to be their son, raised him in a house of love?

What if the shadow had never awakened?

It's all well and good what you did, Natasha, Auden thought to himself, *but it's a little too late for me.*

"I wonder why," Auden muttered, and it was hard to keep the anger out of his tone. He wanted to look at the stranger to see if he was frightened as he should've been. But the moment Auden looked, he knew the possibility of keeping the shadow contained was naught. He kept his eyes glued to a specific piece of broken glass on the ground, wondering if it was a shard that came from his own window.

"Some say that she was doing good in this world. Others say she was looking for someone. She was looking for a specific orphan, but no one knows why. You know how these rumors can be." The stranger paused, before asking, "Did you used to live at this orphanage?"

Auden shook his head. "I didn't," he whispered, wishing that it was the truth.

"Be glad of that, son. I knew a few people who did," the stranger commented, and his voice was sad. "They said it was sort of rough in there."

Rough. What a word for it. Every nightmare that happened to him, each gaping wound that haunted him could be summed up in one simple word: rough. It was laughable, but Auden didn't laugh. Instead, he got to his feet, slowly. He looked over at the man who had come up beside him.

He was a plain looking man, an adult, with dark hair that had begun to gray and an unshaven face. Auden could immediately tell he was from Southside. His outdated clothing made that abundantly clear, not to mention the weathered look in his eyes. The man stared back at Auden with his hands shoved in his pockets, awaiting a response.

Do it then, his mind snapped at him, the shadow utterly prepared to be released. *This man is right here.*

Auden glanced at their surroundings. They were the only two within sight, not another soul near the remains of the orphanage. There were no witnesses to see what he was about to do, no one to report his actions to the authorities. Not that they would anyway. Most people in Southside kept to themselves, to the point they wouldn't even consider getting involved in a situation such as this one, even to save another person. It was the perfect set-up to release this burden, let the shadow do its will. He knew he would feel better afterwards, at least physically. Mentally, the guilt would ruin him, but it didn't seem to matter that much.

So why couldn't he bring himself to do it?

"Do you know what happened to the woman who ran the orphanage?" Auden asked, and his voice was surprisingly calm considering the internal battle that was occurring just beneath the surface of his skin.

The stranger shrugged, looking back at where the place had once stood. "If Natasha relocated the children, I assume she did the same to the people who ran the orphanages. I'm sure they're happier now."

Auden inhaled deeply through his nose, staring at the stranger as he prepared himself to release the shadow in that very moment.

"They say the queen was inspired by the birth of her own child to do this," the stranger said before Auden could finish the deed.

He paused. "The queen had a child?"

The stranger nodded. "A baby girl. She must only be a few months old. They say she saw the baby's face and that was the inspiration she needed to save the children in the orphanages. So I suppose we have the newly born princess to thank for this." He looked down at the ground and smiled. "Reminds me of my own daughter. She's grown now, but she inspired me to be a better person too."

Auden didn't realize he had raised one of his hands slightly the entire time the stranger had been speaking. But upon hearing the last sentence he spoke, Auden froze and slowly dropped his hand.

He took a deep breath through his nose, a gasp for air more than anything. Then he closed his eyes and thought about Marvolene.

"Rider resisted at first. He tried not to love her, but it was futile. He was already so desperately in love with her, needed her the way the moon needed the sun. It was inevitable that she loved him in return."

"Rider had been lost in his own world for a long time, but she pulled him back to life. With every memory they created, he became a little more himself. With each moment together, he became a little more alive. He tried to walk away, but he couldn't. She was too important to him, now, to let go. The demons that haunted him from within were no match for the love she gave him."

"He hadn't dared to hope for centuries, but this woman he loved was the embodiment of hope. With hesitation and joy, Rider let go of the warnings from his past and embraced his love for her. The future belonged to them."

He wasn't ready to say goodbye to Marvolene. He never wanted to say goodbye to her. If Auden used his powers on this man, he would be forced to depart from her life.

He refused to do that.

I am stronger than you, Auden told the shadow. *I am stronger than you.*

It roared beneath his skin, but with less vigor. The strength he had for the last seven days suddenly returned in full force. He wasn't defined by the shadow. Maybe Auden was defined by a lot of terrible things, but not his darkness. He deserved to have a normal life unmarred by this nightmare. He deserved to be a normal person, incapable of atrocity.

I am stronger than you.

It seemed to scream in his ears, but he screamed back at it, until all he could hear was his own internal scream, drowning out any other noise. Then, he stopped.

The shadow was gone.

He waited another moment for it to return, but it didn't.

I am stronger than you.

Auden exhaled, looking back at the stranger. "I'm grateful to her then, the new princess. Orphans deserve a chance to be happy too."

He didn't wait to see what the stranger said.

Auden turned around and started towards Olga's Bakery to go see the woman he loved, his entire reason for existing.

Chapter 9

Things were going a little *too* well for Marvolene Pere.

That foolish little thought hit her in the middle of the day, as unexpected and unnerving as any thought she had ever had. She abruptly stopped in the middle of the street because of it. They had been walking back from watching a street performer down by the harbor, two weeks after they had gone there the first time to walk with her aunt and uncle.

Auden had stopped next to her. "What?" he asked, nudging her with his shoulder with a small smile. Watching the street performer had been ridiculously fun and Marvie was still riding the high she got whenever she was around Auden Frae. Her heart was as light as a feather, and it was hard to keep a smile off her face. Two weeks of seeing him every day and she couldn't imagine it ever getting old.

Marvie glanced at him, and several facts came to her attention all at once.

The first was the most obvious and wonderful one: she was in love with Auden. As silly as it sounded, she had known approximately four days after their introduction. She waited for the logical part of her brain to tell her differently, but it never did. She was wholly and completely in love with Auden Frae, and that was the truth.

Marvie didn't understand how she could possibly care so deeply for someone so soon after their meeting. She couldn't grasp how, at one point, he had been a complete stranger. And now? She didn't remember what it was like to not know him, to not love him. The first time they met, Auden had spoken of knowing someone intimately but not remembering where or when or how you met.

It captured precisely how she felt about him.

They had only known one another for a few weeks, but she knew deep down that it had been a lot longer than that. It was years, decades, centuries. They had met somewhere in a different life, a different world, a different time and existence. Yet, they had found each other again and damned if she didn't spend the rest of her life with this boy.

Even after death, she knew they would find each other again, in the next lifetime. And maybe they wouldn't recognize one another, but their souls would.

Marvie was in love with Auden and she was too scared to tell him, but just knowing was enough for her.

The second fact was simple, but surprising: her aunt and uncle approved of Auden. Their short walk by the harbor had been a nightmare, at least for Marvie. She had to assume Auden hadn't enjoyed it either, getting questioned by the two people who had raised her. Marvie had begged them not to, but Sienna and Hewes couldn't help it. They loved her and wanted to protect her. The questions had just been a means to do that.

It didn't mean Marvie was happy about it.

After they had left the harbor and Auden had departed, Marvie had glared at her aunt and uncle, opening her mouth to unleash her absolute fury on them, but her uncle spoke before she could.

"I like him," Hewes had stated.

Marvie stopped, her angry words at the tip of her tongue. She only managed to sputter, "What?"

"I like him," Hewes repeated.

"Me too," Sienna chimed in, beaming at Marvie as they walked back towards their apartment. "He is such a nice boy, Marvie. I can't believe we didn't get to meet him sooner!"

Marvie had been at a complete loss for words, barely able to keep her feet moving to follow them. They had grilled him about his childhood and his parents and his schooling. Auden's answers weren't exactly revealing, and Marvie assumed her aunt and uncle would be upset about it. She was completely prepared to have an argument with them, a debate about whether or not Auden should be in her life. She had woven a defense of him, an answer to every point that they could possibly bring against Auden.

So what if he didn't have parents? She technically didn't have parents either!

So what if he hadn't gone to school? Not everyone had the opportunities Marvie had been lucky enough to have!

So what if he had no plans to go to university? Marvie didn't either! There was nothing wrong with that!

All of those hypothetical disputes faded away at the simple phrase "I like him".

Hewes was staring at Marvie with narrow eyes. "Do you have something you would like to say, Marvolene?" he asked her, traces of amusement in his quiet voice.

Marvie couldn't help herself; she threw her hands into the air in exasperation. "You like him? It didn't really seem that way when you were questioning him like he was some sort of criminal! The very thing I asked you not to do! You cannot act like that and then claim you actually like him!"

Her aunt and uncle were silent. Marvie's shoulders moved up and down with her rapid breaths from her outburst, her hands slightly trembling at her sides. It had been an emotional last hour of her life. She had honestly thought Auden was about to walk away from her and the fear had been enough to emotionally paralyze her. Marvie was drained, and she knew this probably wasn't the best time for a conversation such as the one they were having.

"Say something," she finally demanded as they turned down the street their apartment was on.

"I don't know what you want us to say, Marvie," her aunt said with a shrug. "I like him. Hewes likes him. Did you honestly expect us to *not* ask those questions of him? I know you're smarter than that."

"But his answers!" Marvie exclaimed. "You couldn't have been happy with them."

Hewes scoffed. "Don't be so harsh on us, Marvolene. We understand that every single teenager in Tenir isn't raised the same. It seems like Auden has had a hard life, but we would never judge him for that. In fact, I admire the boy."

"YOU WHAT?" Marvie almost yelled the words.

Hewes held his hands up in surrender. "I admire him. He's carved a life out at the age of eighteen with no support from anyone. He has his own apartment and a job he uses to provide for himself. Despite this, he seems like he's happy. He was able to hold a conversation with your aunt and me. Oh, and the boy has a good, firm handshake. That's always important. Yes, I found Auden very admirable. Didn't you, Sienna?"

Sienna nodded her agreement. "Absolutely. I like him very much, Marvie. And I know you claim that Auden is just your *friend.*" Her aunt shot her a knowing smile. "But we approve if he's something more as well."

Marvie opened her mouth to respond, but no sound would come out.

"You must bring him over for dinner!" her aunt continued happily.

Her aunt and her uncle approved of Auden. It was too good to be true. When she fell asleep that night, Marvie still couldn't wrap her head around her luck. Starting with finding Auden, but more than that, the fact that the two people she loved most in the world liked him too.

The third fact was a comforting one: her life had fallen into a perfectly mundane routine, and she was nothing short of thrilled about it.

Marvie woke up in the morning and had breakfast with Hewes and Sienna, as she had always done. Then, if she had to work that day, she would get dressed and walk to the bakery. Her shift would fly by and she would basically run out the door to see Auden standing there, waiting for her. The wind would blow his black curls and there would be a smile on his beautiful face as she embraced him, pressing a kiss to his lips that were now so familiar. They felt like home.

Together, they would walk through their city, sometimes to a tavern, sometimes to the harbor, sometimes to a market, sometimes with no destination at all. Auden would walk her back to her apartment, kiss her goodnight, and the routine would repeat itself. Time flew, but every moment was perfect. How couldn't it be, with Auden by her side? He was everything to her now.

The worries about her future had slipped away, disappeared without her realizing it. Marvie didn't want to think about what came next because she was so incredibly happy with what was going on in the present. In the back of her mind, she knew another conversation with her aunt and uncle about university was inevitable, but she didn't care. Auden was by her side now; she would never have to face anything alone again.

And as she stood looking at Auden, the facts played in her mind once more.

One, Marvie was in love with this boy.

Two, her aunt and uncle approved of him.

Three, her life was seemingly perfect with him in it.

Yeah, something terrible happening had to be inevitable.

"Marvie?" Auden asked her, worry creeping onto his beautiful face.

Marvie glanced around. She was on a familiar street, only a few blocks away from her home. She snapped out of her trance, shaking her head and trying for a smile as she wove her fingers through his. "Nothing. It's nothing. Come on, let's keep going."

Auden didn't budge. "Marvolene," Auden said, giving her a look. Marvie matched his expression, simultaneously touched and annoyed that he already knew her well enough to know she was lying.

A few weeks ago, she had not been happy. Obviously, that had changed, but not in the way Marvie wanted it to. Auden was the reason she was happy now, the only reason. He was her source of joy and elation. Which was well and good, except Marvie wanted to be her own source of joy and elation. Auden shouldn't have to carry the burden of being her happiness, even though he didn't know it. She wanted true happiness to come from within, and for Auden to simply be an addition to that happiness.

Auden being in her life hadn't made her previous problems disappear. Yes, it was easier to ignore them. When Marvie thought about Isla and her friends, she let Auden distract her. When she looked in the mirror and hated what she saw, she tried to see herself as Auden did. When the future seemed so big and daunting and uncertain, she imagined facing it with Auden.

Auden had become the answer but a temporary one. Marvie still had to face these problems herself. Starting with her growing anxiety that things were going too well, and some disaster was unavoidable.

When she didn't respond right away, Auden tucked a piece of hair behind her ear, his brow furrowed with concern. "Marvie, what is it?" he asked softly.

Marvie wondered what Auden would do if she just took off running, avoiding the question entirely by abandoning him. She had a feeling he wouldn't like it that much. It was late into the evening, the sun already down below the horizon, the streetlamps lighting their way. Thankfully, there weren't too many people out who might possibly witness Marvie start to cry.

She finally met his eyes. "I'm worried."

Auden raised an eyebrow. "Worried?" he repeated.

Marvie nodded, biting her lip. "Very worried."

"Why are you worried, Marvie?" Auden asked her, his tone so incredibly patient. Her heart throbbed as it often did when she was reminded of how much she loved him. It was always the little things that reminded her. A few days ago, he had laughed at something she said, his head thrown back and sunshine hitting him at the perfect angle, and Marvie had forgotten how to breathe.

"It's just that..." Marvie started and then stopped, rubbing her forehead. Without thinking about it, she blurted out, "Do you still like me?"

Auden stared at her, mouth agape. "I...what?" he stuttered.

Marvie tore her gaze away from his, cheeks burning. Why did she even open her mouth anymore? "I asked do you still like me?" she repeated meekly.

Auden looked around them, as if he were looking to see if anyone else was witnessing this scene. He ran a hand through his hair and his shoulders were shaking. Marvie took a step back, eyes widening. He was laughing at her! He clapped one hand over his mouth to hide it, but she saw right through him. She scowled at him, shaking her head.

"Forget I said anything," she snapped, tearing her hand out of his.

"Marvie!" Auden exclaimed, grabbing for her arm, but she danced out of his grasp, turning around and almost crashing into another person walking in the opposite direction. She barely registered the presence of the person she had stumbled into when a familiar voice chimed, "Why, it's Marvie!"

Marvie blinked twice as she recognized the incredibly beautiful person who was standing before her.

"Isla," Marvie whispered, trying to muster a smile but failing miserably.

And there she was, as stunning as the stars themselves. Isla was wearing some sort of dress that Marvie could never pull off, a dark blue one that accentuated the beauty of her body to a level Marvie didn't believe was possible. Her legs were the star of the show, long and toned and perfect. Isla's short, auburn hair was curly that night, framing her elegant facial features. Her emerald eyes seemed to sparkle in the light of the streetlamps, and Marvie suddenly regretted she hadn't put more time into her outward appearance that night.

"Marvie!" Isla shouted with a grin, pulling her into an embrace. Marvie wrapped her arms around her in return, her face at chest-level because of their height difference. She couldn't help but inhale Isla's perfume and of course, it was intoxicating in the best way. Something floral and sweet, impossible to replicate. Marvie probably smelled like the inside of a bread oven.

Isla finally released her. "It's so good to see you! I've missed you so much! We all have." She gestured to the three other people with her. Marvie nodded and smiled at each of them, her friends who seemed more like strangers. There was Lee, Isla's beloved, tall and handsome, his hand resting on the small of Isla's back. Sera and Evelin stood behind them, two girls whom Marvie had grown up with. It had been months since she had spoken to either of them, yet here they were, grinning at her like they were old friends.

They were supposed to be old friends, but it didn't feel like it.

Marvie's head was spinning too fast to keep up with the conversation. Isla's gaze had fallen onto Auden, and she raised one perfectly manicured eyebrow, before turning to look at Marvie. "And who is your friend, Marvolene?" she asked, laughter in her tone.

Marvie knew, in her mind, that Isla was simply being lighthearted. But a part of Marvie wondered if she was being mocked. Was it so unbelievable that Marvie was spending time with the beautiful boy who stood by her side?

Absolutely it was. It was probably clear, to everyone in the group, that Auden belonged next to someone like Isla, someone whose beauty matched his own. Certainly not Marvolene Pere.

Marvie cleared her throat, looking at Auden, who had been staring at her with narrow eyes. Great. He had obviously picked up on something, whatever was happening right there and then. She hadn't told him about any of her insecurities regarding Isla, but now it appeared she might have to. On top of having to explain the ridiculous question she had posed. *Do you still like me?*

So this was the terrible event that had seemed inevitable only moments ago. Marvie had obviously brought it upon herself. There was no way Auden would want to be with her after this.

"Isla, this is Auden," Marvie said, praying that the slight tremble in her voice wasn't obvious. Judging by Auden's stare, it very much was. "Auden, this is my friend, Isla."

Auden extended a hand, which Isla shook. "It's very nice to meet you," he said politely.

"And you as well, Auden," Isla replied, glancing at Marvie again. Her eyes darted between the two of them before she asked, "I'm sorry, but are the two of you..."

Auden wrapped an arm around Marvie's waist. "We're together," he interrupted, grinning at Marvie and then at Isla.

Isla raised both brows this time. "You're...together?"

Lee nudged Isla in the side. "This must be the reason we never see Marvie anymore," he said, and Marvie wanted to strike him in the face.

"How have you been, Marvs?" Sera chimed in from the back, while Isla continued to stare at Auden.

Marvie's chest ached as she tried to find a reasonable way to answer the question. She subconsciously leaned into Auden for support, and he gripped her waist a little tighter. "I've been...well, Sera. And yourself? How have you been? And you, Evelin? It's been quite a long time."

"A long time since you've spent time with us, Marvie!" Sera exclaimed, throwing her hands into the air, playfully. She shot a joking look at Auden. "But it appears someone else has been preoccupying your time. I suppose that's the reason we don't see you."

"How long have you been preoccupying Marvie's time, Auden?" Isla asked, smiling.

Marvie swallowed back the bile that had risen to her throat. She knew the purpose of the question, knew Isla was trying to prove that Auden *wasn't* the reason she had been distant. Marvie hadn't forgotten that this was the girl she had grown up with. This was the girl who had once been closer than a sister. Isla knew her too well, knew there was something more to Marvie's extended absence.

"Why, I think it's been a few months now," Auden lied softly, pressing a kiss to the side of Marvie's head. For a brief moment, there was peace, but it disappeared as soon as it had come.

Isla nodded slowly. "I see. It must've been right after we finished school then, yes?"

Marvie ignored the churning feeling in her stomach and answered, "I think so." She looked at anything else but Auden or Isla: Sera, Evelin, Lee, the buildings around them, the ground, the sky, anything.

Lee grinned at Marvie. "Have you decided what university you're going to then, eh Marvs? We talked about it so much in school, I figured by this time, you might've chosen one."

Gods, was Lee *trying* to make her throw up all over the cobblestones? She was already pretty damn close; it was as if everything on her insides wanted to be on the outside. That question might push her over the edge. Marvie swallowed back more bile and took a deep breath before answering. "I haven't made a choice yet. What about you, Lee?"

Lee started going on about some university in Lou, but Marvie couldn't hear him anymore. A ringing had crept into her ears as she finally forced herself to look at Isla again. Her old friend was staring back at her, and the rest of the people around them disappeared, including Auden with his one arm wrapped around her tight. For a moment, it was just Marvie and Isla.

There was hurt in Isla's eyes.

It wasn't what Marvie had been expecting to see, but it caused a stabbing pain in her chest.

Isla was hurt.

But how could she possibly be hurt? Isla was just as much to blame for their friendship ending. Isla hadn't tried to reach out the last couple of months, same as Marvie. But the pain in Isla's gaze was apparent and gut-wrenching, and Marvie wanted nothing more than to embrace Isla and reassure her that she had done nothing wrong. Marvie was to blame for all of it.

Marvie was the one who possessed a bitter jealousy for her best friend, not Isla. Marvie was the one plagued by constant comparisons. Marvie was the one who couldn't handle being in her presence anymore, couldn't handle watching the way their friends adored Isla. The distance that had come between them was fully created by Marvie. She thought Isla didn't care, but she might have been wrong.

Marvie managed to mutter, "That's really exciting for you, Lee," when the boy had finally finished his piece.

Lee didn't notice her unenthusiastic tone, just grinned at her and then at Isla.

"We're going to that new tavern by the harbor tomorrow night, Marvs," Evelin told her. "There's supposed to be a popular musician playing too. You've got to come!"

Marvie wanted to crawl into a hole and never come out. Since that wasn't a viable option in this situation, she replied, "What time are you going?" Her voice sounded shaky, even to her.

Evelin opened her mouth to respond, but Isla interrupted her. "It's okay if you don't want to, Marvs. We understand you're busy now, with work and," she shot a sad smile at Auden, "Auden, of course."

"No." Marvie didn't choose to say her next words, they simply leaked out of her without her consent. "What time are you going?"

Isla raised both eyebrows. "You mean you want to go?"

Marvie nodded, the movement unnatural. Auden pulled her a little closer, and she cursed the day she was born. Why did he have to be here to witness this…whatever this was? As soon as they walked away, Auden would undoubtedly have questions to which Marvie really didn't have answers. She had successfully hidden the depths of her insecurities from him in the time they had known one another, but this had surely been a revelation.

Evelin and Isla shared a glance before Evelin said, "We're going at sunset. We were going to meet at the square and walk there together."

"I will…we will be there," Marvie corrected herself, finally meeting Auden's eyes. A single glance told her everything she needed to know. Auden wasn't stupid or ignorant by any means. He had picked up on every undertone in this interaction, every double meaning in her words. A single arched brow made that more than clear.

Isla beamed, and Marvie wondered how it was possible to twist the knife in her stomach even more. But seeing her former best friend's incredibly beautiful smile did just that. She clapped her hands together and glanced at the other members in their group. "Fantastic!" she exclaimed. "This is so exciting! It'll be just like..." Isla hesitated, before finishing, "...just like old times."

Marvie bit down hard on her lip to keep the tears from falling as she mustered a smile in response. "We'll see you tomorrow then," she said softly.

They said their goodbyes, and Marvie watched after them as they started back down the street. Right before they were about to turn a corner, Isla looked back, meeting her gaze with a small, knowing smile. And then, she was gone.

Marvie didn't remember starting to move towards the apartment again, but they had begun walking, Auden's hand intertwined with her own. He hadn't spoken yet and she refused to look over at him. Marvie waited, taking short breaths to try and calm her racing heart, but it did nothing. Tears stung behind her eyes, and she knew at the first word he spoke, she probably would start crying. It was a humbling realization.

Fifteen minutes ago, she had recounted everything that was perfect about her life, and her growing fear that something was about to go wrong. At least she wouldn't spend the next couple of days in anticipation.

It had been five minutes and neither of them had spoken yet. Marvie didn't trust herself to start speaking without bursting into tears, but a part of her wanted to beg Auden to say something. What did he think of her, now that he had a front-row seat to the uncertainty she had been trying so hard to hide? Would it make her less desirable in his eyes? The 'what-ifs' attacked her from all sides, and she bit down on her lip once more.

"The answer is yes, by the way." Auden broke the silence, his sweet voice ringing out and somehow bringing comfort to each of her anxieties.

Marvie stopped at the corner where they would turn onto her street. "What?"

"The answer to your question is yes," Auden told her, picking up both of her hands and pressing a kiss to her forehead.

She wouldn't, couldn't, meet his eyes. "What are you talking about?"

"You asked me if I still like you. The answer is yes, I still do."

Marvie couldn't help herself. She let out a small sob and pressed her hands to her face, as if she could wipe the tears before he saw them.

"Marvie," Auden said gently, pulling her against his chest. She buried her face in his shirt to hide it, actively aware and embarrassed by the fact she was probably staining it with tears. She hated crying, and more so, hated crying in front of other people. Crying in front of Auden was an entirely new level of humiliation. But she couldn't help herself from leaning against him, allowing herself to be held.

Without a word, Auden withdrew from the embrace, taking her arm instead. He started walking, Marvie in his wake, unsure where they were going. It was hard to see through the moisture in her eyes, but she trusted Auden. She assumed he was going to deposit her at the apartment and then never, ever come back. Honestly, she wouldn't blame him for doing just that.

But when they stopped, they weren't at her apartment. They were at the base of a staircase in some alley that led up to a roof. Marvie didn't have time to protest as she followed Auden up the stairs and found herself looking at the rooftops of Tenir, lit up by various lights. In the distance, she could hear waves crashing. For a second, Marvie forgot about everything as she looked up at the sky and the stars that dotted it. They were nothing like the stars that could be seen in the country, and yet, there was something captivating about them, sitting up there, twinkling for all to see.

Marvie took a deep breath and turned to face Auden.

He was watching her, an unreadable expression painted over his beautiful features. His arms were crossed against his chest and for a moment, he faded right into the majesty of their city, the stars, the lights, the pure loveliness.

Too good to be true. The phrase echoed in her head once more as she stared back at him.

"What is this place?" Marvie asked him, looking around at the actual roof itself. There wasn't anything else on it, spare a few broken crates in one corner, and a set of old chairs in another. A lone bench was perched at the edge of the roof, facing the sea. Marvie had a feeling it was the perfect spot to watch the sunset.

"I found it when I was younger," Auden answered softly, taking her hand and leading her over to the bench she had just been observing. "I..." he took a deep breath as they sat down. Auden rested his hand on her knee as he exhaled, looking over at her with a sad smile. "I slept here, once."

Marvie raised both eyebrows. "You did what?"

Auden nodded, closing his eyes. "For a while, when I was younger…I didn't have a home. I sort of bounced from rooftop to rooftop. Mostly in Southside, but occasionally I came to this part of Tenir. I always remembered this one because of this bench and the perfect view it gave of the city and the sea."

Marvie couldn't quite comprehend what she had just heard. Auden didn't have a home when he was younger. It broke her heart into pieces to even imagine it. As someone who had grown up in such a loving, protective home, envisioning a young Auden on his own, *sleeping* on this roof was unfathomable. Auden had revealed almost nothing about his past, but this fact alone raised a million different questions for Marvie, none that she would articulate.

"Auden," Marvie breathed, but he was already speaking.

"Tell me something," he said, brushing a lingering tear from her cheek.

"What do you want me to tell you?"

"Who were they?"

She didn't have to ask who he meant by 'they', but she shook her head, looking away. "It's not important."

"You see, that's where you're wrong," Auden whispered, gently gripping her chin, forcing her to meet his eyes. "It's important to me. You're important to me, Marvolene. You can tell me anything. I *want* you to tell me all the things on your mind, the good, the bad, the sad, whatever it may be. There's nothing you could say, nothing you could do, that would possibly make me leave."

And there it was again, the throb in her chest of the purest and absolute love she had for this boy. If she opened her mouth to speak, she might just confess the very extent of her immeasurable emotions.

But what she couldn't confess was her own problems to Auden. He had just admitted to her that he was homeless as a child. She already knew he had no family, though she wasn't sure of the exact situation. And try as he might to hide it, Marvie occasionally caught a glimpse of the darkness behind his eyes, the only indicator that something terrible had happened to this boy, something he would never speak of. How could she possibly tell him about her own insecurities when they paled in comparison to what he might have gone through?

Marvie didn't realize she was shaking her head back and forth. "No," she mumbled. "It's nothing."

Auden had the audacity to give her a disbelieving look at a time like this. "Clearly, it is not nothing," he remarked, wiping another tear from her face. "You're crying."

"Am I?" Marie choked on a laugh. "I didn't notice."

Gently, Auden pressed a soft kiss to her lips, tangling his hand in the back of her hair. He withdrew, pressing a kiss to her cheek, then her nose, then her cheek again, and Marvie couldn't help but laugh. He smiled at her before kissing her on the lips again.

When he pulled back, Marvie whispered, "It's nothing compared to what you've been through."

He stared at her with those green eyes, as she leaned forward, pressing her forehead against his, his hand still woven through her hair.

"It doesn't matter what I've been through," he murmured, kissing her jaw. "Pain is valid, regardless of whose it is, regardless of why it is. Let me share your burdens with you, Marvolene. Please."

And Marvie opened her mouth and the words spilled out of her like a river.

She told him everything. Every single thing.

She told him about Isla and the growing jealousy she had possessed for her best friend. She told him about Isla being everyone's favorite person, how every trait her friend possessed, Marvie wanted. She spoke of slowly withdrawing from her group of friends, fearing she was dragging them down with her own attitude, yet still being upset when she saw them out together without her, imagining what kind of memories they were creating from which she would be absent.

Auden listened as she spoke of the dreaded future and her intense fear of the uncertainty that came along with it. Marvie described the expectations that her aunt and uncle had woven for her, to choose a university and a career, to choose her life's path when she barely could choose the clothes she wanted to wear in the morning. She explained that another conversation about the future was inevitable, and she couldn't bear to let them down by admitting she wasn't ready to make a choice yet, and maybe she never would be.

Marvie told him things she had never dared to say out loud, like her deep insecurities about the reflection in the mirror, her occasional loathing of the person who looked back at her. She tried to convey how often times, she wished she was an entirely different person, hated herself to a great extent, wished she had never existed in the first place.

The words kept coming and coming, and they filled her with so much relief and so much despair. How selfish was she to be dumping this on Auden, a boy she had met weeks ago who clearly carried his own burdens? And she had the audacity to give him hers as well? But Marvie couldn't stop herself from telling him everything.

Finally, Marvie told him about her eternal pursuit for happiness, except she didn't know what happiness was. She knew she could find it with other people occasionally, but how was she supposed to find it within herself when there was so much pain? The easier option was to embrace the sadness and resign herself to a life of misery, with occasional bright spots here and there.

"And you're the bright spot, Auden," Marvie whispered. She had gotten to her feet, leaning against the edge of the building, facing the sea. Auden sat on the bench, perfectly still, but she didn't look at him. "You're the happiness in my life. I don't think you can understand how much I…" she trailed off as she turned around.

There were tears running down his face.

"I think about you so much," she breathed. "Every hour of every day. There isn't a time when you're far from my mind. Being with you is perfect, of course, but even thinking about you…it makes me happy too. Sometimes, while I'm working, I'll imagine you walking in through the doors, and somehow, a hypothetical situation of being around you makes me smile. I see things when we're apart and I think to myself *I have to tell Auden about that when I see him.* Maybe it hasn't been that long, but I don't understand how I existed without you. You're a part of me now. I'm sorry about it, for your sake, because why would you want to be a part of someone like me? But you are a piece of my heart, the very fabric of my soul. You have made me believe that there was a past in which you and I have met and a future where we will meet again."

Marvie hadn't meant to say the last part. She had only meant to explain some of her life to him, by his request. But looking at him, being with him…how could she possibly exist without professing how much he meant to her? What if she dropped to her death, off the edge of the roof, before speaking? What if Auden never knew how much she cared about him? The only time was the present, and Marvie didn't regret using the present to give him every single shard of her heart.

Auden still hadn't moved, was frozen to the bench like a statue, and Marvie wondered if it had been too much for one person to handle. Maybe Auden *didn't* want the burden she had forced on him, the burden of being incredibly important to someone. Maybe she had unintentionally set expectations that he didn't want to meet. Maybe she had ruined this for good. Marvie wouldn't be surprised. But if this was the end, then there was one more thing she had to say.

"I love you," she whispered, her words floating through the air like music. It was music, to Marvie, to allow herself to say the words she had denied herself for so long. "I love you so much. So much."

If he left, now, at least he knew the full extent of the way she felt for him.

And then Auden was in front of her, grasping her hands, pulling her into his chest, kissing her everywhere, her forehead, her cheeks, her eyelids, her nose, her lips, her neck, before burying his face into her shoulder. "Marvie," he spoke into her skin. "Marvolene." She embraced him in return, running her hand up his back and into his black curls, stroking them softly as she wept.

There were many reasons why she was crying, but one stood out above all the rest. She had bared her heart to someone and it was quite possibly the scariest thing she had ever done in her entire life.

Yet Marvie couldn't focus on the fear because Auden had lifted her chin and pressed his lips against hers once more. It was different than any other kiss before; those had been gentle and soft. The kiss Auden gave her was desperate and wild, his hands moving over every part of her, and Marvie shivered, feeling his touch throughout her entire body. She had no idea what she was doing but released herself to the instinct that had awoken through Auden's touch.

He pulled back, after a long while, his eyes glossy with unshed tears as he spoke, in a raspy voice. "I have read a thousand different ways to say I love you, in stories and songs and poems, but each of them are ridiculously meaningless as I try and fail to say it to you. Words are a pathetic attempt to express the depth of what I feel for you, Marvolene. But by the will of the gods, I will try."

"I love you more than I love the air I breathe, Marvie. I love you more than waking up in the morning to greet another day. I love you more than any person, any place, any single thing I have ever encountered. I've been in love with you since the day I saw you and I swear to the gods that I will love you until the day I die. A thousand miles couldn't separate you from my love, Marvolene Pere. I have spent my *entire life* wondering why I existed, what sort of purpose I had in this dark and cruel world. But it is you, it has been you this entire time. I survive, I exist, I live, all for you, Marvie. I love you, Marvolene. My gods, I love you."

She was shaking with sobs now, her face nestled between his shoulder and neck because she couldn't bear to meet his eyes. The last shred of her heart that had been her own drifted away. All of it, every broken piece of her heart, every part of her soul, every fiber of her being belonged to him. Her head was spinning from his words and if not for his arms around her, she would have collapsed to her knees.

Things like this didn't happen to her. Marvie wasn't the type of girl that people fell in love with. She wasn't the person that people lived their lives for. This was a dream, and any minute she would wake up and realize Auden was a figment of her imagination.

But right now, he was real, and this moment might've been her entire purpose. She had been born and lived her entire life just to experience this moment.

His lips brushed her ear as he spoke once more, barely above a whisper. "And in the event that you and I don't last forever, I will draw comfort in the fact that we end up together in a thousand different worlds."

"Auden..."

"But we will, Marvie. We will last forever," Auden assured her, and she believed him. She believed him like it was the gods themselves coming down to proclaim the truth and the truth was that she would be with this boy forever.

"I know," Marvie cried into his shoulder, finally forcing herself to meet his eyes. As she gazed into them, she saw, so clearly, their future together. Right in front of her, at her fingertips, was the rest of her life that she had to spend with him. Marvie wanted nothing more than to plunge herself into that future with the same level of disregard she had cast herself into Auden's life with.

"Do you believe me now?" Auden whispered raggedly, using his thumb to brush away another tear. He replaced his thumb with his lips, pressing a kiss to where the tear had been.

"Believe what?" Marvie managed. She was surprised she was still capable of speech. What she was feeling in that moment was more than one human should be allowed to feel. Marvie wondered if she was radiant. She wanted to throw her arms in the air and spin around and bask in whatever this emotion was. Calling it happiness was a ridiculous understatement; this was more. If she had the privilege of getting to experience this a second time, she would consider herself the luckiest girl in the world.

"Believe that I still like you," Auden said with a smile, rolling his eyes.

Marvie didn't respond. Instead, she ran a hand through his black curls before kissing him with everything she was.

Because everything she was belonged to Auden Frae. And in some distant corner of her mind, she knew that it always would.

Chapter 10

There was always that moment, right after one woke up, where there was complete and utter ignorance. It happened to Marvie so frequently, she would rise from sleep with no idea where she was or what had happened the night before. She had about ten seconds of this ignorance before the previous day's events would descend upon her. And typically, the descension caused her stress or pain or apathy.

But not this morning.

This morning, the purest of ecstasy overcame her the moment her eyes opened and she couldn't help but smile, the biggest, brightest smile she could muster. Marvie's eyes hadn't even adjusted to the ceiling of her own room, her brain hardly grasped where she was, but she could not stop smiling.

Auden loved her.

Auden Frae loved Marvolene Pere.

For a few seconds, Marvie wondered if last night had been a dream. Indeed, the entire scene on the roof, from start to finish, seemed like it could only come from the depths of Marvie's imagination. It was something out of a storybook that Marvie read. She would envy the main character of the story for getting to experience something so magical, something Marvie herself would never experience because she wasn't in a storybook; she was in the real world, and in the real world, magical moments did not exist.

Marvie had been wrong. She had never been happier to be wrong about something.

Auden loved her.

Her heart was thumping in her chest as she closed her eyes and tried to bring herself back to the roof and everything that occurred. It had started off as one of the scariest times in her life and then in an instant, it was perfect. Time had stopped, just briefly, last night on the roof, allowing Marvie one single second of crystal clarity in which she realized that this might be the most perfect moment of her entire life.

She savored the moment as if it were a priceless treasure she had been given. She cherished the moment, tucked it deep down within her soul and locked it up tight. Marvie basked in the knowledge that no matter what happened with the rest of her life, she would always have that moment to fall back on. Her world could crumble apart, she could lose everything that ever meant something to her, but that moment would still be there, in her heart, a core part of who she was. Marvie would hide that moment, not share it with anyone else, because it belonged to her and her alone.

Auden Frae loved her. That one simple fact replayed in her mind as she got out of bed and went directly over to her mirror. Her hair was disheveled and her eyes were droopy with sleep, but the smile that stared back at her was gleaming. She couldn't stop. Her cheeks were starting to hurt, but Marvie could physically not stop smiling at the reflection that smiled back at her.

Because that girl in the mirror, the girl Marvie had been with since the very beginning, the one she loved and despised and encouraged and scorned, was the girl that Auden Frae was in love with.

He had said so himself.

The doubts were still there, but they were such a distant shout Marvie couldn't hear them. No doubt they were trying to convince her that she wasn't worth loving, that she wasn't worth much of anything. They wanted her to believe Auden had made a mistake, that this was all some joke or trick, because who in the world would fall in love with Marvie Pere? There was nothing special about her, right? The voices tried so hard to infiltrate her happiness, but it didn't work. Marvie's elation was too powerful, it was almost a force within itself.

"Marvolene Frae," Marvie whispered to herself as she turned to wash up. She hadn't consciously said the words, but they rose to her lips and rang through the air and sounded so perfect. Marvie had to say it again, "Marvolene Frae. Marvie Frae." She wanted to sing it, to shout it, to proclaim it to the world. She wanted to skip down the street and dance and laugh and announce that she, Marvolene Pere, was in love. Was there a way she could spread it to other people in Tenir? Because every person in their world deserved to feel the way she was feeling right now. She wanted each soul to have their very own Auden Frae.

But not *actually* Auden, because he belonged to Marvie and she was his. Every broken piece of her, every insecurity, every anxious thought or word or feeling, every fear and every heartbreak. It wasn't hers alone; it was theirs.

And one day, maybe not soon but someday, Auden would share the same with her. He would share his broken pieces, his insecurities and anxious thoughts, fears and heartbreaks. And Marvie would be there, hearing every word and slowly letting his burden become her own. She had only the slightest of ideas what his past held; yesterday he had revealed he had been homeless at one point in his life. She desperately wanted to find out why, where his parents were, what had happened in his past, all of it. But more than anything, she wanted to know why she could sometimes see darkness in his eyes. Yet Marvie wouldn't pry. She wouldn't push and shove until Auden confessed. She would allow him to tell her on his own time, and then, they would share their burdens together.

Because Marvie loved Auden.

"I love Auden Frae," Marvie sang to herself as she pulled on a pair of pants and a shirt. She had nothing to do today until Auden came to pick her up to go to the new tavern with Isla...

...Isla.

The elation within Marvie dimmed but only slightly.

Last night had distracted her from the plans she had been forced to make. She and Auden were going to meet up with Marvie's old friends to see some musician at a new tavern near the harbor. Guilt was the driving emotion behind that decision. Guilt because Marvie had looked into Isla's eyes and seen hurt there. Her former best friend was hurt at the extent to which Marvie had pushed her away. Marvie hadn't realized Isla cared at all, but it was clear that she did.

It didn't matter. Marvie would fix things tonight because the joy she felt was enabling her to fix everything about her life. She was determined to be happy because, damn it, she wanted to be happy. She was tired of being sad all the time, hating her life for no good reason. She was tired of the smallest things dragging her down and keeping her there. By some will of whatever gods watched over them, Marvie was in Tenir, living and breathing and existing, and by gods, if she had to be here, she would be happy. Why shouldn't she be happy? Other people got to be happy, why not her?

Auden made her happy, but it would be more than that. Marvie was going to make herself happy, seek happiness out with unwavering perseverance. With the gods as her witness, she was going to be happy.

The first step was resolving things with Isla. What that resolution would look like, Marvie didn't know. Maybe it was a goodbye, a sense of closure on their dying friendship. Or maybe they would start over from the beginning, because why turn their backs on what had once been a good thing? Regardless of what happened tonight, Marvie would not let it get in the way of her new pursuit of happiness.

After tonight, she would begin to deal with the other issues that plagued her. Her insecurities and fears of the future, her anxieties and struggles. One by one, she would settle these obstacles between herself and happiness. And if that didn't work, there was always Auden Frae. He was a viable solution to any of her troubles.

Marvie smiled again as she thought of him, and then smiled at herself in the mirror. She had combed out her blonde hair and put on her favorite jacket. For a second, Marvie was confused at her reflection. She looked beautiful.

She had never thought that before in her entire life. Her range of emotions about her outward appearance ranged from disappointed to mildly apathetic. But as Marvie stared at the smile that looked back at her, her bright eyes, her hair and skin and everything, she thought she might look sort of beautiful today.

Marvie smiled at the ground as she whispered again, "I love you, Auden Frae."

"MARVIE!"

Marvie jumped at the sound of her aunt calling her name and she started to blush. She had been so lost in her own thoughts about Auden that she almost hadn't heard her aunt. Marvie shot one last smile at the mirror before starting downstairs.

Sienna and Hewes weren't sitting down when she entered the kitchen; both were standing beside the table, observing something on its surface. Their heads snapped towards her at her entrance, faces painted with matching grins. Sienna gave her a knowing look, "Well, good morning, dear."

Marvie raised an eyebrow. "Good morning?" she said unsurely. She wouldn't be surprised if her aunt and uncle could immediately pick up on her happiness. She was filled with so much joy she was positive it was spilling out of her.

"There was a box outside for you this morning," Hewes told her with a grin.

Marvie was moving before her uncle finished speaking, almost flying to see what they were looking at on the table. It was a small white box with a black bow on it, a creamy colored envelope on top. Marvie glanced at her aunt then her uncle. "This morning, you said?"

Sienna nodded. "I think I know who it's from," she said, almost singing the words as she clasped her hands together. "Open it! Open it!"

Marvie already felt the red creeping up her cheeks, but more so than that, another additional wave of elation. The gift was obviously from Auden and she almost didn't want to open it, just bask in the anticipation and the knowledge that Auden had thought about her even when she wasn't around him. What a sensation to feel. To know that someone was thinking about her outside of her physical presence, that she was special enough to make that happen. It might have been the most addicting feeling of Marvie's life. Trying to hide her excitement, Marvie quickly ripped open the envelope lying on top of the package.

Marvolene,

It read in Auden's script.

I wanted to give you something that is special to me, because you are special to me. This is a book I've had since I was a child. I would read it and dream of going to the faraway places it talked about, all by myself.

But what's even better, now, is that you and I get to go there together.

I love you.

-Auden

Marvie read the words over and over again, hearing them in her head as if Auden were standing beside her speaking them. She pressed the letter to her chest and wished he were here right now. Marvie wanted to laugh; she missed him. She had seen him less than twelve hours ago, and yet, it could've been ages, for that was how much she wanted to see him.

Special to him. She, Marvolene Pere, was special to him. It wasn't believable.

"Well for goodness sakes, Marvolene, what does it say!" Sienna demanded, trying to read the letter over her shoulder.

Marvie swatted her away and stuffed the paper in her pocket. "Nothing for you," Marvie laughed as she pulled the ribbon off the package. Slowly, she opened the box and found herself looking at a book with a dark green cover. In golden lettering, it was titled *Legends of Our Fabled Past.* Below the words was a drawing of a stag. The book was worn, as if it had been read before. Marvie skimmed through the pages and saw different drawings. She knew right away she would spend the entire day reading this book just so she could talk to Auden about it when they were with one another later that night.

"What is it?" Hewes asked, observing the book from beside Marvie.

"A book," Sienna answered him, and Hewes gave her a look.

"It's Auden's book," Marvie explained. "He said it's special to him and he wants me to read it." She hugged the book to her chest and smiled.

Her aunt and uncle both stared at her for a moment, before sharing a knowing glance.

"What?" Marvie sputtered.

Hewes pulled a chair out from under the table and slid into it. "Oh nothing, Marvolene. How about some breakfast?"

"Why did you look at me like that?" Marvie asked her aunt, who had gone back into the kitchen, a small grin glued on her face.

"Like what?" Sienna said innocently as she transferred the eggs, sausage, and toast to the table, before taking a seat herself. Marvie stayed standing, gripping the book, unable to wipe the smile off her face no matter how hard she tried.

"Sienna!"

She beamed at Marvie. "Oh Marvie, we are just so happy to see you so happy!" she exclaimed. "I haven't seen you look like that in...oh, I don't even remember!"

"She's in love, Sienna," Hewes sighed, but he had a small grin on his face. "It might be hard to believe, but you once smiled like that because of me."

"Oh Hewes, stop it," Sienna chided. "You know I still get excited about you. But Marvolene is absolutely giddy and it is the cutest thing I've ever seen."

Marvie's cheeks were getting warmer and warmer. "I am not giddy!" she protested, hugging the book tighter to her chest.

"Right," Hewes snorted.

Marvie opened her mouth to respond and closed it. Instead, she giggled into her hand before running back upstairs.

"Don't you want some breakfast?" Sienna called after her, but Marvie was already in her room with the door shut. She had hours before Auden was going to pick her up and she would spend every minute of that time diving into this book. For her, it wasn't even a book; she was diving into Auden's world. He had written that he had read this book over and over as a child. It was a chance to delve a little deeper into the inner workings of Auden's mind, a place that Marvie had not seen much of. She would absorb every detail she possibly could and try to puzzle out a little more.

It was clear to Marvie, by the first page, that she could not focus to save her life. Instead, she pulled out the note that had come with the book and read the phrase *special to me* over and over until it rang through her mind like a divine harmony.

Despite her lack of concentration, Marvie kept the book hugged to her chest, a physical symbol of Auden's thoughtfulness that she wanted to hold on to forever.

The day dragged by as Marvie attempted to read the book, absorb the story. She only made it a few sentences before her mind inevitably drifted to the boy she was in love with and the coming ordeal of spending time with Isla. The actual plot flew over Marvie's head, some tale of a boy named Jo who wanted to go on adventures. Marvie knew once she sat down to read the book, she would fly through it and probably love it as much as Auden.

But not today, and if Auden made fun of her for not reading it, she would promptly put the blame back on him. "It's not my fault I wasn't able to think of a single thing other than the magical words you proclaimed to me last night, a lasting truth you carved into my soul, a permanent mark I'll never be able to forget."

Eventually, Marvie tucked the book below her bed, stashing the note under her mattress in case a curious Sienna came looking for it. She went to the mirror once more and braided her hair, undid it and braided it again, before being somewhat satisfied with the final product. She dug through the clothes in her wardrobe, slipping into a dress before throwing it on the floor with anger. A slightly bitter feeling had crept up on her as she did this. Marvie tried to avoid imagining what beautiful outfit Isla would don, but it was impossible. No matter what Marvie chose to wear tonight, Isla would most likely upstage her.

She had forgotten what it was like to be in a group of people along with Isla, but as she threw more clothes on the floor, the sensation resurrected itself. Isla was the life of the party, the heart of a crowd. She had a way of bewitching people, enchanting them with her fascinating conversation and stories. Marvie had a distinct memory of comparing Isla's laugh to some sort of celestial melody. Any sort of person, loud, quiet, happy, angry, tired, vibrant, could sit in front of Isla and come away feeling entertained, feeling like they were the most important person in the world. Isla had a way of making people feel important, and Marvie was no exception.

The happiness drained out of her quicker than she imagined it would.

Marvie realized her hands were shaking slightly as she thought about Auden in Isla's presence. Their introduction last night had been brief, not enough time for Auden to be possessed by Isla's charm. But tonight? They were about to spend hours with the girl. In other words, an adequate amount of time for any normal human to be bewitched. What if Auden finally realized that Marvie was incredibly mundane? What if he realized he had so many better options than a quiet girl with a normal face? And what if one of those options suddenly became a beautiful girl with short auburn hair and eyes you could lose yourself in?

Marvie scowled at herself in the mirror. *Are we forgetting that this is the same boy who professed his love to you last night? The same boy who swore to the gods that he would love you until the day he died?* But Auden's words from last night seemed far away. Besides, promises were easy to make, the words easy to say. It was so simple to release little oaths into the world like they were nothing, not realizing that the person on the other side believed you with every fiber of their being.

Auden said those words and Marvie breathed them in like they were keeping her alive. What if it had been a slip of the tongue, an accident? Were those words that Marvie would have to work hard to forget after Auden left her?

A single tear fell out of her eye as she looked down at the dress she was wearing. It was a pale yellow one with white stripes; it was one she once found beautiful, but now as she looked at it, it seemed boring. Especially considering Isla would probably be wearing something that the gods themselves would find stunning.

Marvie was so lost in her own thoughts that she almost didn't hear the knock at her door.

"I'm getting dressed, Sienna!" Marvie said without moving to open it, whilst trying to prevent her voice from shaking. Her floor, which had been clean that very same morning, was now covered in clothes she hadn't deemed good enough for Isla to see. It was a tragic symbol of her own insecurity, her admission that she would never be good enough for Isla.

"It's not Sienna," a beautiful voice said through the door.

Marvie froze as she turned around and stumbled across her room, avoiding tripping over the clothes scattered about. She went for the door handle before stopping. "Give me a moment," she sputtered, quickly gathering everything into her arms and shoving it into her wardrobe. She glanced at the mirror, wiping the few tears away and straightening her back up, taking a deep breath and trying for a smile. It was convincing enough, but knowing him...

She sighed. There was no point; it was abundantly clear Auden could pretty much read her mind.

When she opened the door, Marvie smiled at him.

He stood there, leaning against the doorway, beaming. Immediately, she felt a wave of relief, but she sort of resented it. Why couldn't she create her own solutions to the problems she brought upon herself? Still, one look at Auden and it all came back to her, last night's perfection. She looked at him and promises echoed in her ears like music and the fake smile suddenly wasn't fake anymore. Auden, of course, looked ridiculously handsome in a gray long-sleeved shirt and black pants, his black curls smoothed down in an attempt to be tamed. His green eyes were glowing and Marvie had a feeling he was thinking about the same moments she was.

"Hello," she said breathlessly.

Auden didn't respond, but took one step forward, wrapped one arm around her waist, and pulled her in for a kiss. The moment his lips met hers, the gnawing thoughts disintegrated completely and it was just Auden, and all the beautiful, beautiful things that lay between them. Marvie brought one hand around his neck, weaving the other through his curls as he closed the door behind him, kissing her harder, a shadow of what had almost transpired last night had Auden not insisted she go home to her apartment instead of his. Marvie gasped as his lips found the soft skin just beside her throat and she clung onto him tighter.

"MARVOLENE?"

Both of them froze, Auden's lips still pressed against her neck.

"Yes, Uncle Hewes?" she managed to yell in reply.

"I want that door to be kept open if Auden's going to be in your room." Her uncle's tone was firm, but there was amusement in his voice.

Marvie sighed as Auden released her, taking a step back with a large grin on his face. "Yes, Uncle Hewes," she shouted as Auden opened the door wide. He turned back to her and shrugged.

"Oops," he said without a trace of regret in his tone.

Marvie's shoulders were moving up and down with her gasps for breath and her heart was pounding through the yellow dress she hated. Still, she gave him a disapproving look, trying her hardest not to slam the door shut and resume what had almost started. "You're a bad influence on me," she told him, her voice trembling slightly.

Auden snorted. "Believe me, I am well-aware."

Marvie turned back to her mirror, pretending to fix her hair even though her hands were trembling and couldn't fix much of anything. She simultaneously cursed and thanked her uncle. If that would've continued…well, they wouldn't have made it to the tavern tonight, that was for certain. "What are you doing here?" Marvie asked him, glancing at him in the mirror's reflection.

Auden sat down on the edge of her bed, his face glazed over with a resting smile. Marvie couldn't help but blush as she met his eyes because that smile said it all. It was an inside joke between the two of them, their little secret, something only the two of them knew. That *something* was the entirety of the night before. Marvie almost expected Auden to deny it had happened and for her to realize that yes, it had been a dream, but the small smile dancing on his lips seemed to say otherwise.

"I seem to recall that we're going to a tavern tonight," Auden said and even his voice seemed to brim with joy. He watched her through the mirror and Marvie blushed even harder as she tore her gaze away from his and let it settle on her toes.

"It's early," she replied.

"I'm right on time, Marvolene," Auden countered. "You told me an hour before the sun went down."

Marvie glanced out the window and saw it was, indeed, exactly when she had told Auden to arrive. The day had slipped through her fingers like water. She supposed that was what happened when one spent the day reliving a dream over and over again. Time apparently didn't exist in fantasies of the past and future.

"Oh," was her only reply as she pretended to fiddle with her hair.

And then, Auden was right behind her, wrapping his arms around her waist and burying his face into her shoulder. She laughed as she spun around and embraced him in return. He picked her up off the ground and spun her around the room and she could barely breathe from laughing so hard. He was laughing too and he set her down, pressing a single kiss to her lips before resting his forehead against hers, grinning wildly.

"Hey," he whispered, his breath tickling her lips.

"Hey," she giggled in reply.

"What's wrong?" he asked, and Marvie shook her head.

"Nothing. Nothing at all," she whispered, and it was the truth.

He didn't reply, but his smile didn't disappear and that was all she needed.

"What is with you right now?" Marvie asked, laughing again as he picked up one of her hands, bringing it so it was resting on his shoulder. He wove the other in his hand, and then rested a hand on her waist. He began to hum as he rocked her back and forth. In Marvie's tiny bedroom that had just been covered in her discarded outfits, they were dancing.

Auden had his eyes closed, but she couldn't stop staring at him as they swayed back and forth to the rhythm of whatever song he was humming. She didn't know it, but she knew she would never forget it. Like the words he had proclaimed last night, this moment would be with her forever.

She managed to say, "What's going on?"

Auden stopped and opened his eyes. He tucked a piece of hair behind her ear and, in a similar fashion to Marvie herself, smiled down at the ground. "Nothing's going on, Marvie," he breathed, before looking back up at her again. "I think I'm just happy."

"I…" She tried to respond but couldn't think of the right words as the darkness was in his eyes again, but there was something else there too. How was it possible that this person in front of her, this boy who she had given her heart, could be the most familiar person in the world while still being a stranger?

"I think I'm happy, Marvolene," Auden said, taking a step back, and running a hand through his hair, rustling the neat style he had it in. "I don't think I've ever really known what it feels like to be happy before," he whispered, looking down at his hands. "My whole life has been a fluctuation between bad and worse. The good days were never good, they were just less terrible. On the best days, I was just content, resigned to surviving another day in this world, but right now…" He smiled up at her and she could've sworn his eyes were glassy. "Right now, I'm happy."

Marvie made a promise, right there and then, to herself. She didn't believe in promises very much, but the one she was about to make suddenly became the most sacred agreement she had ever dared to take; she was going to preserve his happiness. Auden's happiness was a flame and she would protect it from the wind, shielding it from the cold, keeping it aglow and alight. She would protect it until the darkness behind his eyes was gone. *I don't know who broke you, Auden Frae. But I'm going to put you back together again. I'm going to take your broken pieces and love you until you're whole. With the gods as my witness, I will make you whole again.*

She wanted to tell him that, wanted to grab his face and force him to look at her as she swore on her life she would protect him from whatever darkness he was carrying, whatever scars from the past he bore. She wanted to make known to him that never again would his best days be days where he was…resigned to surviving another day in this world? What had happened to make his good days the days where he didn't want to die?

It didn't matter. She would take away all the pain, make it her own if she had to. Marvie wanted to declare that to Auden, but instead, she took his hand and squeezed it.

"I think I'm happy too," she told him.

Chapter 11

"**D**oes the dress look okay?" Marvolene asked Auden for about the tenth time as they walked hand and hand towards the tavern, the light from the streetlamps guiding them and the rest of the crowd.

"Marvolene, do you think I was lying to you the last ten times when I told you the dress looked beautiful?" Auden replied, his tone patient if not amused. He looked over at her and rolled his eyes, smiling. "What will it take for you to believe me, hmm?"

She shrugged as she slowed their pace just slightly, hoping Auden wouldn't notice. They were getting closer and closer to the tavern and had fallen into a crowd of people who were all going in the same direction. Marvie had a feeling they were probably going to the same tavern. Great. More people to experience her misery, maybe even absorb it from her.

She was in the predicament of teetering on the brink of absolute elation and intense fear. Elation because it seemed every conversation she had with Auden became her new favorite memory. She thought nothing would be able to top the previous night's confessions on the roof, but alas, she had been proved wrong.

I think I'm just happy.

Five tiny little words that would never leave her.

Auden held her hand, swinging it back and forth as he whistled under his breath, excited for the night's events. Despite the nervousness that was gnawing at her stomach, Marvie smiled. She had noticed, at times, when they walked on the streets, Auden would be alert, observing every single person who passed as if they were going to be attacked. She didn't know why he did that, but she had her guesses. Auden had grown up in Southside and had, at one point, been homeless. She was sure it was a habit to be aware of his surroundings.

But as they walked side by side, Auden Frae seemed carefree, as if he hadn't a trouble in the world.

I think I'm just happy.

"It wouldn't hurt for you to tell me one more time," Marvie pointed out as they turned onto another street, the brick buildings of Tenir towering above them, a comforting, nostalgic vision. There were no horses on this road, as it was so busy with people that they spilled off the walkways. It was common knowledge, for any Tenir native, not to attempt bringing a horse to this part of town. And indeed, the street was overflowing with people, talking and laughing in Orinthian. There were other couples around them, holding hands, linking arms, smiles spread across their faces. There were groups of friends, stumbling down the cobblestones, laughing loudly. All around her, memories were being created, joyous memories that made Marvie remember why she loved this city so much. Yes, it had its problems, but there were so many wonderful things to see, if one simply knew where to look.

Auden looked over at her and sighed, though there was a smirk on his face. "Marvolene Pere, you are the most beautiful woman alive."

Marvie cocked her head as they turned onto the street that led to the harbor. Her chest had turned into a drum, thumping as she tried to swallow down the lump in her throat. Still, she managed to reply, "That's more like it."

Auden laughed softly under his breath, wrapping his arm around her waist and pulling her in closer.

The music was growing louder and louder and Marvie took a shaking breath in, trying to calm herself before Auden noticed her anxiety and tried to fix it for her. He was happy; he would stay happy. She would figure out the complications between Isla and herself all on her own.

The little voice in the back of her mind was dying to contribute to her internal dispute. *And if Auden falls in love with Isla the way everyone else does? If he leaves you for her, what then? Will his happiness matter then?*

That was the punchline of the whole thing; if Auden fell for Isla tonight, Marvie would let him go. Because, somewhere between that day she walked into his store and now, his happiness became more important than her own. And if Isla was going to be the person to secure that happiness, Marvie would walk away and not look back.

"Marvie?"

Marvie took a deep breath as she looked over at him. His smile had disappeared and he had one eyebrow raised.

"Is everything alright?" Auden asked.

They hadn't stopped moving even as he questioned her. She opened her mouth to reply as she caught a flash of red hair standing outside the tavern they were bound for. It was housed in a two-story brick building and the doors were flung open, an enormous crowd outside waiting to get in. The party had spilled over, filling the square next to the harbor, where Marvie could hear, but not see, the waves crashing into the wall. A makeshift stage had been created in the middle of the square, so the musician was high enough that even people at the back could see him. There was a steady stream of people entering and exiting the tavern with drinks to get a better look. It appeared he hadn't started his performance but was fiddling with some sort of stringed instrument. The noise of the crowd was almost painful to the ears, but Marvie managed to shout back to Auden, "Everything's magnificent."

Marvie caught the flash of red again and this time, Isla spotted her in return. She grinned widely and waved them over to where she was waiting in line to get into the tavern. Marvie took a deep breath, not allowing herself to fully observe her friend yet, as she pointed her out to Auden. "There she is."

Auden's gaze followed hers, settled on Isla, and he dropped a hand to the small of Marvie's back as he guided them through the crowd and towards their group.

After a minute of navigation, they approached where Isla was waiting for them. She was dressed in a deep purple gown that almost touched the ground. It had no sleeves, showing off her naturally toned arms and smooth skin. Her short auburn hair was curly and her face had just the right amount of cosmetics on it so that she looked innately stunning. A few different sorts of jewelry hung from her body, drawing attention exactly where she wanted it. But it was the dazzling smile that did it, that was all white teeth and red lips and pure beauty. Lee was with her, arm linked through hers, but Marvie hardly noticed him.

Isla let go of Lee and embraced Marvie, pulling her in tight. Marvie hugged her back, trying not to inhale, but she couldn't help herself. Isla released her and shot a smile at Auden.

"I'm so glad you were both able to make it!" she exclaimed, clapping her hands together.

Lee extended a hand to Auden, which he shook, keeping his other hand on Marvie's back. "We're glad too," Auden said warmly, smiling at Marvie and then Isla. He gestured to the scene around them. "Apparently we're not the only ones who heard about the performance tonight." His point was made clearer by the fact he had to raise his voice to be heard.

Lee whistled under his breath. "Tell me about it! We've been here for almost half an hour and the line to get a drink has hardly moved!"

Isla nodded her agreement. "Evelin and Sera arrived here a few minutes before we did and they made it inside. But we haven't seen them since."

"We'll make it in sooner or later," Marvie said, hoping her voice sounded level. Subconsciously, she wove her fingers with Auden's. He squeezed her hand tight as she continued, "After the performer starts, we'll probably get a chance to go in and get a drink." And she needed a drink.

"You're right, Marvs. In a few minutes, we'll all have cold drinks in our hands, serenaded by the musician. I think his name is Pip or something," Isla surmised. She clapped her hands together and beamed at Lee and then Marvie. "I heard they will eventually clear part of the street for dancing. Isn't that magnificent?"

"Wonderful," Marvie croaked out, making a silent promise right there and then that she would NOT be dancing tonight. It's not that she didn't enjoy dancing; she did, especially with Auden. But dancing in the company of Isla would be an entirely different scenario. She had seen the way Isla moved, with all the grace and rhythm of a professional. There was no way she would stand up next to her and attempt the same thing.

"So Marvie," Lee began and with the hand that wasn't holding Auden's, Marvie dug her nails into her skin in order to force a smile to her face, "how are your aunt and uncle?"

She tried not to breathe an outward sigh of relief. It was a simple enough question. Nowhere along the lines of 'why have you isolated yourself for the last five months?'. "They're wonderful," Marvie answered, almost shouting the words to be heard over the crowd. "My Uncle Hewes still works in construction and my aunt does odd jobs here and there."

"I miss them!" Isla exclaimed. "Aunt Sienna was almost a second mother to me growing up." There were traces of sadness in her words, though they were true. Isla had constantly been at Marvie's house throughout their childhood and vice versa. Marvie still remembered Isla's mother and father claiming Marvie as their "second daughter", as Isla only had brothers. There was some strange mixture of sadness and regret and nostalgia as Marvie thought about it.

Trying to swallow it back, Marvie asked, "How is your family, Isla?" The line moved slightly forward so they were crowded into the doorway of the tavern, halfway inside, halfway out. Marvie could smell Orinthian wine and body odor, a scent that wasn't necessarily bad, as it just made her think of Tenir. All the tables and chairs of the tavern had been stacked on the far side of the room, leaving a large space that was completely full of people standing in line to get to the long bar that took up the other side of the room. There were two levels of this tavern, the balcony that lined the perimeter of the tavern was also filled. The people leaning against the railing had drinks in their hands and contributed to the absolute roar of noise taking up the whole of the place.

Isla had to yell even louder to respond. "They're good too!"

Marvie couldn't hear a thing as Auden's grip on her hand grew tighter. "WHAT?" she yelled.

Auden stepped between them as they moved farther into the tavern. "Marvie, why don't you and Isla go get us a spot to watch the musician." He gestured at Lee. "Lee and I will get us some drinks and find you. At this rate, we'll be so far back we won't be able to see the man."

Marvie stared at Auden, hoping her wide eyes were conveying what she was thinking, which was no, no, no, absolutely not, please don't do this to her. By the small smile on his lips, she knew that Auden was being purposeful in his actions, as always. But before she could protest, Isla had woven her arm through hers and said, "Lee, darling, I would like a very large glass of Orinthian wine." She looked at Marvie pointedly, as if daring her to get out of this.

Marvie let go of Auden's hand, shooting him a look as she said, "Same for me."

Auden grinned at her. "Lovely."

Isla started pulling them outside as Marvie glared at Auden one last time. He gave her an innocent look and a shrug before disappearing from her sight.

She was glad that Isla was pulling them along because the anxiety running up and down her body was enough to make her want to collapse. Her hands were shaking and her knees would've been doing the same if they weren't being forced to move, forced to weave in and out of the crowd as they made their way closer to the stage. The crowd was loud, but in that moment, it sounded distorted to her, because she could only focus on Isla. The way her curls bounced as she marched them closer, the way she walked, so smooth even as she dodged people stumbling about. Marvie couldn't help marvel at the way her dress flowed behind her, as if it were being moved by its own wind. And here Marvie was with her, a pebble next to a prized diamond.

Abruptly, Isla stopped, when they were a short distance from the stage. There was still a large number of people separating them from the musician, but they were close enough to see his eyes. Isla turned to Marvie and gestured around them. "What do you think?" she asked, and her melodic voice in harmony with the waves crashing against the seawall was enough to make Marvie want to cry.

But she didn't. She mustered a smile and nodded. "Perfect." She looked back towards the tavern, hoping to catch a glimpse of Auden, but there were just too many people. "I hope they'll be able to find us."

Isla scoffed. "Who cares if they do or don't! I'm just eager to talk to you, Marvs."

Marvie met Isla's gaze. Her old friend was staring at her as if she were waiting to hear something. The hurt was back, and even though Marvie had prepared for it, it still struck a chord deep within her, a chord of guilt. "How is your family?" Marvie asked, though it was the least of what they needed to say to one another. "I couldn't hear you back there."

"Oh, they're fine," Isla said with a smile. "My brothers all left for university. Tray is in Lou and Reta is in Abdul. They were eager to explore another city besides the one we live in."

"And you?" Marvie questioned. "Have you made the decision they've been begging us to make since we were ten years old?"

Isla snorted, running a hand through her red hair. "They have been nagging us for quite a long time, haven't they? The answer to your question is no. I haven't decided what university I'll go to, or even if I will go at all. I don't know what I want to do tomorrow, Marvolene. How am I supposed to decide what to do every day for the rest of my life?"

Marvie laughed, a genuine laugh and Isla's head snapped over to her, a grin appearing on her beautiful face. "What's so funny?" she asked, laughing along with her.

"Nothing, nothing. It's just that I think you stole the words from my mind just then."

"You haven't decided either?"

Marvie shook her head. "No, I haven't. My aunt and uncle are impatient for me to do so. They've set aside some funds for me and they're eager for me to use them, to get a proper education and all of that, but every time I imagine going to university, I just hate the idea of it. It's not to say I'll never go. Now is just not the time and I wish they would understand that."

Isla threw her hands into the air. "Gods, can you please come talk to my mother and father to prove to them I'm not the only one who thinks like this?"

Marvie beamed, the anxiety and guilt easing just a little bit. "Only if you promise to talk to Sienna and Hewes."

Isla's smile disappeared as she sighed. "Things were much easier when we were small, weren't they?"

"Oh, yes," Marvie agreed. "There were days when our biggest problem was getting caught for stealing chocolate from Miss Greta's desk."

Isla laughed again and this time, it attracted the attention of some of the people near to them. Marvie watched as those people all seemed to smile. Isla's joy was contagious; it had always been like that. "I forgot about that!" Isla exclaimed. "We were eight, weren't we? And Miss Greta bragged about the special chocolate her brother had brought back from Grady. She talked about it for so long and then, when she took us outside for break, you and I snuck back in, found where it was hidden, and ate every bite. Oh boy, I remember the punishment for that like it was yesterday."

Marvie giggled, pressing a hand to her mouth. "I wasn't allowed to eat chocolate for a month. I don't think my aunt and uncle have ever been more upset with me."

"I'm sure; I received a thrashing from my mother," Isla snorted. "Do you remember what we did only a few days after?"

"We stole chocolate from Tray's room and ate every single bite. And then we blamed it on Reta."

"Reta still hasn't forgiven me for that," Isla told her. "That boy will go on to get an education, get married, have children of his own, and he still won't forgive me for the time I stole Tray's chocolate and let him take the punishment for that."

"I don't blame him," Marvie laughed.

Isla laughed along with her as the crowd slowly began to hush. Marvie exchanged an excited glance with Isla before directing her attention towards the stage. The musician, Pip, had picked up his guitar and stood at the ready. The stage was built in a manner to amplify the sound of the music, though the crowd had almost gone silent in anticipation. Without thinking about it, Marvie grabbed Isla's hand, squeezing it tight. Isla looked over at her, trying to meet her eye, but Marvie kept her focus glued to the stage.

And then the musician began, playing his instrument with the skill of a professional, the music ringing out for all to hear. For a few minutes, he plucked the strings, creating a beautiful melody before he joined in with his voice, the beginning of an old Orinthian folksong. The moment he began to sing, the crowd joined in and the riot resumed, with clapping and shouts of praise. Marvie and Isla both clapped along with them. For one serene moment, Marvie forgot where she was, what she was doing, and who was beside her. She lost herself in the perfection before Isla called over to her.

"You seem to like Auden quite a bit."

Marvie wanted to laugh at that statement. 'Liked Auden quite a bit' didn't begin to describe the immense feelings she possessed for him, but still, she nodded, meeting Isla's eyes. Her friend had her brows raised, lips twisted into a knowing smile. "I suppose he's alright."

Isla snorted. "Oh Marvs, you forget how long I've known you. You had boys here and there, but none who you looked at like you look at Auden."

Marvie felt the heat creep into her cheeks and she smiled at the ground. "Well, yes. I suppose I like him…quite a bit." Imagine if she told Isla that it had been only the previous night when she had confessed her love for him like a crazed lunatic. Isla would probably find the whole thing amusing.

"And Lee?" Marvie quickly spoke before Isla could ask anything else about Auden. She wasn't sure she wanted to divulge all the details of their meeting and the aftermath. Part of her was afraid Isla would laugh at her for being stupid enough to feel this way for a person she hadn't known that long. The other part was afraid Isla would see it as a challenge to take Auden away from her. It was a ridiculous thought and somewhat insulting to Isla, given her friend had never done anything of the sort before, but Marvie's anxiety loved to create fake scenarios and convince herself that they would inevitably come true. The movement of fear in her body resumed.

"What about him?" Isla said with a smile.

"It's been, what, three years since you started going with him?"

She nodded. "Something like that."

"And you're not growing tired of him yet?" Marvie asked jokingly.

Isla stared at her. "Marvolene, I'm going to marry that boy."

Marvie opened her mouth wide, grasping Isla's hands. "You're serious?"

Isla bit her lip. "Well, not anytime soon. But one day, we will. We've talked about it time and time again, and oh Marvie, I feel any day he's going to ask me! I love him. I love Lee so much. I haven't decided what I'm doing for university or where I'm going, but I would follow that boy anywhere. I'm going to marry him and I'm going to be happy." She grinned after the last sentence and threw her hands up to the sky. Over the music and the crowd, she yelled louder, "I'M GOING TO BE HAPPY!"

Marvie laughed as Isla shouted again, "I'M GOING TO BE HAPPY!" She dropped her arms to her side and smiled at Marvie. "Do it. Tell the whole world you're going to be happy. Don't let life have a choice in the matter. If you scream at the world you're going to be happy, the world will let you be happy. Do it, Marvie, do it!"

Not totally in control of her body or actions, Marvie threw her hands into the sky, staring up at the colors that the sunset had created, and shouted, "I'M GOING TO BE HAPPY TOO!" She giggled, looking over at Isla, who nodded at her enthusiastically. The music was loud, but Marvie was even louder as she shouted again, "I'M GOING TO BE HAPPY!"

She dropped her hands, grinning wildly, as a wave of thoughts washed over her. She thought about Isla and the rest of her friends she had let slip away. She thought of the reflection in the mirror, the yellow dress and blonde hair she had despised, the internal battle to love who she was when she wanted to be someone else. She thought of the relentless way she refused to be happy, always coming up with reasons to be sad instead. Marvie gathered everything, all of those thoughts and feelings, those barriers between her and her happiness, and released them into the night air, letting them be carried away with the wind and the music. "I'm going to be happy," Marvie said again.

Isla had taken ahold of her hand, stepping in front of her, and once again, everything around them disappeared. Marvie stared back at her friend, seeing her at every different stage of life. When they first met, when they were just children, when they stole the chocolate, when they skipped through the city streets together, when they stayed up late talking about trivial things, making up stories, laughing until sleep claimed them. She saw Isla in taverns with her, having a good time. She saw Isla in taverns without her, still having a good time. She saw Isla in every form as her friend opened her mouth to speak.

"Did I do something to upset you?" Isla asked, and even though her voice was soft, Marvie heard the words like they were being screamed into her ear.

Marvie shook her head. "No. No, Isla. You didn't do a thing," she whispered.

Isla picked up her other hand so that they were clasped between their two bodies. "Then what happened to us, Marvie? Why did you disappear? Why'd you stop coming to things and letting us all go? Why did you...why did you let me go?"

Marvie opened her mouth to respond, but no sound came out. The guilt showered over her like rain and she was dripping with it, dripping with regret, dripping with words she wanted to say but didn't know how. How was she supposed to confess to Isla, her former best friend, what a terrible, jealous person she was? What if her friend cast her away after it seemed like they had figured things out again?

Before she could think of the right words to say, Isla looked down at the ground. "I thought you thought you were too good for us...too good for me. I thought you grew tired of our childish exploits, and I didn't blame you for it."

The song came to an end and the crowd around them exploded into cheers and applause, but Marvie kept ahold of Isla's hands. "What are you talking about, Isla? That I thought I was better than you?"

Isla shook her head and one single tear fell onto her cheek. Marvie wanted nothing more to wipe it away, but she couldn't bring herself to move. "It's just that...Marvie, look at you. You're so beautiful and you're so intelligent. Sometimes when you speak, you sound like you've already been to university, like you've already lived ten lifetimes. I love listening to you talk, I could listen all day. And you know how to have fun, of course, but I thought you might have outgrown the taverns and the dancing and all of it. Someone who speaks like you do, who looks like you do and acts like you do...you should be around people who match your level of cleverness. And well, me and Lee and Sera and Evelin and the rest...I don't think we do. That's why I thought you had left us."

Marvie was paralyzed with shock, her muscles frozen like they had been coated in ice. She stared at this girl, this incredibly stunning person who she had known her whole life, but as she looked back at Isla, she saw a stranger saying nonsensical words. Marvie was not beautiful, she was not intelligent, she was not clever. What was Isla saying? That Marvie had outgrown both Isla and the rest of their friends? It was so far from the truth. Marvie had believed that the whole group had outgrown her, were content with leaving her behind in the dust.

But it seemed Isla felt the same way Marvie did.

"Isla..." she whispered and a tear fell from her own eye to match the one resting on Isla's cheek. "Oh, Isla."

Isla mustered a smile. "I told myself I was okay with it. That's part of life, right? People you think are going to be in your life forever disappear in the blink of an eye. Friends who were once like family grow apart until they're gone. I told myself we had moved on from each other because you were above us..."

Marvie shook her head. "I'm not above you, Isla, I'm not."

Isla didn't stop speaking. "I convinced myself it was okay, but the truth is, Marvs, I miss you terribly. I love the rest of our friends, and Lee of course, but I always thought it was you and me, Isla and Marvie. I don't want to grow apart from you. I want you in my life forever. I want you standing next to me when I marry Lee and maybe I can stand next to you when you marry Auden. I want you to hold my first child and second child and all the rest. I want to watch your own children grow up. I want to get together with you every week over glasses of Orinthian wine and complain about all the drama in our lives, but underneath we're so damn happy because we told the world we're going to be. And I'm so afraid that's gone now."

The single tear turned to dozens, streaming down her face as Marvie held onto Isla's hands like she was anchoring her to the world. The crowd, the music, all of it had fully disappeared. Even the loudness of her mind, the volume of her anxiety and guilt had faded until it was just Marvie standing in front of Isla, with the desperate need to convey the truth. "It's my fault, Isla. It's my fault we've grown apart, but it's not because I think I'm better than you. On the contrary, Isla, sometimes," her voice cracked and she wondered whether she should say this out loud, if Isla would curse her for it, but it was too late to stop, "sometimes, I'm so jealous of you."

Isla's mouth opened until it made the shape of a circle. She stuttered, "Jealous of me?"

Marvie nodded, wanting desperately to tear her gaze away and look at something else, but she couldn't. "I'm jealous of you, Isla. You say I'm beautiful and it makes me wonder if you've ever looked in the mirror before. You remind me of a star, Isla, you shine so brightly. The way you light up a room when you enter it, light up people's lives the moment you meet them. I felt so special to be your friend, and then something soured in me and it's all my fault, all mine. I just thought you didn't need me anymore, because of how perfect you seemed on the outside. I'm a jealous and bitter person and I wouldn't blame you if you walked away from me."

"Marvie…"

"…but if you don't. If you decide to give me another chance, I miss you too. I miss everything about our friendship. I miss your laughter and your hugs and our jokes and everything in between. It would be an honor to be in your life, for every big moment and every small one."

Isla didn't say a word, just stared at her with bloodshot eyes, tears falling at the same rapid rate. She took a breath, as if to speak, but stopped herself as she suddenly grabbed Marvie and embraced her. Marvie let out a strangled sob as she buried her face in Isla's shoulder and hugged her tightly in return. There was so much to say, but neither spoke, just held tight to one another like the world depended on it. An unspoken promise seemed to pass between the two of them, and something else too, an apology of sorts, an acknowledgement that life was strange, and people were stranger. But life had brought them back together and Marvie would be damned if she would let anything tear them apart.

She wasn't sure how long they stood there, holding each other. But when they pulled apart, eyes wet and smiles large, Marvie saw that they had finally cleared a large space away for dancing. Most of the crowd had joined, spinning around in a display of organized chaos. A few other people had joined the musician on stage, singing along with him, playing other instruments, contributing to the show.

Isla grabbed her hand and grinned through the tears. "Dance with me?"

The jealousy that had once been a living force in her shattered like glass and she left the pieces behind as Isla pulled her through the crowd towards where the masses of people were dancing. Isla in her purple dress, Marvie in her yellow one, both of their hair down and wild. There were smiles on their faces, large and vibrant, and Marvie realized that this was life. These moments, the one she was experiencing right now, last night on the roof, any moment she shared with Auden…these were the moments that made life worth living.

There was pain, yes, and there would always be pain. But Marvie could bear it if she collected these moments like coins.

Isla pulled her into the mass of dancers and there wasn't a hint of embarrassment within Marvie as they began, spinning around with one another, spinning around with strangers, dancing with the sunset behind them as the perfect backdrop. Marvie's cheeks were hurting, but she couldn't stop smiling as they kept going. Her heart was pounding and sweat covered her skin, but not because of the anxiety creeping through her. No, it was the happiness. It blossomed throughout her body, bringing relief to each of the hurts of the past and worries of the future. She didn't let go of Isla's hands the entire time.

She felt young. She felt free.

Marvie was happy.

It could've been hours, but it passed like mere seconds before they managed to break out of the crowd, laughing, the tears long gone. A lot of things had disappeared for Marvie, and she didn't want any of it back. The jealousy, the insecurity, the pain. It was gone.

And as she saw Auden standing there among the crowd, holding a glass of wine and smiling at her, Marvie tried to fill the empty spaces where those things had disappeared with what she felt in that very moment.

Isla let go of her hand and went towards where Lee was standing a short distance from Auden, but Marvie kept walking forward until she was right in front of him, wrapping both arms around his neck and pressing her lips to his.

Auden kissed her lightly before pulling away with a laugh. He wrapped one arm around her waist, holding out the glass of wine with the other. "For you," he said softly.

Marvie beamed at him as she accepted the glass, taking a long drink before looking over at Isla. Her friend also had a glass of wine in her hand and she raised it towards Marvie with a grin. Marvie raised hers in return before looking back at Auden.

He was looking at her thoughtfully. "How was it?" he asked, and she didn't need to ask what he was referring to.

Marvie shook her head. "I thought I was going to be mad at you for leaving me alone, but I'm glad you did. Everything's okay now, Auden. I wish I would've talked to her months ago."

Auden brushed a piece of loose hair out of her face and looked her up and down. "You must be okay. You and Isla looked like you were the center of attention out there," he laughed, nodding at where the dancing had continued.

Marvie shrugged. "It comes naturally, what can I tell you?" and he laughed harder at that as she took another drink of her wine, the happiness growing with every sip.

"Auden?"

"Yes?"

"I love you."

Auden wrapped his arm tighter around her and his smile was so large as he replied, "I love you too."

"Well, I love you more," Marvie said pointedly.

"Marvie…" he began to protest, but she put a hand over his mouth.

"Nope. I love you more. That's all there is to it." She finished the rest of the wine and set the glass on the ground before grabbing his hand and pulling him towards the dancing. "I love you more," she said again.

"Marvolene," Auden said, shaking his head. "What's going on with you?"

Marvie stopped right before they were about to be swept away with the dancers. She wrapped both hands around his neck and caught Isla's glance over his shoulder. Her friend smiled at her again and raised a glass for the second time. Marvie grinned at Isla and then at Auden and shrugged.

"You know, Auden? I think I'm just happy."

Chapter 12

He had to tell her.

Auden realized he had to tell her quite early into the evening but refused to actually consider the weight of the realization. If he were being honest with himself, he realized it sometime within the last few days, somewhere in between the perfect moments with Marvolene Pere. The awareness began to spread through him after their confessions on the roof. The voice was a quiet one, whispering to him *you have to tell her, you have to tell her.*

And then the voice grew louder after his own admission in Marvie's bedroom. He hadn't been planning on saying those words at all, but he couldn't help himself. Marvie was staring at him in that yellow dress, flushed and smiling, and an elation grew in his chest, a phenomenon he had never experienced before. He discovered that it was a familiar word but an altogether foreign sensation: happiness. He was happy. He had heard of happiness before, but they had never become acquainted with one another. Yet standing there in front of the woman he loved, he knew that dizzying feeling within him was happiness.

I think I'm just happy.

The voice spoke a little louder right then. *Auden, you have to tell her.*

Auden ignored the voice and together, he and Marvie had gone to see that musician, but he knew this night did not belong to him. No, this night was for Marvie and her friend, Isla, to figure out what was between them, whether there was something there worth salvaging. Auden was more than happy to step aside and allow them space to do just that. He and Isla's partner, Lee, had gone into the tavern for a long while.

When they finally reached the front of the line and returned outside with the drinks in their hands, Auden had stopped because time had stopped. He watched Marvie dance, her hands thrown in the air, a look of pure glee painted on her beautiful features, moving like the gods themselves were watching and Auden had to force himself to breathe. She danced and danced and he could've watched this girl and her joy for the rest of his life.

Some voice in the back of his head whispered to him, *You get to be with that girl for the rest of your life.*

And as that sacred reality set in, filling Auden with more happiness than he thought he was capable of feeling, the other voice screamed *YOU HAVE TO TELL HER.*

Auden couldn't ignore the voice anymore. Even after Marvie stopped dancing, finding him in the crowd and kissing him, pulling him into the dancing himself. Even after he had one of the greatest nights of his life with her, listening to the music and enjoying life for everything it was offering them. Even on the walk home, his hand woven through Marvie's, listening to her drunkenly sing Auntican songs and laughing with her. Even after he kissed her goodnight, leaving her at her aunt and uncle's apartment, walking back to his own, hands almost trembling with joy. Even after he locked the door behind him and splashed water in his face, tempted to pinch himself to wake him up from the dream that had become his life.

Even after all of that, the voice was relentless. *You have to tell her.*

The voice managed to speak through him the moment he stepped into his washroom. He looked at his reflection in the mirror and the voice took over. "Auden," his reflection said, "you have to tell her."

"No," Auden whispered in reply, grasping both sides of his basin and not meeting the reflection's eyes. "I can keep it a secret."

"No, you can't," the reflection argued. "She deserves to know the truth, the entire truth."

"NO!" Auden yelled back. "I CAN'T!"

"You see the way she looks at you, Auden. She loves you. She told you so herself. But would she love you if she knew all the terrible things you've done? Would she love you if she knew about that body in the alley? Would she love you if she knew how you lied and manipulated as soon as you were able? Would she love you if she knew about the people watching you, the people who might know exactly who you are? And ask yourself this, Auden, would she love you if she knew about the dark, evil power that you possess?"

Auden clamped his hands over his ears in an attempt to block out the inner voice, but he couldn't. He stumbled back, crashing into the door of his washroom before tripping over his feet to get away from the reflection. He managed to land in a heap on his bed, yanking the covers tight around him, pulling them over his eyes as if it would hide him from his conscience. It didn't work. The questions repeated themselves over and over again, the truth in them stinging like salt in a wound.

It was painful because it was true; Auden had to tell Marvie everything.

Marvie was content without knowing the details of his past. But he knew that eventually she would start asking more questions and when she did, how could he possibly answer them with the truth? The truth was an ugly nightmare that Auden couldn't escape from. What kind of person would he be to subject Marvolene to that truth? Expose her to the reality of who he was?

It was more proof he should leave Marvolene while he had the chance. But after that very night? After the previous night on the roof? It was too late for him; Marvie was his world now. Marvie was the air he breathed and the stars that lit his way. Leaving her would crush him and he wouldn't do it, no, he wouldn't do it.

Which left the only other option: telling her the truth.

Auden slowly let the covers fall onto his chest so he was staring up at the dark ceiling. He wished Marvie was lying there next to him, bringing the comfort that could only be found in her presence.

But because she wasn't, Auden spoke aloud.

"Marvolene…Marvie…there's something I need to tell you."

Knowing Marvie, her instantaneous reaction would be to panic. It was just like Marvie to assume the worst of everything and jump to the most extreme conclusion. Marvie would automatically believe that Auden was leaving her. In fact, she would probably believe he was leaving her to go pursue Isla or some ridiculous notion such as that. Yes, Marvie's friend was beautiful, but no one could compare to Marvie anymore. Auden could only see her at all times and everyone else's beauty became irrelevant.

Marvie would assume the worst, but then she would be surprised. Not in a good way. She would be surprised because Auden would tell her something much worse than she expected: that he possessed a dark power that had the capability to kill people and manipulate people's minds. He had discovered this power when he murdered a boy who had been at the same orphanage as him.

And speaking of an orphanage, Marvie, that's where he grew up. A children's home that really shouldn't have been called a home at all. It was a dangerous place full of people who were born with burdens they couldn't bear, cast away, robbed of any love or nurturing. It was a place where one was forced to

SUMMER SULLIVAN

grow up at such a tender age, exposed to just how cruel the world could be. It was that place, Marvie, where he was hardened to his breaking point, except his breaking point had been the death of someone else. His breaking point had awoken something in him that he couldn't control.

It had only been a week ago that he went to Southside and almost hurt an innocent bystander, just because his shadow was craving it. The same shadow, which had been silent for the last few days in lieu of Auden's newfound happiness, surged through him. Auden took a deep breath, trying to calm it, but it wouldn't be tamed. It was almost screaming as loud as the voice in his head was screaming.

TELL HER. TELL HER. TELL HER.

There were tears starting to form behind his eyes as he tried again. "Marvie, I have to tell you something. It might change the way you look at me, but I hope it doesn't change the way you feel about me." His voice cracked mid-sentence as he imagined the look on that beautiful girl's face once she found out his truth.

Auden remembered the way she began to cry at the harbor, right when he was about to walk away from her. Her lips started to tremble followed by her hands, and her eyes filled with tears that she rapidly tried to blink away. Auden would be lucky if his truth warranted that reaction. Marvie would probably scream in fear and then cast him away. No, she would probably run away before he could finish, run away while begging him to leave her alone. She would call him a monster, and he wouldn't be able to deny it. She would flinch at his gaze, wake up from the nightmares of his memory, once she realized what he was capable of.

"I'm not like you," he said, his voice raspy. "In many ways. You're...good, Marvolene, and I'm not. I don't know how you can't see it. I'm not good. I can't pretend to be good. I won't pretend to be good. Sometimes I think that might be the reason I can't stay away from you; I just have to be around a person who is pure goodness."

Auden rushed to correct himself, hearing the ghost of Marvie angered at the implication of his previous statement. "That's not the only reason, Marvolene, not even close. I love you because of who you are. But there is something in you that erases the darkness in me and I can't let that go. So please. Don't leave me."

She would curse him. She would spit in his face. She would run to her uncle and send the man to kill Auden. Auden might let him. A life without Marvolene was not a life worth living.

He rolled over in his bed, dragging the covers with him until he was lying on his stomach. He buried his head in his pillow, grabbing at his hair and tugging it to distract him from the pain within. When he spoke, his voice was muffled. "This changes nothing. I know I've lied to you about who I am and where I come from. Well, not lied, but I certainly haven't given you the truth. But everything I feel for you is real, Marvie. When I tell you I love you, it is the truest words I've ever spoken. At least understand that. Even if you walk away, just tell me you know how much I love you," and on the last word, Auden realized he was sobbing.

He didn't speak again, couldn't bring himself to keep talking. The longer he played into the illusion, the more real the vision of Marvolene became, casting him out of her life forever. He couldn't tell her; it was just that simple. They would go on the way they had gone on for the weeks, with Auden dodging her questions like he was dodging arrows from a bow.

Auden squeezed his eyes shut, begging his body to escape to slumber, save him from these paralyzing thoughts of the future, but the voice was speaking again. *There's no room in love for lies, Auden. You don't lie to someone you love.*

He exhaled slowly and nodded into his pillow. "Okay," he said out loud to the emptiness of his apartment. "Okay. I'll tell her. I'll tell her."

He didn't know if he meant it or not. He prayed he did, because that stupid voice in his head was right. If he professed his love to Marvie without the truth, was it really love? He wanted to spend the rest of his life with her. How could that happen if it were all based on a lie?

And if she left him after hearing it? Well, at that point, he would probably let the shadow consume him. With that comforting thought, Auden drifted into a deep sleep and dreamed of Marvolene.

When he awoke the next morning, he was firm in his decision. Auden stared at his reflection in the mirror and made a promise. "I'm going to tell her," he said, and his voice didn't even shake. His eyes weren't swollen with tears anymore, but the darkness was there, as apparent as it always was. Maybe the truth wouldn't come as a shock to Marvie; maybe she had been more observant than he thought. Maybe the revelation that Auden possessed a dark power would be more of a confirmation than anything else. Maybe he was panicking for no reason.

No, there was absolutely no way Marvie could've guessed he had the shadow. If she did, she would not be with him anymore. She would have run far away and Auden would've let her.

After the performance last night, they had made hasty plans to meet one another during Marvie's break at work. Today was one of the days where she worked longer hours but received one hour of free time at midday in return. He was planning on stopping by and walking with her to the creek where they had their first kiss. It seemed like a good idea while he was making the plans, but now he dreaded returning to that place with her. The place had become sacred for him, and now, he risked desecrating it by delivering the truth to Marvie there.

He peeked out the window and saw it was just before noon. Auden quickly changed into fresh clothes and splashed water from the basin onto his face. He made a valiant attempt to smooth out his curls, but it was for nothing. They stuck out in all directions, having a mind of their own like they always did. He shook his head at his reflection in the mirror, the same reflection forcing him to do this dreaded task to begin with.

As the urge to talk himself out of it grew even more, Auden thought of what Lee had asked him the previous night as they waited in the tavern for drinks.

"Marvolene seems to really like you," he yelled over the roar of the crowd.

Auden gave him a warm smile. "I should hope so," he said in reply. "And it appears Isla likes you."

Lee grinned as he shrugged. "I should hope so," he snickered, repeating Auden's words.

Auden thought that was the end of the conversation, but Lee suddenly asked, "Are you two planning to get married?"

The question was so frank that it took Auden a moment to fully register what had been said. He managed to sputter, "M…married?"

Lee gave him a strange look. "Yes, married. You know, when two people take vows and have their companionship recognized by Orinthian officials. Marriage?"

"I know what marriage is," Auden chuckled nervously as he wrung his hands together.

"Weren't your parents married?" Lee asked.

After all this time, one would think questions like that wouldn't warrant a reaction from Auden, but still. The thought of his parents was a punch in the gut, a swift strike to his throat. He avoided images of his father and the ghost of a mother he would never know as he asked his own question of Lee. "Are you going to marry Isla?"

Lee beamed, the former inquiry immediately forgotten. "Oh yes. I'm actually planning to ask her…"

Lee kept talking, but Auden had lost focus as he thought about the concept in the middle of that crowded tavern. Marriage. His mind reeled with a thousand questions. The most prominent was an echo of Lee's query. Had his parents been married? In the few times he met his father, the man had never spoken of the woman who had given birth to Auden. If his mother and father had been married, then maybe Auden didn't want it at all. It must not have meant that much if his parents were gone and Auden was abandoned.

Auden tried to let those thoughts dissipate as he considered the idea of marrying Marvie. A part of him rejected the concept. First of all, weren't they too young? Marvolene was only seventeen, Auden a year her senior. And secondly, why did they have to have what was between them validated by Orinthian officials? Wasn't it clear enough to the both of them that they were in love? Why did they need it confirmed by another person when it was so powerful, so real?

Yet the seed was already planted in his head. Standing with Marvie in a temple, proclaiming in front of people and below the gods themselves, that he would be with her forever. It was just right.

The conversation with Lee, the aftermath of his thoughts of marriage, all of it replayed in his mind because Auden knew if there was any chance of marrying Marvolene, she would most definitely have to know the truth about him. The truth he planned to deliver today. Auden took a deep breath, drained the basin, grabbed his small sack of coins, and left his apartment, bound for what might be the most painful goodbye of his life.

As he walked towards Olga's, not even the familiar sights of Tenir could bring him comfort. Instead, his senses were overloaded, mind not equipped to handle the assault of sounds and sensations. The light of the sun was too bright, shining on the brick city, the colors too vivid. The shouts of shopkeepers, the knock of horse's hooves on the cobblestones, the constant lull of people talking; it was shrieking in his ears and Auden wanted to scream at it to stop. Everyone needed to quiet down, stop looking so damn happy. Didn't they know this was the day Marvolene Pere was going to walk away from him? Didn't they know this was the day the darkness would return?

Apparently, they did not. Because as he grew closer and closer to Olga's, the deafening chaos didn't stop. It only grew, seemingly proportional to Auden's shadow. The noise was loud; his shadow was loud. It was enacting revenge on him for the neglect of the past few weeks and he gasped for breath trying to calm it. The attempt was null. The people, the sounds, the sights, all of it were food for his dark power.

Auden stopped at the corner, one street away from Olga's, and inhaled slowly through his lungs, closing his eyes and blocking it all out. The shadow numbed, if only slightly, but enough that he didn't fear it exploding against his will. He took a few more breaths before turning onto the street that Olga's was on.

This street was as crowded as the rest of them, as it contained mostly shops, taverns, and inns: a hub of activity. There were hundreds of people cramped onto the stretch, but Auden could only focus on one person.

She was already standing outside the bakery, leaning against one of the streetlamps, blonde hair appearing to glow in the beams of the sun. Marvie was glancing around, picking through the faces of the crowd with her eyes narrowed. Auden was only a short distance from her, but a wave of people separated them, and he found both of his feet were planted into the ground. He didn't want to move closer to her, begin the conversation that would inevitably end him. He just wanted to watch her, memorize the details like he always did. The way her skin shone in the light. The way the crowds didn't bother her like they bothered Auden. The way Marvie just belonged. With her face in the sun, its beams dancing around her, Marvolene was born to exist in the light.

Auden dug his nails into his skin and resisted the impulse to turn around and run. Run back to his apartment, run back to his bed. Become that little boy who hid under the covers when the older boys in the orphanage were looking for him. Only this time, he would be hiding from the truth, the reality he could never stand in the light like Marvolene did, completely free from darkness. If he hid long enough, maybe the truth would pass him by just like the boys used to. Maybe reality would spare him out of laziness and uninterest. Auden would make up some sort of excuse tomorrow of why he didn't see her; he would tell her Kalen came to him and asked him to work. He would lie to her, because he simply could not see her today in the state he was in.

And then, Marvie turned her head and locked eyes with him, through the entire mass of people on the street. Her gaze flashed with recognition and one brow shot up with what must have been curiosity, probably as to why Auden was frozen on the street looking terrified.

She smiled at him.

The people streamed around her and streamed around him, but they didn't exist. It was just Auden standing there, Marvie standing across from him with a smile on her face.

Auden could not breathe.

The shadow melted away and for an intoxicating second, he was free of it as he stared at her smiling.

He had thought that their moment on the roof was the most powerful thing he had ever experienced. There was no way, in his mind, he would ever feel more love for her after that. Immediately he had been disproven. Standing there watching her dance the night before; that had been the most significant time of his life, watching the girl he loved dance with her head thrown back laughing, the picture of carefree bliss. That memory would stay with him to his grave, he was sure of it. Nothing would come close.

Auden had been wrong again, so incredibly wrong.

Because Marvie standing there in the street smiling at him was more momentous than any of it. The rest of his life had been one, meaningless joke in comparison to her smiling in the sun, the shadow a distant memory, a power he no longer possessed.

And he saw it. He saw their future. He saw him and Marvie together, traveling to distant lands with each other just for fun. He saw them in a stupid temple getting some stupid Orinthian official to confirm what they already knew, that they loved one another and wanted to be with each other for the rest of time. He saw a house that became a home, a baby that became a child, a love that became something greater than two teenagers could comprehend. He saw everything he could have if the shadow wasn't his, everything that seemed just out of reach.

Auden snapped back into real life and the people returned and Marvie's smile had turned into a quizzical gaze, her head cocked as she started towards him. What was she seeing right now? She smiled at him and Auden just cracked. Maybe he didn't have to tell her; maybe his impending breakdown was enough to send her away.

Then, Marvie was right in front of him. "Auden?" she asked, grabbing one of his shaking hands. "Auden, what's wrong?"

Auden blinked twice, looking down at her. Marvie was glancing up at him, concern painted over each of her beautiful features. The noise of the city had resumed, people brushing past them to get where they were going, the chaos continuing.

"Auden?" Marvie repeated.

I'm a monster. You're of the light, but I'm of the darkness. I killed someone, left him in an alley when I was fourteen years old. I can barely control my power, this darkness that runs through my veins, gives me the capability to do terrible, terrible things. But you're of the light and I love you. You make me light. This changes nothing for me, Marvolene.

This changes nothing.

"Hello," he whispered, squeezing her hand that was grasping his.

"Are you okay?" Marvie asked, brushing a stray curl out of his face.

Auden smiled at her. "I'm wonderful, Marvolene. How are you?"

She didn't answer the question. "Auden, you look like you've seen a ghost. You're pale and shaking."

This...changes...nothing.

Auden shook his head. "I just grew dizzy for a moment in the sun, Marvie. I promise." He forced himself to smile at her, to make the lie seem a little more convincing.

"Are you sure?" she demanded as she wove her arm through his. Together, they started moving with the crowd. He was glad Marvie was holding onto him because he was still right on the brink of collapsing. Her skin was touching his and underneath it, the shadow was reeling. Not even Marvie's presence calmed the power; on the contrary, the lies he kept from her seemed to strengthen it.

"I'm sure, Marvie," he answered, his voice trembling.

You have to tell her.

"Good, because you have *got* to hear what happened at the bakery today," and Marvie launched into some story that Auden wished he could concentrate on. He loved hearing her talk, he loved watching her tell stories, and he loved her, but he couldn't hear a thing. He could barely see the street in front of him.

This changes nothing.

Marvie continued talking and Auden constructed phrases in his head on how exactly he should go about telling her. Well, he couldn't while they were walking. The crowd was too loud and they were moving too fast. He would wait until they were sitting on the bench by the creek. Well, no, he really didn't want to spoil the memories the bench held for them. Maybe on the walk back to the bakery. He couldn't; Marvie would leave him in the middle of a crowded street, with so many witnesses. In front of the bakery? No, he wouldn't ruin the rest of Marvie's workday.

Besides, how could he break the news to her after she stared at him across the crowded street and smiled at him? That vision was enough to last him a lifetime and he refused to spoil it with the truth.

You have to tell her.

NO, I DON'T. He finally snapped and screamed back at the voice in his head. He took a deep breath through his nose, grinning at Marvie as she got to a certain part in her story, but in his mind, he made a promise.

I'll tell her tomorrow. I'll take her to a quiet spot, sit her down, and tell her everything. I promise I will but not today. Not after the smile. Not today.

They rounded the corner to where the bench by the creek was and Marvie's voice finally cut through his inner turmoil.

"Auden?"

Auden helped her sit down and sat next to her, wrapping his arm around her, clenching his fist to stop it from shaking. She leaned against him and he clenched it even harder to prevent the rest of his body from trembling too.

"Yes?"

Marvie's gaze flickered to her toes and then back at him, a shy smile creeping onto her face. "Can I tell you something?"

"Of course you can, Marvie," he replied, and a part of him wanted her to tell him goodbye. Cast him away for some trivial reason before she knew the dark truth. Let her memories of him be perfectly preserved. He was just some Orinthian boy she met, nothing atypical about him. Remember him as someone capable of living in the light.

"I just wanted to say thank you for last night. It was really wonderful and I'm very happy about the way things played out. If it wasn't for you…I don't think I would've tried to make up with Isla at all. And now that we have, I wish we would've done it months ago. Still, it's because of you so I wanted to say thank you." She spoke quickly, rushing to get the words out.

Auden couldn't help but wrap his arm around her tighter. "You don't have to thank me, Marvie. I didn't do anything; it was you." She should be doing the opposite of thanking him; she should be cursing him for coming into her perfect life to begin with.

Marvie waved him off. "I don't think you understand but just know I appreciate you…"

You have to tell her.

"…and I'm really really glad that I met you…"

She needs to know the truth.

"…and I can't imagine my life anymore without you in it…"

This changes nothing.

"…I sort of wish I would've met you a long time ago…"

I'll tell her.

"…and I guess what I'm trying to say is that I love you," she finished with a small smile.

Auden leaned over and kissed her lightly on the lips before pulling back and speaking softly. "I love you too. More than you know."

She shook her head. "I love you more."

"Marvie…" he laughed, but inside he was breaking. *It's because I love you that I need to tell you that…*

"No, I do," she said with a grin. "I love you more."

"Alright, Marvolene," he conceded, kissing her again before saying, "alright."

I'll tell her but not today.

Marvie cheered in victory before launching into another story about the bakery, which Auden tried desperately to focus on instead of the shadow creeping through his body. He stopped planning the phrases in his head and let it fade away until there was only Marvolene Pere staring back at him, the sun creating a crown around her head, her smile giving off its own warmth.

Not today.

Chapter 13

Auden didn't tell her the next day either.

It wasn't his fault, or at least that was what he told himself. He had planned it all out. After he dropped her back off at the bakery, Auden made a plan. He offered to take Marvolene on a walk by the harbor that very night. It was the slowest night of the week, so therefore the taverns would be less busy and the harbor district less crowded. The sun would be going down and there would be quiet; in other words, the perfectly imperfect backdrop for him to deliver the news to Marvolene. He would break her heart and his own, but at least the city around them would be beautiful.

Everything proceeded accordingly. Auden waited outside the bakery until she came out, covered in flour but looking lovely nonetheless. It broke his heart just a little more as she took his arm excitedly, already telling him all about her day, completely unaware of what was going to happen.

They made it to the harbor district and, just as he had expected, few people were walking along the dock. It was almost disappointing. If the walkway would've been flooded with people, it would've been an excuse to put off telling Marvie about the shadow just a day longer. But no, it was as if the gods were pushing him to tell her the truth by providing the perfect place to do so.

And as they stepped onto that same walkway, arm in arm, Auden took a breath to begin.

Marvie beat him to it. "Have you ever thought about getting married?"

Auden's mouth stayed open as he looked over at Marvolene, who was watching him with wide eyes. She clapped a hand over her mouth and blushed furiously. "Oh my gods. I didn't mean to say that out loud!"

Auden couldn't help himself; he started to laugh. Marvie moved her hand so it was covering her face and shook her head. "Forget I said anything," she mumbled, refusing to meet his eyes.

His mission to tell the truth disappeared as happiness bubbled up within him like a spring. Marvolene had just asked him about marriage. And there was only one reason she would ask him about such a thing.

"First of all, Marvie, I don't know how many times I have to tell you, you never need to be embarrassed of anything you say to me," he said, still chuckling as he wove his fingers through hers. "And secondly, yes, I have thought about marriage. I never have before, and then I met this girl. And, well..." he trailed off.

Marvie was still blushing, but she grinned at him through the cracks of her fingers. "Oh? Is she nice?"

"As nice as they come," he confirmed, squeezing her hand tightly.

Marvie dropped the hand from her face and raised an eyebrow. "This girl must be sort of charming, if she's got someone like you thinking about commitment."

Auden nodded seriously. "She is *very* charming," he agreed. "Extremely beautiful as well. And get this, she bakes! The best cherry tarts I have ever had in my entire life."

Marvie's smile faded and she furrowed her brow. "Auden, I don't actually make the cherry tarts; I just sell the baked goods."

Auden pretended to look confused. "I wasn't talking about you, Marvolene. I was talking about the love of my life, my very purpose for existing. You might know her, her name is Olga. She owns a bakery and I swear to the gods I'm going to marry that woman."

Marvie started to glare at him, but it was too late as she threw her head back and laughed. She smacked him hard in the arm. "You had me going there for a minute," she told him, rolling her eyes, but the laughter didn't cease.

Auden couldn't breathe through his own laughter as he turned to her, stopping them in the middle of the walkway, and pressed his lips against hers. She was still giggling even as they kissed. When they pulled apart, Marvie rolled her eyes at him. "I hope I'm invited to the wedding, at least. Seeing as I'm the one who introduced you and Olga."

Auden nodded thoughtfully. "Oh yes. I imagine you might even be the guest of honor."

Marvie snorted. "I might have to kill Olga now."

Auden gasped. "Before the best day of her life, her wedding day? I'm ashamed of you, Marvolene!" And Marvie laughed again, resting her head against his chest. He leaned down until his lips were on the top of her head.

"You already know we're going to be together for a long time, right?" he murmured.

Marvie shrugged. "If I can get Olga out of the way, then I suppose so."

Auden flicked her ear and she giggled, pulling back and kissing his cheek. "Of course, I know we're going to be together for a long time."

"Somewhere in between now and the rest of our lives, Marvie, we'll get married. How does that sound?"

Marvie pretended to ponder it as they began to walk again, Marvie tucked into his side, his arm draped around her shoulders. "I don't know if I like the sound of Marvolene Frae."

"How about Auden Pere?"

"We could combine them. Marvolene FraePere?"

"Or Auden PereFrae."

"We'll combine our first names. Marvoauden?"

"Or Audolene."

And then they were laughing again, the sound cutting through the silence of the harbor, spare only the waves in the distance. The sunset was perfect, as always. Somewhere down the street, music could be heard, and it all seemed to compliment the sound of their laughter intertwining. None of the sights or sounds compared to what he felt inside, the pure elation of being around Marvie.

When she had finally gotten ahold of herself, Marvie managed to choke out, "Let's combine the two of them. Audolene FraePere."

"It's a deal," Auden wheezed. "I now pronounce you Audolene FraePere," and they couldn't stop laughing once more.

It took another two minutes before they were capable of speech. Marvie said to him, seriously, "I think I want to move back to Auntica at some point. Are you okay with that?"

Oh Marvie, you have no idea just how *okay* with that he would be. The idea of leaving Tenir, leaving all of this behind him…what a wondrous possibility. Of course Auden knew he could've left a long time ago, but something had always kept him here, prevented him from leaving the place that had been home. He now knew that Marvolene was that something.

Auden picked up her hand again and swung it back and forth. "You could tell me you wanted to move to the other side of The Shadow Wall and I would go with you, Marvie."

Marvie beamed at him. "You don't have to worry about that."

"I'm glad," Auden chuckled and they continued to walk for the next few minutes in silence. It was a beautiful silence, a silence where they enjoyed the simplicity of just being in one another's presence, words or no words.

"For the record," Auden said as they turned around and started back the way they had came, "I really like the sound of Marvolene Frae."

"For the record," Marvie smiled, "So do I."

The rest of the night was quite simply one of the best nights he had ever had in his entire life.

It was only when he had left Marvie at her apartment, made his way back home, cleaned up, and tucked himself into bed, did he realize he hadn't told her the truth. The elation of seeing Marvie and the lightness in his heart completely disappeared and a bitter despair crashed over him. Auden had a *plan*. He had taken her to the harbor for silence and seclusion, the perfect place to confess. Instead, they had laughed so hard that tears streamed down their faces.

He supposed it was a symbol of what Marvolene did to him. He had brought his darkness and she turned it into light.

Auden attempted to formulate another plan to tell her, but the peace she brought him allowed him to sleep easy. He dreamed of Lola.

"I marked the page where we left off, Lola," Auden told her as he settled into her couch, his head back, munching on a biscuit.

Lola sighed, setting her quill down and picking up the book from its spot on her desk. The covers had begun to wear from the number of times she had read the book to him, but Auden also suspected that Lola read it by herself sometimes. There was something so addicting about the story of Rider Grey.

Maybe his story was so heartbreaking, it made what they were going through pale in comparison.

"I don't like the parts we're getting to, Auden," Lola groaned as she opened the book. "Can't we go back to the beginning? When Rider Grey meets the first love of his life?"

Auden shook his head. "We have to finish the story, Lola. Let's keep going."

She sighed again but opened her mouth and continued.

*"Rider was determined that this time would be different. He had fallen in love again; it was a reality he had to accept. But the situation hadn't changed. The woman he loved would grow old and he would stay young. There had to be something he could do to prevent the same heartbreak he had experienced centuries earlier. First, he wouldn't have children with his new love. Watching his first wife die had been painful; watching their children die had been excruciating. And second, he had to tell his new love his cursed predicament, that he was trapped in the body of an eighteen-year-old boy. He had to be completely honest with her, try to explain that, if they were going to be together, they would be together for the rest of **her** life."*

"He would live on, even after she died."

"It would break her heart, he knew, because it broke his heart. Part of Rider wanted to leave her now, spare both his love and himself the pain of loss. But it was much too late for him; walking away wasn't possible. Which left him only one option and that was to tell her the truth. If he didn't tell her, she would eventually find out on her own, when she realized the love of her life hadn't changed in decades."

Auden interrupted her at this point. "What would you do, Lola, if you were Rider Grey?"

Lola looked over at him, and her eyes were glazed over the way they often were when she was deep in thought. "If I were Rider Grey?"

He nodded. "Would you tell your new love about your curse, or let her find out on her own?"

Lola took a breath as she drummed her fingers against the surface of her desk. By the time she answered, Auden had finished his biscuit. "Honesty is the foundation of any relationship, Auden. Whether that be lovers or friends or family members. A relationship without honesty will eventually crumble. So I suppose if I were Rider Grey, I would tell her the truth from the beginning. And if she stayed, I would know our relationship was built on honesty. And if she left…well, I guess Rider Grey wouldn't have to worry about losing her anymore, would he?"

Auden forced himself to wake, pulling himself out of the dream that was getting close to a nightmare. Sweat coated every inch of him and he was gasping for breath as he sat up, Lola's voice echoing in his head. *Honesty is the foundation of any relationship, Auden.*

The inner voice of his mind decided to join in with her. *Why haven't you told Marvie yet?*

Auden wanted to scream, but instead, he stumbled to his basin and splashed water in his face. Then, he started planning another occasion to tell Marvolene.

He planned to tell her a few weeks after his first attempt. They had seen each other every day, but the occasion was never right. The city was always so damn busy. A few times, Isla and Lee had been with them and Auden couldn't very well confess his darkness to the three of them. He had a perfect plan to tell her over drinks at a quiet inn on the outskirts of town, but then Marvie had invited him to dinner with her aunt and uncle. What was he going to do, say no? He had swallowed back the truth and put on his best face for Sienna and Hewes. By the way the dinner proceeded, Auden suspected they were starting to like him.

It should've made him happy, after the disaster that had almost occurred during their walk at the harbor. He should've rejoiced that the two people who had raised Marvie were beginning to approve of him. But the longer he stayed at their apartment, laughing and talking around the table, feeling like a family, the more his anxiety grew. He was becoming a part of something bigger than just him and Marvie. He was being embraced into her life by all those in it. Sienna. Hewes. Isla. Lee.

He. Had. To. Tell. Her.

Finally, exactly three weeks after he had attempted to tell her the truth at the harbor, Auden took her to a garden in the tourist district of Tenir. The garden was highly manicured with stone trails that wove throughout the trees and flowers that had been planted in the middle of their city. He had come here by himself a few times throughout his life, and its serenity made it the perfect place to tell Marvie about his shadow. A place of beauty to reveal an ugly truth.

Marvie didn't work that day, so she had worn a white dress with blue flowers on it, her blonde hair piled on top of her head. Auden hid a long sigh when he saw her for the first time. Of course she had to choose that day to dress like a princess. With the sun shining on her skin and hair, creating a ring of light around her, he could've stared at her forever. And there was the smile that never seemed to leave her face; Auden was a finished man.

His mood was a sour one, but apparently Marvie didn't pick up on it. She whistled as they wove throughout the garden, swinging their clasped hands back and forth. Occasionally, when she thought Auden wasn't looking, she would glance over at him and her smile would grow even wider. Auden cursed himself as he continued pushing back his confession. Why couldn't he have chosen a dark, dismal alley on a cloudy, rainy day to tell her the truth? Now she would always attach this garden to the memory of finding out the boy she thought she loved was capable of evil things.

The voice in his head roared louder and Auden clenched the hand that wasn't holding Marvie's. He flexed it and looked over at Marvie. And once again, she spoke first. "Do you ever want to have children of your own, Auden?"

Auden blinked twice, stunned for a paralyzing moment at the question. He waited for Marvie to start blushing or try to take back the question, but she stared at him, awaiting an answer with wide eyes.

Instead of scrambling to find one, his mind drifted away.

Rider Grey took his second love to a village a few miles from where they lived; it was quiet and there was no risk of seeing a familiar face. She had brought a blanket with them and laid it on a grassy field, the sun sparkling down upon them. Together, they laid on their backs, side by side, hands intertwined, listening to the wind's music.

"I have something to tell you, my love," Rider whispered to her.

"I have something I must tell you, Rider," she replied softly, leaning over and resting her head on his chest.

Rider grew nervous. "What is it?" he asked her.

"You tell me first," she responded and Rider shook his head.

"No, my love. You tell me." He would put off telling her the fate of their love as long as he possibly could. He avoided the images of his first wife, the ghost of his former lover suddenly haunting the air around them. The memory of the pain, in that moment, was as fresh as the day he had lost her.

"I was going to wait to tell you for a while. But then you took us out here to this beautiful place and the sun is shining and I can't keep it to myself anymore…"

Rider's heart was falling, the pieces of it raining down around them in that field, because he already knew what was coming.

"I am…we are…going to have a baby."

Lola stopped reading and pressed the book against her chest, exhaling slowly. Auden looked over at her and realized a single tear had fallen onto her cheek. He didn't say anything, just watched its path down her face, moving along the edge of her jaw before falling off her chin and onto the very page that was opened. Auden opened his mouth to say something comforting, but no sound came out. He just watched the woman who raised him, wishing he knew what was going on inside of her head.

"Auden?"

Marvie's voice snapped him out of his trance. He was still staring at her and they had stopped walking in the middle of the garden, on the stone path. There were no people close to them, but a thicket of bushes on either side, flowers blooming from the ends, exuding a heavenly scent. In the distance, Auden could see the brick buildings of their city. His mind had drifted so far from the present; it was somewhere in the Southside, in the rubble of an orphanage.

"Auden," Marvie repeated, and she had let go of his hand.

Auden tried to snap out of it. "I'm sorry…what did you say?" he said breathlessly.

Marvie shook her head. "Nothing. Nothing. Let's keep going." She took a few steps forward, but Auden didn't move, his feet glued to the stones. His hand subconsciously reached out to brush one of the flowers as he stared after Marvie. She looked over her shoulder and asked, "Are you coming?"

"I guess I've never thought about it, Marvolene," he said softly, answering her first question about children, while fading back to the past.

The months flew by. His lover's stomach grew and his love for her grew and the burden grew. Everything continued to grow but himself. Rider was being haunted, now, by more than his deceased first wife. Their children she had borne followed him around as well. He saw their faces in the city streets, among the crowds. He caught flashes of their hair and found himself running after them. Once or twice, he had grabbed their shoulders, crying out their names only to come face to face with a confused stranger. Rider would mumble an apology and then break a little more as he realized, once again, that his wife and children were dead. They had been dead for centuries; they weren't coming back.

Rider wanted to run away. A few times, he packed a bag and stared out the window at the world that beckoned him. He heard something deep within his heart, begging him to spare himself from the pain that this entire ordeal would bestow. But every night, he came back to her, his love who made the pain worth it.

The pain was just a phase. After a few weeks, it, along with the ghosts and memories, disappeared. Weeks later, as Rider held his newborn daughter in his arms for the very first time, the pain was expelled completely, replaced by the same love and devotion he had felt centuries ago. Only this time, it was for his second wife and the daughter they had created from their love.

"I shouldn't have asked," Marvie mumbled, kicking one of the stones off the path and Auden quickly closed the distance between them, picking up her hands.

"Remember a few weeks ago when we agreed we were going to be in each other's lives for a long time?" Auden asked her.

Marvie bit her lip and nodded, refusing to look at him.

Gently, Auden grabbed her chin and brought her gaze up to meet his. "I was being serious about it. Were you?"

Marvie gave him a look. "What do you think?"

"Well eventually it's something we have to talk about. Children, I mean. I haven't thought about it because I've never met someone I would want to start a family with."

Marvie raised an eyebrow. "Olga?"

Auden pretended to ponder it as they began walking again. "While I'm sure children with the combination of our features would be stunning, I wasn't thinking of Olga."

The corner of Marvie's mouth twitched. "I don't know. Olga's gray hair, your green eyes? They would certainly be beautiful sons and daughters."

Auden laughed fully this time as they made their way through a patch of blue flowers that vividly brought out Marvie's eyes. Auden stopped them just so he could look a little longer. He set his hands on her shoulders. "I want to be with you forever, whether there are children or not. You're always going to be the person I love most in the world. Do you understand?"

Marvie titled her head slightly. "Are you sure I'm not second after Olga?" she asked, laughter in her tone.

Auden rolled his eyes and pressed a kiss to her forehead. Her skin was warm, having soaked up the rays of the sun, and he once again thought of her as a manifestation of light rather than a regular person. When he pulled back, she was smiling up at him.

"I'm glad I met you, Auden Frae," she whispered.

"You have no idea, Marvolene, just how glad I am that we met."

With that, they finished walking the length of the garden and made their way back into Tenir to eat dinner.

He had spent the entirety of the day with her before going back to his apartment. This time, he was already in bed and on the brink of sleep when he realized the opportunity to tell her the truth had passed him by. But dreams had claimed him before the guilt of his inaction could.

Rider Grey watched his daughter grow into a young girl. He watched his wife grow into an older woman. Rider looked in the mirror every morning, praying to the gods that he would see a single wrinkle, a strand of gray hair, some indication that he was aging. He prayed that his bones would crack when he stood, that his hands would begin to shake, that his vision might begin to fail him. But he was as spry as the day he turned eighteen.

When his daughter turned ten years old, Rider took a trip to a large city. He told his wife it was for business, but he found the keeper of scrolls deep within the heart of the city. The keeper was an old man and the moment Rider met him, he was filled with a deep jealousy of his age. Rider wished he could wrap his youth up like a present, put it in a box with a ribbon on top, and give it to this wrinkled, white-haired man.

The keeper asked him what he wanted and Rider answered before he thought about the implications of his words.

"I want death," Rider whispered, and the keeper looked frightened. Rider couldn't help but repeat himself. "I want death."

The moment his eyes opened, he went to the bakery. Marvolene was there, but Auden couldn't take joy in her presence. He forced a smile on his face as to not worry her and asked if she would meet him at the roof with the bench on it, where they had first confessed their love. Marvie agreed and they set a time. Auden left before he changed his mind and bailed on the plan.

He didn't want to go back to his apartment. It was too cramped for his current state of mind and the reflection in the mirror would chastise him for having waited so long to tell Marvolene. But after he left the bakery, his shadow crept up on him and being around people was too difficult. Auden settled on walking into a mostly empty tavern. He barely observed the place, just went directly to the bar and ordered an ale. Auden rarely drank, as possessing the shadow required him to be in complete control at all times, but the ale calmed his nerves. It soothed all the possibilities that ran through his head of how Marvie would leave him. He drank three of them before stumbling out of the tavern.

Auden didn't remember much of the trip to the roof. He simply found himself sitting on the bench, watching the sunset and feeling nothing inside. There was a ghost in the corner of that roof where a thirteen-year-old Auden huddled, using an old burlap sack as a blanket, desperately trying to sleep. He was cold and miserable, but at least he wasn't in the orphanage, right? The ghost was shaking so badly that Auden had to tear his gaze away from him, praying the ghost would fade away.

"Marvie," he whispered to himself, "I'm still the same person you met those months ago."

He thought of the harbor and how he had failed and the garden and how he had failed and every other time had failed. He had lost count of the times he had attempted to tell Marvie about the shadow. He would not allow himself to fail tonight.

"I love you and I care about you and I want to spend the rest of my life with you. None of that has changed," he whispered to the air.

This changes nothing.

Please don't leave me, he begged her in his mind. *Please don't go.*

"Auden?"

She had already arrived. Auden assumed she worked until sundown. He stood up and turned around to face her. Marvie was still in her clothes from the bakery, her hair messy, her face coated with flour. But with the sunset behind her, she might've been the most beautiful person in the world. Not even the darkness taking root in his heart stopped him from smiling at her. "Marvie," he said softly.

She smiled at him as she crossed the roof and wrapped her arms around him with a soft sigh. He hugged her back, wondering if this was the last time they would embrace, the last time she would feel safe in his arms. Together, they sat down on the bench, Auden keeping one arm wrapped around her.

He cleared his throat. *I have to tell you something.* "How was work today?"

Marvie shrugged. "Oh the same as always. How was your day?"

I wouldn't tell you this if I didn't love you. Lola once told me the foundation of every relationship is honesty. I want to spend the rest of my life with you, so I guess I have to be honest. "It was alright," Auden replied quietly, keeping out the fact he had spent most of it in a tavern.

"I was thinking about something today," Marvie told him.

I have a dark power. I call it the shadow because it's a shadow of darkness. I can kill people with it, Marvie, and I have before. It was in self-defense, but still...I killed someone. "What were you thinking about, Marvolene?" Auden asked her, and he wondered if she could hear the tremor in his voice.

She hesitated. "Well, it was sort of slow today at Olga's, so I had a lot of time to think about random things, you know?"

I can manipulate with it too. In fact, before I met you, it's all I did. I manipulated people to get the apartment I live in. All the food I ate, the clothes off my back, each and every one of my possessions. I only got my job to keep me somewhat entertained. Using the shadow to control people was just too easy and too tempting. "That happens to me sometimes at The Wooden Barrel," Auden replied, and he was almost breathless.

Marvie still didn't notice. "I just started thinking about the first time we met."

I don't know how I got the power, Marvolene. I don't even know my own mother. My childhood was one dark fog of misery and to be honest, I think it's affected me in ways I will never be able to understand. You grew up with love and sometimes I envy you for it. I grew up with pain. That's got to leave some sort of mark, doesn't it? "Did you now?" he asked with a shaky laugh.

"There's something I want to know about that day."

Maybe I was born with the darkness or maybe it grew in me like a disease because of that place. But it's disappeared in me...well, most days it has. There's a lightness in me now and it's because of you. If you can come to accept who I am and who I've been, I'll never leave your side. We'll be with each other forever, Marvie. I love you and this changes nothing.

"What do you want to know?"

This changes nothing.

"What did you think the first time you saw me?" Marvie asked and her voice was both nervous and excited. After asking the question, she tucked her head tighter into the space between his chest and shoulder.

Auden closed his eyes. *Tell her.*

He looked down at her and smiled. "Why do you want to know?"

Marvie shrugged as a slight pink flushed her cheeks. "I don't really know. Well...I guess my thoughts were so crystal clear the first time I met you to the point I can almost recall them now. I wanted to know if you thought the same things I did or if you're just with me to get closer to Olga."

Auden laughed and for the first time all day, he felt a semblance of happiness within him. He kissed the top of her head. "I can tell you, absolutely and most definitely, that I am not with you to get closer to Olga."

"I'm still not convinced," Marvie snorted, placing her hand on his knee.

"Let me think about it for a moment," Auden said softly and he closed his eyes, thinking back to that day where a beautiful girl with blonde hair stumbled into The Wooden Barrel after a man spilled water all over her.

"At first, I was surprised at how rude that man was," Auden told her. "Spilling his water on you like that without an apology." He left out the fact he almost used the shadow on the man to demand one. "I watched after him and then I looked at you. I really looked at you."

"And?" Marvie whispered, leaning in closer.

"I thought, well, maybe today isn't so bad. There's a beautiful girl in the store," he said, and Marvie began to laugh even though it was the biggest lie he had ever told her.

He couldn't tell her what he really thought, though the words flew through his mind and heart and soul, desperately trying to escape so maybe this girl would have some idea of how much she meant to him.

I didn't know why I existed. I didn't know why I kept trying. Why I kept waking up in the morning and living every single day. I told myself to survive, and I did, but I never asked myself why. What was the point of this survival business? What exactly was I waiting for? My life was not supposed to change, not supposed to get any better. I was teetering on the edge of falling to darkness. I guess it was a waiting game of when it would eventually happen, when I would snap and hurt someone once more. Maybe surviving was a way of testing myself, seeing how long I could go without being a monster. But there was no reason to play this game of survival.

And then you walked in the door of the shop.

All at once I realized there was a point to the surviving. Every day I wanted to throw it away, every time I forced myself to keep breathing and to keep living, every time I asked myself why. I thought I was surviving, but it was never surviving, Marvolene. It was waiting. I was waiting for you. I didn't know it, but someone did, and that's the reason I could never throw my life away. Somewhere, deep inside me, I knew you. The moment I saw your face, the lifetime of survival all pointed towards one person: you.

I've been waiting for you my entire life, Marvolene. You'll never be able to understand how much I love you. You might say you love me more, but my darling, you can't possibly love me more than I love you.

"What about you?" he asked her hoarsely.

She was expecting the question because she answered right away. "I saw you and I thought I'm going to be in this boy's life whether he likes it or not." And then, they were laughing again.

TELL. HER.

The voice was a shriek in his brain and it took everything within him not to clap his hands over his ears because of it. He took a shuddering breath.

"Auden, I told my aunt and uncle I was staying at Isla's tonight," Marvie suddenly blurted out.

"Why?" he whispered, the truth on the tip of his tongue.

Marvie wrapped her arms around his neck and kissed him hard. It was a long time before she pulled back, keeping her forehead against his as she said, "Because I want to be with you. Because I love you. Because I think what's between us is bigger than you and me. Do you understand?"

There had never been a question so easy to say yes to. He did understand. He understood it like he understood how to breathe, like his heart understood how to keep beating, night and day. The love that they shared was bigger than them, bigger than the city, bigger than the whole continent. Auden felt himself standing, grabbing her hand as he led her off the roof.

He held her hand the whole walk back to his apartment. There was every opportunity to stop in one of the quiet streets of Tenir and tell her everything, but he didn't. The voice had disappeared, the shadow had fled, and there was only Auden and Marvolene.

He said a prayer to the gods as he led her up into his apartment.

That it would always just be Auden and Marvolene.

Chapter 14

He was laying on the floor of the orphanage, on the one area of clean carpet in his room. He was laying there, breathing in and out, listening to the sounds of the city through the crack in his window. Sunlight was streaming through the glass, soaking into his skin and bringing him a warmth he could find nowhere else in this dismal place. He wondered if he lay there long enough, would his skin glow? Would beams of light shoot out of his fingers? His thoughts moved through his head lazily as he lay there, clinging onto that moment of peace.

Auden opened his eyes.

He wasn't in the orphanage; he was in his bed in his apartment. Normally when he woke up, there was a surge of despair as the shadow awoke with him, a cold reminder of what he was capable of. It typically took an hour or so before the grim feeling went away and he tried to embrace the good things in his life.

Until a few months ago, there had been no good things in his life.

But that morning, something was different. He heard noise coming from his kitchen, the sound of something sizzling in a pan, someone's melodic humming along with it. There was a heavenly smell drifting through his space for the first time ever. Auden never used his kitchen, besides the ice box when he used to drink frequently and heavily. Auden reached over to the space next to him in the bed; it was empty but warm, as if someone had just risen from it.

But that was impossible because he had spent his entire life isolating himself, physically, emotionally, mentally. No one had ever been in this apartment but him. No one had ever made it past his heavily guarded soul. He never allowed anyone inside because they would hate what they found. He knew this because he hated what was in him; how could someone find it within themselves to love him? Auden sat up slowly, brushing his hair out of his face, and exhaling slowly as he glanced out his window at the sparkling sea in the distance.

Marvolene.

Like the beams of sun through the window of the orphanage, the memory of the previous night crashed into him.

Marvolene was in his apartment.

Marvolene had stayed the night.

Marvolene didn't know the truth.

Marvolene loved him.

Auden was out of bed and on his feet before his mind comprehended his movements. He pulled on a pair of pants laying on the floor and stumbled out into the kitchen, stopping in the doorway and bracing the side of it with one hand.

She was the source of the humming, singing under her breath as she moved around the kitchen, her blonde hair falling down her back, slightly messy. But her cheeks were flushed and there was a lingering smile on her face. Her head snapped up when he entered the room and the blush grew redder. She immediately glanced at the ground and said, "There wasn't a lot in your ice box, so I made do with what was there."

Auden crossed his arms. "What are you doing right now?" he asked, fighting off a smile of his own. Marvolene was here, in his apartment, with him. The light of the morning sun was dancing across her skin, shining on one of his shirts that she had on.

She gave him a strange look. "Making breakfast?"

Auden rolled his eyes and crossed the room. His kitchen consisted of a large central counter with cabinets underneath it filled with dishes he had never used. Against the wall was stove and his icebox. There was a pan of something over the fire of the stove, but Auden didn't even glance at it. Instead, he grabbed Marvie by the waist. She let out a little yelp as he lifted her onto the counter and sat her down, pressing a kiss against her forehead and then her lips. She kissed him back, but she was smiling and then laughing and he was laughing too.

Finally, he drew back, resting his forehead on hers as he whispered, "Hi."

"Hi," Marvie giggled back.

"How are you?"

"Oh, you know." Marvie pretended to ponder the question, using one hand to push him back and the other to stroke her chin. "I guess I've been better."

Auden raised both eyebrows, trying to make a serious expression and failing miserably. "Oh?"

"Ahhh no. Never mind." She beamed at him, the biggest, brightest smile he thought he had ever seen. "Remember how the other day I told you that I thought I was happy."

He nodded, picking up both of her hands and holding them in his own. He couldn't let go, couldn't stop reminding himself that this was real. Not just last night, but every minute in this girl's presence. Auden didn't deserve this; he didn't deserve her and yet here she was, smiling at him like he was worth something.

"Well, I don't think it anymore, Auden, because I know I'm happy." She looked down at their clasped hands and then back at him. "I am happy," she repeated, leaning forward until their foreheads were touching again.

Auden kissed her and whispered in reply, "I'm happy too. I have never been happier."

"I love you, Auden Frae," she said softly, running a hand through his curls and then resting it behind his neck. "I used to worry I would never find someone who would love me in return. And now I never have to worry again. I get to love you for the rest of my life. I never want to be with anyone else. Just you…forever."

The sun wasn't just shining on him; it was inside of him, buried in his heart and trying to get out, for that was what it felt like. There was a glowing energy in his chest, shining from within him, extinguishing the darkness that had always had a home there. But no longer. The sun was shining and the darkness was no more.

"Marvie," he tugged her closer to him. "It's hard to believe in good things when you live in this world. I never believed in them, and then I met you. And suddenly I want to see the good things in everything…including myself. I want to make the bad, better. I want to make the good, great. I want to bottle up this feeling and sell it at the harbor, because I bet people would pay in gold to feel what I feel when I'm with you. I guess what I'm trying to say is I love you too, Marvolene Pere."

She smiled up at him again and then tucked her head against his chest, sighing quietly. Auden didn't know how long they stayed like that, Marvie sitting on the counter leaning against him. He could've stayed there forever, as every moment they had shared together, from the day they had met to the previous night, played over and over in his head.

Eventually, Marvie wrinkled her nose and used both hands to push him away from her, jumping off the counter. She gasped as she saw the smoke that was now streaming from the pot she had been working on and she scowled at Auden. "You distracted me!" she exclaimed. "The breakfast is burnt!"

Auden peered into the pan and saw that whatever Marvolene had been concocting was, indeed, burnt. He waved his hand over it, trying to lessen the smoke to no avail. He couldn't help but laugh as he grabbed a pail of water and poured it over the smoke. It sizzled and hissed in protest. Marvie had her arms crossed and was trying to maintain a glare, but the smiles continued to prevail. Auden took the pot off the fire, put out the flames, and glanced at Marvie.

"How about we go get breakfast somewhere other than here?" he asked with a sheepish grin.

Marvie rolled her eyes as she stomped back towards his bedroom. "Let me get dressed," she grumbled, but he could hear the laughter.

Minutes later, they were walking down the streets of Tenir, bound for a tearoom Marvie had suggested. Auden wasn't sure what was brighter, the sun shining down upon the brick streets and buildings, the beautiful girl on his arm, or the glowing energy spilling out of him.

As they walked, Marvolene planned.

"I think we'll go to Grady first," she told him. She had changed into a pair of his clothes that fit her better, a white shirt and gray pants. Her hair was still down and loose, gently blowing in the salty breeze and with her cheeks still slightly flushed, Auden was quite possibly sure it was the most beautiful she had ever looked.

"Grady?" he repeated.

"Yes," Marvie replied enthusiastically. "After we get married, let's take our celebratory trip to Grady. I've heard such wonderful things about it. White beaches with soft sand, the kind you want to feel in between your toes. And the water is as blue a thing as you've ever seen. They say the sun is always shining there. There are different sorts of plants and trees and fruit than Orinth. It's a paradise! I would love to go there."

He would go anywhere with her, but truthfully, he didn't see the need to go to Grady. Wonderful place? Sun always shining? Paradise? It sounded like any moment he spent with Marvie. Still, he replied, "I bet it's the kind of fruit you bite into and the juice drips down your chin."

"Oh yes," Marvie agreed. "By the time the fruit arrives here, it's not the same. If we ate it in Grady, I think it would taste better. We could go swimming too!"

Auden raised an eyebrow. "Swimming, huh?"

She gave him a look. "By that time, I think I'll know how to swim."

He held his free hand up in surrender. "I believe you," he insisted.

Marvie rolled her eyes but smiled nonetheless. "And if I don't," she said pointedly, "we can still lie on the beach and soak up the sun and let time pass us by without a care in the world."

Auden closed his eyes for a brief moment as they turned a corner and imagined it. He opened them and smiled over at her. "Perfect," he said.

"At night, we'll go to the same spot and look at the stars," she continued and her eyes had gotten a faraway look. In her mind, Marvie was already in Grady, lying on that beach, soaking up the light as if she needed any more of it. "It's hard to see the stars here, don't you think? The city makes the sky sort of foggy. But in Grady, I bet the sky is clear as glass. I bet you can see every star in the sky. I bet they feel so close you could pluck one from the clouds and wear it around your neck."

He saw the tearoom for which they were bound in the distance, but he didn't want to reach it just yet. Something about this moment made him want to stop. Talking to his lover about all the things they were going to do, all the time they had to fill with one another. "I wish I could do that for you, Marvolene," Auden murmured. "Pluck a star out of the sky and give it to you to wear around your neck."

"Auden, don't you know you've already done that?" she asked him incredulously. Before he could answer, she was speaking again, "I hope things calm down in the Wilds because I want to go there too and see the mountains. Maybe I'll finally see something the same shade of green as your eyes."

He tried to cut in, but she wasn't done. "Nagaye too. I've never been to the desert. I want to see a camel," Marvie added with a chuckle. "I want to see the red sand and the strange plants that exist within it. I want to try their strange foods. Sienna went there once when she was young and she said they have the strangest cuisine."

"And Auden…I want to show you Auntica. I want to show you the place where I was born. Though, I suppose I'm not as familiar with it as I should be. I've been there less than a dozen times. Maybe that's even better. We can learn about my home together and make it our home. Doesn't that sound perfect?"

Auden was so caught up in the future she was weaving for them that he barely managed to utter, "Perfect."

Marvie sighed, glancing up at the blue sky. "I just want to go everywhere with you, Auden, and see everything. There are all these experiences I've always wanted, and now, I get to experience them with you…" her voice trailed off and she closed her mouth, blushing just a little. "Sorry," she mumbled, "I didn't mean to get carried away."

Auden stopped them right as they were about to enter the tearoom. "I love you," he said, hoping it was an adequate response for the wishes she had just professed to him. Judging by the way her face lit up, it was enough. He held his hand out to her and together, they went inside.

Auden was still so caught up in the future it took his eyes a moment to adjust. First, he observed the room. He had never been inside the place. It was small, with only a few tables scattered atop a white marble floor. There was a counter pressed against the far wall made of clear shelves with dozens of delicacies crammed behind glass. Behind the counter, Auden could see employees moving around in the kitchen. The walls were covered in frames of pressed flowers and light streamed in through the giant windows that provided a view of the Tenir street. There was only one open table left that Marvie was already leading him towards, tugging on his hand.

Just as he began to follow her, Auden noticed a flash of movement out of the corner of his eye as an employee stepped out of the kitchen and into the dining room. He turned his head and he froze; Marvie didn't seem to notice as she continued to the table, releasing his hand, but Auden was stuck in place.

The person had stopped in the doorway, frozen just like Auden. It was a person whose face he had tried to expel from his memory like he had expelled every other face that was in the alley that day. And yet here he was. Auden tried to recall his name, recall anything about him besides the fact that he had been one of Conli's most loyal followers, had followed him until the very end. He was shorter than Auden and stocky, with beefy arms and a broad chest. His face was narrow, his eyes too close together. His brown hair was cut right to his scalp. He was dressed in the same uniform the rest of the employees were wearing, a white jacket and black pants, quite the contrast to the rags they all used to wear.

Auden's hopes of escaping were already dashed; the man's eyes were on him and his mouth opened up in a phantom scream.

The man dropped the tea pot he had been holding and it shattered onto the ground. The noise in the entire establishment stopped and there was a ripple of gasps as every head turned towards the waiter who had dropped it. His hands were trembling and he picked one of them up, slowly pointing at Auden as the recognition fully settled in and he realized who he was seeing. Auden had to imagine there was quite a difference upon seeing him in the flesh versus seeing him in nightmares.

The rest of the boys stumbled back as their leader fell to his knees, shrieking in pain as Auden felt the anger rush through him. He rolled over, still cradling his gut, but his eyes were on Conli. Anger at him, anger at his parents who had left him, anger at the world and the gods who allowed such evil.

With one eye swollen shut, Auden watched with the other as Conli began foaming at the mouth, shaking so badly that he could hear the cracks of his bones. The screaming hadn't ceased, but Auden could barely hear it over the ringing in his own ears, the mass of anger that had suddenly been awakened.

Conli collapsed to the ground, a final scream ringing out. His body convulsed once, then went still.

Auden had managed to sit up, his head and entire body throbbing from the pain he had just been put through. He dragged his eyes up to where the group of boys now stood, huddled together in fear, staring at where Conli lay on the ground. "Get out of here or I will kill every single one of you," Auden breathed, though it didn't sound like him speaking anymore.

The place was silent as the young man stumbled back into the counter, bracing it with both hands as he rolled over it and scurried into the kitchen and out of sight. Auden still hadn't moved, hadn't dared to look around at the other patrons, hadn't dared to look at Marvie. Instead, he turned around and walked out the door, slamming it behind him as he walked out into the street.

Chyles. His name was Chyles.

Auden's first thought was the strangest. He wondered how Chyles had escaped Southside. The only reason Auden had been able to leave that place was because the shadow enabled him to. His dark power had been a rope thrown to him, pulling him out of one place of evil into another deep within. But Chyles didn't have the shadow. He had been stuck in the orphanage, doomed to the same fate as Auden, the same fate as anyone from Southside: surviving and nothing more. How had Chyles gotten to the other side of Tenir? And earned a job in a tearoom nonetheless.

Auden's second thought was pondering whether or not he should go back there and kill him.

Chyles had never done anything to him, but that was exactly the problem. He had been the person to stand back and watch as Conli and the rest beat him and mocked him and belittled him, took the last shreds of his dignity and cast them to the wind. He had allowed the torment to continue, never speaking up, often contributing to the games they played with him. Chyles had seen the horror and looked away; he might have been worse than Conli for that. Auden expected Conli to be a monster; Chyles had been witness to a monster.

Auden had already fallen into a group of people, but he could hear Marvie calling after him. He didn't stop, didn't turn around because he couldn't. His shadow had returned in full force, like flames starting at the bottoms of his feet, flaring and licking around his body, threatening to consume him. He clenched his fists, digging his nails into his skin, desperately attempting to calm it before Marvie caught up to him. He could not be reeling in the shadow while she was near.

A small voice in the back of his head chimed in. *None of this would be a problem if you would have told her in the first place.*

Auden argued back. *She probably wouldn't be here if I had told her.* The shadow seemed to enjoy that comment, its intensity growing at the words and their meaning.

Marvie caught up to him, tugging on his hand. "Auden!" she yelled and pulled him so he was face to face with her in the middle of the street.

Auden yanked his hand away from hers, like it had burnt him. He couldn't touch her when underneath his hands were powers with the capability to kill her, to torture her, to manipulate her. She couldn't be near him like this.

She should have never been near you in the first place the same voice added and Auden couldn't help but agree with it.

The expression on Marvolene's face was enough to break him. "Auden, what just happened?" she asked, her lips already trembling.

Auden took a step back, putting his hands behind his back so she couldn't see how badly they were shaking. A thin layer of sweat was already coating his skin and it had nothing to do with the sun beating down. A few minutes ago, the sun had been a lovely representation of the way he was feeling inside, but now it was burning him, a man who belonged in the darkness. "Marvie," he managed to gasp. "Could you give me a moment?" He didn't wait for her to respond; he moved out of the way of the crowds and stepped into a shaded side street tucked between two tall brick buildings, praying Marvie had enough sense to see the blazes behind his eyes and retreat.

In typical Marvolene fashion, she did not see the warning signs. Or she did and decided to ignore them. Either way, she followed him. "Auden, tell me what is going on," she demanded, but her voice lacked confidence. Instead it was filled with fear and Auden had a brief moment of triumph. *Finally*, the inner voice whispered. *Finally, you have the sense to be afraid of me.*

He could force her to leave, send her away using the shadow so he could have a few moments of peace, a few moments to talk himself out of doing something stupid. Was stupid the right word? Was walking into a place crowded with people and using his shadow to choke the life out of a boy who played a major part in his traumatic childhood 'stupid'? Or was it evil? Or was it just? Auden didn't know, but Marvie was standing between him and where he wanted to be.

AUDEN. Reason seemed to shriek in his ears and he winced, using a hand to brace the wall of the alley. *You did not actually consider using the shadow on Marvie. Please tell me that didn't just happen.*

"Marvie," Auden said, and his voice came out much calmer than he was expecting it to. That was always the way when plagued by the shadow: inner turmoil with absolute serenity on the outside. "Marvie, go home for a while. Please. I'll explain everything later. I'll come by and explain what happened, but right now, I need you to go." His calm cracked with the last word, the utter desperation leaking through.

Marvie crossed her arms, even though her whole mouth was still shaking and tears threatened to spill out of her eyes. "No."

"Marvie," he said, his voice taking on a dark tone that, once again, should've been an enormous indicator that he was not right, not good, not safe. He dropped his hand from the wall and turned to her, exhaling. "Go home."

"No," she repeated and the shadow flared again, seemingly enjoying this entire scene. A part of it urged him to make her leave. Another part begged him to make her forget about the morning altogether, make her forget the utter terror in Chyles' eyes as he beheld Auden, the man he had watched murder his friend. Bend Marvie's mind so her only memory was of last night rolling into an equally perfect morning and nothing more.

A sliver of his mind wondered if he shouldn't erase himself from her mind altogether. Let there be no Auden. Let her go on living her beautiful, glowing life without him in it. He would never have to tell her about the shadow if Marvolene forgot about him completely.

But then he would have to erase himself from the minds of everyone who knew Marvie was in love with him, a list that had grown in the past few weeks.

On top of the fact that losing Marvie would destroy him in the most prolific way possible.

He could still erase the morning, though. Auden hadn't used the shadow in weeks. Was using it bad if it spared Marvie from a harsh reality of his past? It wasn't using it for evil then; it was a bad thing being used for good, right?

AUDEN the voice shrieked again.

"Marvie, please," he whispered, almost whimpered, his voice losing all traces of confidence. He was a broken man controlled by darkness. He wasn't worthy of being with this girl, wasn't worthy of the happiness and light she bestowed upon him. The shadow crept up his arms and swirled in the palms of his hands, begging to be released, begging to fix what had just happened.

"When are you going to understand that I will never walk away from you?" Marvie asked, her voice cracking midway through. She stepped closer to him and he winced. She froze, before slowly reaching for his hand. "When will you understand that I'm here for good?"

Auden shook his head. "You don't want to be, Marvie," he said softly as she picked up his hand that was currently possessed by the shadow. The moment her skin touched his, the shadow fled, retreating back to its origin in his chest, leaving his fingers trembling as her hand closed around them. She waited a moment to see what he would do before picking up his other, holding their clasped hands between their two bodies.

"I do," she responded and a single tear fell onto her face.

He had broken his promise. Weeks ago, he promised to never make her shed another tear and the inevitable had happened. He was so bad for her, the worst possible thing that could've happened to her. He needed to gather the strength to leave, but as she took a step closer to him, the shadow dimmed just a little bit more. Auden squeezed his eyes closed, refusing to meet her gaze. A dull ache had crept into his head and it was throbbing with the effort it was taking to resist the temptation to use his shadow. The space between his ears was flooded with a chorus of different voices, each urging him to do something different.

Use the shadow on her. Make her forget. Use the shadow on her. Kill Chyles. Let her go. Kill Chyles. Say goodbye forever and leave this place before she gets hurt.

Take her in your arms and never let her go. Tell her everything. She told you everything, confided in you even the most broken parts of her. Do the same. Maybe she'll leave you and hate you and fear you, but maybe she won't. Maybe she'll be with you forever and all those things you were saying about the future…going to Grady and the beaches and The Wilds and the mountains and Nagaye and the desert…all of it will come true because you were honest. You laid the foundation. You can be with her forever. Just tell her the truth and stop bearing this burden on your own.

"Marvie," Auden said and a tear fell onto his own cheek. He regained his motions and grasped her hands, pulling her closer because he couldn't help himself. "There are things I must tell you…that I'm just not ready to tell you."

More tears fell out of her eyes as she nodded slowly. "I never asked you to tell me anything," she said, her tone somewhere between defensive and meek.

"I know," he whispered, gently touching his forehead to hers. "I know, but I want to tell you. My past is complicated and messy. I'm not like you."

"I know that, Auden."

"No, you don't," he insisted softly. "You don't know. Marvolene, you are the first person in my life that I have ever wanted to share the past with. I've never loved another person the way I love you; I've barely even loved another person. I can't tell you these things because I don't know how."

"Auden…" Marvie cried.

"But I'm going to learn, okay? I'm going to figure out a way to share my past with you because I love you and I want to be with you for the rest of my life. I need time. Can you give me that, Marvolene? Time to find the right way to give all of myself to you?"

Marvie's chin sunk down and her hair fell in front of her face. Auden touched her chin, gently bringing her gaze up to meet his. He wiped away the few lingering tears on her cheeks as more of his own fell. The shadow had numbed, but it was still there. He was staring at Marvie, but a part of him was still with Chyles, wanting to destroy him because maybe destroying him would destroy the past and then he would never have to tell Marvie anything. Maybe killing Chyles would kill the part of him he didn't want her to see and they could be together with nothing between them.

No.

The voices screamed at him from every angle, but one rose above the rest. The one that knew killing Chyles would only kill the good part of him, the part that Marvie saw. It wouldn't bring Auden anything but pain, and he wasn't sure he could bear much more of it.

"Okay," Marvie whispered, staring up at him, blinking back more tears. "I can wait."

A profound relief flushed over him and his shoulders physically sagged as the tension drained out of them. "Really?"

Marvie nodded, trying to muster a smile. "I don't care about your past, Auden. I just care about you. I don't care about that waiter, and I don't care about who your parents are, where they are, or why sometimes you look like the saddest person on the continent. None of it matters to me...well, it does, but if I have to choose between the truth and you, I'll choose you in this life and the next."

In his head, the response to her statement was loud and clear. *You shouldn't.*

But he didn't say that. He didn't push her away to return to the tearoom and tear that boy apart. He didn't use the shadow on her, but he was distantly aware that once it sunk in he had considered using his powers on her, the guilt would ruin him.

Instead, he pulled her close to him and buried his face into her hair and she held him tightly in return. And he realized, as more tears were falling, that he was silently sobbing. Hopefully Marvolene couldn't tell, but his body was shaking as he relived a thousand memories at once. There was Lola, the orphanage, the boys, the alley, and the blood flowing through the cobblestones. There was Conli, his ghost, his screams, and the nightmares that followed. There were four years of darkness, the shadow, the manipulation, and the high that came with using it.

And then there was a girl in a shop, looking at him like he meant something, the same girl who now clung to him like he might disappear.

He wanted to disappear, fade away until his burdens were no more. But for Marvie's sake and maybe his own, he held on tight, praying the shadow would leave him, no...leave *them* be.

"My love," Rider said as he grasped the hands of his wife. Their daughter was playing outside and he had finally worked up the courage to tell her. She was sitting in the middle of the house that was theirs, waiting for the truth that he was ready to give. "My love, there's something I must tell you."

"Yes?" she asked simply.

"It's not good," he whispered and he fell to his knees, still grasping her hands. "It might break you because it broke me."

"Then don't tell me," she said simply.

He stared at her. "But..."

"Please don't tell me," she pleaded. "I don't want to know."

"But my love," Rider insisted, "it has to do with why..."

"Rider," she interrupted him. "Do you love me?"

Rider was taken aback. "More than anything," he managed to reply.

"Does what you're about to tell me change the fact that you love me?"

"My love, there is not anything in this entire world, anything on this entire continent, that could affect my love for you, that could take it away, that could change it. I'll love you until the end of time, and I think I'll even love you after that." The statement was truer than the woman in front of him would ever realize.

"Then I don't need to know whatever you're going to tell me," she whispered. "Your love is enough for me. It's always been enough for me; it will always be enough for me."

Rider didn't respond as the desire to tell her the truth drained out of him faster than he could comprehend. It drained and drained until there was nothing but his love for her. Love and something else.

Regret. Regret that he let himself fall in love for a second time when there was only one way it could end...in pain. The regret disappeared as she opened her mouth to speak again. "You will always be enough for me."

And Rider wondered if the pain he was feeling was worth the absolute love he received from her.

Chapter 15

Auden had mastered using a fake smile ever since he had stopped using the shadow at his job. Without the power as a crutch, he had gained the valuable skill of pretending to be happy, pretending like he was legitimately enjoying his life and its goings-on.

He never thought he would have to use the skill on Marvie.

Yet after they had walked out of that alley and down a few more streets to another tavern that Marvie liked, Auden had plastered a grin to his face and feigned being happy. He grinned at the server who sat them and brought their food. He smiled at the other patrons in the establishment, at the passersby peeking in through the window. He responded to everything Marvie said, laughed at her jokes, listened intently to her stories, attempting to be as normal as he could be. But inside he was an empty shell, a puppet pulling his own strings for Marvie's sake.

She could tell something was off, but of course she could. Auden had practically admitted to her that there was something terribly wrong with him, with the promise he would work up the nerve to tell her. He was honestly surprised that statement alone hadn't sent her running, but it was Marvie. He was starting to realize that his lover was blind to darkness, choosing only to see the light in others. What a beautiful blessing, a strange, peaceful, ignorant life.

Marvie didn't draw attention to his fake smiles and laughter. She didn't mention anything about their conversation in the alley or the man who had dropped the teapot less than an hour ago. It seemed Marvolene was playing along with the game. When they had finished the meal and Auden offered to walk her home, she politely declined. It was only then Auden knew she was truly upset.

They had walked out of the tavern and Marvie had kissed him on the cheek, making no plans to see him for the rest of the day or even the next. Auden wanted to apologize again, fall his knees and beg her for forgiveness, but he didn't. He said goodbye and watched her fade into the crowd.

Even after she disappeared, he stood in place, leaning up against the wall of the tavern, trying to gather his bearings. It was difficult considering the shadow resumed its torment the moment Marvolene disappeared from sight.

Closing his eyes, Auden slid to the ground so his back was leaning against the building. No one paid him any attention as they walked past and he was glad for it; he needed time to think. His mind ran through each truth one by one.

Last night had been out of a dream and here he was, living his worst nightmare.

The past had finally caught up to him. He had killed Conli when he was fourteen and now he was eighteen. Had he really expected to avoid every other person he grew up with when he hadn't left the city? He had murdered a boy and stayed in the same place where he committed the crime. This had been inevitable.

But why…why did it have to be with Marvie?

The next truth cut into him like nails. Auden had actually considered using the shadow on Marvie.

His reasons might have been logical. The first was her safety, because after seeing Chyles, the shadow was close to the breaking point. His power was uncontrollable and when it reached that "breaking point", Auden didn't know who or what it could affect. He would've simply used the shadow to send Marvie away for her own sake, protecting her from what might have happened if he truly did reach the breaking point.

Auden found it very easy to lie to other people but took pride in being honest with himself. And if he were being *honest* with himself, he wanted to use the shadow on Marvie as a matter of convenience; he did not want to answer the questions that came after the scene with Chyles. He didn't want her to pry about his past and his parents and Chyles' fear upon seeing Auden. He just wanted her to remember a perfect night rolling into a perfect morning, and it would save them both a lot of heartache.

So, there it was. Auden Frae had considered using the shadow on Marvolene Pere.

The ever-present voices were mocking him, their chorus of conscience growing with each truth Auden embraced. Today had been a consideration; tomorrow might be more. How much more temptation would it take until Auden snapped and used the shadow on her? And when that happened, how could he be sure he could control it? He would try to limit the damage, of course, but it was the shadow. At the end of the day, it did what it pleased once he released the hold on it.

And if he released the hold around Marvie…

Auden brought his legs to his chest and lowered his head until it rested between his knees. The noises all around him faded, replaced by the voices in his brain embraced in an intense, brutal argument.

He was never selfish as a child. He had spent most of his childhood taking care of other people, though he didn't have much of a choice. He took care of Lola, took care of the other children at the orphanage, tried to take care of himself. That was the opposite of selfish, right? Auden had eventually left the orphanage, which could've been considered selfish, but he had no other choice. The other boys would have eventually killed him if he stayed.

Once he discovered he could manipulate people's minds using the shadow, the selfish part within him grew until it utterly consumed him. Auden took whatever he wanted without a smidge of regret. The self-indulgence within him spread like a disease, took root in his heart and stemmed outward like ivy on a castle. For so many years, it had been Auden's world. No one else existed but him; there were no other needs but his. He had been the very definition of selfish.

When he met Marvie, Auden had thought that had disappeared. He thought he had reverted back to the person he had been as a child, a human free of darkness. He thought the selfishness had drained out of him until it was nothing.

Auden had been wrong.

He knew this because what he was about to do was selfish.

Slowly, Auden dragged himself to his feet. He observed his surroundings, ensuring that Marvie wasn't watching from somewhere. When he was positive she had actually gone home to her apartment, he started to walk. There were other people around him, yes, but he couldn't see them, couldn't hear them. They didn't exist to him because for the first time in a long time, it was back to being Auden's world.

It was selfish to stay in Marvie's life. From the very beginning, his conscience had pleaded with him to leave this poor, lovely girl alone. Every time he thought Marvie was about to walk away, he was fully prepared to let her go without argument. In his mind, in his heart, in his soul, he knew it was better for her to be far, far away from his dark, messy life.

But being the selfish bastard he was, he had allowed Marvie to crash into his life, to consume him almost as fast as the shadow had. Less than an hour ago, he had almost used the shadow on her. Was there a more glaringly obvious sign he should leave her than that?

He stuck his hands in his pockets as he walked, staring down at the cobblestones. He didn't have to watch where he was going; his body knew exactly where it needed to be, the shadow growing with each step.

Last night had been perfect. The night before last had been perfect. Every day with her had been perfect, but it didn't have anything to do with Auden; Marvolene was perfect so therefore being with her was perfect. Auden was sure that everyone who knew her felt the same way. He had been lucky enough to meet her, but she had been so terribly unlucky to meet him.

The battle between voices grew louder and Auden wanted nothing more than to clap his hands over his ears and scream at them to shut up, shut up, shut up. He glanced briefly at the street he was on, wondering if he could stop the voices by drowning himself in ale or something stronger. But no, the shadow had never been stopped by physical vices; it would only numb before eventually coming back more powerful than before.

Half the voices told him he was the worst person to ever walk this world, and Auden believed it. But it was that side of his mind telling him to leave Marvie. Leave Tenir so she could never find him. Break her heart for her sake.

Auden didn't want to hear those voices, but the other side might have been worse. Stay with Marvie because she was his light. Sure, being around him was dangerous and he was a walking nightmare who might explode at any given moment, but how could he let go of her now, after all that had passed between them?

Selfish. All of the options were selfish. It was too late to do the right thing; the right thing would've been to leave her alone to begin with.

"You skipped a part," Auden piped up from the couch.

Lola looked up from the book, blinking a few times as she pulled herself out of the book. "I did?"

Auden nodded, his eyes closed, hands folded upon his stomach. "You skipped the page after Rider went to see the keeper of scrolls."

Lola paused for a moment, flipping through the pages before she scoffed, "You're right!" She sighed as she glanced over at Auden. "You've made me read this book so many times when we eat biscuits and honey that the pages are sticky, Auden."

Auden chuckled as he tucked his hands behind his head. "Will you read me that part too, Lola?"

Lola shook her head as she clicked her tongue, but she turned the pages back. "I don't know why you couldn't have gotten obsessed with a happier story than this one, Auden. There are stories about knights and warriors and dragons and princesses and things that are fun. And instead, you choose the story about the man who can never die, falling in love with people who are doomed to do just that. That's the story you make me read over and over and over again."

"I don't know, Lola," Auden whispered in reply. "There's just something about this story that I love."

Lola didn't respond, just stared at him for a moment longer before she started up again.

"The keeper asked him what he wanted and Rider answered before he thought about the implications of his words."

""I want death," Rider whispered and the keeper looked frightened. Rider couldn't help but repeat himself. "I want death," he said again."

"The keeper was frightened for a moment. He thought that Rider was there to kill him, desiring his death, but Rider immediately assured him he wanted nothing of the sort. The keeper still remained wary, and Rider tried to explain himself. As the words came out of his mouth, Rider realized how otherworldly his predicament sounded."

""You see, sir," Rider began, "I have been alive for centuries. I look like I'm eighteen years old, but I have lived so many lifetimes. I cannot die. It used to be a blessing, but there are so many people who I love. There were so many people who I loved long ago and I had to watch them die. Have you ever had to watch someone you love die?""

"The keeper was looking at him like he was deranged, but the man still answered, "I saw my mother die when I was just a boy.""

Lola took a deep breath before continuing. "Rider nodded. "I'm sorry you had to go through that. But imagine you had to watch your mother die a dozen times, no, two dozen times. Imagine you had to watch your wife die before your eyes. Imagine watching your children and your children's children follow her to the grave, bound for the one place you can never follow. Can you even conceive the amount of pain from living that over and over?" Rider didn't mean to start sobbing with each word, but he couldn't help himself. He fell to his knees and pressed his hands against his face, trying to hide the tears and the agony. More than anything, he tried to hide from the image of his current wife that flashed behind his eyes, the pain that lingered on the horizon if this keeper of scrolls couldn't help him.

"The keeper shook his head. "I can't imagine," he said, and the incredulity of his tone had been replaced by pure sympathy."

""That's why you must help me," Rider begged him. "Please. I will do anything. I will give you anything. Just tell me how to get rid of this curse. Give me the power to follow my wife into the Beyond. To follow my children. To move past this life and into the next. To escape what should never have been inescapable.""

"The keeper grabbed Rider by the shoulders, pulling him to his feet. "I will do what I can to help you," he promised, but Rider could take no solace in that face. Instead, he looked up at the man and spoke."

""They told me it was a blessing," he whispered. "They told me I should be thankful, that I could be the most powerful man in the world if I put my mind to it. Maybe once, it was what I wanted. But now I just want to be with my wife, in the way that I should be. That's all I want. I want to be with my family, to live with them, to die with them. It's the only thing I dream of. It was never a blessing at all; this much power was always intended to be a curse.""

It took Auden precisely fifteen minutes to return to the same tearoom they had been at an hour ago.

He didn't go in; it would be much too obvious if he went in. Instead, he ducked into an alley across the street and found access to the roof within minutes. Apparently, his honed skill of finding roofs to sleep on had not diminished a bit since he was a homeless teenager. Auden crept to the edge of the building and peered down at the tearoom. He settled into a sitting position, once again bringing his knees to his chest.

And then, he waited.

The place was still busy, with a constant stream of people moving in and out. An employee dropping and breaking a teapot in the middle of the dining room, evidently, had no effect on the number of patrons supporting it. A part of Auden wondered if Chyles had fled the scene the moment Auden walked out the door. He assumed not; Chyles would probably believe Auden was waiting for him on some side street and wouldn't dare to leave the safety of the witnesses in the restaurant. Auden assumed it and hoped it; he wanted the man to be in the establishment.

Auden sunk into a state of subconsciousness while still remaining acutely aware of who was entering and leaving. To his knowledge, there were two entrances to the building, the front door and a back door in an alley. From his vantage point, he could see both the front and the mouth of the alley where the back door was. Eventually, Chyles would have to leave through the front door or come out of the alley.

And when he did, Auden would be ready.

Hours passed. Rider waited and waited and waited as the keeper went through scroll after scroll, book after book, parchment after parchment, desperately searching for the answer to every one of Rider's despairs. The longer time went on, the more hope he lost, though there had not been much hope to begin with. Rider wanted to help him, scan the scrolls with the same vigor the keeper displayed, but he could only sit there at his table, staring down at his hands, thinking of the lifetimes he had lived, the people he had loved, the people he currently loved who would one day be claimed by the past.

Rider could only hope he would be claimed with them.

But as the keeper continued to file through all the knowledge he possessed, Rider began to conclude another goodbye, another dreaded goodbye, might be inevitable.

Another voice had joined the chorus, but it wasn't one of his internal consciences trying to convince him he was a monster or convince him he deserved something good. No, the voice was Marvie, begging him to leave the roof and come find her.

Auden let out a shaking sigh as his mind wandered back to her. He had been trying not to think about her because she was the only person he had to be good for. He simply did not care about anyone else. The world was full of monsters; what was one more?

But he didn't want to be a monster to Marvie; he wanted to be a light to her like she was to him.

A light. Auden Frae, a light in someone's world. Laughable. That was the only word to describe the notion. Would a person of the light be sitting on a roof, awaiting a certain person with the intention of confronting them, harming them, and possibly killing them?

If only Marvie could see him now, crouched on a roof, scanning the face of every person who left the tearoom, hoping and praying one of them would be Chyles. She told him she loved him, but she wouldn't love him like this. She would hate him the way he hated himself for what he was doing.

A part of him thought he had healed from what happened in the alley. Auden would never be completely over it because how could one be completely over something such as that? But the past didn't control him anymore, or so he had told himself. He wasn't that boy curled up on the cobblestones heaving his guts out before he reached out his hand and awakened a dark power within. He could control it now and he would never kill with it again. Conli was the first and the last; hadn't it been self-defense? Auden wasn't a monster for defending himself.

Deep within his heart, Auden believed he had come to terms with it. In some warped way, he convinced himself he had forgiven Conli, forgiven the rest of the boys who had been there that day. Not for their sakes, because gods knew they didn't deserve mercy, but for Auden's own sake. He had to let go because it might ruin him if he didn't.

But Auden hadn't let go. He held onto the pain of that day, the nightmare of it. He blamed them, not just for what happened in the alley, but for every ugly memory before that. If not for them and what they had subjected him to, maybe the shadow never would have awakened in the first place. What if he had met Marvie as a completely normal person? How much better, how much purer would their love be?

The hatred for the boys hadn't disappeared; it had just been buried so deep that Auden could pretend it wasn't there.

Then he saw Chyles and realized that the hatred and malice and contempt and all the things the shadow fed on were still there, as strong as the day in the alley. Hatred, if not resolved, festered and grew until it was uncontrollable, enabling one to do terrible things. For Auden, it was worse.

For Chyles, it was much, much worse.

Marvie was still in his ear, imploring him to walk away, but he shut her out until her voice faded and all he could feel was the shadow, biding its time, waiting to strike. It had been biding its time for a while, Auden realized. Since that moment he had denied it in front of the remnants of the orphanage in Southside, barred it from preying on an innocent bystander, it had been waiting. Maybe it wouldn't get to do its will on a bystander, but it was patient. Auden would eventually see someone he wanted to use it on, and when he did, the shadow would be ready.

Auden had used the shadow every day for four years straight. Denying its usage had been more difficult than he admitted to himself, but now, he was granting it full permission to do whatever it desired to Chyles, the boy who had allowed Conli to do whatever he desired to Auden.

The keeper was speaking to him, but Rider wasn't really listening. He only had to hear the first two words to know he was doomed.

"I'm sorry," the keeper had began and Rider faded away until he wasn't standing in the library any longer, but in the past, making the decision to never love anyone again.

He had tried so hard. He had left his family behind, a most painful undertaking. Somewhere in the world, at that very moment, his kin were walking around, living, breathing, existing, and he would never know them. It was better that way, he convinced himself, because he wouldn't know them and wouldn't lose them. The decision had been calculated, a careful weighing of options to spare himself pain.

He had chosen not to love for a reason; Rider couldn't do it all over again.

But he had broken the promise he made to himself. He had fallen in love and now he had a daughter. And that daughter would probably get married and have children of her own, children Rider would come to know, come to love, come to lose.

All of this pain could have been spared if he would've kept his promise and never loved someone again.

The keeper of the scrolls had been his last hope.

Rider would live. The people he loved would die.

The only thing that would live as long as Rider was his regret and despair. It was the only thing he could think about as he walked out of the library without another word to the keeper.

The sun was beginning its descent when Chyles finally walked out of the tearoom.

The shadow blazed within Auden and he could feel its glee as he began to move. He found his way back to the street whilst keeping out of sight. Chyles had not forgotten seeing Auden that morning, because the stocky boy glanced around with plain fear in his gaze. He searched the crowds outside the establishment, the waves of people walking down the street. It gave Auden ample time to climb back down to the street and remain in the shadows until Chyles, satisfied Auden wasn't close, began to walk.

Auden started after him, clenching his fists to keep the shadow at bay. *All in good time,* he promised the power within him. *All in good time.*

It was easy enough to track the boy through the crowded streets of Tenir, keeping his eyes glued to the back of Chyles' head, the brown hair cropped to his head. As they walked, Auden tried to recall if he had always looked like that. He tried to remember more details about Chyles as a person. What had the boy been like? Did he contribute anything to their orphanage, helping out with chores, watching the smaller children, protecting them from the horrors outside the walls, the horrors within? But Auden couldn't recall anything about him besides the fact he had stood by and let Conli persecute him his entire life.

It was the only thing he needed to recall.

For Auden, the rest of the people on the streets disappeared. There was only Chyles.

Auden's memories of his childhood had always been distorted by what had happened in the alley. It was hard to remember exact details before that, besides the prominent memories of Lola and a few of his father. But as he followed Chyles through the streets, Auden remembered things he had forgotten.

There had been older children in the orphanage who turned to different substances to make life a little easier. For some of them, it was drinking; for others, it was stronger stimulants that could be ingested a hundred different ways. Lola discouraged it heavily, but what could she do? How could she stop them when the substances were the only way they thought they could survive?

There was one boy Auden remembered specifically, not his name, only his face. He remembered that the boy had the happiest smile for someone who was so sad. The boy had counted on stimulants for so long to get him through. One day, the boy had gone missing for days. Auden remembered not thinking much of it, as the older children from the orphanage disappeared all the time, Auden included.

When the boy finally returned, he swore to each and every one of them he would never touch the substances he loved again. He never explained what had changed his mind, but there were horrors in his eyes that hadn't been there before.

For months and months, Auden watched the boy deny anything offered to him, even the smallest of drinks. He kept proclaiming he wanted to face life all on his own, with no crutch. A part of Auden was jealous; he didn't have any crutches, but he knew one day he would probably end up like the rest of them. It wouldn't be his fault; it was just their world. There was too much pain to bear it alone. To watch this boy begin to face it without assistance made Auden feel like he had to do the same.

The boy was set to get adopted. Two people had come in, a young couple, and expressed interest in adopting one of the children. It was such a rare feat, willing couples showing up to their orphanage in Southside to look for a child, when there were so many others in Tenir with better options. But this couple had shown up and selected the boy to be their new son.

The paperwork was completed; the date was set. The boy had found the escape that he had once sought at the bottom of a tankard or in a pill that could fit in the palm of his hand. He had no need for those things anymore, now that he was about to be saved.

And then, at the last possible moment, the couple pulled out of the deal. The date they were supposed to adopt him came and went; they never arrived. The boy's escape was eliminated, with no explanation. Auden remembered hearing that the boy had searched for his two almost-parents to no avail.

It took two days before the boy was drinking again. Two more days before he was using stimulants and within the week, he was gone from the orphanage. Auden never saw him again.

It was a strange and sad thing to remember. A part of him wondered where the boy was now. But in that moment, following Chyles down the street, Auden saw himself in that boy from the past.

The shadow had been his crutch since the very day he discovered he could use it. It was his tool of survival, his method of getting through each day. He couldn't live without it. It was the air he breathed, the blood that ran through his veins.

Marvolene had entered his life and brought hope, just like the couple had done for that boy. Auden had no need for his crutch anymore because there was finally some light in his life of darkness.

Marvie hadn't left like the couple had, but Auden had faltered so easily and so quickly, just like the boy. It didn't matter how much time separated him from use of the shadow. His addiction to the power was too strong to give up. He desperately needed the crutch.

Auden thought about the boy as he followed Chyles, the sun disappearing beyond the horizon, like Auden's hopes of ever being a normal person.

Chapter 16

Chyles walked far past where he should have turned to get to Southside. In fact, he was bound for where the businessmen of Orinth lived and worked, a far cry from the slums where he and Auden had grown up. Beneath Auden's mass of anger and hatred, there was confusion. Where was Chyles going? Was he on his way to go steal something from the rich, a hobby Auden used to partake in quite frequently?

Chyles was maybe two or three years older than Auden; there was no way he would still be living in a children's home. Especially not the one they had grown up in, considering the remnants of it were crumbled bricks and broken glass. Yet Auden had expected him to still live in Southside, because without the shadow, how would one escape from there?

The door between Southside and the rest of the world was made of one thing: money. If you didn't have it, you didn't get to leave. Which was why most people of Southside were born there, grew up there, and eventually died there. Auden had bypassed the bridge because of the shadow, but how would someone like Chyles pull himself from the slums? Auden didn't need a stellar memory to recall that Chyles was as dumb as a rock, the perfect candidate for Conli's henchmen. He followed along with whatever Conli did with no questions asked. Chyles would not have escaped the Southside with his brains, as the rare few had accomplished.

Auden reverted to his first conclusion. Chyles was on his way to make money in the true Southside fashion: taking it from someone else.

As they moved closer to the business district of Tenir, the crowds seemed to thin. On a night like this, people were bound for the harbor district and the town square, where the action would be. The further they moved away from those areas, the fewer people there were. Eventually, Auden had to duck into the shadows, away from the light of the streetlamps in case Chyles looked back and spotted him.

Not that it would matter. If Chyles discovered he was being followed, he would run, but Auden would catch him. The result would be the same regardless, but now a part of Auden followed him to see what exactly this bully from Southside was doing in this part of Tenir.

The shadow had been a steady presence throughout the entire walk, but Auden realized there was a relentless feeling of anxiety that had crept up on him. There was barely anyone around and the shadows seemed to grow; the spaces in between the brick buildings could've been a mile long. Auden wondered what faces lived in those shadows, watching Auden walk down the street. Southside was the most dangerous by far, but Tenir was simply a dangerous city. People didn't discriminate when it came to the areas they committed their crimes.

Nothing could threaten him, not really. But that didn't mean he was safe.

Auden, for the first time in three years, allowed himself to think about a memory he had tucked far away. The dark streets had resurrected it for him, brought it to the forefront of his mind so it could not be ignored.

Three years ago, he had been attacked on a dark street walking home from a tavern. He had never gotten a good look at his assailant and the person had scurried off before he could identify them. They had jumped him in an alley he was using as a shortcut. At that time, only months after discovering the shadow, his instincts he had learned from the Southside kicked in. He flipped the assailant off his back and kicked him hard in the gut. The shock of the encounter was so great that Auden didn't know what to do other than to stumble back. He realized that his dark powers could protect him, but before he could use them, the man had disappeared.

Auden had always told himself that he had been the random victim of a street thief, something quite common in Tenir. But in the back of the mind, he wondered if the attack hadn't been random at all, if someone knew who Auden was and had followed him, hoping to catch him unaware.

Even thinking about it in the present moment, Auden denied it. It was random. Nothing of the sort had happened since then, which was more evidence it was random.

Auden was desperate to believe that, because if it hadn't been random, the implications were too terrifying to explore. If it hadn't been random, then someone knew who Auden was, knew what he had done, and tried to kill him for it. It had always occurred to Auden that there had been several witnesses to his crime. Those first few weeks after Conli's death, Auden jumped at every noise, flinched when he made eye contact with people, grew startled anytime a door opened. He was just waiting, *waiting,* for Orinthian guards to burst in and arrest him, marching him to his execution.

As time went on, Auden started to trust in the boys' silence. In order to report Auden to authorities, they had to admit that they were a part of a gang of people who had cornered him into an alley and attempted to beat him to death. Had it not been for the shadow, Auden would've died. Even with the shadow as his defense, he had still knocked on death's door. The rest of the boys would not have admitted to their deed.

Plus, it was the unspoken rule of the Southside: don't get involved in things you don't have to. If they reported Auden's crime to authorities, the boys would become a part of an investigation. What was the point of bringing justice to Conli? The boy was dead and no one had ever really cared about him. Reporting his death to authorities wouldn't bring him back. The most Southside thing to do was leave his body in the alley and never speak a word of what happened to anyone ever again.

Auden didn't worry about it often; it was why he buried the memory deep away along with so many others. But walking down the street, with the brick buildings towering over him, shadows being cast in every direction, a strange feeling was in the air, Auden couldn't help think about the fact that one of the boys might have said something to someone. Maybe not the Orinthian authorities, but someone else.

Maybe he wasn't as concealed as he thought he was.

Auden forced those thoughts out of his head as Chyles finally started to slow down. A quick glance around told Auden they were right on the border of where the business district began and the center of the city ended. It wasn't the nicest part of Tenir, but it was certainly nicer than Southside. Chyles had stopped in front of a dimly lit storefront where the slight sound of laughter could be heard coming from under the door. There were a few people lingering outside of the place, smoking, and Auden watched as they greeted Chyles. He was too far away to hear their exact words, but he saw one of them slap Chyles on the back, a large grin on his face. Chyles beamed back at him, shaking his hand earnestly.

Auden paused for a moment. He had never seen that expression on Chyles' face before. He had seen sneers and smirks and scowls but never a real smile. The boy didn't look so ratty when he smiled. The lights were dim, though, and Auden didn't have a great angle. Maybe he still looked conniving and evil, and Auden just couldn't see.

Auden leaned up against a building across the street, staying out of sight under an awning, away from the light of the streetlamps. The shadow, which had been steady up until that point, was now on the edge of exploding as Chyles was in his sight, waiting to be destroyed. And Auden was more than happy to do that, but not yet, not with the people outside of wherever they were. There was no sign indicating what was in the building, but judging by the general aura of relaxation, Auden guessed it was a tavern. He had never been to this one, but if he tried to go to every tavern in the entire city of Tenir, he would die of old age before he finished the task.

Auden was patient. Clearly Chyles was going to go into the tavern, maybe have a few drinks, and then eventually make his way home. Maybe that was the reason he hadn't gone to Southside yet. He was stopping at this tavern and then he would walk back across the bridge to the place where they grew up, the place where they belonged.

After speaking to the people outside the tavern for a few minutes, Chyles slapped them on the back and entered the place.

Auden waited exactly a minute before he crossed the street, hands stuck into his pockets like he was a friendly passerby and not a man about to explode and kill someone. He didn't enter the place but ducked into the alley right next to it, that was lit only by the light pouring from the windows. Auden used those windows to peer into the tavern, careful not to get too close so that someone on the inside would see him.

The tavern looked just like any other, with its brick walls decorated with Orinthian art and wooden tables scattered about a wooden floor. There was an empty stage in one corner and a full bar spanning the opposite wall. Every stool at the bar was taken, but none of them held Chyles.

No, Auden watched him stand at the door, smiling and laughing with the keeper of the tavern. Once again, Auden wasn't looking at the Chyles that lived in his memories, the one laughing at his pain, orchestrating his torment. This Chyles had a hand on the shoulder of the keeper, talking animatedly to him. If Auden had seen him for the first time, there was no way he would've guessed he was from Southside. His people didn't smile, didn't laugh as freely as Chyles did. Auden didn't let himself get distracted by the confusion. His shadow was seething underneath his skin, waiting.

"Just a little while longer," he promised it. He might be patient, but the shadow was not. No, the power deep within him was furious at the constant denial for weeks and weeks, and then again today, when he had prevented himself from using it on Marvie. Enough was enough, the shadow seemed to say. Just let go. "A little while longer," Auden said again, gripping the pane of the window so tightly his fingers began to cramp.

Chyles clapped the keeper on the back one final time before he started towards one of the tables, greeting several of the people sitting at the bar, who returned his greeting with wide smiles and shouts. Auden couldn't hear what they were saying back to him, but he could read their lips and imagine.

"Chyles, you bastard! Where have you been?"

"There's the man I wanted to see!"

"Let me buy you a drink, Chyles, you look tired!"

A few of them even stood up to embrace the man. Chyles embraced them back, that same stupid smile not leaving his face.

The shadow was boiling now as Auden gripped the window pain, beads of sweat dripping down his back and forehead. Thank the gods there was no one else in that empty alley, for if there had been, it would've been too much. Auden could barely stand up straight. His knees were shaking, his mouth trembling like Marvie's had been hours ago. It was too much. He might not be able to wait. He might have to march straight into the tavern and kill him right there and then.

No, no, no! He screamed at himself. Chyles had basically greeted every patron of the establishment. What was he going to do, murder him in front of his friends? The boys in the alley had stayed silent about Conli's death, but these people in the tavern would certainly not do the same. In a few days, Auden's face would be plastered on posters all over the city. He would never be at peace here again.

If he killed Chyles in the shadows, he could continue living his life the way he did.

Auden knew he was a fool if he believed that was true. If he killed Chyles, his life was over. He would have to leave Marvie; he would have to leave Tenir. He would probably have to leave the continent. But in that moment, he, no, the shadow did not care. It needed blood and it needed it now.

Auden could barely stand as he watched Chyles finally remove himself from the people at the bar. He walked slowly towards a table in the back corner, a table where two people were waiting for him.

Well, no, not two people. A woman and a child.

For the first time since that very morning, the shadow faltered.

Chyles practically ran the rest of the way over to where the woman was waiting for him. She was already standing as she embraced him, beaming from ear to ear. He picked her up and spun her around; Auden could almost hear her laughter through the glass. She couldn't have been much older than Auden, maybe twenty or twenty-one, and she was ridiculously beautiful. Well, he thought she was. Anyone was beautiful with that much elation painted on their face. She had bright red hair and a smattering of freckles across her pale skin. She was a head shorter than Chyles and wearing a blue dress that brought out her red hair.

But Auden had already stopped paying attention to her.

His eyes were on the child standing at their feet, raising her hands to the sky as she laughed along with them.

Auden watched as Chyles picked the little girl up and spun her around like he had done to the woman. The little girl shrieked, eyes squeezed closed with laughter. Chyles threw her into the air, caught her, and then threw her again. The woman smiled at the entire scene and when the two were finally done, Chyles leaned over and pressed a kiss to her lips.

The little girl was still in his arms, resting her head on his shoulder with a large smile on her face. The girl had short, bright red hair, the exact same color as her obvious mother, but her facial features were all Chyles. She was tiny, probably not any older than three, and she held onto her father fiercely.

Chyles looked at the woman and his daughter before he gestured at them to sit. The woman sat down across from Chyles, whose back was to the window. The little girl remained on his lap, sandwiched between his arms as the same person who had greeted Chyles at the door came up to their table with drinks.

The shadow was shattering and rising all at once. It was falling to pieces, but Auden was trying to gather those pieces enough to do what he knew he needed to.

Chyles was a father. Chyles had a woman in his life, a woman who loved him; even a blind person could see it. Chyles had a daughter who looked at him like he had hung the sun in the sky. And Chyles looked at them like they were his one sole purpose for living, which they probably were.

Auden collapsed to the ground, his muscles finally giving out on him. He rested his head against the wall as he pulled his knees up to his chin before burying his face in between them again, squeezing his eyes shut, trying to hide from the only thing he could see now: Chyles' family.

When he thought of Chyles as a bitter, lonely man who still lived in Southside, the idea of using the shadow on him to get revenge was incredibly appealing. No one would miss him. Auden would send him the same place he sent Conli and all the wrongs would be made right. That little boy from his past, laying on the carpet of his room, desperately trying to soak up some light from the sun, would be avenged. Maybe he would force Chyles to tell him where the rest of the boys from the alley were, and then Auden would *truly* right every wrong.

But Chyles wasn't a bitter, lonely man. Chyles was a father and a lover and a friend, Auden had gathered that in the five minutes of watching him in the tavern. Chyles had people who loved him, but Auden guessed those people mattered very little compared to the woman and the child sitting at that table.

Auden couldn't take Chyles away from them.

No. He could. He wanted to. Because why in the world did Chyles deserve to be happy after all the terrible, terrible things he had allowed to happen to Auden?

Chyles had tormented him his entire life and his punishment for it had been, what, a woman and child who adored him? A group of people who were happy to see him? A job at a place that wasn't in Southside, and probably a life that was worth living? That wasn't a punishment at all. It was almost as if the gods were mocking Auden by *rewarding* Chyles with the things that every human person in their world worked to have.

People worked to find a means to survive; Chyles had that with his job at the tearoom.

People looked for human companionship, for friends who would make the bad days better and the good days great. Chyles had found that, apparently, from the people within the tavern that Auden trembled against.

More than anything, people searched for love, for another person to share their life with, to share the highs and the lows and everything in between. Chyles had found that within the eyes of the woman and within the soul of the little girl who sat on his lap. Chyles had found what so many people never did, and he was only a few years older than Auden himself.

Auden had to take those things away from him. He couldn't live in a world where bad people were rewarded with the things others dreamed of. He couldn't allow Chyles to be happy. The boy who made his life miserable was living a dream and Auden simply would not let it be. He would wait to follow them home, ensuring not to harm the woman or the child. He would wait until they were all tucked in and then he would use the shadow to manipulate Chyles into coming out of his home and into some deserted alley somewhere. And then,

Auden would set things right by taking away the wonderful things that Chyles had done nothing to deserve.

Auden had nothing but a dark power that had fallen silent. Chyles had everything and Auden had...

Well, Auden had Marvolene Pere.

A single tear fell onto his skin as he thought of her for the first time in hours.

In life, there were three things that were so difficult to find: a means of surviving, friends, and love. Chyles had all of those things, all the ingredients in a recipe to be happy, and it was clear that he was.

But Auden had those things too, didn't he?

He had never really needed a livelihood, but he had one nonetheless with his job at The Wooden Barrel. He had the same thing Chyles did, a way to provide for himself that wasn't the shadow. A way to make a little money so he could take the woman he loved out for a night on the town.

Auden didn't have many friends, but he could change that, if he wanted. He could go to a tavern and make an effort to talk to people, look them in the eye, smile at them. He could eventually walk into the same tavern and those friends would cheer upon seeing him, insist on buying him a drink. He chose not to have friends because of the shadow, but why not? Why shouldn't he have other people in the world who cared about him?

Then he remembered there was only one person in the world he cared about caring about him.

Auden had love. Auden had Marvie.

He had a girl whom he had fallen in love with instantly, from the moment she stepped into his life and every moment afterward. Marvie had pulled him from the darkness so much so that he was able to deny the power that had controlled his life for four years. Marvie expelled that darkness with the light that was within her, and she didn't even know. Auden had never experienced happiness in his life and yet, Marvie brought him so much; sometimes, it was overwhelming because Auden wasn't used to being happy.

A part of him wanted to push Marvie away because he was scared of that happiness. He was scared he would do something to lose it. He cradled the happiness in his hands like a piece of glass he was desperately trying not to break. That frightened part of him wanted to ruin it right now and spare himself the heartbreak.

But the rest of him was going to cling onto Marvie Pere like she was the one thing keeping him alive, mostly because she was.

Auden choked back a sob, the sound muffled by his knees in his face, as he came to a strange revelation; all the things he was livid at Chyles for having, he possessed already. And instead of cherishing those things, here he was, thinking of stealing them from someone else. Not just from Chyles, but his lover, his child, and the rest of his friends in the tavern.

Auden lifted his head, experiencing a moment of crystal clarity.

It didn't matter that Chyles was happy because Chyles didn't matter. Chyles had no effect on Auden's life and his ability to appreciate the woman he loved. Why in the world should Auden destroy someone else's happiness just because he thought they didn't deserve it? Gods, Auden didn't deserve to be happy either and yet, he still allowed himself to fall in love with Marvolene.

The shadow made one last attempt, flaring up suddenly, shrieking at him to go into that tavern and kill the boy who had witnessed his pain and done nothing about it. Take away the happiness that Chyles had no right to have. Auden dragged himself to his feet, glancing back into the tavern with one arm braced against the wall.

The woman still sat at the table, but Chyles was on his feet, holding the little girl in his arms and dancing with her, spinning her around the room with a large grin on his face. The little girl shrieked with laughter and the woman watched the whole scene smiling.

Why would Auden concern himself with destroying other people's happiness when he could be spending that same time cherishing happiness of his own?

Auden slammed walls up against the shadow and started walking before his mind caught up with his actions. He strode out of the alley and through the empty streets without a trace of fear in his mind. He walked, street by street, until it began to grow crowded towards the center of town. He walked, looking straight ahead, until his feet began to hurt and the muscles of his hands hurt from clenching his fists. He walked, wondering if he should've killed Chyles, but he didn't turn around. He kept walking.

The question haunted Rider Grey, the question of whether this pain was worth the love. When he returned from the city, returned from the keeper of the scrolls and his lack of answers, he walked into his house, looking for his wife and daughter, but they were gone. He didn't know where they were, but he wasn't worried. They often went on excursions, just the two of them. Besides, he wasn't sure if he was in the right state of mind to see them. How was he supposed to look them in the eyes and enjoy his time spent with them, knowing that he was going to lose them and there was nothing he could do about it?

So Rider laid down on his bed and tried to sleep. The tears had stopped coming, but the pain was just as fresh, the keeper's words repeating in his mind.

"I'm sorry."

Rider fell asleep, but it wasn't a restful sleep. He saw so many faces of so many people he once loved. In the dream, they were standing in front of him, just far enough away that he couldn't reach them. He stretched his arm out, desperately trying to embrace them, or even just touch them to see if they were real. But they were always too far away.

He didn't wake up screaming, but tears were falling once more as he sat up.

Only his wife was sitting on the side of the bed, right next to him, looking down at him with love in her eyes. For one precious moment, time froze and all he could see was her. The window behind her was filled with light and she was glowing as she smiled. Her smile disappeared as she saw the tears and her mouth was moving, but Rider couldn't hear her. He could only see her beautiful face, the face he had fallen in love with so long ago. He saw past her face, saw everything they had shared with one another, all the words of love that had passed between them. He relived seeing her for the first time, their first kiss, big moments and little ones. He lost himself in who this person was to him, the incredible depth of what he felt for her that he would never fully understand.

The moment passed and her voice cut through to him. "Rider? Rider, is everything alright?" She had her hand on his knee and the other cupping his face.

Rider sat up and, without responding, kissed her before pulling her tight against his chest, burying his face into her hair and exhaling softly.

"Rider?" she asked again, but she embraced him in return.

"I'm sorry," he whispered. I'm sorry for even considering that you weren't worth it. I know pain is on the horizon, as inevitable as the sun rising. But I won't waste these precious moments I have with you fearing that pain. I'll cherish every second and love you as best as I can. You are worth it. I would do this a million times over if it meant I got to love you again.

"For what?" she questioned, but Rider didn't answer. He only held her tightly and tried not to think of the day when she would be gone and he would be alone.

Auden started to run. Walking was too slow; walking wouldn't get him to her fast enough. He wove throughout the crowds, mumbling apologies and ignoring insults, and it still wasn't fast enough.

It seemed an eternity until he was standing outside of her door after practically hurtling himself up the stairs. He couldn't help himself; he pounded against the wood of the door. Auden wanted to just burst in unannounced, grab Marvolene, plead for her forgiveness and then never let her go, but her aunt and uncle might not like that. So he continued pounding on the door like a maniac instead.

Within a half-minute the door was opened by Marvie's uncle, Hewes. He had a quizzical expression on his face replaced by recognition and then confusion again. "Why, Auden! Is everything alright?" he asked, and Auden wondered what he was seeing right now. Sweat stained his clothes and his face was flushed. Not to mention the pure chaos that was in his gaze, the result of the entire day being one, long nightmare.

Auden managed a nod. "Everything is fine, sir. Is Marvolene here?"

Hewes opened the door wider. "Come in," he insisted, and Auden stepped into her apartment. Sienna had walked into the room and smiled when she saw him.

"Oh hello, Auden!" she exclaimed. "How are you?"

Auden glanced around for Marvie, but she wasn't in the room. Auden forced a smile on his face as he returned the pleasantries. "I'm well, ma'am, and how are you?"

Sienna waved him off without answering. "None of this sir and ma'am stuff, Auden. It's Sienna and Hewes to you."

Auden couldn't even appreciate the meaning behind her words; he just had to see Marvie. Still, he replied, "I appreciate that, ma'am. Oh, I mean, Sienna. Is Marvie home?"

Hewes had already started back towards the kitchen, where Auden could smell something heavenly, but he hadn't been hungry since he followed a man across the city with the intention to kill him. Hewes called over his shoulder, "She's been up in her room sleeping for the last few hours."

Sienna nudged him in the shoulder. "Go wake her up, Auden. Dinner is going to be cold by the time she gets down here, but you know how Marvie is with her sleep. Wake her up and come join us, yes?"

Auden was already on his way up the stairs as he nodded back to Sienna. He heard Sienna call something after him, but he was already at Marvie's door. He knocked gently and when there was no reply, he opened it.

Sure enough, Marvie was in her bed, sleeping on her side. The only sound that could be heard was her soft breathing. Auden left the door open as he walked quietly over to the side of her bed, sitting down and picking up her hand. He brushed a piece of stray hair out of her hair before he said quietly, "Marvie?"

She stirred but didn't wake. Auden said again, "Marvolene?"

Her eyes fluttered open, darting around the room before coming to land on Auden. She smiled at him, but he saw pain there, too, at what had happened earlier. Marvie quickly sat up, looking around and then looking at him. "Auden," she yawned. She squeezed his hand once and then scratched the back of her head. "What time is it?" she asked, her voice uncertain.

"Marvie, I'm sorry," he answered, bringing a hand up to her face and touching her cheek. "I'm so sorry," he said again. And at that moment, with Marvie staring at him with droopy eyes, her hair slightly messy from being slept on, he almost told her everything. Starting with his childhood in the orphanage and ending with the events of his day, where he almost killed a boy with his dark power.

"For what?" Marvie asked, putting her hand atop of his on her face. "You haven't done anything wrong."

It took all his willpower not to throw his head back and laugh. He had done so many things that were wrong that it baffled him. But he was pulling himself from the darkness, embracing the happiness that was possible if he only let go of the past. And that happiness began right here, in the eyes of the girl he was in love with.

"Remember a few days ago when we were talking about going to Grady and The Wilds and Nagaye and all those places?" he asked her.

Marvie nodded, the corners of her mouth upturning. She leaned forward until her head was resting on his shoulder. "We'll lay on the sand and look up at the stars. You'll pluck one out of the sky for me so I can wear it around my neck."

"We're going to go to all those places," Auden promised, "and more. Anywhere you want to go, I'll take you. You're my future, Marvolene. I'm going to tell you about the past someday, but I realize, in the end, the past doesn't matter; the future does, and my future lies with you, wherever you want to go, whatever you want to do."

"Oh really?" Marvie said with a shaky laugh. "What if I want to go down to the vendor square and buy new clothes and jewelry and cosmetics. Will your future lie with me then?"

Auden threw his head back and laughed. If there were any lingering remnants of the shadow, they had disappeared. The shadow might come back, though, he realized. It might come back even when Marvie was around. But he was stronger than it. He had proven it time and time again, so long as he had things that were worth fighting for.

As long as this girl was in his life, he did.

"Anywhere, Marvolene," Auden promised her. "Anywhere."

Chapter 17

The days turned into weeks and the weeks turned into months, but Marvie hardly noticed. She measured the passing of time, now, by the time she spent with Auden Frae. Moments with him, memories with him, things she knew she would never forget, tucked deep within her heart to think about on nights she couldn't sleep.

She was happy, so happy she didn't know what to do with the happiness she possessed. It felt as if she were holding a cup overflowing with wine, spilling over the sides of the glass and dripping down her arm. Marvie tried to share the happiness, but no matter what she did, she still held an overabundance of happiness, carried it with her every single place she went.

The best part about it was her happiness extended past Auden.

Well, mostly. Marvolene was well-aware that Auden was the main source of her happiness, but she took pride in the fact that he wasn't the *only* source of her happiness.

She had her aunt and uncle, like she had her entire life, yet her appreciation for the people who raised her had grown in the months since she had met Auden. Although Marvolene didn't know about his past completely, she knew that he hadn't come from a loving home like she had. It made her have a deeper understanding of just how lucky she was to have Sienna and Hewes. They had raised her as a daughter, given her an education, made her into who she was today. She would never fully comprehend how blessed she was, given that she would never see the alternative, but Marvie made a point to thank the gods for them every single night.

And on top of that, the inevitable conversation about university had come to pass.

Marvie had returned from whatever outing she had been on with Auden in the early evening. Auden had kissed her goodbye and she entered the apartment with a smile on her face. The smile quickly disappeared when she saw her aunt and uncle sitting at the kitchen table waiting for her.

"What's wrong?" Marvie asked immediately, shutting the door behind her and bracing herself for the worst. Hewes had lost his job. Sienna was sick. They were getting evicted. *No, Marvie*, she internally scolded herself. Since meeting Auden, she had tried not to jump to the worst possible conclusions. Marvie didn't understand just how much she did that until Auden pointed it out to her a few weeks ago, after she had asked him if he were leaving her when he didn't say "you're welcome" when she said "thank you".

"Nothing is wrong, Marvie," Sienna told her, amusement in her voice. She gestured at the empty chair at the table, the chair that had been Marvie's since she was just a little girl. "Take a seat. Your uncle and I have to talk to you about something."

This is it then, Marvie thought to herself as she moved across the room and slid into the seat. They were going to tell her that they disapproved of Auden and never wanted her to see him again. As much as she respected and loved Hewes and Sienna, she would defy them for the first time in her life if they said that. Not after a long argument that would probably end up in screaming and tears. *ENOUGH* her mind screamed at her. *Just wait and see what they have to say!*

"What is it?" Marvie asked carefully, trying not to reveal just how terrified she was. Her heart was pounding and she drummed her nails on the surface of the table quickly.

"Marvie, calm down," her uncle immediately said, not failing to notice her impending panic attack. "It's nothing bad, we just want to have a conversation with you."

That statement did everything but make her less anxious. "What is it?" Marvie repeated and this time, the shaking of her voice was loud and apparent.

"Well, Marvie," Sienna began, glancing at Hewes and then her, "we just wanted to talk to you about your plans for the future."

Marvie's breath caught and she swallowed back a massive lump in her throat as her chest seized up with the implications of the question. It had been months since they had attempted to have a conversation like this with her. They hadn't tried since she had met Auden, which had almost been eight months ago. In fact, it had been so long since they had asked her about the future, it hadn't occurred to her to fear another conversation like this one. She had been blind-sided, and she said a quick prayer to the gods not to burst into tears.

"What about them?" Marvie asked nervously.

Hewes reached across the table and set his hand on top of hers. "Marvie, dear, this isn't a confrontation. We just want to know what you're thinking. About university. About Tenir. About Auden. About any of it."

"Auden?" Marvie questioned. Of course, out of all the things he had listed, Auden was the one she focused on.

Her aunt and uncle exchanged another look before Hewes said, "Yes, Auden. We know he's a part of your life, Marvolene, and we want to talk about if he's going to be a part of your future."

"But that will come later," Sienna added. "First, we want to know what you've decided about university."

Marvie tried not to blink. Blinking to hold back tears was a habit she had since she was about three years old, as well as her mouth trembling to the point where she couldn't speak. The moment she did either of those things, her aunt and uncle would see her as a child and this would cease to be a conversation between three adults. Slowly, Marvie tried to speak, but Hewes interrupted her first.

"It's been months since you finished school. You've already missed the beginning of one term, which is fine. But the beginning of a new term is on the horizon. If you're going to university, now is the time to start making plans, which is something Sienna and I need to be involved in."

Marvie closed her eyes and took a long, deep breath through her nose, and released it through her mouth. She thought about Auden, as she always did when she felt anxious. She thought about his green eyes and his smile and all the beautiful words he had spoken to her. But more than that, Marvie thought about how she had changed, how she had grown in the last few months.

She didn't need to fear the future anymore.

Marvie opened them and said, "Aunt Sienna and Uncle Hewes, I love you both very much. But, I have to tell you, I'm just not ready to go to university yet."

Sienna tried to speak, but Marvie didn't stop. "It's not that I don't want to go. I do want to get a higher education and use it to do wonderful things in this world like the two of you. But I'm not ready now. I love my life so much. I love working at the bakery, saving up money for the future. I love spending time with my friends in this city and I love spending time with Auden. I'm not ready to let those things go just yet. Next year, I will start researching universities and deciding what I want to do with my life, but right now, I just want to live it."

Marvie exhaled when she finished and held her chin up a little higher. She hadn't rehearsed that, but the conviction in her voice was firm and true. Maybe her aunt and uncle would be furious and scream at her, but at the end of the day, the decisions she made about her life were hers and she would stand behind them.

Sienna and Hewes were silent for enough time that Marvie's confidence wavered. Their eyes met one another's and then landed back on Marvie, the expressions on their faces betraying nothing. Marvie wanted to scream at them to say something, but she held her ground, folding her hands in front of her and waiting. If Sienna and Hewes did scream at her, Marvie promised herself that she would walk out the door and go to Auden's apartment. That would be the consolation prize.

And then, Hewes beamed at her. Without a word, he stood up, crossed the distance between them, and embraced her. Marvie let out a long sigh of relief as she embraced him in return and then Sienna was behind her, embracing the two of them. Marvie couldn't help laughing, but it was a half-sob as she finally broke down into tears because the future was scary, uncertain, daunting, and real. It didn't escape her knowledge that one day, she would move out of this apartment that had been home for so long. She would move away from her beloved aunt and uncle. Yes, she would be moving with the love of her life, but there was a strange bittersweetness there, and right now, it was more bitter than anything.

"That's exactly what we wanted to hear, Marvolene," Sienna told her, her voice muffled because it was buried in Marvie's back. "We just want you to be happy and make your own decisions. We raised you to be an independent thinker and your answer shows us that we succeeded."

"Your timeline is your own, Marvie," Hewes added. "What Sienna and I did doesn't have to be what you do. We know that whatever it is you choose is your path, you will pursue it with dedication and determination. But right now, if you choose to enjoy your life and enjoy your youth, we wouldn't dream of stopping you."

Marvie tried to respond, but she couldn't find the words to convey just how much relief and hope their words brought to her. For months, she had been dreading this conversation, one she thought would be a confrontation. The idea of talking about the future kept her up at night, plagued her during the day, and this entire time, her aunt and uncle were ridiculously reasonable about the entire situation. She almost wished they would've had this encounter sooner; it would have certainly spared Marvie some sleepless nights.

They stood there for a long time and when it was over, they found comfort in the mundane, sitting at the table, playing cards and drinking Orinthian wine like they always did.

Things with her friends had been just as amazing as with her aunt and uncle. At least once a week, the entire group went out. Only now, Auden was there too, making the good nights even better. More often than not, it was Marvie, Auden, Isla, and Lee. And a lot of times, it was just Isla and Marvie, like the good old days.

They were making up for lost time. Though they had been out of each other's lives for months, they had fallen back into the role of being best friends so easily. They went shopping and drinking and dancing and shopping again. They gossiped about everything, laughed about the past, and basked in the fruits of friendship. Many nights, Marvie ended up at Isla's house and they stayed up late, talking about so many things before dawn came. In the same way she knew moments with Auden would never leave her, Marvie knew those midnight conversations with Isla were in her heart just the same way.

Marvie could look in the mirror and be happy with what she saw. And if she wasn't, she tried to remember how other people saw her. How they saw her smile and laugh, how maybe her beauty wasn't as profound on the outside, but it was obvious within.

And then, of course, there was Auden.

He was her whole world. Not a single bad thing had happened since that morning in the tearoom that Marvie still couldn't explain. But it didn't matter to her because he had promised, when the time was right, he would tell her everything, about his past, about the darkness in his eyes, about everything.

Marvie didn't push him and she never would. She was a very patient person and she reminded herself that they had the rest of their lives for Auden to tell her. Maybe he would tell her when they were twenty-five or maybe he would tell her when their skin was wrinkled. They would be together forever, and that made Marvie happier than the idea of discovering Auden's past ever would.

She saw him every day, and when they weren't together, she relived those moments in her head, closing her eyes and imagining them as clear as day. Half the time, she would go home to her aunt and uncle's, but most nights, she was at Auden's. Staying with him made the future that much more attainable, that future where she woke up next to him every morning in a house that was theirs.

Every memory she made with him clarified that future in her mind. She wasn't ready to tell him about that future yet, but for her, picturing the future was a daily ritual. It started with a cottage. She didn't know why she imagined a cottage, but there it was, a little one on the edge of a forest, close enough to a city to work, but far enough away that it was their world. She added furniture to the cottage and a portrait of them hanging on the wall. There were flowers she planted in the boxes outside the windows, maybe a dog or two they kept as pets.

The sun streamed through the windows of their future cottage and Marvie opened her eyes to see Auden in bed next to her, smiling because in this strange, puzzling world, they had found each other. They wouldn't speak because how could words possibly be enough for what was between them? No, they would just hold hands and wonder how something so perfect could be real in a world that could be so cruel.

In the vision, Isla and Lee came to visit and they drank wine outside as they watched the sun go down. Hewes and Sienna were there too; they moved to be closer to Auden and Marvie.

And then one day, the vision had a child, a child with blonde hair and green eyes, the perfect mix of their mother and father, the physical manifestation of the love that was between them. Marvie thought that there would never be anyone she loved more than Auden. Then there was that child in the vision, and Marvie's love for her child surpassed her love for Auden.

The vision came in flashes and she saw them growing old together, loving each other far past the time their youth had faded. But it didn't matter, because that old man would always be the boy in Tenir she fell in love with.

Marvie held onto that future so tightly, clinging to it with every fiber of her being. One day, when she gathered the courage, she would tell Auden about the future. But what was the point? She didn't need to tell Auden about that future because he was that future, and he would live all of it beside her.

Every time she thought she had a favorite memory of Auden, he surprised her. Her current favorite memory had happened only weeks ago, and she had no idea how it would possibly be replaced, but inevitably Auden would do something so perfect and sweet that even this memory would be topped.

She had stayed the night at his apartment again. At this point, her aunt and uncle knew that Marvie was doing so, but they didn't protest. In fact, they had suggested to Marvie that he come live in their apartment until the two of them eventually moved in together. Sienna and Hewes knew Auden didn't have any family, so they had made it their goal to become his family. One day, they really would be his family, when Marvie married him and became Marvolene Frae. Sienna and Hewes would almost be another set of parents to him, by Orinthian law.

Marvolene had opened her eyes and blinked a few times, trying to remember where she was. She felt a warm pair of arms around her and a heavy breathing in her ears and she immediately was overcome by waves of elation as she turned around in the bed, looking up at him.

Auden was already awake, eyes half opened, a smile on his face. "Hello," he said softly.

"Hello, my love," Marvie replied, but she switched to Auntican.

Auden furrowed his brow. "What did you say?" he asked.

Marvie laughed. It was still amusing to her that Auden didn't know Auntican. Of course, most citizens in Orinth hadn't bothered to learn the language of their neighboring country. Marvie and Auden, however, had talked it through and the plan to move back to Auntica was almost definite. If Auden was to live and work in her home country, he would have to learn the language at some point. So, for the last few weeks, Marvie had begun teaching him, but Auden was as Orinthian as one could get. Auden had revealed nothing of his past, but it was fair to assume there wasn't a drop of Auntican blood in this boy.

"Auden, that was an incredibly simple phrase. Have you retained nothing?" she asked exasperatedly.

Auden flicked her across the nose and she feigned a gasp of pain. "I'm trying my best," he told her stubbornly. "Here's one." Auden cleared his throat and spoke in Auntican, his Orinthian accent so thick the words were barely audible. "The sky is blue."

"You knew "the sky was blue", but you don't know the word for "hello"?" Marvie asked skeptically.

Auden tried to glare at her but had already begun to laugh. "Here's a deal for you: I will master Auntican if you learn to swim."

Marvie snorted and then, in clear Auntican, she answered, "I will learn to swim the day you ask me to marry you."

Auden's laughter disappeared. "What did you say?" he asked, his tone serious.

Marvie giggled and spoke again in her language. "I take it back. I will learn to swim the day we stand in a temple and have our love recognized by the Orinthian officials. Not a moment before then."

"Marvie," Auden pleaded, and she laughed again.

Auden rolled his eyes and said, "You being able to say things to me I can't understand is incentive enough for me to be fluent in Auntican by the month's end." And then he kissed her.

The kiss lasted for a long time, and even though it was familiar, Marvie's heart still pounded when he drew back. She couldn't help but give a giddy smile as she brushed a stray curl out of his face. She loved the way Auden looked in the morning, his curls matted and messy, his eyes droopy with sleep. She couldn't wait to wake up to that for the rest of her life.

"I can't believe I didn't know you a year ago, Marvolene," Auden whispered.

"What do you mean?" Marvie asked, resting her head against his chest. He was so warm that she snuggled even closer.

"It feels like I've known you forever," he murmured. "I can't believe there was a time in my life I was just walking around the world, not knowing that somewhere, you existed."

"I know what you mean," Marvie agreed. "It must have been hard to exist without me." And she started to laugh, but Auden was nodding, expression completely serious.

"It really was," he whispered. "I never want to do that again."

"Do what again?"

"Exist without you. Be a living, breathing, human being who has to be in this world without you to keep me sane."

Marvie stopped laughing. The conversation had taken on a serious undertone she hadn't been expecting. She considered his words, considered that at one point, she had been a living, human person without Auden in her life. She had been completely unaware that the person she would fall so desperately in love with existed. She woke up every morning and went to bed every night, totally clueless to his presence. It was strange.

The strangeness of it slowly transferred into intense joy and then into ecstasy as Marvie slowly came to a realization. She pulled back from him until they were side by side, her head resting on the pillow, looking into his eyes.

"We never have to be alone again," she whispered.

Auden raised an eyebrow. "What do you mean?"

"What you're talking about? You living without me, me living without you? It never has to happen again. I'll never have to wake up wondering if I'm going to be alone for the rest of my life and neither will you. If something bad happens, I'll never have to worry about facing it alone, because I'll be able to come home to you and talk to you about it. When we come to these huge, momentous life decisions, they won't just be my decision, or your decision; they will be our decisions." Marvie beamed at him. "Isn't that something? We'll never have to decide anything on our own again."

Auden didn't respond, just stared at her for a long time expressionless. Marvie's smile faded. "What?" she asked. "Did I say something wrong?"

"No," Auden whispered. "I just want to know what in the world I did to deserve someone like you."

Marvie buried her face in her hands. "Auden," she mumbled, and heat crept into her cheeks. How was it, after everything they had shared, she could still be embarrassed? Still, she was blushing hard.

Auden removed her hands from her face and pressed his lips against hers softly before pulling back. "I'm serious," he insisted. "I've never done anything good in my life before." Marvie tried to protest, but he kept going. "Never. And the gods still decided to put Marvolene Pere in my world." He shook his head in disbelief. "I can't fathom it."

"Auden…"

"You want to know something?" he interrupted her.

"What?"

Auden grasped her hands in his own. "I can't wait to make every single decision with you. Big ones, small ones, insignificant ones, terrifying ones. I am so excited to make them with you every day for the rest of my life."

Marvie's heart bubbled over and warmth filled her entire body as she tore her eyes from his, for fear that she would cry tears of joy from those words. "Every decision," she repeated.

"We'll be at a tavern and I'll say 'Marvie, should I get Orinthian wine or Auntican ale?'"

Marvie scoffed. "That's a very obvious answer, Auden."

Auden grinned. "Yeah, yeah."

"I can't wait to help you make the most important decision of your life," Marvie told him.

"What would that be?" he asked.

"Olga or Marvolene?"

Auden snickered. "The most difficult decision for my life, for certain," he said with mock seriousness.

Marvie laughed and Auden dropped the subject, asking her what she wanted to do for the day, but his words lingered in her heart and mind and soul.

I can't wait to make every single decision with you.

Forever was a stupid, silly word. Forever was a myth they put in stories to give people unrealistic expectations of love. Marvie had never believed in forever, never allowed herself to believe in such a ridiculous concept. Forever didn't exist because one day, they would die and pass onto the next phase of existence, the Beyond or something else. Their time in this life, the events that had seemed so important, the memories that had been so real; all of it would fade into nothingness. Life would go on and new people would inhabit their world and one day, no one would remember a girl named Marvolene Pere.

She had always thought that and then she had met Auden.

Marvie believed in forever because she was going to be with Auden Frae forever.

They would die in this world, yes, but their love was so strong they would find each other in the next lifetime and the next and the next and if they eventually drifted to the Beyond, they would find each other there too.

I can't wait to make every single decision with you.

Marvie wanted to add to it.

I can't wait to make every decision with you, forever, in this lifetime and the next. Into the Beyond, into eternity.

Forever.

Marvolene Pere and Auden Frae.

Forever.

Chapter 18

It was one of those moments when Marvie was able to remove herself entirely and have a moment of crystal clarity that she was experiencing something so perfect. And once she had that realization, she returned to the moment and tried to cherish every detail.

She was sitting at the dining room table of her childhood home, a glass of wine in her hand. Auden sat across from her, with her aunt and uncle on either side of them. They were all drinking something, Auden and Sienna deciding on ale while Hewes drank Orinthian wine like Marvie. The four of them were all talking at once.

It had been Hewes who suggested they play a game of cards after Sienna had made them a feast for dinner.

Two hours had passed since that suggestion and the game hadn't ended.

"You're cheating!" Sienna shouted at Auden, but there was a wide grin on her face as she pressed her cards up to her chest.

Auden stared at her in disbelief. "How?" he asked, trying and failing to keep a straight face.

"You saw my hand!"

"I did not!" Auden exclaimed, his mouth open wide, as if he were shocked at the suggestion. "Besides, it's not my fault if you keep flashing me your hand," he added with a shrug.

Sienna gaped at him. "So you DID see it!"

Auden glanced at Marvie and then at Sienna before he started laughing. "Well, maybe," he admitted and then looked at Hewes. "In my defense, she pretty much showed them to me."

Hewes snorted. "She's been doing that since the first time I played cards with her, what, twenty-five years ago?"

"I do not!" Sienna defended herself, but her giggling in between words seemed to convey the truth. She shot a desperate look to Marvie. "Marvolene, you have to defend me. They're teaming up on me!"

Marvie held her hands up in surrender. "Don't bring me into this," she pleaded before smiling at Auden, who beamed back at her.

They were playing a classic Orinthian card game, one Marvie had known for her entire life. It had never had a name and the concept was quite complicated, with pairs, runs, drawing, discarding, and several other moves. All four of them were familiar with the game. They were on almost the eleventh round and it was currently a tie for first between Marvie, Auden, and Hewes, with Sienna trailing behind. Marvie couldn't foresee the game concluding anytime soon, if Sienna had any say in the matter.

"You better be careful, Auden," Hewes told him. "Sienna has an extremely long memory, *especially* when it comes to card games."

Auden's eyes widened and he turned his cards around so they were facing Sienna. "Here you go," he said hurriedly.

Sienna threw her head back and laughed as she swatted his hands away. "Oh Auden, dear, you know I'm only teasing you," and then they were all laughing again.

Marvie looked at each of their smiling faces and tried to memorize them, paint them in a picture she could look at forever. She tried to memorize the intense joy within her chest, the feeling that she might explode with elation because she was with her family. Sienna and Hewes, of course, but more than them, Auden.

One day, she would leave this place, leave Sienna and Hewes.

The boy sitting across from her, grinning as he ran a hand through his black hair was more than her family. He was her future, and Marvie's ecstasy only grew when she thought of the countless nights like these that were to come. Right now, with Sienna and Hewes, but maybe someday, they would be sitting around a table with children of their own, laughing so hard that tears ran down their faces.

Even though she knew nights like this one would be frequent, she savored this moment like a priceless wine, considering herself lucky she even got one sip of it.

An hour or so later, when the game couldn't continue because of the laughter and the tantrums, Sienna stood up and announced, "I think it's time for dessert!" She collected a few of their empty dishes.

Hewes cheered loudly and threw his cards down on the table. "Good. I'm not sure I can take much more of this," he said, shooting Auden a smile.

Marvie didn't think she knew a happiness more profound than seeing her uncle get along with her lover. As Auden smiled back at Hewes, that happiness only grew.

Sienna cleared her throat, putting her hands on Marvie's shoulders. "Would you mind helping your dear old aunt in the kitchen, Marvolene?"

Marvie stood up and took ahold of Sienna's arm. "Of course, my dear old aunt. Come on, let me help you wobble your way out there."

Hewes and Auden chuckled as Sienna smacked her in the arm, but together they left the dining room. Marvie reached for the ice box, but Sienna continued walking towards the stairs that led to their rooms. "Where are we going?" Marvie asked her aunt, glancing at where the pies sat on the kitchen counter. She could still see her uncle and Auden sitting at the table, as a wall partially separated the kitchen and dining room.

Sienna sat down on one of the steps and patted the space next to her. "Sit down, Marvie," Sienna said softly. Gone was the laughter of the card game, replaced by something different. Marvie sat down slowly and picked up her aunt's hand.

"What is it, Sienna?" she asked.

Her aunt smiled at her, and Marvie realized there were tears behind her eyes. Marvie squeezed her hands tighter. "What's wrong?"

Sienna shook her head. "Nothing, Marvolene," she whispered. "Absolutely nothing. I just wanted to tell you something is all." She leaned over until her head was resting against Marvie's shoulder.

"Am I in trouble?" Marvie asked with a shaky laugh.

"Oh no, never," Sienna snorted, before she took a deep breath. "Well...I know we don't talk about your parents very often, Marvie, almost never. Gods rest their souls, I miss them! I miss your mother especially, Marvie. My sister, Alissya Lois. But your father too, Tomas Pere. It's been so long since they were alive, but sometimes, when the light hits you just right, I see your mother."

Tears started to sting Marvie's own vision as she thought of the parents she had never known. They had died when she was only a toddler; she didn't even have a picture of them in her mind. To Marvie, her mother and father were Sienna and Hewes; those were the people who had raised her, made her into the person she was today. "Why are you telling me this, Sienna?" Marvie asked, resting her head on Sienna's shoulder.

"Because I know they would be proud of you," Sienna told her. "They would be so proud of how you're choosing your own path, seeking out happiness and grabbing it by the collar. I know, Marvie, that they are looking down upon you with smiles on their faces because of the smile on yours."

The tears spilled out of her eyes, rolling down her face. Marvie knew Sienna's face matched her own. She squeezed her aunt's hands once more. "Well, I'm glad to hear that," she replied gently. "But if that's true, they know how much of that they owe to you and Uncle Hewes...everything. They...I...I owe everything to you."

"Oh Marvie," Sienna said, her voice choking up as she turned and wrapped her arms around Marvie' body.

She embraced her aunt in return and let out a small sob into her shoulder. When they pulled apart, Marvie wiped her tears with the back of her hand and glared at her aunt. "You're getting sentimental on me, Aunt Sienna."

Sienna didn't bother trying to wipe her own tears. Instead, she asked, "You remember all that time ago when I asked you if you were happy?"

Marvie nodded. It had been almost ten months ago, the very same day she met Auden in The Wooden Barrel. How ironic was that? It was as if the gods knew exactly when she needed him. Marvie had never really believed in the gods, but meeting Auden had not been a coincidence. Maybe there was truly something bigger than the two of them going on here. She would ponder the concept later.

"You were lying to me when you said yes, weren't you?"

Marvie chuckled but nodded. "Apparently I didn't do a very good job of it," she admitted.

Sienna waved her off before asking, "And now?"

"Now what?"

Sienna leaned forward and kissed her niece on the forehead. "Are you happy, Marvolene?"

Marvie smiled widely and a few more tears spilled onto her cheeks. "Sienna," she told her, "I don't think I could possibly be happier," and then, they embraced again.

Sienna finally pulled back, burying her face into her hands and mumbling, "I am getting too sentimental."

Marvie laughed. "I think I am too. Come on, let's go get those pies, and definitely some more wine."

Sienna gestured at her to go ahead. "I need a few minutes to collect myself before I return out there, dear. You go ahead and give them the pies."

Marvie kissed her aunt on the top of the head before she started back towards the kitchen. The conversation with her aunt had blindsided her, but in a way, it touched her. Maybe her birthparents really were watching over her from the Beyond, and maybe they really were proud of her. Alissya Lois and Tomas Pere, her mother and father. She wished she could've met them, wished they could've met Auden.

Strangely enough, Marvie had a feeling they would've been proud of him too.

Marvie turned the corner to enter the kitchen before stopping as she heard the sound of Auden and Hewes' voices coming from the dining room. She was hidden behind the wall and she waited there, as a part of her was curious to see what kind of things Auden and her uncle talked about. There was never a moment in her life where she was afraid to leave Auden alone with her friends or family. The previous week, she and Isla had gone shopping while Auden and Lee sat in a tavern nearby. When they returned, Auden and Lee were in a deep discussion about the economic effects of the war with the Wilds. Isla had met Marvie's gaze and rolled her eyes, but Marvie could tell her friend was just as happy to see their two loves bonding.

So, Marvie pressed herself against the wall and listened. She heard Auden clear his throat.

"Mr. Courtright, I know Marvie's father passed away when she was only little. Since that is the case, and you're the one who raised her, I figure you're the one I should tell my intentions."

Marvie clapped a hand over her mouth to keep from screaming or crying or both. She stayed absolutely still, her muscles tense and frozen, waiting to see what her uncle would say in reply.

"And what are those intentions, Mr. Frae?" Hewes asked in reply.

Marvie's entire body had gone from calm to trembling in the span of ten seconds. The time in which it took Auden to answer seemed like an eternity, the silence stretching out tortuously long. Marvie's hands were shaking beyond reason and her knees were trembling as well; she could hardly stand upright with the anticipation that wracked through her, awaiting Auden's response.

"I intend to marry your niece, Mr. Courtright," Auden said, his voice quivering just slightly.

Marvie leaned her head back until it touched the wall and slid down until she was sitting on the floor. She pressed her hands against her face and another round of tears began because Auden was going to marry her. Marvie wanted to sob; she wanted to scream. She wanted to leap into the air and dance around the room and then fall to the ground weeping. More than anything, she wanted to charge into the next room and tackle Auden with an embrace.

Auden didn't stop with the first statement. He continued, "I'm in love with her and I would do anything to protect her. I've been saving money for a long time and I have enough to provide for us. I'm asking for your blessing. It would mean the world to me...us."

If waiting for Auden to state his intentions had taken forever, awaiting her uncle's reply took a dozen eternities.

And then her uncle Hewes spoke, words she knew would seal her future, seal the fate that she was now convinced the gods had planned for her. "I was wondering when you were going to ask me this Auden. And it fills my heart with joy that you have."

Marvie silently sobbed harder into her trembling hands. The vision of her cottage, no, their cottage on the edge of the forest grew clearer. She saw the two of them in a temple, professing their love to one another. She felt the phantom presence of a ring on her finger, the ghost of Auden's hands clasping her own as they sealed their matrimony with a kiss. She could almost hear the cheers of their friends and family as Marvolene Pere became Marvolene Frae, the name she would carry to her grave.

"You're both young, but I've never seen such passion before. Of course you have my blessing. I never had a daughter of my own, but I was lucky enough to raise Marvie. She is a wonderful, special girl and I can't imagine a better man for her than you."

Sienna and Hewes sending them off with their blessing. Riding across Auntica, but taking a trip first, to Grady, to Nagaye, to all the places they had talked about. Laying on the beach looking up at the stars, dancing on the sand, kissing under the light of the moon. Then to the cottage that awaited them in Auntica. At first, Marvie saw just the two of them, and then, there were others. Children with blonde hair and blue eyes, children with black curls and green eyes, running in their front yard. She saw them taking those children to all the places they loved, but even more than that, nurturing them with the love that was theirs.

Marvie saw the future and it was so close that she could almost reach out and touch it. She wanted to. She wanted to reach out and grab that future by its collar, just like her happiness. Auden was doing that for them in asking for her aunt and uncle's blessing of their marriage.

Marvie smiled into her hands that were now wet with her tears. She was going to marry Auden Frae.

"You...you're serious?" Auden asked her uncle and his voice was so uncertain that it took everything in Marvie's willpower not to dart out from the wall and kiss him just to provide him with reassurance.

She heard her uncle stand up and she could almost imagine him shaking Auden's hand. "I'm serious. You have my blessing. It might be worth a conversation with Marvie's aunt, but I have a feeling she'll bestow her blessing upon the two of you as well. Tell me, Auden, when do you plan to ask my niece?"

Auden exhaled and Marvie could hear the relief. She closed her eyes and imagined the grin that was spreading slowly across his face. "I'm not sure yet. I want to find a place that is really special. Marvie deserves all that and more."

"Oh yes," Hewes agreed. "Do you have enough money for the wedding?"

"I have a lot saved," Auden replied.

"Well, Sienna and I would be happy to contribute. Gods, our niece is getting married. I can scarcely believe it." Her uncle sighed softly. "We'll miss her desperately, of course."

"I don't know where we'll go yet, Mr. Courtright. But I promise you I'm going to take good care of Marvie. And I have a pretty good feeling she'll take care of me, too."

Marvie physically couldn't bear it anymore; she was either going to burst out from her hiding spot or reveal her location by squealing into her hands. She did neither; she jumped to her feet and darted past her aunt and up to her room. She opened the door and shut it behind her, sliding down once more until her knees were hugging her chest and she pressed her face against her hands once more.

Marvie laughed. She laughed and then she sobbed because she was so damn happy.

Then, she whispered, her voice quiet and muffled.

"I never really believed in you before; I'm sorry for that. It might speak poorly of me that something wonderful had to happen in my life for me to acknowledge that you exist. But this...him...I just know now. You're there because you must be. This can't be a coincidence. Loving him can't be an accident. I think...I think he was made for me. Maybe there is some sort of divine plan, because he came into my life exactly when I needed him to, and honestly, I think I did the same for him. What I'm struggling to say is thank you. Thank you, gods, for Auden Frae. Thank you for the boy who's going to marry me."

At the last word, she broke down into sobs again, but they were entirely joyful. For one minute, she allowed herself tears of joy on the floor before she stood up, stumbling to the mirror and wiping them away. She had to gather herself, pretend that she hadn't heard what she had heard. When Auden asked her to marry him, she would act surprised and do that face that everyone did when they were proposed to. She would clap her hands over her mouth before tearfully nodding and embracing him.

One day, years from now, she would tell him that she had heard the conversation with her uncle, and that it had brought her an ecstasy unlike anything she had ever known. But tonight, she would return downstairs and pretend like everything was normal, when deep inside her, she was grabbing for their future with everything she was.

Chapter 19

Auden had thought of everything.

It had been months since he had walked away from Chyles in that tavern, months since there had been even a hint of the shadow. It had been a few weeks since he had asked her aunt and uncle for their permission to marry Marvie. In between then and now, he had pondered and prayed and practiced, and tonight was the night it would happen. As he held Marvie's hand, navigating through the crowded streets, he went over it all in his mind.

A quiet place for them to talk had always been what he lacked when trying to tell her the truth before, or at least that was what Auden told himself. If he only had the right environment, the right moment, he could comfortably tell her about the shadow, the alley, and his past. The fear that she would hate him and cast him away was still there, but it had lessened in the last couple of months. He had a feeling that Marvolene needed him as much as he needed her. Maybe she would require a few days to adjust to the harsh realities of his past, but Auden didn't think she would leave.

Once he told her, he was more than ready to get down on his knees and swear that he was done with the shadow, had been done with it from the first moment they met. He would do anything to keep her trust, make her believe that he was still the same person she had fallen in love with, mostly because he was.

Auden had found a place in Tenir they hadn't gone yet, which at this point, was quite a feat. He had to believe they had been to every tavern in this city, had graced every sort of entertaining place they could find. Yet, they weren't bored of them, because everything was exciting when they were together. A few days ago, under the recommendation of Kalen, Auden had made reservations at a restaurant on a rooftop. There weren't many availabilities because of the exclusivity of the place, but he was able to secure a table for them. For Auden, it meant a quiet spot he could tell Marvolene the truth about himself.

Outside of his prepared speech of honesty, they would be celebrating exactly one year together.

It baffled him. Almost one year ago, Marvie had walked into The Wooden Barrel and changed his life forever. No, changed seemed too simple a word to describe what Marvie had done. Marvie hadn't changed his life; she had given him life. She had given him a purpose, a reason for existing, a face to picture the moment his eyes opened, a face to imagine right before he went to sleep. Marvie had given him something more valuable than anything he had ever possessed: love.

And yet, strangely, it didn't feel like a year. It felt like it was only days ago that she stumbled into the shop and stared at him like she was seeing a ghost. On the other hand, it was an eternity ago because it felt like he had known Marvie his entire life, not just one single year. He was convinced he had known her even before this life and their souls recognized one another from lives of the past.

If the rest of the years of his life contained even half as much joy as the year with her had brought him, he would consider himself a lucky man.

As he walked with her, their hands woven, he felt a weight in his pocket. He tried not to focus on the weight and focus instead on Marvie as she talked about what she and Isla had done during the day, but he couldn't. His attention stayed with the weight in his pocket.

That was the other goal for the night: ask Marvie to marry him.

Sienna and Hewes had given him their blessing. Auden had bought the ring with his own money from a store in the harbor district. He had practiced his speech a thousand times in the mirror of his apartment, but more than any of that, he knew that this was the girl that he intended to spend forever with. That knowledge alone was enough to prepare him for this night.

They were almost to the rooftop, weaving in and out of big groups of people between the tall brick buildings. There was some sort of holiday tomorrow that Auden wasn't aware of, but apparently, the rest of the city was, because the streets were filled with people. Music and laughter spilled out of every place they passed and there were even some celebrations on the cobblestones. Marvie yelled over the crowd, "Are we almost there?"

Auden observed the street they were on and replied, "A few more minutes, love."

"Where are we going?" she asked in reply, swinging his hand back and forth. It was at least the tenth time she had asked the question because he refused to tell her where they were celebrating their one year together. Marvie, being Marvie, had not stopped pestering him since finding out about a surprise.

Auden rolled his eyes at her, smiling. "It's a surprise," he repeated his words once more.

"Why don't you tell me!" she exclaimed, throwing her head back with a laugh, blonde hair whipping against her face. It was almost as if Marvie knew something special was going to happen that night; she had dressed like a goddess. She wore a light blue dress that perfectly matched her eyes. It was sleeveless and stopped just above her knees. Part of her hair was piled on the top of her head, and the other half was down and curly. But, as always, it was the smile on her face that Auden couldn't stop staring at.

"Because," Auden said, pulling her closer and pressing a kiss to the side of her head, "it wouldn't be a surprise if I told you."

Marvie chuckled in response, squeezing his hand tight.

They had about five more minutes before they would reach the building whose roof housed the restaurant. That left five minutes for Auden to rehearse his speeches before he had to make them to Marvie.

Auden took a deep breath and thought of the words he had to say.

The first time I told you that I loved you, I said that words are a pathetic attempt to express what I feel for you. That statement seems even more relevant in lieu of what I'm about to ask you. Yet words are the only thing I know how to use. I wish I knew how to sing or dance or perform some grand gesture so that you would know how much you mean to me. Alas, I only have my humble words. Despite that, I will try to use them to ask you what I have wanted to ask you from the first day.

There is no Auden Frae without Marvolene Pere. You might ask, what about all that time before we knew each other? The sentiment holds true. I was only half myself without you, Marvie. I only lived half a life until I saw your face. And if I ever had to live without you again, I could never be whole. Luckily for us, we don't have to worry about existence without one another.

I love you and you love me. Your family knows it. Our friends know it. Anyone who lays eyes on us knows it, and sometimes, I think the gods themselves know it. I guess the only thing we have to do now is get it recognized by Orinth. Let the whole country know that you and I are together and will remain that way until death.

But there's a part of me that knows, Marvie, we'll be together beyond death. We'll be together in every lifetime, in every universe, in every realm. Wherever we are, we will find one another. Wherever I am living a half-life, you will find me and make me whole once again.

So, marry me, Marvolene Pere. I'm asking you to marry me. Will you marry me?

Tears stung behind his eyes as he looked over at Marvie, the words fading away. She glanced around at their surroundings with a resting smile on her face, as if she were anticipating the happiness that was waiting for them that night. He was ready, so ready to say all of it. He had to hold himself back from stopping Marvie on the street, dropping to his knees, and saying it right then and there. Forget the rooftop overlooking Tenir, forget the fancy food and drinks. So much of their love happened in these city streets; wouldn't that be special too?

It would be, but before he could say those words, he had to say the other ones.

Auden's joy faded but only slightly as he rehearsed them once more.

I have given all of myself to you but one part, Marvie. The past. I don't want to do it. My past is ugly and it might be a blemish on our love. But someone once told me that honesty is the foundation of any relationship and I want to be with you forever. So, I'm giving you all of me, even the parts I don't like.

He stopped himself. Auden knew what he was going to say; he didn't need to run through it again and dampen his own mood. When the time was right, the words would come to him and whatever happened, happened.

Auden made a promise to himself; he wouldn't ask her to marry him until she knew about his past.

If he did propose and Marvie said yes, he would be selfish. He would continue to push off telling her until they were standing in a temple and the wheels were already in motion. The excuses would begin. He could almost hear himself making them now. *I can't tell Marvie right now; we're on our wedding trip! We're happy! It would dampen the mood. I will wait to tell her when we return.* And then, *Now is not the right time; we just bought our own apartment together. It would be miserable if I told her while we're trying to settle in. There will be a better time.* On and on until there was no good time to tell her and the burden of his own secret would weigh so heavily upon him that he would crumble.

To avoid that, he planned to tell her before asking her to marry him. If she ran away, then he didn't have to worry about the proposal. And if she stayed, then the future belonged to them.

When Auden saw the building for which they were bound, he exhaled slightly. Right. It was time. He would wait until they were seated on the roof at their table and then tell her. Well, no, better wait to get drinks. Maybe the news would be easier to bear if they both had wine in them. At that point, he might as well wait until the food was served; Marvie wouldn't be hungry after hearing about his past. So they would sit down, have drinks and food, and then he would tell her. Well, no, what if Marvie threw up after hearing about how he murdered a boy at the tender age of fourteen? He would give her stomach some time to settle and *then* he would tell her.

Auden shook all the thoughts away and tried to be in the moment. He would enjoy every second with her until he had to tell her. If Marvie ran away after hearing the truth about him, then that meant this night was their last night. He would spend his time cherishing every minute.

Auden pointed to the base of the stairs at the side of the building, the entrance to the rooftop. He let go of Marvie's hand and wrapped his arms around her waist. "Here we are," he whispered, kissing her once more.

Marvie looked at him and then at the stairs. He watched her eyes follow the stairs up to the roof, where the tables with smiling patrons could be seen. She looked back at him, the corners of her mouth beginning to upturn. "Oh, Auden," she said softly and he grinned at her.

They were ushered up the stairs and seated at a table right on the edge of the roof. The view was even more stunning than Auden could've imagined. He could see the familiar buildings and the sea on the horizon, the water a hazy orange in the light of the setting sun. A group of musicians were playing soft, instrumental music on the roof, serenading the other five or six tables scattered about the place. In other words, the perfect place to celebrate a perfect year.

Auden pulled a chair out for Marvolene and made a grand gesture at her to sit down. She giggled, pressing a hand to her lips, before taking a seat. Auden took his own as Orinthian wine was brought out. A waiter poured them each a glass, explaining that they would be served various dishes of Orinthian cuisine that was specially curated by expert chefs. Auden tried to listen to the man, but he was too busy staring at Marvie nodding animatedly, obviously thrilled with the meal that was about to commence. She thanked the waiter profusely as he went to bring them the first course.

Marvie's gaze snapped over to him and she shook her head. "I can't believe you did this." She gestured at the scene around them: the cityscape, the sea, the music, the other couples. The table with their glasses of wine also contained a single candle, flickering gently.

Auden shrugged, but he couldn't help smiling. "Believe it or not, it's true."

Marvie opened her mouth and then closed it. "I'm glad you kept it a surprise. Because while I'm trying to keep my expression in check, I am absolutely shocked and excited, but above all, reminded that you are the most amazing man I have ever met," she admitted.

"I bet that's a pretty easy claim to make when I take you to a place that's giving you endless wine and food."

Marvie grinned sheepishly. "It doesn't hurt."

Auden leaned forward and grasped her hands. She squeezed them in return as he opened his mouth to speak. *Right now,* his mind suddenly told him, *tell her right now and you won't have to spend the rest of the night in anticipation.*

But he didn't. Auden reminded himself that this could possibly be the last few moments he had with her. So he took her in once more, as if he were seeing her for the first time and hadn't seen her every day for the last year. Her smooth, soft skin, dazzling blue eyes made even more vivid by her blue dress, her flowing blonde hair, her perfect lips and every other feature that made her so attractive. And yet, not one of them compared to what he knew was on the inside. Marvie's kindness, her love, her sense of humor, her imagination, and her ability to see the good, to create good, in everyone she came across. None more than Auden himself.

"Do you know why we're here?" he asked her softly. Music and laughter could still be heard, but per Auden's plan, the roof was mostly quiet and peaceful.

Marvie pretended to ponder. "Well, it seems to me that around this time last year, a clumsy nitwit stumbled into that store you work at."

Auden started laughing before he could give her a disapproving look. He rolled his eyes. "Marvolene."

She grinned at him. "What!" she exclaimed. "You know I'm not wrong!"

"I would never describe you as a clumsy nitwit."

"Let me try again." Marvie stroked her chin as if in deep thought. "Around this time last year, you met the love of your life, the woman you want to spent forever with: Olga, owner of the infamous Olga's Bakery. Your life hasn't been the same since."

Auden almost choked on the wine he was attempting to sip and Marvie's face was pressed in her hands as she tried to contain herself. When they finally recovered, Marvie leaned across the table and kissed him on the lips. "A year ago today," she whispered, "my life changed in the most wonderful and extraordinary way. I don't know where I would be without you and I am so happy that I never have to find out."

Auden basked in the sensation of the flush of love he had for her, the feeling of her lips against his. Memorizing it like it was the last time, in case she didn't take the news about his past well. He wished he could freeze her staring at him, the city of Tenir and the sea behind her. He wished he could bring in a portrait artist to capture the moment so he could see her like this forever. Auden made a silent promise to himself that every day on their anniversary, they would come to this very spot.

"Wonderful," Auden replied, "You, this, all of it."

Marvie smiled at the ground and back up at him.

The waiter interrupted the moment when he brought a plate of fruit and for the next hour, they feasted like they never had before. Every time they finished one course, there was another delectable cuisine in front of them. The conversation shifted solely to talking about the food, debating what they liked best and how they would try to recreate it. The wine didn't stop coming and at three glasses, Auden stopped himself. If they were going to have this discussion tonight, he would need to have a clear head. But Marvie kept going because, as he well knew, there was really nothing in the world she liked better than Orinthian wine.

He asked her, somewhere in the middle of it, "If you had the choice between me and Orinthian wine, which would you choose?"

Marvie burst into laughter. "I am not answering that."

He pressed her. "Come on. If you stay with me, you can never drink Orinthian wine again. But if you choose the wine, I'm gone. Which do you like better?"

Marvie buried her face into her hands. "The two things I love most in the world pitted against one another. Why would you even make me consider it? Well, I hope you think of me when you drink Orinthian wine, Auden, because you know I'm not choosing you."

Auden clutched at his heart overdramatically. "Ouch."

Marvie shrugged. "Don't ask questions you don't want the answer to." She grabbed his hand and kissed it. "Thankfully, I'll never have to make that choice. I'll get Orinthian wine and Auden Frae for the rest of my life, best enjoyed together, of course."

They eventually ate the last course, a chocolate cream sauce slathered onto different berries. Auden let Marvolene eat most of it, as his stomach could handle no more. His heart had begun to pound in his chest because everything he waited for was past. They had drunk, they had eaten, they had laughed. He had ample time to cherish their last few moments, if fate decided they were to be their last. It was time to tell Marvolene the truth and pray to the gods she still wanted him afterwards.

Swirling her wine in the glass as he opened his mouth to speak, Marvie looked up at him, smiling, cutting him off before he had the chance.

"This is incredible," she said, taking a long sip of her drink. "I truly can't understand how you found this place."

Auden exhaled slightly. Well, he had said he would give their stomachs a chance to settle. Let this conversation play out and then he would tell her about the shadow. He shrugged, mustering a grin despite his ever-growing anxiety that tonight might be the end. "I have my ways."

"I love you," she told him.

The smile on his face was genuine. "I love you too. More than anything."

She shook her head. "Not more than I love you. I'm serious."

Will you love me after you know the truth? Auden ignored the question as he rolled his eyes and laughed. "You're so stubborn, Marvolene. Just let me tell you I love you more."

"Never. Not in a million years."

Auden laughed. He couldn't count the number of times they had this exchange over the last year. Marvolene loved to insist she loved him more, and most of the time, he let her. A few of what he thought were good-natured arguments would turn brutal quite quickly, sometimes ending with Marvie screaming *I LOVE YOU MORE DAMN IT* at him. He had learned his lesson.

"Okay, Marvolene," he said, picking up his nearly empty glass. "Whatever you say."

For a few peaceful minutes, they listened to the music and enjoyed the scene in silence. Eventually the waiter returned with the bill for the meal and Auden knew that their time with one another was running out. Soon another couple would take this table and create their own memories. He had to tell her and he had to tell her now.

"It's hard to beat Orinthian wine," Auden said, not sure why those words in particular came out, instead of *Marvie, I possess a dark power that I used to kill another boy when I was fourteen.*

"You can say that again," Marvie replied, finishing off her glass. "This is the nectar of the gods."

"I'm sad the night is ending," Auden told her, and it wasn't a lie. By 'the night', he meant 'the time he allotted himself to not tell her the truth'. That time was coming to an end and he just needed to get it over with.

"I'm not," Marvie said curtly, and for a moment, Auden was stunned. She broke into a grin. "Why would I be sad that tonight is ending when I know we have a hundred, no, a thousand more like it that we get to experience?"

Auden breathed a sigh of relief. "What do you mean?"

"I mean for the rest of our lives, we have time to have these special nights, create these memories. This was fun, Auden, and in ten years, when we sit on a roof and eat dinner, drink, and laugh, it'll be fun then. The future, Auden," Marvie whispered, and for a moment, her eyes looked glassy. "The future is ours."

Auden leaned across the table, picking up her hands once more. "What do you see when you think of our future?"

Marvie raised both eyebrows. "Honestly?"

He nodded.

"I see a cottage."

"A cottage?"

Marvie nodded, her eyes taking on a faraway look. She had transported to wherever the cottage was, leaving Auden on the rooftop in Tenir by himself. He closed his eyes and tried to go to the cottage with her. "I see us in a cottage on the edge of a forest, with no one else around for miles. I used to think I wanted to settle in a city, that I needed to be near people to be happy. Now, I realize I just need to be with you, wherever that may be. For me, it's a cottage on the edge of forest." She sighed dreamily.

Auden could see it as clear as day, the cottage that she spoke of. He saw them as they were right now, teenagers. But he could see past that, to when they were older, maybe with children of their own. He saw even further to when those children were gone and it was just the two of them, but the love still remained. The love would always remain.

"The future is ours," Auden repeated her words from moments ago. He opened his eyes and found her gaze. Marvie stood from her seat, crossed over, and slid onto his lap, wrapping her arms around his neck. She pressed a soft kiss to his lips and then said, "I love you."

It would have to wait. He refused to ruin this perfect moment with his past; his past had ruined enough for him. They were talking about the future, talking about each other. They still had the entire walk back to her apartment for the truth. Right now, this moment was for them.

"I love you too," Auden whispered. "Endlessly."

Marvie rested her forehead against his, sighing softly, and Auden wanted to scream at the world to just stop for a moment. Let time take a break so he could stay right there forever. On a rooftop in his favorite city holding the love of his life. Marvie said they had so many more nights like these, but he just wanted to live in this one for all eternity. He breathed her in and memorized the way she felt in his arms. Safe. Holding onto her was safe, a familiar feeling he never wanted to go away. Her hair tickled his skin and she smelled of something sweet. He could feel the way her heart was pounding against his; his own heartbeat matched hers beat for beat. If he stayed still enough, he could almost imagine they shared one heart, beating in perfect harmony. He held her tighter, petrified of letting her go. He held onto Marvie like she was anchoring him to the surface of the world. In a way, she was, and always had.

Auden held onto Marvie and in his mind, he whispered, *I was only half myself without you, Marvolene. I only lived half a life until I saw your face.*

The moment was over before Auden knew it. Marvie scrambled back to her seat just as the waiter approached, bidding them a goodnight. Marvie stood up and stretched, then yawned. "You think he will remember us the next time we come to this place?"

Auden couldn't move. His arms felt so empty without her; his skin so cold and bare. He managed to get to his feet, immediately grabbing her hand. "He'll remember you; it's hard to forget someone so lovely."

"Oh Auden," Marvie laughed. "You don't have to flatter me like that anymore."

Auden leaned down and kissed her lightly on the lips. It was wonderful, but it didn't come close to what had happened moments ago, the sensation of holding Marvie in his arms and trying to stay locked in that moment infinitely. "Marvolene, I'm going to remind you how much I love you every second of every day for the rest of our lives. Is that going to be a problem?"

They started walking towards the stairs that led back down to the streets. "Not at all, so long as I get to remind *you* of the same thing." She smiled sweetly at him.

Auden's heart throbbed once as he whispered. "Come on, let's go home."

Chapter 20

She had worn her favorite dress. She had spent about three hours on her hair and cosmetics, redoing it until it was perfect. She had smiled at the mirror until her cheeks hurt and practiced the words over and over again, ensuring they would be perfect once Auden asked her.

Yes, I will marry you. Why did it take you so long to ask me?

It had been weeks since Marvie had heard Auden ask her uncle for his blessing of their matrimony. Since that night, Marvie had been ready every single day for Auden to get down on one knee and ask the question she had been dreaming of. He hadn't asked her yet, but the moment Auden told her about a surprise he was taking her to, Marvie knew it was time; she was determined to be ready for it.

Throughout the dinner on the roof, in between the food and wine and drinking and music and laughing, she had waited. Auden would take a breath to speak and Marvie's heart would stop, ready for the question, ready to give him an answer without hesitation. But the question had not come. It didn't matter to Marvie, as the dinner had been so beautiful, a perfect way to celebrate being with Auden for a year, an even better way to celebrate all the years to come.

When they got up to leave, Marvie felt the slightest surge of disappointment. She quickly pushed it away. They still had the walk left to her apartment, plenty of time for Auden to propose to her. Even if he didn't do it tonight, he obviously was planning to at some point. Why else would he ask Hewes for his blessing? Marvie couldn't deny, however, that she was getting impatient.

She was just so ready to become Marvolene Frae and begin the rest of her life with Auden.

As they walked the city streets, hand in hand, Marvie's heart pounded in her chest. She hoped Auden didn't notice the clammy way her hands had become in anticipation. She paid special mind to take slow, deep breaths, but they didn't help; Marvie was about three seconds away from getting down on her own damn knee and asking Auden herself. She had drank enough wine at dinner that the idea wasn't completely absurd.

The streets were surprisingly empty for this time of night, but Marvie guessed it was the gods giving Auden the perfect setting to propose, with just the two of them. They walked in silence, and Marvie waited and waited and waited.

Auden opened his mouth and began to sing an Orinthian song.

Marvie looked over at him and beamed. It was the same song they had sung in the tavern, the second time they had spent time with one another. She would never be able to hear the song the same way again without thinking about that memory. She began to sing along with him, their voices echoing through Tenir.

As she sang, Marvie thought about where she wanted them to get married. There was a temple down by the harbor with windows that opened up to the sea. There was something about the music used to praise the gods mingling with the sound of waves that made it a divine experience. The temple smelled like salt and sunlight would stream through the colored windows, casting beams of red, blue, and green. Marvie hadn't been there in a long time, but she still remembered the spiritual experience it had been, even as a young girl.

They would get married there. She could see it now, proclaiming their love in front of the gods and Orinth, with the waves crashing in the distance. The sound of the crowd would probably still pour into the temple, but it would be perfect because that was the music of Tenir. The sea and the people. What better music to wed Auden to, when they had met and fallen in love in this beautiful city.

Aunt Sienna and Uncle Hewes would sit in the front row. Sienna would cry, probably sniffle and sob throughout the entire ceremony. Hewes would pretend like he wasn't crying but secretly keep dabbing his face with a handkerchief.

Isla, of course, would stand up next to Marvie as she made vows to Auden. Isla was the closest thing Marvie would ever have to a sister, and it would only be right if her sister was next to her on what would surely be the greatest day of her life. Isla would probably wear a purple dress with flowers in her hair and shed the prettiest tears as she watched her best friend marry the love of her life.

Marvie would wear her mother's wedding dress. It had only been a few weeks ago that Sienna had given her the beautiful white gown, the one possession of her sister that she had kept. Marvie had tried it on and sobbed like a baby when it fit her perfectly. It had been hours that she stared at herself in the mirror, imagining what Alissya Lois and Tomas Pere would think of Auden Frae. For the first time in her life, she cried for the parents she would never know, and then, she cried in gratefulness for the parents she already had. Still, it would be quite fitting to wed Auden in the dress her birthmother had worn to marry her father.

Auden would probably wear something black. He would try to tame his curls, but they would still be messy and in disarray. His eyes would be glassy and his vows would be perfect, more words to carve into her soul. The priest would declare them as one, husband and wife, and Marvie would wonder if she was about to wake up from a dream. Then, Auden would kiss her and she would realize, not for the first time, that it wasn't a dream. It was her life, and it was perfect.

The celebration would last all night, at the tavern by the harbor. They would have a feast worthy of royalty and enough wine to drown the whole of Tenir. There would be dancing; they would dance until their feet hurt and their eyes couldn't stay open. And while the others continued to dance, Auden and Marvie would slip out of the tavern and go to the apartment that was now theirs.

Auden and Marvolene Frae's.

The future was theirs.

Marvie thought about it all, over and over again, until there were tears in her eyes and joy in her heart. She sung the words to the Orinthian song with Auden in a shaky voice, because in a few moments, he was going to ask her to marry him and she was going to say yes, and all the things she had imagined, all the wishes she had made, and all the dreams she hadn't dared to speak aloud would come true.

She wished Sienna would ask her the same question again. *"I just want to know, Marvie, are you happy?"*

Oh Sienna, happy seemed too weak of a word to describe the way she felt. Not just about Auden, but about her entire life. The pieces had finally come together, the pains had gone away, and her life was her own. Marvie was wise enough to know she might not always feel this happy, but on the bad days, she would remember a very important realization she had learned in the last year.

Happiness was never a destination.

Marvie had spent her whole life thinking she was on a journey to being happy, but that was never the case. Happiness wasn't a treasure and life hadn't given her a map to find it. Happiness wasn't an achievement, a present she would open once she had proved herself worthy.

Happiness was something to be found in every moment of every day. Happiness was enjoying the uncertainty of life and youth, accepting you never had as much control as you thought you did. Happiness was seeking joy, both in the good days and the bad. Some days, happiness was obvious, in joyful memories and laughter. But many times, happiness was one single thing to pick out of a bad day: the sun drying your tears, a friend soothing your hurts.

Marvie would never reach her original destination of happiness because she had already obtained it. It was hers to have and hers to share with others, and she would spend the rest of her life trying to do just that.

Especially with the boy beside her, who swung her hand back and forth as the song finally came to an end. Auden looked over at her and she saw her own happiness mirrored in his eyes as he smiled at her.

"I miss you already, Marvie," Auden said, his eyes glassy. "I miss you even when you're with me."

Marvie's heart seized up in her chest and her entire body tensed with the most blissful anticipation because this was it! He was going to ask her! They had eaten, drank, talked, sang, and there was only one more thing that this night held: a proposal.

Marvie could barely get words out to respond. "But I'm right here!" she exclaimed.

He shook his head. "Just the thought of having to leave you and walk home by myself makes me sad."

Marvie looked over at him with a smile. But for a moment, she didn't see him as Auden walking with her through the streets of Tenir. She saw him in their cottage on the edge of the forest, dancing with her in the home that was now theirs. She saw him in the morning, every morning for the rest of their lives, waking up and smiling because they had found each other. Life was cruel, fate was a tease, and they had found each other.

"My uncle and aunt have told you time and time again you can stay permanently. You would never have to worry then," Marvie replied and with the hand that wasn't holding Auden's, she dug her nails into her hand to prevent from collapsing to her knees and sobbing with joy.

Auden laughed, but Marvie didn't see him laughing on the cobblestones. She saw him laughing in their front yard, playing with the children that they would one day share with one another. She saw their heads of blonde hair and black curls. Auden hugged them in his arms and threw them up into the air, their shouts of glee reaching Marvie's ears. She saw Auden turn his head and meet her eyes and smile, because they had found each other.

"I would still miss you," Auden told her, drawing her back into the present moment. "When you closed your eyes at night and fell asleep, I would miss you then. That's how much I love you, Marvolene. I would miss you when you're sleeping."

So many words were on the tip of her tongue as she saw the children grow up and leave the two of them behind at the cottage. But they still had each other, and they always would. Marvie could almost look past this world and see into the next lifetime, where they would be born as strangers and spend years unknowingly searching for one another.

A girl would stumble into a shop. A boy would fall in love with her and it would begin again. They would live and they would die and they would find each other over and over again until they found The Beyond, hand and hand, to spend the rest of eternity together.

It was at her fingertips if he would only ask her. There was no one else around but the two of them walking on the empty streets, and Marvie knew there wouldn't be a better moment than this one. She wanted to tell him that, but she squeezed his hand and said, "So, I'll never fall asleep then. How about that?"

Auden laughed. "I know how much you like to sleep so I wouldn't ask you to do that."

Marvie nudged him with her shoulder, letting the visions slip away so she could be with him fully. "You know me so well."

"I do, don't I?" Auden pondered. "It's hard for me to fathom that it's only been a year. I feel like I've known you forever."

A wave of elation swept over her. He was leading into it; she knew he was. But she couldn't let him know that she knew what he was about to do. Marvie would act surprised like she had been practicing for weeks. She snorted. "What do you want?"

Auden grinned at her. "Nothing! Why do you ask?"

Because I want you to ask me to marry you! "Because you're being so ridiculously romantic and making me fall even more head over heels for you."

"I don't want anything, I swear," Auden insisted. "I'm just realizing how lucky I am to have you, Marvie, really. You saved my life."

And now I want to spend the rest of my life with you. Will you marry me? He was missing so many opportunities just to do it. "From what?" Marvie asked him.

"I can't even explain it."

Well, try harder. Marvie laughed into her hand and calmed her mind. He would ask her. If not today, then someday. They had the rest of their lives; they would be married one way or another. So she squeezed his hand and said, "You're crazy."

"Crazy for you," he corrected.

She snorted again. "Now you're actually being crazy," but she couldn't wipe the smile off her face.

Auden stopped suddenly and turned to her, taking her other hand in his own. Marvie's heart exploded in her chest. It was time! His expression had turned serious and he took a deep breath. Time slowed, as Marvie experienced a profound moment where every vision of their future flashed before her eyes. She saw their wedding, their trips, their cottage on the edge of the forest, their children in the yard, their empty house filled with love. She saw this in a hundred different worlds, a hundred different lives, a hundred different times that they defeated fate and found one another once more. In a split second, she saw it all as she waited for Auden to ask her to marry her.

"Listen, Marvie, there's something I need to tell you."

I love you. Will you marry me? Marvie could almost hear the words and avoided the urge just to scream yes before he even had the chance to ask.

And then something whizzed past them, barely missing her head. Marvie's first thought was wondering if she had imagined it, before another flew by. Her chest seized up in panic and confusion. She opened her mouth to yell in fear, but Auden was already speaking.

"Run," he commanded, and her instincts took over as she took off running down the street, her mind reeling trying to figure out what was happening. Had it been a large bird? She hadn't seen what it was, only felt it almost graze her skin. Were they being attacked by street thieves? What was going on? Auden was right behind her and for the first time in a long time, fear bubbled up within her.

They were close to her apartment and as Marvie turned the corner to get to a more familiar street, she screamed as her head exploded in pain. One moment she was standing and the next she was on the ground, the pain racking through her. She tried to keep her eyes open, tried to see what had struck her, tried to find

Auden, but she couldn't move. The brick buildings towering above her multiplied and dots of black danced in front of her vision until she didn't have much vision at all. Marvie opened her mouth to scream and no sound came out. She tried desperately to stay conscious, but she was fading.

The last thing she heard was Auden screaming her name. "MARVIE!"

The visions of the future were overtaking her, but she couldn't lose herself in them. She had to stay awake to figure out what was happening, to protect Auden, but the temptation was too great. Marvie closed her eyes, the agony of her throbbing head fading away.

In the vision, she was carrying a child. Auden's child.

"What names do you like?" Marvie asked him. *They were leaning against an unfamiliar balcony overlooking the sea. Marvie had one hand on her stomach, the other intertwined with Auden's, who was leaning next to her.*

Auden smiled. "Whatever ones you like, darling."

She gave him a look. "Auden, this child is both of ours. We need to come up with a name we both like."

"Marvie, I will like anything you like," he told her.

"Oh yeah? What if I want to name the child Auden?"

Marvie fought to open her eyes, but another part of her grasped onto this dream of the future. She didn't want to wake up from it, whatever it was.

"Never mind. You can't name the child," he said and Marvie laughed as she slid into a seat that was on the balcony. She subconsciously fiddled with a ring on her finger, a wedding ring that Auden had given her after she told him she was pregnant with his child.

Marvie yanked herself out of the dream and there was so much pain. She couldn't see anything but felt Auden kneeling next to her. There were voices, but she couldn't recognize any of them but Auden's. She could hardly comprehend anything that was being said; every time she tried to think, her head throbbed. She managed to murmur, "Auden."

His hand was in hers and he squeezed it. "I'm here," he whispered, but his voice was worlds away. He was so far away from her, even though his hand was in hers, and she tried to scream for him, but no sound came out.

"This must be the lovely Miss Marvolene Pere," a stranger said, but his voice was as far away as Auden's. He kept speaking, but Marvie stopped listening, fading back into the vision of the future that was so much better than whatever was happening to her and Auden.

"Marvolene," the Auden of the vision whispered to her. "The first time I told you that I loved you, I said that words are a pathetic attempt to express what I feel for you. That statement seems even more relevant in lieu of what I'm about to ask you. Yet words are the only thing I know how to use. I wish I knew how to sing or dance or perform some grand gesture so that you would know how much you mean to me. Alas, I only have my humble words. Despite that, I will try to use them to ask you what I have wanted to ask you from the first day."

She fought to return to real life. They were in danger. She didn't know what was happening, that much was apparent. Marvie didn't care about herself, but the idea of Auden being in danger was enough to break her.

The strange, distant voice spoke again, this time to her. "Marvolene, I'm sorry. You were never supposed to be part of it. But your Auden? He's a bad man. He's dangerous to the future of Orinth and we would all be better if he was dead."

That's not true! Marvie tried to scream at the voice, but the agony was too great. She fought to open her eyes and stand and save the boy she loved, but her body wouldn't respond. The only thing she could feel was Auden's hand grasping her own and his shaking voice that shouted, "Don't say a word to her!" Marvie felt herself slipping until there was nothing but the voice of Auden of the future, whispering softly in her ear.

"There is no Auden Frae without Marvolene Pere. You might ask, what about all that time before we knew each other? The sentiment holds true. I was only half myself without you, Marvie. I only lived half a life until I saw your face. And if I ever had to live without you again, I could never be whole."

When she pulled herself out of the fog, she was in Auden's arms, and he was carrying her through the city streets. Marvie tried to speak to him, ask him where the voices had gone, but it came out a painful moan and Auden clutched her tighter to his chest, whispering things she couldn't hear. She slipped back into subconsciousness, silently begging the gods to take the pain away. It had spread from her head, through each and every limb, an incessant ache. Take her back to being on the roof with Auden, waiting in hopeful anticipation for him to ask her to marry him.

It's not too late, she told herself. *It's not too late.* The pain would go away and she would wake up and Auden would be there. There would be some rational explanation for all of this. Tenir was a city of criminals and they had been unfortunate victims, but why would it have any effect on their love? They would be more cautious. No, they would move to Auntica like they always planned. Everything was fine, everything was fine, everything was fine.

The next thing she knew, Marvie was laying in her apartment, body draped across the couch, the pain not ceasing. There were more voices, but she could only hear Auden.

"I'm sorry, Marvie," he whispered and there was more regret in his voice than she had ever heard before. She thought about all the times she saw darkness in his eyes, but this time, she was hearing the darkness within him. *I'll save you, I'll fix you, I'll make you whole again* she tried to say, but the suffering had spread from her head and moved throughout her body. She managed to whimper, "Why does it hurt so bad?"

"It's going to be okay, I promise," Auden said, and she believed him. Auden could promise her anything and she would believe it, but darkness was dripping from each of his words, a type of pain she couldn't grasp. She was reeling with her own anguish, but she would take it three times over if she could just take the pain out of his own voice.

"Auden!" she screamed, a plea for him to give her his darkness, to allow her to share his burden. They were so close, so damn close. The future was right in front of them. "Auden, Auden!" She wasn't in control of her own body. She was twitching and shaking, cloaked in sweat from head to toe.

"I'm right here, darling. Right here," he said, choking back a sob, and the regret was even stronger.

Marvie didn't know why she felt the need to say her next words. Auden leaving her hadn't been a fear since the beginning, but the way he sounded in that moment forced her to beg him, "Don't leave me, please." The pain she felt in that moment would be nothing compared to the pain of his absence. She spoke again, "Please don't leave me."

She was fading again. The last thing she heard was Auden saying over and over again, "I'm right here, Marvie. I'm right here."

The visions of the future became vivid and real and Marvie plunged herself into them. She would live them right now, and when she woke up and Auden asked her to marry him, she would live them again. Everything was going to be okay. The future was still theirs. It was alright. She repeated reassurances in her mind, but for some reason, she couldn't make herself believe them.

Marvie tried to find the cottage on the edge of the forest, picture it in her brain as crystal clear as it had been earlier in the night. For some reason, she couldn't find it. The cottage wouldn't reveal itself to her, the yard with their children had all but vanished.

She tried to see their wedding again, but she could only see darkness, feel the phantom pain. She searched for Isla standing next to her, her aunt and uncle in the front of the temple, Auden standing across from her, holding her hands as they professed their love for one another. Nothing but darkness.

Marvie searched for the beaches of Grady, laying in the sand looking up at the stars, her hand intertwined with Auden's. She searched for the mountains of the Wilds and the fields of the Darklands and the deserts of Nagaye. She searched for the familiar streets of Tenir and the place she was born, Auntica. Marvie looked for the visions of she and Auden traveling to those places, making memories with one another that would last forever, but she couldn't find them.

The future was fading and Marvie tried to scream at it to come back, but her body wasn't working.

And then, Auden spoke to her, a whisper in her ear from miles and miles away. She couldn't tell if it was real or in her head, but she clung onto the familiarity and peace that his voice brought her, soothing the pain albeit slightly.

"Marvolene Pere, I know you always get to say you love me more, but you're not awake right now, so I guess I get to say it."

Marvie smiled inwardly. She always got to say she loved him more because she did. She tried to tell him that, open her mouth and proclaim her love again, but it didn't work. The Auden of her vision kept talking, but she still couldn't tell if it was truly a vision.

"You saved my life. I love you more than anything in the entire world and because I love you, I have to protect you. And the only way I can protect you is to leave you. Go far away and make it so you can never find me because if you found me, I couldn't say no to you. I love you, but I promised to make you safe, and I can't do that. Dammit, Marvie, if we were in a different place and I was someone else, maybe we'd have a shot. But I couldn't live with myself if I was the reason you were hurt. Even tonight is too much for me. So that's why I have to go."

NO! Marvie tried to scream. *NO, NO, NO.*

She reminded herself it was just a vision, a nightmare brought upon by the pain of her wound. Auden had promised, over and over again, that he would be in her life forever. This was an ugly delusion, the side effect of whatever had happened that night. It wasn't real, just like the cottage on the edge of the forest had never been real. It was alright. Everything was alright.

"I love you," Auden told her.

I LOVE YOU TOO she tried to scream.

"Please, please know I love you."

It's just a dream, she told herself again. Not a dream, a nightmare. The visions hadn't stopped since she had lost consciousness and this was no different. It was alright. It was alright.

"I love you."

I love you too. And when I wake up, it'll be the first thing I tell you. I'll ask you to marry me because I'm tired of waiting for you to do it. You'll say yes and the vision of us in the church will come true and then the visions of us in all the places we talked about and the cottage and the future. I wish I would've told you 'I love you' more, but it won't matter. I'll wake up and tell you and everything will be alright. This is just a bad dream. Maybe I had too much wine and passed out. Maybe you'll make fun of me for the rest of our lives about this.

Marvie let go of reality and allowed herself to drift off into sleep. It was going to be alright. She would wake up and everything would make sense. The future, the one she had been dreaming of for so long, was still intact. It was time to sleep, and when she woke up, Auden would be there. The very thought of it brought a wave of peace to her, lulling her into slumber.

Auden's voice echoed in her dreams. *Tomorrow will be better, so long as you and I are together, Marvolene Pere.*

Gods, let them be together for the rest of her tomorrows.

Chapter 21

Rider loved her.

From the very beginning that had been the problem. He loved her the moment he saw her in the street and for every moment after. Love was something sought after by many, but for him, it had always been a tortuous burden. Yet he had it for her and she for him and they were doomed, no, he was doomed from the start.

Rider wondered if there was something he could have done differently to spare him from this.

Maybe not. Maybe some people were just meant for a life of suffering.

He thought these things and so many others as he knelt in front of her grave.

The first woman he loved had grown sick and died; they had known for weeks that her time was coming. Rider had been there, at her side on her deathbed, looking down at an old woman and seeing someone entirely different. They had been surrounded by their children and grandchildren, who were used to Rider's unchanged appearance. A stranger would have thought it curious that an eighteen-year-old boy knelt down next to her, not one of the several older people in the room. But to his family, they were seeing a familiar sight, this young man clinging to this old woman with everything he was.

Rider had never intended to fall in love after that horrible day. But when he did, a part of him always expected it to end the same way. In a room with his second love, with their only daughter and her children, their grandchildren. He would be at her side, a young boy by an elderly woman, and the love, the agonizing love, would remain.

His wife was forty-four years old, their daughter was a teenager. There were no grandchildren yet. It was just the three of them.

He had awoken that morning and went for a walk around the city, leaving his wife sleeping beside him. His daughter was already at school. Rider walked around the city and when he came home, he made breakfast in their kitchen. His wife's favorite: porridge with honey. He set the table and put flowers in the center of it, blue flowers to match her eyes. Then, he went to wake his wife. Rider was surprised she wasn't already awake, as she always loved to watch the sunrise. He smiled as he internally planned to watch it with her the very next morning. He entered the room and saw his wife's sleeping figure in the bed they shared.

She was dead.

Rider shook her. She was just sleeping deeply.

But no. She was dead.

Rider didn't cry. He didn't scream or sob or shake her body that was perfectly still. He just laid next to her, watching her face that was so perfect, waiting for her to open her eyes and stare back at him. She would smile and move closer to him. He would be able to feel her heartbeat, beating in time with his own. He would try not to think about how her heartbeats were numbered, while his were endless, an unlimited source of his suffering. But she didn't open her eyes; she just laid there, hair spread over the pillow, framing her head like a crown.

Rider didn't know how long he stayed there next to her. In his mind, he knew he needed to move. He needed to get their daughter and gently break the news that her mother had passed. He needed to see the gravedigger and the priest who would conduct the ceremony for her passing. He would have to arrange some sort of celebration of life afterwards. There was so much to do, but he was frozen in this moment, hoping and praying with everything he was that it was just an illusion.

They were supposed to have more time than this.

For Rider, time meant nothing. It was an infinite thing, meaningless in his eyes. But when he thought about his time with her, it was treasure. Gold, silver, diamonds, gems were nothing, nothing, nothing. They may as well be the dirt beneath his feet. But the time he had left with her was his most prized possession; it was sand slipping through his fingers. His time with her was water cupped in his hands, slowly draining away until there would be nothing. His time with her was the only thing in his life that was limited.

It was gone. The sand had slipped through, the water drained away. He thought they had so many more days and nights. They would never have forever; Rider had accepted that. But they had the rest of her life to cherish the love that was between them, bask in it like they were basking in the light of the sun. They had so much left, so many plans they had made. When their daughter went to university, they were going to travel to new places, see the world together. They were going to sail on ships, climb mountains, swim in the sea, hike across the plains, see everything there was to see before it was too late. They would take their time whilst also hurrying because the seconds were ticking away, the sand slipping faster than they knew.

Rider didn't remember much after that. One moment he was laying next to her in their bed, the next he was kneeling by her grave.

He had lived many lifetimes. He had watched empires be built and empires crumble. Rider had learned as much as he possibly could, having all the time in the world to experience life. In some ways, he considered himself the most brilliant being in their world, simply because he had the "advantage" of living forever. He had loved two women, created a life with them, raised a family. He had lived.

The people in their world put value on so many things except the thing that really mattered: time.

He wanted to give it to them. Give them his abundance of time, the minutes that weighed down on him, choking the air out of his lungs and the will from his heart. There were other people who needed the time more than he, starting with the woman who was buried beneath this grave, a woman who Rider would never see again, separated by the expanse between life and death, an expanse Rider would never be able to cross.

Rider moved until he was sitting on the ground in front of the gravestone, resting his arms on the knees. The ceremony had happened hours ago, the priest long gone from the graveyard. His daughter had left too, embracing her father one last time before going home to grieve her mother. Rider knew he should be there for her, soothe her own pain and hurts. He tried to follow her, yet there he still sat, at the grave.

Rider thought there was only one thing that was endless for him: time. But he had been wrong.

The pain. It was as unending as his heartbeats, as unrelenting as his breaths.

And Rider realized it always would be.

He looked around the graveyard, at the other markers that were next to his wife's. The pain gave way for a burst of envy. All of these people had been able to achieve what he never could: death. The gravestones mocked him, a symbol of what he would never have, a trophy given to the people who could go where he could not. He could almost hear them laughing at him, this boy who had once thought eternal youth was a gift.

He hadn't even gotten to say goodbye. Maybe it was better that way. Maybe it wasn't. Rider didn't know.

He had lived forever and he didn't know much of anything.

He walked back to his house. He cleared the table of where the porridge and honey still sat. He called his daughter into the room and embraced her, wiped away her tears, and told her to pack her bags. They were going to live with her mother's sister, in the city. Rider packed his own bag, taking the possessions that had been his for centuries, enough riches to take him everywhere except where he wanted to go. When they were finished, they rode to the city.

His sister-in-law welcomed them with open arms, devastated at the loss of her sister. They talked and Rider tried to seem as normal as he could. He kissed his daughter goodnight and waited until they had all gone to bed. Then, he sat at the table and wrote his daughter goodbye. He was a coward; he couldn't do it to her face because she would convince him to stay. He wouldn't tell her no and then he would watch her grow up. He would watch her get married and have children and Rider would love those children. He would watch them grow up too until his daughter died and her children died and their children died and everyone would die and Rider would just be standing there, begging the gods to let him die too.

He couldn't do it, not again.

He wrote her goodbye and left the city. The next day, he was on a ship.

The captain had said where they were going, but Rider hadn't really heard him. If the destination wasn't The Beyond, he didn't care. He just wanted to…go.

He wouldn't live in a city. No, he wouldn't take the chance of meeting someone again, of loving someone again. He couldn't die, but Rider truly believed if he had to fall in love again just to watch them grow old and die, it would kill him. A part of him wanted to try it, see if it would send him into The Beyond to experience that much pain again. But knowing his luck, he would be alive and the pain would continue to punish him for eternity.

He would sail and land and if there were people there, he would keep sailing. Rider would run until he found a place he could be alone.

Rider had lived a long time; he knew that loneliness, with all of its perks, could be agonizing.

But it couldn't possibly be more agonizing than losing the people he loved over and over again.

Rider would run until he was truly alone. He would find some way to pass the time, whatever that may be, doomed to this eternity of pain. Maybe he would pass the time praying that the faces of his past would fade into nothing, finally providing him with relief. Yet he knew the scars on his heart would never truly fade, that he would always feel the wounds of their loss, especially his second love, whom time had stolen from him.

The cold reality was, it was easier to be alone than in pain, pain as endless as Rider's life. In the sea, he caught a glimpse of his own reflection. An eighteen-year-old boy looked back at him and Rider laughed, tears falling from his face like rain.

He thought of his first love. He thought of his second love. And he thought of that naïve boy from his past, who thought that eternal youth was something to celebrate. What a foolish boy, Rider thought to himself. What a stupid, foolish boy.

So Rider sailed, cursing so many things, but nothing more than the curse that was his own.

"Goodbye," he whispered to the wind, not sure who he was speaking to. His first love, his second love, his family, himself? He didn't know. He was saying goodbye, but he knew the world was truly saying goodbye to him, as he would never exist within its people again.

The wind seemed to whisper back, words he knew would be with him forever.

"Goodbye, Rider Grey."

Auden stared at the city that had been home for so long. It was strange; he had never seen this view of it. The sea sparkled on the horizon and the brick buildings stood sturdy and proud. He could almost hear the lull of the crowds and the music spilling from buildings, the sounds of his entire life. Tenir was home and it would always be home.

He would never return here.

There was nothing. Where he should feel sadness, anger, despair, pain, anything, there was emptiness. It was better that way, he thought. If he allowed himself to feel what he wanted to, he would ride back into the city to be with the girl he loved. The promises they had made to one another, the conversations about the future, the dreams they had shared and created, everything but the vows echoed in his ears; he ignored them. If he stopped ignoring them, he would be in her arms within the hour.

That was impossible now.

They had been attacked the previous night on the way home from the place where he was going to tell her about his shadow.

It seemed like a sign.

There had been so many signs for Auden to leave Marvie alone. He had ignored each and every one, choosing the happiness that came from being with her. There had been warnings and he had brushed them aside, basking in the light that Marvolene brought him, the first light that had been in his life. He had curled under the window of the orphanage, absorbing the sun and being at peace, neglecting the indications that being involved with him was a disaster.

Last night had been a warning he could no longer ignore.

He didn't know who they were, the men who had attacked him. He only knew he had left them dead on the street, three corpses whose manner of death would never be solved. Auden had promised himself long ago he would never kill again, and yet, he had. The guilt that he felt after killing Conli was chillingly absent from him at that moment. He felt nothing. He didn't want to feel anything.

He shouldn't have walked into the bakery after meeting her for the first time. That had been the first mistake. When she walked away that moment by the creek, Auden should have let her, allowed her to act on her instinct that something was off about this boy. When he had gone to the Southside to kill someone, he should have had the will to walk away on his own. He should have understood that he was too dangerous to be with someone like her, someone good and worthy of love, but not his love. When he followed Chyles that day, he should have left her, understanding that the shadow was too powerful a thing to control, even if he convinced himself he was able.

The signs were countless and yet, he had made his choice to stay in her life. They had created so many memories. Marvie had brought him back to life, made him whole again. They had spoken so many words to one another, words he never thought he would understand but did. Every moment had been perfect. These were things he knew he would never forget.

That was his punishment. He would never forget her; he would never love another. Auden would be in love with Marvolene Pere every day for the rest of his life, yet he could never be with her. He had risked her life by allowing her to be with him, and this was the gods' retribution. For one glorious year, he had known what it was to live a full, beautiful life of light.

Now, for the rest of his days, he would live the half-life he had lived before her.

Auden's emptiness faltered when he thought of her, laying on that couch in her aunt and uncle's apartment. She would wake up and he would be gone. Gods, he was breaking so many of the promises he made to her, destroying the future they had planned, but what choice did he have? People he didn't know had attacked him the night before, speaking of things he didn't understand, saying he was a threat to the future of Orinth. Though he didn't fathom the words, he believed them. Even more so, he now knew that there were people who knew who he was and what he had done to Conli. They knew what he was capable of and wanted him dead.

Auden would be an evil man if he subjected Marvolene to the same danger he was now in. Last night, they were lucky. An arrow had grazed her head, but what if it had hit its mark? What if Marvie had died because of the people who wanted to kill him? What if it was his fault that Sienna and Hewes lost their niece, that Isla lost her friend, that the world lost a kind and beautiful soul? He wouldn't be able to live with the guilt; he would surely die.

Marvie would probably hate him when she woke up, but maybe that was for the better. She would hate him and curse his name, but it would give her the will to move on from him. There would be a painful few months and then she would open herself up to love once more. She would meet someone able to love her the way she deserved to be loved, to give her the life she deserved to live.

Auden was not that person and he never would be. How could he stay with her when he knew that?

"I'm sorry," he whispered to the city, hoping his words reached Marvie's ears.

He was never going to see her again.

"I love you."

He was never going to love another.

"But forget me," he told her. "Let me fade away until I am nothing. Find another and love them. Let them love you and live a life that is safe and perfect. Forget me until I don't exist."

Because for Auden, he didn't really exist anymore.

He had searched his life for a reason to survive and he had found it. Now, he was leaving it behind which left the one thing he had always known how to do: survive. He would leave this city and face each painful day, surviving, surviving, surviving. This time, there would be no light at the end of the tunnel, no hope that he would find the reason. He had found her and left her. Auden would now just survive for the sake of surviving.

"I love you," he whispered again and a tear worked its way down his face, burning like acid.

Would it be better if he never met Marvolene? Maybe for her sake, but at least now he had something to tuck deep into his heart. He had spent so much time memorizing her, cherishing their memories. He would relive them if he had to, praying they would give him the will to keep surviving, even if he knew those memories were all he would ever have of her.

Auden had always wondered why he forced Lola to read the story of Rider Grey to him over and over again. The story was tragic and depressing, and there was enough tragedy in the orphanage already. But still, he had memorized every word of that story.

Now, he knew why.

Rider Grey was doomed to suffer the same way he was. Maybe Auden wouldn't live forever, but he would live without love to spare himself and others pain, just like Rider Grey.

He was just like Rider Grey.

He was Rider Grey.

Auden tightened the grip on his horse's reins as he took one last look at Tenir before turning around.

"I'm Rider Grey now," he said to himself.

Auden Frae belonged with Marvolene Pere, and because that was impossible, Auden Frae was dead. The boy from the orphanage who had suffered so greatly and loved so deeply was dead. He was a new man now, one who would isolate himself to protect others. He would resign to living half a life for their sake. Auden Frae was nothing.

Goodbye, Auden Frae.

"My name is Rider Grey," Auden said, and he began to ride towards the horizon.

Chapter 22

She dreamed about Auden. It wasn't really a surprise.

But the dreams were memories of everything that had happened to them before he left.

"Have you ever met someone for the first time, but deep inside of you, you know it's not the first time at all? That somewhere, at some time, your paths have crossed. You just can't remember where or when. But you just know. Has that ever happened to you?"

The first time they had met one another. She wondered if it had been a mistake. Marvie would never have known their deep love, but she would have never known this pain either. And maybe losing one was worth not having to experience the other.

"I don't know what I'm trying to say, Marvie. I know we just met, but why do I feel like I've known you my entire life? Why, when you walked into the shop yesterday, was it like I was seeing someone coming home, someone who had been apart from me for a long time? Why is that I can barely breathe when I look at you, Marvolene? Gods, I'm nervous just sitting here next to you. Can you explain it to me?"

She couldn't explain it then and she couldn't explain it now. Why had they loved one another in the way they did? They didn't have much in common. Their personalities were so incredibly different, and yet, she loved him more than anything and anyone in the entire world, and she knew she would never love that way again.

"I have read a thousand different ways to say I love you, in stories and songs and poems, but each of them are ridiculously meaningless as I try and fail to say it to you. Words are a pathetic attempt to express the depth of what I feel for you, Marvolene. But by the will of the gods, I will try."

"I love you more than I love the air I breathe, Marvie. I love you more than waking up in the morning to greet another day. I love you more than any person, any place, any single thing I have ever encountered. I've been in love with you since the day I saw you and I swear to the gods that I will love you until the day I die. A thousand miles couldn't separate you from my love, Marvolene Pere. I have spent my entire life wondering why I existed, what sort of purpose I had in this dark and cruel world. But it is you, it has been you this entire time. I survive, I exist, I live, all for you, Marvie. I love you, Marvolene. My gods, I love you."

Marvie woke up screaming. It wasn't uncommon these days.

It had been three weeks since the day she woke up on the couch, a numb throbbing in her head, but other than that, she was normal.

The moment she sat up, her aunt and uncle were at her side, embracing her, hugging her, demanding to know how she felt, shoving a cup of tea in front of her, asking if she were hungry, overwhelming her as she tried to remember what had even happened. Their voices continued as she recalled the events of the previous night, coming up with nothing after being on the roof with Auden. Marvie yelled, "STOP!"

Both Sienna and Hewes froze, their eyes wide, their mouths open. There were tears running down Sienna's face and Marvie couldn't understand why. She used the silence to try and piece together what she was doing here, why her head hurt and...

"Where's Auden?" Marvie asked, her voice trembling as bits and pieces of the night began to come back to her.

Her aunt and uncle exchanged a look and Marvie asked again, "Where is Auden?"

"He's not here, Marvie," Sienna said gently. "He left late last night."

Marvie didn't remember much after that. She had stumbled to her feet and out the apartment door, to her aunt and uncle's protests. She had careened down the streets, her body knowing the way to get to the place she had spent almost every night for the last few months. Her head was pounding and her vision was faltering, but she managed to climb the stairs until she was knocking on his door, screaming, "AUDEN!"

In her heart, she already knew. But her head wouldn't accept it yet, which is why she continued to knock and scream his name. "AUDEN, AUDEN!"

He didn't answer. It was alright, Marvie told himself. Maybe he was still sleeping. No, maybe he had an early shift at The Wooden Barrel that he had forgotten to tell her about. It didn't matter; Marvie burst in through the door anyways.

The apartment was empty.

The furniture was still there as well as a few items on the kitchen counter, but everything else was gone. Auden wasn't messy, but there were always clothes on the floor, books on the tables, half-drank glasses of water balanced on surfaces throughout the place. It was all gone. Marvie went straight for his bedroom, the reassurances playing on repeat in her mind. Maybe he decided to straighten up before he went to work. Maybe he had hired someone to clean the place.

His bedroom was empty. The bed was made, but every drawer of his wardrobe had been stripped of his clothes. The few books he kept on his nightstand, the ones that were the most important to him, were gone. The satchel where he kept most of his money was absent. It could have been a stranger's apartment for how bare the place was.

Marvie's knees were shaking, but she wouldn't let herself collapse yet. If she did, it was an admittance that he was gone, and she wouldn't believe that. No, Auden had just moved into another apartment without telling her. Or perhaps that's what he was trying to tell her last night. He had bought them a new apartment that they would move into once he married her, and he was going to marry her. He had told her. He had promised her. Marvie had simply ruined the surprise for herself.

She clasped her hands together to stop their trembling. Her lips shook so bad she couldn't speak. Reality threatened to crash upon her from all sides, but still, she blocked it out.

"I think I'm just happy."

She made him happy. When she had met him, he hadn't been happy. Marvie could tell by the darkness she saw in his eyes, darkness that never really went away, but she made it better. She knew she did. That darkness would one day disappear completely because she would fix him. She would make him better, share his burdens, soothe his hurts. Auden told her she made him happy. They were going to get married and live in the cottage on the edge of the forest, just like they talked about.

"I wish I could do that for you, Marvolene. Pluck a star out of the sky and give it to you to wear around your neck."

So many words and promises. So much potential. Love like theirs shouldn't exist between two people as young as they were. Auden wouldn't walk away from that. Auden wouldn't walk away from her.

And as Marvolene slowly sunk to the ground, she heard a whisper of last night.

"I love you more than anything in the entire world and because I love you, I have to protect you. And the only way I can protect you is to leave you. Go far away and make it so you can never find me because if you found me, I couldn't say no to you."

No. No, it wasn't true. It had been a dream, no, a nightmare. It hadn't been real. She had hit her head and it was a painful illusion, a side effect of the agony she was feeling. There was no possibility that the voice in her head had *actually* been Auden's.

"I love you, but I promised to make you safe, and I can't do that."

She sunk to the ground and curled into a ball, hugging her knees to her chest and burying her head between them. It hadn't been real. This wasn't real right now. She was still lying on the couch, suffering from a headache that was making her delusional. Auden was right beside her, waiting for her to wake up. The voice in her head was a part of the delusion, she knew it was.

Because Auden, her Auden, would not do this to her.

"Dammit, Marvie, if we were in a different place and I was someone else, maybe we'd have a shot. But I couldn't live with myself if I was the reason you were hurt. Even tonight is too much for me. So that's why I have to go."

"No," Marvie whimpered, the tears beginning to fall rapidly. "No. Wake up, Marvie. Please wake up."

"I love you."

"NO!" she screamed, her voice bouncing off the empty walls of Auden's apartment. "NO, NO, NO! WAKE UP, MARVOLENE. WAKE UP!"

"Please, please know I love you."

"GODS, MAKE IT STOP!" she shrieked, rocking back and forth, gasping for air. "MAKE IT STOP! MAKE IT STOP! MAKE IT STOP!"

"I love you."

She saw everything from last night. She remembered it all, and yet, she didn't stop rocking back and forth, waiting to wake up from this nightmare. Auden would be by her side and maybe right there and then, he would propose to her. It wouldn't be romantic, but it would be real. She just had to wake up. This nightmare was becoming too realistic.

"AUDEN!" she screamed, hoping he would be the person to pull her from the terror. "AUDEN!"

He wouldn't do it. He wouldn't leave her. He wouldn't do this to her.

"No, gods, please," she sobbed, pressing her face to her hands, choking on her words. "Please, gods, no. No, Auden. No. Please."

She dragged herself to her feet, stumbling over to his bed and falling onto it. She buried her face in the covers that still smelled like him. She inhaled deeply, almost expecting to turn over and see him next to her, like so many mornings where she had awoken in bliss. She reached for him, reached to be in his familiar arms and feel safe once more, but the bed was empty. "No," she whispered. "Please don't do this to me."

She stayed there for hours waiting for him to come back.

He did not.

It was okay, though. Maybe Kalen had him stay later at work. Maybe he was at her own apartment, not knowing where she was. Maybe he was at the apartment he had bought for them, making a special dinner where he would ask her to marry him. He wasn't gone. He couldn't be gone. There was no way, after all the promises he had made her and all the words he had spoken, that Auden could walk away.

It had been three weeks since then and he hadn't come back.

She had spent every day of those three weeks in her bed waiting for him. When she was awake, she held the book he had given her to her chest, rocking back and forth. Somehow, the pages smelled like him and she would breathe it in and out, pretending he was there. Her mind still fed her reassurances. Maybe Kalen had sent him out of town on some sort of business trip. Maybe he had gone to Auntica to find them a house, and when he returned, he would sweep her away to start their lives together. Her mind hadn't stopped and she continued to believe what it said.

Marvie didn't talk to anyone, just held the book in her arms and waited. She didn't talk to her aunt when she begged her to eat something more. She didn't talk to her uncle when he pleaded with her to get up, get some fresh air, let the sunshine soak into her face. She didn't talk to Isla when her best friend sat in front of her and asked what happened. She wouldn't talk to anyone until Auden came back. And Auden would come back, she told herself. He wouldn't just leave her behind, knowing exactly what his leaving would do to her.

The Auden she knew wouldn't subject her to that pain.

In the nights, she dreamed of him. She saw their memories, relived them over and over again. She heard his voice and his promises and it made her believe all the more that he wasn't really gone. He would come back and there would be a rational explanation for all of this. He would reassure her that she was the love of his life and had done nothing that would cause him to walk away. He would beg for her forgiveness and she would give it to him willingly, because it was Auden, and Auden could do no wrong in her eyes.

So, she hugged the book and she rocked back and forth and she waited. Barely eating, barely drinking, just waiting.

Marvie knew Auden was coming back, but being without him was still difficult. He was a consistent part of her life. She had grown used to his smiles and his laughs and their conversations, almost expected them in her daily routine. Auden was a part of her, and to go from being with him always to not being with him at all was like being plunged into icy cold water and held there to drown.

But he was coming back. Marvie held onto that belief with everything she was. Auden was coming back.

Would the same Auden who had talked about the future with her really abandon her like this? They had talked about going to Grady, laying under the stars and swimming in the ocean, climbing mountains in the Wilds, hiking through deserts in Nagaye. They had talked about getting married, proclaiming their love in front of the gods, for all of Orinth to see. They had talked about the cottage on the edge of the forest where they would start a life together, raise their children together, grow old together. Auden wouldn't just be saying goodbye to her; he would be saying goodbye to that future they had planned.

The Auden she loved wouldn't do that.

Auden Frae was a part of her now; there was no Marvolene Pere without Auden Frae.

Days passed. Weeks passed. No Auden. She waited for him, imagined him bursting through the door and falling to the ground. She imagined crashing back into his arms. He had been gone for almost four weeks now, but it could've been an eternity. She would never let him go if he came back, would cherish how his arms felt around her because she missed it desperately. Being with Auden was as necessary as breathing. If she didn't do it, she would eventually die.

At the end of the fourth week without him, Marvie got up to relieve herself. The moment her feet touched the floor, she collapsed, screaming in pain. Physically, of course, because she had barely ate or drank anything, but mentally, the anguish was worse. It was getting harder to justify his prolonged absence. He should be back right now, from wherever he was. He should have returned to her. And if he hadn't...

NO! Her mind screamed at her. *I WON'T LET YOU THINK THAT WAY.*

Her head didn't stop screaming at her even as her uncle burst in the door of the room, shouting in alarm because she was on the floor. The reassurances that Auden was coming back didn't cease, even as Hewes scooped her into his arms and she passed out. In the darkness, she saw him, reached for him, screamed for him, but Auden faded into the distance without even looking at her. She heard the words again.

"I love you more than anything in the entire world and because I love you, I have to protect you. And the only way I can protect you is to leave you."

Marvie screamed at the voice to stop, but her mouth wouldn't move. There was only pain; she had become a being of agony, the torment ripping through her. Her heart was falling apart, piece by piece, each shard of it cutting into her soul. Her brain was trying to get out of her head, to stop hearing the voice and seeing his face. Her entire being was turning on itself, a war between letting him go and holding onto the desperate hope he was coming back. In the blackness, the war with herself continued.

"Dammit Marvie, if we were in a different place and I was someone else, maybe we'd have a shot. But I couldn't live with myself if I was the reason you were hurt. Even tonight is too much for me. So that's why I have to go."

"SHUT UP!" she screamed at the voice. "SHUT UP!"

YOU PROMISED. YOU PROMISED YOU WOULDN'T LEAVE ME. YOU PROMISED ME FOREVER. YOU PROMISED.

"I love you, but I promised to make you safe, and I can't do that."

IF YOU LOVED ME, YOU WOULD STAY. IF YOU ARE TRULY GONE, THEN YOU NEVER LOVED ME. YOU LIED TO ME. I HATE YOU, NO, I DON'T. I LOVE YOU MORE THAN ANYTHING BUT I NEED YOU TO COME BACK BECAUSE I AM NOTHING WITHOUT YOU.

THERE IS NO MARVOLENE PERE WITHOUT AUDEN FRAE.

YOU CAN'T DO THIS TO ME.

"Marvie?" A soft, familiar voice pulled her out of the nightmare and she blinked a few times as she adjusted to the light. She was lying in a bed that wasn't hers, staring up at a blank ceiling she had never seen. She prayed, *prayed,* the voice was Auden's, but when a pair of arms helped her to sit up, she was staring at her uncle Hewes, her aunt Sienna, and an older-looking woman whose face she recognized but didn't know why.

"I...where are we?" Marvie asked, and she was distantly aware that it was the first time she had spoken to her aunt and uncle since she asked them where Auden had gone all those weeks ago.

"This is the healer, Rivera. We're in her office," Hewes explained gently.

The familiarity settled into place. She knew the healer from the few times in her life she had grown ill. The healer was a kind woman who knew her craft, but Marvie didn't know why she was here. She looked around the room for Auden before turning back to the three adults. "What happened?" she managed, her voice sounding raspy. She barely recognized it.

"Marvie," Sienna began, her voice shaking, "you were barely eating or drinking anything. You collapsed and wouldn't wake up." She began to sob as Hewes wrapped an arm around her. Through her cries, she continued, "We thought we were going to lose you. We got you here just in time so Rivera was able to save you." Her aunt broke down into more sobs, pressing her face into her hands.

Marvie opened her mouth to speak, to muster some sort of apology, but no sound came out. Had she really done that to herself? Neglected herself in such a way that she had almost...died because of it? How could she do that? What if she would've died and Auden would've returned to find his lover in a grave? The guilt in her grew, almost trumping the lingering pain. "I'm sorry," Marvie said, tears beginning to roll out of her own eyes. "I'm sorry," she repeated.

Sienna shook her head, desperately trying to hide her face. "Don't be sorry, Marvie. You haven't done anything. I would react that way too if I was going through what you're going through."

"I...what? What are you talking about?" Marvie asked, her hands trembling so much that they were growing numb. "What am I going through?"

"Oh sweetheart," Hewes whispered. "I'm so sorry."

"FOR WHAT!" Marvie shouted. "WHAT ARE YOU SORRY FOR?"

"Marvie..."

Rivera cleared her throat. "I'm sorry to interrupt," she said, "but there are really some things we need to talk about, Marvolene." She set a tray on the table next to the bed Marvie was laying on. There was a tall glass of water and a bowl of something steaming. "I need you to eat the stew and drink the water slowly. And after that, I'll bring you more. We need to get your strength back quickly if what I suspect is true."

"What you suspect..." Marvie trailed off, her head beginning to pound from the onslaught of things that were happening.

Sienna and Rivera exchanged a look. "Marvie," Sienna said carefully, "we know you've been throwing up every single morning for weeks now. We can hear you. It's been happening consistently."

Marvie nodded. Her throat felt like it was bleeding as she spoke. "It's just with everything that's happening, I don't feel well."

"There's that," Rivera agreed. "But Marvie, can you tell me when your last cycle was?"

Marvie blinked twice. "Come again?"

"Your last cycle. When did you have it?"

Marvie felt a tear slip out of her eye and there was a ringing in her ears that began to grow in volume. "I can't remember," she whispered. "It's been over a month."

No. This wasn't happening. It wasn't real. She was still locked in the nightmare. An endless nightmare where Auden told her goodbye and she woke up in some healer's office with her aunt and uncle. Maybe she had drank some bad wine when they ate on the roof together. Maybe she had hallucinated the last four weeks of her life. Maybe she was dead and had gone to the Beyond and the gods were punishing her for what she did in the world. It was the most logical explanation for what was happening right now.

Rivera looked at Sienna and then Hewes and gave a slight nod. "There are other signs," she told them, as if Marvie weren't in the room. "I'll give you some space while I go get more soup and water. Please tell her and make sure she eats what's on the tray." With that, the healer left, leaving the three of them alone.

Marvie tried to ask so many things but only managed, "Why are you sorry?" The question came out cold and accusing.

Sienna sat down on the side of the bed and handed Marvie the glass of water. Despite herself, she drank the entire thing. The relief it brought her was not enough to distract her from the disarray of emotions. She looked at Hewes, at the sympathy in his eyes, and demanded again, "WHY ARE YOU SORRY?"

"Auden is gone, Marvolene," Hewes said softly. "We checked with his boss. We checked with his landlord. We even checked with Isla. He left the city four weeks ago and no one has seen him since. He's gone."

Marvie started shaking her head from his first word. "No," she whispered. "That's not true. He's not gone."

"Marvie…"

"He wouldn't do that to me. He wouldn't hurt me like that. There has to be some rational explanation for his leaving, but he'll be back."

"He's gone, Marvie," Sienna sobbed, setting a hand on her knee under the blankets. "He's gone."

"NO!" Marvie screamed, jerking out of her grasp and scrambling against the wall. "HE'S NOT GONE!"

"Marvolene," Hewes said and his voice was serious. "Auden is gone."

She wasn't sure why it was her uncle's voice that was finally able to cut through the walls of lies she had been feeding herself for the last four weeks. Her own logical mind had tried to tell her this time and time again to break her out of the trance, to spare her from the disappointment of her hope that he would return. And yet, in that moment, Hewes' three simple words cut straight to her heart, destroying it with the reality that Auden was truly gone.

Marvie let out a sob and collapsed into her aunt's arms.

Auden was gone.

She sobbed into her shoulder and the voices finally faded away. There was nothing in her head as she cried, her heart an empty and meaningless thing. Hewes sat down next to them and wrapped his arms around her, but even the steady arms of her uncle couldn't save her from the pain that was going to be hers. It hurt now and it would hurt so badly and nothing could protect her from the reality that Auden Frae was gone.

He had left her.

He had broken her.

He had said he loved her, but how could someone who loved her inflict this sort of torture on her?

Had any of it been real?

She didn't know. She didn't care. The agony was too great to have comprehensive thoughts. Instead, Marvie sobbed into her aunt's shoulder, begging the gods for some sort of reprieve from this burden. *Spare me,* she told them, *spare me. Let me forget about him right now, in this moment, for I would rather forget about him than face the cold and lonely days ahead. Take him away from me, I don't want his ghost. Take it away, take it away, take it away.*

"Marvie, there is more," Hewes voice cut through the sobs of both her and Sienna. Marvie wanted to let herself go completely, but something made her meet her uncle's gaze. Sienna held onto her, squeezing her tight, the only thing separating her from collapsing to the ground in a pool of despair and staying there until the pain went away. But deep down, Marvie knew this pain would never truly go away, no matter how many years separated her from it.

For some reason, she was able to stop crying enough to hear him. She tried to ask him what more there could possibly be, but he was already speaking.

"We talked to the healer. About how you've been throwing up every morning, how you've been sick, and how you haven't had a cycle in quite some time. I don't know how else to say this, Marvolene; you're with child."

Marvie stared at him with no reaction. She heard the words, but Hewes could have been speaking another language, for she had no comprehension of that statement that just came from his mouth. She looked down at her stomach and then back up at him, waiting for a laugh or a smile. It would be just like Hewes to make some sort of joke when both she and her aunt were crying, but his expression was deadly serious.

She. Marvolene. Pregnant.

His ghost spoke to her and she wanted to shriek at it to leave her alone.

"I want to be with you forever. Whether there are children or not. You're always going to be the person I love most in the world. Do you understand?"

It wasn't possible. Marvie looked back down at her stomach and whispered, "With child?"

Sienna had begun to speak, but Marvie wasn't listening. She could only hear his voice and see his face and feel the love she would never feel again. She set one hand on her stomach, searching for some sort of proof that it was real, that she was actually carrying Auden's unborn child. There was nothing, so she didn't believe it.

Marvie had done everything she could to be a good person. Would the gods truly punish her both with Auden's departure and his abandonment of the child that was theirs?

Well, they had. She had nothing. No love. No future. No Auden.

Just a child.

Marvolene looked up at the ceiling as if she were looking into the sky above and asked the gods why. Why did they do this to her? Why did they make this happen? Why had they given her such a beautiful blessing only to have him leave? Why would they bring a child into this, when Marvie could barely take care of herself among the pieces of her broken life? What was the reason? What was the purpose? Why had they done it?

But Marvie didn't have answers to those questions, no relief among the torment.

She only had a child.

Marvie wasn't sure if she should love the child or hate the child. But the reality was Auden was gone and the baby inside her womb was all she had left. The future that, four weeks ago, had contained a wedding, traveling the world, a cottage on the edge of a forest, and an eternity with the person she loved most, was gone. It had slipped through her fingers before she even knew it, leaving her with only one thing: a child.

Auden was gone.

Keeping one hand on her stomach, Marvie pressed the other against her face and begin to sob once again.

Fifteen Years Later

Rider knew he should be paying better attention to the king at this meeting of economic handlers. After all, he and Tieran had strategized about this specific meeting for weeks and weeks. It was the moment they were going to launch a new strategy for helping smaller businesses remain afloat in Abdul, a decision that would surely bring them prosperity. They had gone over it so many times, but now that Tieran was in their council room, speaking loudly and confidently, Rider couldn't focus on anything but her.

He probably should have stayed in his room today, citing that he was feeling ill. Tieran wouldn't have questioned him and he would have had hours of peace, hours to think about his life without interruption. But a part of him was scared to be alone with his thoughts, scared to let the walls he had built up so high around him down for just a day, to think about the person he tried not to think of at all. So he went to the meeting and tried to give Tieran nods of approval when the king looked his way.

It had been fifteen years since the night on the roof. Sixteen years since the day he had met her in that shop, set eyes on the girl who stumbled into his life and changed it forever.

Most days, Rider fought between wanting her to disappear from his mind and desperately trying to hold onto the memories he had of her, the image of her that continued to fade as the years went by. He wanted her to leave him alone and let him live without regret, but at the same time, haunt him for the rest of his days because at least that meant she was in his life.

He tried to think about some happy memory they had shared together, when he was young. He tried to picture them dancing by the harbor, but it wouldn't come to his mind. He thought about a bench on a rooftop under the stars and words about love and life and the future, but those words had long disappeared from his mind. He tried to think of anything, but it was gone, all gone, just as his future with her had been for fifteen years.

Marvolene Pere had made him a new person. She made him good, an impossible feat considering who he was and the past that haunted him. She had taken his broken pieces and made him whole, for one beautiful year of his life. He thought that once he left her, he would fall apart again. The anguish of her absence left a hole in him, but he remained intact, drawing from her memory to conquer the shadow underneath his skin. He would be a person she could be proud of, even if he never saw her again.

Rider refused to wonder where she was or what she was doing or who she had become. They were questions that plagued him when he allowed himself to think about Marvolene. Was she still in Tenir or did she flee from the city where they had fallen in love? Marvie never had any idea what she wanted to do with her life. Had she figured it out or did she still walk throughout the world, doing whatever she desired and being happier than people who seemingly had it figured out? Had she fallen in love again? He prayed that she had. He prayed she had found someone who could love her in the right way, love her innocently. He wondered if Marvie ever went to that cottage on the edge of the forest, the place she was always talking about, a place he would never see. Did she have children of her own, playing in the yard of that cottage, beloved by their mother who was the manifestation of goodness and light? Those questions would never have answers and that was his burden to bear.

When he left Tenir fifteen years ago, he thought his life was over. In a way, it was.

But Rider had found out the truth from his father, the truth about his mother. It was strange; for so long, he had cursed the woman who had given birth to him, the woman who had abandoned him to the horrors of the orphanage. To find out that it wasn't her fault at all? That Rider had been ripped from her arms before she had the chance to know him and love him like a mother should? Rider didn't let himself go down those roads; he already had more regret than one person ought to bear.

It took him six years to work up the nerve to contact her. In the meantime, he survived, just like he always had. There was no joy in his life and the only pain came from Marvie's ghost. But Rider had always been good at surviving, breathing in and out without feeling much of anything; this was no different.

His life had changed since then.

He thought he was doomed to a life of surviving until he met his mother, the late Queen Natasha. He loved her in his own strange way, and she loved him back. She took him into the castle and let him work, never acknowledging that Rider was truly her son, whilst still letting him be a part of her life. Natasha loved him, but when she looked at him, she saw the years and years that he had been beyond her reach, the years he had just been a boy in a dream, her son she would never know. Rider sometimes believed there was so much brokenness between them they would never have a healthy relationship.

And then, his mother would invite him to tea, just the two of them. They would talk about trivial things, like their favorite color or their favorite place. They would talk of the kingdom, the king, and the princess. In those conversations, when they would smile and laugh together, Rider was grateful he had the opportunity to know her. They would never get over what had happened to separate them, but she was his mother and he was her son. That simple fact allowed Rider to love her, and for Natasha to love him.

She had died and it had been painful, but Rider's life had not ended because he had someone who made his life worth living.

Rider shook away his thoughts and looked over at the girl who was sitting next to him. Her brown hair hung down her back, her brown eyes narrowed. She wore an olive-green dress, one she wore frequently, and a small crown adorned her head.

Alida Goulding, the princess of Orinth. Alida Goulding, his half-sister who didn't even know it. Alida Goulding, his best friend.

Lida, the one who made his days more than just surviving.

Alida had joined them in the economic meeting, as she had started taking a bigger role in matters of the kingdom, slowly preparing to one day be a queen. Her chin was buried in her hand and she was absorbed in her father's words. She was mouthing some of the phrases with him, as she too had heard the speech a thousand times. She nodded along with the others in the room, until she noticed Rider looking at her. She raised an eyebrow and then shot him a smile.

When she smiled, he was transported back to the moment he saved her in the cave.

Natasha had asked Rider not to tell Alida about their connection, that they shared the same mother and were half-siblings. Rider never had. He watched her dart around the castle, knowing he could never be the person who sparked a friendship with her.

He had saved her from the cave and Alida made the choice herself.

They spent every second together, or at least, every second they could spare. When she was younger, she would beg Rider to play with her, to go on rides, to swim in the nearby springs, to walk through the city to get candy and pastries from the vendors of Abdul. Rider had always obliged her. When their mother was alive, he remembered seeing her smile at the pair of them when she saw them together.

He thought his life was over. But in those moments with Alida, his little sister who had grown into his best friend, Rider's life began again.

Auden's life began again.

His life would always have a hole in it, a gap where Marvie should've been. But the boy he used to be, Auden Frae, had been wrong. He wasn't living a half-life without her. Maybe at one point he had been, but Alida had made him whole once more. His sister, his best friend, his reason for surviving. The shadow went away when she was with him, the ghosts of his past ceased to haunt him. Even when she was little, the love she had for him made it disappear.

As Alida grew, as their conversations became deeper and their friendship more meaningful, Rider came back to life. He no longer wanted to survive; he wanted to do something in this world. He wanted to make a difference, to make other people's lives better. As an advisor to the king, it was something he was capable of. After the queen died, Rider took over the reformation of orphanages around their country and the revival of safe children's homes, where kids could live until they were adopted by loving parents.

Rider had the power to make sure no one had the childhood he had. He would be damned if he didn't use it.

His life had meaning again and it was because of Alida Goulding. As he looked over at her smiling at him, he was reminded of that fact.

Somewhere in the world, Marvolene Pere existed. Rider hoped her life was perfect and she was happy. He had left her to keep her safe, and he prayed to the gods she was better off for it.

As for Rider, he had his sister and his job in this castle, a responsibility to make other people's lives better. In some strange way, he was happy too. He would've been happiest with Marvie, in that cottage on the edge of the forest. Knowing that could never be a reality, with the shadow as a constant threat, Rider knew he was living the next best option.

"What?" Alida mouthed to him.

Rider shot her back a smile and shook his head while trying to hold back tears. For some reason, right then, it hit him how grateful he was for his little sister, even if she didn't know he was her older brother. They were in one another's life and that would always be enough for him.

Alida stuck her tongue out at him before returning her attention to the king.

An hour later, after the meeting dispersed, Rider ducked out of the room before Tieran could find him to have a conversation. Although he was happy, he had always spent this day mourning the loss of Marvie. He would spend the rest of the night alone, thinking about her and the life he could've had. He stuck his hands in his pockets and walked back to his room. When he reached it, he went right over to his balcony overlooking Abdul. He leaned against the rail and looked out at their city, wishing for one moment that he was looking at Tenir instead.

He hadn't been back to the city and, for many reasons, he never would. First, if Rider ever saw Marvie again, he would probably beg her to allow him back into her life, to resurrect the future that would've been had he stayed fifteen years ago. He wouldn't do that, wouldn't put her in danger. Secondly, it was the city where he had let the shadow consume him, control him, do its will through him. He would never be that person again and Tenir was just a reminder of what he was capable of. He would remember the city as the place he fell in love with Marvolene, but he would never return.

Rider felt tears stinging behind his eyes as he thought about her, as he thought about himself from the past. Marvolene Pere and Auden Frae. Two teenagers who thought they had it all. Maybe they did. Maybe they did.

Rider sometimes remembered words he had spoken to her. He couldn't remember where or when he had said them, but they were still in his heart. *"And in the event that you and I don't last forever, I will draw comfort in the fact that we end up together in a thousand different worlds."*

They didn't get to be together in the world he was in. But perhaps, in some other realm, there was an Auden Frae and a Marvolene Pere who were together, in that very same moment, happy and in love. Maybe they had gotten the future they talked about. Rider only wished he would've gotten to be *that* Auden Frae, instead of the one who fled because of the shadow. Yet a small part of him drew comfort in the fact that somewhere, in some place, he and Marvie did end up together.

He hadn't heard the door to his room open, but he heard her voice, "Rider?"

Rider blinked a few times so the tears wouldn't be visible in his eyes before turning around. Alida was leaning against the doorway that led to the balcony, her arms crossed. She was still in her green dress and crown which led him to believe she had followed him straight from the meeting. He only hoped she didn't sense that something was wrong with him.

"Lida," he said softly.

"What's wrong with you?" Alida demanded and Rider wasn't surprised in the slightest. She walked forward until she was leaning against the railing, her gaze locked on him. He turned to observe the city, wondering if he shouldn't just tell her everything. Alida was fourteen years old, but she was so wise for her age. He could tell her about Marvolene and his past and the cause of the shadow, and Alida would listen. Knowing her, she would know the exact right things to say to make it all better. For one moment, he was tempted.

Then he remembered he wasn't supposed to tell her about being her brother. If he told Alida about Auden Frae and Marvolene Pere, she would inevitably figure out there were inconsistencies in the story they had told her, about Rider's father fighting alongside Tieran. He couldn't tell her. Like always, it was his burden to bear.

"Nothing, Lida," Rider said softly in reply. "Nothing at all."

Alida crossed her arms, unconvinced. "You seem like something is wrong."

"How do you think your father's speech went?" Rider asked her.

"Rider, you can't distract me with unrelated questions," she snorted. "Tell me what's wrong."

Rider laughed softly. It was so Alida to know when something was truly wrong, without knowing just how deep the hurt ran. Maybe one day, he would tell her. Not today. "I don't know, Alida," he admitted. "I'm sad, but I don't know why. I guess it's one of those days."

Her demanding aura seemed to disappear as she put a hand on top of his. "I get it, Rider. I think we all have those days sometimes," she said.

"Oh, yes," he sighed.

"A very wise person once gave me a sage piece of advice," Alida told him, squeezing his hand tightly.

Rider chuckled. "Oh?" He brought his other hand to rest on top of hers.

Alida nodded. "He told me that you're lucky when you have a bad day."

Rider remembered this conversation well. Alida had been upset about something a few months ago and he had been there to comfort her, just as he always had. He had wrapped his arms around her and given her the advice he knew she was about to give him. So Rider wrapped an arm around her and pulled her in close. "Lucky? How can I possibly be lucky? I just told you I've had a bad day!" Rider mimicked the words Alida had told him.

"Well, Rider," Alida said profoundly, tucking herself into his side and wrapping her other arm around him. "It's almost nightfall. And you see, that's the thing about bad days. They always have to come to an end." She repeated the exact words that Rider had told her.

Rider laughed softly and they stood there for awhile, arms wrapped around one another, looking out at the kingdom below them.

"Hey Rider?"

"Yes?"

"I love you."

The tears stung behind his eyes once more and it wasn't lost on him that he was holding onto the person who had saved his life. Rider had saved her life in the caves, but it was nothing compared to what Alida had done for him. She would never understand. "I love you too," he replied, and the words seemed too little a thing to describe just how much he loved her. It wasn't the romantic love in which he shared with Marvolene, but a love just as powerful; the love a brother had for his sister.

She let go of him and said, "You have five more minutes to mope and then let's go play cards. I'll run down to the kitchen and steal us a few pastries and maybe you can get us a bottle of wine." Rider snorted, but Alida ignored him as she continued. "We'll play cards and eat and drink and make this bad day a little better. How about that?"

"I think that sounds wonderful, Lida," Rider replied. "I'll mope for five more minutes while you get the pastries, and then I'll meet you in your room. Okay?"

"After you get the wine," Alida corrected him with a grin.

Rider rolled his eyes but couldn't help but laughing. "Fine. I'll get us some wine too, but don't you dare tell your father."

Alida pressed a hand to her mouth and swore, "My lips are sealed." Then, she embraced Rider tightly. Rider hugged her back before she released him and started towards the door. "I love you! See you in five minutes!"

Rider waited until she had left his room to reply. "I love you too," he whispered, the tears finally spilling onto his cheeks.

For five minutes, he thought about Marvie. He thought about everything that had happened between them. Some people might call it young love, but

Rider knew it was as real of a thing as he would ever feel. Auden had loved Marvie and Marvie had loved Auden, and for one year, the world was theirs. Maybe they didn't get that future, but at least they had that one year. Rider thought about all of it and he cried for her.

He missed her with a desperation that might kill him if he didn't have something else worth living for now. He loved her as deeply as the day he left her.

When the five minutes ended, Rider wiped his eyes, took a deep breath, and smiled.

That's the thing about bad days; they always have to come to an end.

Rider turned around and went to go play cards with the other girl who had saved his life, his beloved sister Alida Goulding.

A cottage at the edge of the forest

Ali Lois wanted to be sad that day, but her daughter was not allowing it.

The moment her eyes opened, she prepared to spend the day in mourning. Mourning for a boy she once knew named Auden Frae, mourning for the girl she had once been, Marvolene Pere. But before she could convey that to her husband and daughter, Sawny had burst in the room with a plate of eggs and bacon, proclaiming with pride, "I made you breakfast, Mom!"

Before Ali could protest, Caleb marched in from behind her, carrying a cup of coffee. He shot Sawny a pretend scowl. "I think you mean 'we', Sawny, my dear."

"I did most of the work, Dad," Sawny shot back as she climbed onto the bed and slid next to her mother, setting the plate of food on her lap. She looked at her mother and nodded seriously. "It's true. Most of the food on that plate was made by yours truly."

"The mountain of dishes in the sink was also made by that same person," Caleb chimed in, grinning at Ali as he offered her the mug of coffee.

Ali had been seconds away from bursting into tears, from closing the door to her bedroom and isolating herself for the day, as she had to do every once in a while. But she threw her head back and began to laugh, the despair draining out of her body until there was nothing but love for her daughter and her husband. She wrapped an arm around Sawny and squeezed, pressing a kiss to the top of her head. "This is such a treat. What did I do to deserve this?"

"Only be the best mother in the world," Sawny responded with a grin, putting her head on Ali's shoulder. Ali smiled at Caleb as she took the mug of coffee from his hands. Her husband smiled back at her and she felt a wave of love for the two of them. The day's plan of being sad seemed to drift away as Ali dug into the breakfast that Sawny had prepared and began to converse with the two people she loved most in the world.

It wasn't the first time Sawny and Caleb had saved her from a day of mourning.

There had been a time when Ali thought she could never be happy again. Then she remembered that happiness was never a destination, but something to squeeze out of every day, a light in the darkness no matter how hard it was to find.

Ali had managed it, even in those days right after it had happened. It seemed such a difficult task, to find one good thing in a day of misery. How was she supposed to be happy when she was completely alone, spare the child growing inside of her that she would never be able to care for, the nameless, faceless baby who she despised? But each day, Ali found a light, even from the smallest of places, a flame flickering in a sea of night. It was the only thing that kept her going.

Ali thought her life was over. Until in a medicine house in Auntica, her daughter, Sawny Lois, was born.

The tiny human she held in her arms that day was the resurrection of a person who she assumed was lost forever. Happiness came from the smallest of moments, but also, from the smallest of people, from the baby that was hers. They would build a new life together, just the two of them. They would find happiness in each day, with one another. She didn't need much of anyone anymore, except for Sawny Lois, her beloved baby girl.

As Sawny grew older, her face began to resemble Ali's more and more. They had the same cheeks and lips, the same wide smile and blonde hair. Sawny liked to keep hers long, just like her mother. But those green eyes came directly from her father, the man Ali had loved, the man Sawny would never know.

Ali thought it would be just the two of them for the rest of their lives, until she met her now-husband and Sawny's adopted father: Caleb Ore.

Ali truly believed that the gods themselves had sent Caleb Ore. He had walked into the place she worked almost eleven years ago, when Sawny was just a toddler. It wasn't a passionate, overpowering love, like the first time. No, Ali grew to like the shy, sweet boy from the Darklands, with his sandy blonde hair and brown eyes, his toned figure from years of being a warrior. He was full of nervous smiles and quiet laughter, profound words to share if someone would listen to him. It wasn't an instant love, but Ali began to adore Caleb Ore until that adoration became love, powerful and true.

They were married only three months after meeting, in a tiny church in Illias. They lived in an apartment while Caleb built them a cottage on the edge of a forest, just outside of Illias. A year later, they moved into it and turned it into a home, their home. Sawny started calling Caleb 'father' within weeks, loving him with everything she was.

It wasn't the life that Ali had imagined for herself, the life she had dreamed of and prayed for. But her life was her own and she loved it. She loved Caleb Ore and she loved Sawny Lois and she loved herself and who she had become, despite the brokenness of her past, the piece of her heart that had been stolen long ago.

Yet once in a while, the pain would hit her and she would withdraw into her room, taking the day to herself. Caleb understood and tried to explain it to Sawny. Ali had never told Caleb about Auden, but he knew that something painful had happened to her long ago. On those days, she laid in the dark, trying to remember the memories she had worked so hard to forget. His face had faded from her mind, and she would try to recall it, his black curls, his green eyes, his sad smile. She would try to remember the exhilarating feeling of loving someone that deeply. Her love for Caleb was steady and consistent, a warm feeling in her chest, the knowledge he would never leave her and break her like Auden had. But on those dark days, she tried to remember the feeling of overwhelming, absolute love for someone, the type that consumed people.

It was supposed to be one of those days today, but Sawny and Caleb had stopped it before it could even begin. Ali was grateful.

"So, Mom," Sawny began, her voice completely innocent. "Dad and I have a question for you."

Ali gave Sawny a look. "So that's why you made me breakfast," she said, looking pointedly at Caleb, who held up his hands innocently, as if he had no idea what was coming.

"I made breakfast because you are a wonderful mother," Sawny scoffed. "I can't believe you would think anything else!"

Ali snorted loudly. "What do you want?"

"Well, since *you* asked," Sawny said sheepishly, shrugging her shoulders, "Dad and I were thinking that we would take a picnic out to the spring and go swimming this afternoon. The sun looks like it's going to shine all day and we wanted to take advantage of the warmth. But we want you to come with us, even though you're not," she cleared her throat, "great at swimming."

Ali faked a frown. "Ouch."

"Hey, neither are me or Dad," Sawny countered. "You're just the worst of the worst."

"Sawny," Caleb said, clapping his hand over his mouth as he laughed. "You are really not helping our case."

Ali couldn't help but burst into laughter at the whole scene and the fact Sawny and Caleb had tried to bribe her by making her breakfast and delivering it straight to her bed. They were dedicated, she would give them that.

Caleb had been the one to teach her how to swim, in a spring near the Forest Dembe. After years and years of not knowing, her husband from the Darklands had taught her. Ali adored it, adored the feeling of being in the water and using her arms to keep herself afloat. It seemed a strange symbol of her life since the incident, using her own skill to prevent herself from drowning. Years after Caleb had taught her, they had taken Sawny to the spring and taught her as well.

They had done all the things that she had imagined doing with Auden and they had brought her just as much joy. It brought her joy even when Ali couldn't help but wonder if she would be happier if it was Auden raising Sawny with her instead of Caleb.

Those hypothetical questions became meaningless when she remembered happiness was a state of being, not a destination. Ali was happy. That was what mattered. The "what ifs" faded when she simply remembered that she was happy.

"You don't need to convince me, Sawny," Ali told her, pulling her daughter in tight. "Let's get ready and go swimming."

Sawny shouted in glee, kissing her mother on the cheek as she leapt back to her feet. She hugged Caleb, whispering something in his ear that he laughed at, before darting out of the room, calling over her shoulder, "I'll get the food ready for the picnic!"

Caleb watched after her before he turned around, beaming at Ali. "She's had that planned for weeks now; I hope you know that." He sat down on the edge of the bed beside her, taking a large bite of the eggs.

Ali rolled her eyes at him, grinning. "She didn't even have to make me breakfast. I would've said yes, regardless."

Caleb shrugged, removing the plate from her lap and setting it on the nightstand beside the bed they shared. "Yeah, well, you know Sawny."

"I know her well," Ali agreed.

Caleb picked up her hand and pressed a kiss to it, before leaning in and pressing a gentle kiss to her lips. Ali kissed him tenderly in return, a warmth creeping into her chest, completely casting out the sadness that she had planned to wallow in that day. When Caleb pulled away, he whispered, "I love you."

"I love you too," Ali told him, and she meant it. She did love Caleb. She loved him with her entire heart.

It was not, and would never be, the astounding love she had shared with Auden. But that didn't mean it wasn't true. Love didn't always have to be something that took the air from a person's lungs and rendered them incapable of speech. Love could be something steady and reliable, easy as breathing, calm as a gently flowing stream. Loving Caleb was as simple as loving the sunset. She wanted to be with him until the day she died.

Caleb stood up, still smiling. "I'm going to go get the picnic ready, because gods know Sawny won't." With that, he walked out of the room and closed the door behind him, almost knowing Ali needed a moment to herself.

There was one regret, in all of this. There had once been dozens of regrets, but Ali had conquered each and every one of them until they disappeared. She was left with the regret that Auden would never get to meet Sawny.

Well, not never. Ali hoped that one day Sawny would meet the man who was her birthfather. Ali hoped that one day she had the courage to tell her daughter about him, to sit her down and explain that Caleb was not the man whose blood she shared, though her husband was Sawny's father in every other way.

If not, Ali had written a letter.

She remembered her journey back to Tenir, years ago, as if it were yesterday. Sawny had been eleven years old.

Her Uncle Hewes had passed away years before. It was devastating to Ali, discovering the news in a letter. Since fleeing from Tenir, she had seen her aunt and uncle one time, meeting the pair of them between Tenir and Illias when Sawny was just a toddler. They had stayed in an inn in a village and spent a few days with one another before parting ways. Ali loved her aunt and uncle, but their life was in Tenir, while Ali's wasn't.

She had gone back to Tenir for two purposes: to visit her dear aunt and see her oldest friend.

Ali had given her aunt the letter she wrote to Sawny, in the case that she never got to tell her the truth about Auden. Sienna had promised that, if something happened to Ali, she would make sure that Sawny received the letter and learned about her birthfather. Ali had spent the night at her old apartment after a long, wonderful conversation with her aunt. Even that one night had brought too many painful memories, forcing Ali to leave the next morning.

As she walked through the streets of Tenir, she couldn't help but search for him, praying for just a glimpse of his face. She didn't know what she would do if she saw him. She was married, now, and had a life that was happy without him in it. But if she saw him and he saw her...well, she wouldn't let him go without a long conversation, that much was for certain.

But she didn't see him. Eventually, Ali reached the tavern where she had asked Isla to meet her.

Isla didn't look any different than she had fifteen years ago. Her auburn hair was as perfect as it had always been, her green eyes glowing with happiness. They embraced one another for a long time and Ali couldn't help inhaling. Isla smelled like the past. They sat down and ordered drinks and a conversation Ali always knew she would hold close to her heart began.

"How are the children?" Ali asked her, sipping on Orinthian wine that brought back so many memories.

"Oh, they're wonderful," Isla answered, her eyes still glassy with unshed tears. They sat in a tavern they used to frequent when they were teenagers, Orinthian from the pictures of scenery that adorned the walls to the empty stage that would surely be filled that night. Ali knew she could only stay in here for a few hours before she would break down. "May is starting school soon and Chelle just learned to read a few weeks ago! And how is darling Sawny?"

Ali smiled. "With her father in the Darklands, visiting his family."

"That's incredible. How is Caleb?" and the small talk continued.

Ali's plan, upon fleeing Tenir for the first time, was to utterly abandon every part of her life there, including her old friends. But the thought of Isla not knowing what had happened to her was too painful to bear, so Ali had sent her a letter from Iyria, telling her of Sawny's birth. Isla responded right away, congratulating her while demanding to know what had happened. And although Ali had planned to hide the full extent of what had happened in Tenir, she wrote it in a letter and confided in the girl who had been her friend for so many years.

Their correspondence hadn't ended. Since those first letters were exchanged, it had continued. Isla had written to announce her marriage to Lee, the birth of her two daughters, May and Chelle, the purchase of their home on the outskirts of Tenir, and every moment in between. Ali, in return, had written about Sawny, about Caleb, about her job in Illias and her new life in Auntica. After the first letter, they didn't mention Auden or the life she had once had in Tenir, as Marvolene Pere.

They talked in that tavern for a long time, and as the conversation began to end, Ali leaned in a little closer to Isla.

"I'm glad we've stayed friends for so long," she said, and she meant it.

Isla smiled at her, her eyes still glassy. "I'm glad for it too."

Ali took a deep breath. "Because I wouldn't ask this of anyone else, Isla."

Her smile disappeared. "What is it, Marvie?"

Isla didn't even notice she had let her old nickname slip and Ali didn't correct her. Instead, she took an envelope out of her jacket pocket and slipped it across the table. In her own script, the name 'Auden' was neatly written on the front.

Isla's eyes widened when she saw it. "What…what is it?" Isla, of course, knew all about Auden's abrupt, unexplained departure right before Ali discovered she was pregnant with their daughter. She knew that Ali had searched for him for months before going to Auntica to start a new life, and she hadn't seen or heard from him since. Isla was possibly the only person who understood the deep wound that had been created within Ali, one that was healed, but the scar would always be there. Therefore, Isla fully understood the implications of an envelope with his name on it.

"If you ever see him again, I need you to give this to him," Ali said softly.

"Marvie…"

"Don't worry, Isla," Ali said with a half-smile. "It's not a profession of my love. I have Caleb now and I'm happy. But I still want…" she took a breath, struggling to say his name out loud, something she hadn't done in years, "…Auden to know that in this world, there is a piece of him, a piece of us. I want him to know his daughter and I want Sawny to know her birthfather. It's an explanation of everything. If you see him, he'll finally know about our daughter. Will you do that for me, Isla? Will you give him this letter if you have the opportunity?"

The tears spilled out of Isla's eyes as she nodded. "Of course I will, Marvolene," she whispered in reply. "I don't know if I will ever see him. But if by the will of the gods I do, I will give him this letter."

Ali stood and embraced her old friend, burying her head in her shoulder and letting out a muffled sob. But in that moment, she thought of Auden and Sawny and the void that existed between them. In reality, she didn't even know if

Auden was still alive. Maybe he would never know his real daughter, but Ali held onto hope that one day, the two of them would be united.

She had said goodbye to Isla and ridden back to Auntica to resume the life she had created for herself there.

And now, Ali was about to go swimming in a spring with her husband and her daughter. There wasn't much she could be sad about, but sitting there on the bed, she allowed herself exactly one minute of regret.

After giving Isla the letter and going back home, Ali sometimes found herself looking at the horizon, waiting for a man on horseback to find the location she had described. Auden would probably recognize it anyways; it was the cottage on the edge of the forest that Marvolene Pere had always talked about. Well, Marvie got it, just not with him. In fact, she had everything from the perfect future she had once dreamed of, everything besides Auden.

Auden would ride and Ali would greet him with a sad smile. She wouldn't demand an explanation. She wouldn't scream and cry and curse his name. Whatever had happened between them was past, though she knew a part of her would always love him. But she could never be with him again because she loved Caleb. Caleb hadn't left her; Auden had. She would simply lead him into the cottage and introduce him to their daughter, Sawny Lois, and pray they could have some sort of relationship. It was all she wanted out of Auden now; not the future they had dreamt of, not his love, not his apology, but to know and to love their daughter.

Ali would be lying if she said she didn't wonder about what their life would've looked like together. They had made so many plans, so many promises. Deep in her heart, she knew it would have been perfect, just like the year they had spent together. She still believed that the love between them was real and everlasting; a part of her loved Auden and always would. She hoped that, wherever he was, he had found the same happiness she had found in the absence of each other.

Wondering why he had left was a fruitless task. Ali would never know and a part of her never cared to find out. In the end, she had her cottage, she had her husband, and more than anything, she had Sawny Lois, her light in the darkness.

If Marvolene Pere didn't get to share life with Auden Frae, she prayed Sawny would.

But, in that moment, about to leave the cottage with Caleb and her daughter, Ali was happy. Despite the scars and the ghosts of the past, she had found happiness in every day, and would continue to find that happiness until the day she died. She would teach her daughter to seek out happiness and claim it for herself, not allowing anyone else to dictate what would make her happy. Sawny was only a teenager, but she already understood. It didn't surprise Ali; Sawny was steadfast.

Ali took one more deep breath and thought about Auden one last time.

She whispered to him, hoping her words would carry on the wind until they reached his ears, wherever he was. "I love you. I always have and I always will."

Ali stood up, wiping the single tear off her cheek and mustering a smile. "But I'm happy."

"My name is Marvolene and I choose to be happy."

With that, Ali walked out of her bedroom to join her daughter and husband for a day that would undoubtedly be filled with the most precious happiness one could find in their world.

Acknowledgments

First, I would like to thank my friend Amanda B. for giving me the idea to expand upon Marvolene and Auden's story. I never thought to dive deep into what happened between Sawny's parents. Now, I can't imagine what the story would be like without it.

As always, thank you to the people who worked on this book. Thank you to John Sullivan, Lisa Leach, Cheri Sullivan, and the people who read the story before publication! This book wouldn't be what it is without you!

Thank you to my family for their unending support. Thank you Mom, Dad, Savannah, LeMay, and Rem. Thank you to my friends for always encouraging me in my writing. Thank you to the people who are in my life, and the people who are not, for inspiring me to write about this strange world that we live in.

More than anything, thank you, reader, for being on this journey with me. You give me the motivation to keep going, the knowledge that there is someone out there who cares about what I have to say. Writing has changed my life in profound ways, and I owe a lot of that to you.

If you enjoyed the book, please leave a positive review on Amazon, Goodreads, etc. You can also tell me all about it on falltodarkness.com. Check out the website for updates on upcoming novels, new merchandise, and more!

About the Author

Summer Sullivan is a writer who grew up in rural Northern Michigan and attended a small high school. After writing a story for fun during the pandemic, she decided to publish her work and the world of Fall to Darkness was born. Now, Summer lives in Northern Florida, working and writing as much as she can. Summer enjoys biking, playing guitar, cooking, and spending time with friends and family.

www.ingramcontent.com/pod-product-compliance
Lightning Source LLC
Chambersburg PA
CBHW060606030726
47498CB00005B/1558